DEEP DOWN THE RABBIT HOLE

T. R. Hill

T. R. HILL

ISBN:
979-8-9926478-0-8 Paperback
979-8-9926478-1-5 Ebook

Published by T R Hill
trhill.author.wordpress.com

Cover design by: T. R. HILL

For my family, who never gave up on me—even when I gave up on myself.

For a list of trigger and content warnings, visit
trhillauthor.wordpress.com/trigger-and-content-warnings/

CONTENTS

"I wouldn't mind being a Pawn, if only I might join —though of course I should like to be a Queen, best."

ALICE'S ADVENTURES IN WONDERLAND, LEWIS CARROLL

ONE

Kinsley: July 3, 2008

My heart rattles under the silk of my Chanel sundress like the train barreling through town. Overhead, the crystal chandelier trembles as boxcars blur on the other side of the chapel's window. The reverend's denture-perfect smile fades to a grimace as he looks down at the black fabric I roll between my fingers. What kind of a bride wears black to her wedding? Perhaps the kind who wore a white christening gown to her mother's funeral.

We wait. And wait. And wait for the train to pass before continuing the ceremony. I swallow the nervousness creeping up my throat. It tastes like this morning's tequila sunrise. Anxiety—or unmetabolized alcohol— swirls in my gut as if I'm about to do something irreversible, but that's not true. Divorce is as easy as marriage. It all boils down to a piece of paper in the end.

When the train passes and the room quiets except for the hum of the air conditioner, the reverend continues. "Do you, Kinsley Samantha Holland, take this man to be your lawfully wedded husband?"

"I do," I say and watch the ring Landon bought me slide into place just past my knuckle.

"I now pronounce you husband and wife," the reverend says with a wink. "You may kiss the bride." As my husband leans in to kiss me for the first time, I close my eyes.

❋ ❋ ❋

June 14: Three weeks earlier.

"Keep them closed," he tells me, and I squeeze my eyes tight in response. Landon takes my hands—I know it's him even with my eyes closed. His hands have known every inch of my body since I was fifteen. I would know his touch in my sleep.

"Open them," he says and I do. He no longer sits next to me at the table but has moved his chair out of the way to kneel before me, his blue eyes sparkling with excitement.

Oh, my god. This is happening.

I glance across the table at my best friend, Nikki, and try to read her smile.

"Kins…" Landon runs his thumb over my knuckles. "We've been through a lot, and it hasn't always been easy, but we've come a long way from that summer Ben abandoned us." He teases, his eyes shifting to Ben.

"And, looking back, I'm really glad he did because there's no way he would have let me date his little sister if he wasn't off in the desert taking out bad guys."

Shallow laughter erupts from our dinner party, and I steal a glance at my dad. Landon's teasing of the past is innocent—after all, it was nine years ago, but for my dad and Ben, it might as well be yesterday. Their war continues to rage on.

"But, you're mine now, and there's nothing Ben can do about it." Landon winks. His teasing voice shifts to sincerity as he produces a little black velvet box and opens it before me. "Kinsley Samantha Holland, will you marry me and be mine forever?"

Oh, my god. This is happening.

From the moment I opened my eyes, I knew it was coming but it still takes my breath away. Yes, we've dated off and on for almost nine years, but the last few months felt like we were slowing down, not speeding up. It's as if someone scooped up our drowning love and breathed new life into it.

"Yes, of course, I will." I lean down to meet his lips. "I love you so much." The restaurant fills with applause, cheers, and a few whistles.

"Here." He pulls out the ring and places it on my finger. "It's perfect, isn't it?" Landon beams. "Do you love it?"

I lay the palm of my hand against his Oxford blue Burberry dress shirt. The Asscher cut diamond twinkles under the restaurant's pendant lights. Its layered facets remind me of viewing a mirror inside a mirror. You can keep going and going, deeper and deeper—there is no end.

"I do. I love it, Landon."

"Congrats, you two," Ben says, giving me a side hug. "Guess I knew this day was coming. But Landon…" He stops, eyes set on him. "Don't make me come back here and kick your ass." Landon has returned to his chair, and I watch his eyes squint as if trying to discern Ben's meaning. Not more than a second later both men are laughing.

"I know you love her, man," Ben says. "I'm really happy for you guys." He releases me from his embrace and reaches for his glass. "A toast. To the happy couple." I take my glass in hand and join them, along with my dad, Nikki, and her boyfriend, Chase. If only I could lock them in this moment how much easier it would be.

"And to Kinsley," my dad says, still raising his glass. "Charleston Holland Industries' newest and youngest Junior Vice President."

"To Kinsley," they say in unison. I finish off my wine, and the moment is over.

* * *

I stand in front of the bathroom mirror, reapplying my lip gloss and checking my face for food or smudged makeup. It has been the longest day. First, my graduation from business school, then the reception that followed, a quick stop at the house to change before the celebratory dinner, and now the proposal. But the parade of emotion is far from over—tonight I'll say goodbye to Ben, and by this time tomorrow, he'll be halfway around the world.

"Girl, you gotta watch where you're flashing that thing. It's blinding me." Nikki teases as she joins me in front of the mirror. "Gimme." She takes my hand and admires the ring.

"Maybe Chase will give you one next," I say, wiggling my eyebrows.

"Please, you know we're not *that* serious."

"Mm-hmm, we'll see. You might just realize you can't live without him next week on our girls' trip. Reception is spotty in some of those RV parks."

"I'll be fine. But you should let Landon know about the spotty reception. Don't want him calling the cops if you miss his call."

"Nik–"

"I'm only teasing. You know I'm happy for you, right?" Nikki's expression changes from playful to concerned. I turn my gaze back to the mirror, hoping to avoid the conversation that's coming, but Nikki continues. "I know it was super romantic and exciting, but are you sure you want to–"

"Are you serious right now?" I wave my hands under the faucet sensor and begin washing them just to have something to focus on other than the attempted intervention. *I am not having this discussion.*

"Kins, come on. Just be real with me for a minute. Last week you weren't even sure if you'd make it to the end of the summer, and now–"

"And now I know we will." I yank a sheet from the paper towel dispenser, refusing to look at her.

"Why? Because of the ring?"

"No, of course not, Nik. With my finals and graduation, and his mom's diagnosis, we hardly had any time together. It was just a rocky period–"

"A rocky period? Kinsley, no less than six weeks ago I was scraping you off the floor at Buddy's. I know you were hammered, but you can't tell me you don't remember any of that."

"I remember. Thanks for throwing it in my face."

"I'm not throwing it in your face…or at least I wasn't trying to. I'm just looking out for you."

"I know you are, Nik, but we're fine now. It was just a misunderstanding. Can we move past it?"

Nikki agrees with a tight-lipped smile. Our fifteen years of friendship have taught me the meaning of that smile. I know it's a lie—I accept it anyway.

* * *

When I return to the table, Landon is mid-spiel. "It opens up a world of possibilities for drilling. We could make billions from it. No joke."

"What's no joke?" I ask.

"The horizontal drilling I've been pitching my dad. My uncle can help me with it if my dad would just give me a chance."

Landon pulls out his phone, checking a message on the screen before sliding it back into his pocket. "Hey, babe," he says, nuzzling my ear and waking goosebumps on my neck. "I need to stop by and check on my mom. You okay dropping Ben off and meeting me at my place after?"

I nod. It's better this way—I don't want to put a damper on our engagement night. Landon hates seeing me all tear-stained and worried about Ben. He only ever tries to reassure me that Ben will come back in one piece. I'm overreacting, but the goodbyes never get easier.

* * *

"Think you'll stay at the house next time?" I ask Ben as I pull up to the Will Rogers Inn. He doesn't answer, just forces a smile. The last time he slept at home was the night before boot camp. I know it's unlikely he'll stay at the house even though his old bedroom remains untouched. He's still angry. So is our dad. Ever since Ben announced he was joining the army instead of going to college and joining the company, I've been caught in the middle of their war.

I park the Jag between faded lines. "Thanks for coming home for graduation. It means a lot to me that you were here."

"Kins, you know I would have done anything to be here." He reaches over and gives my hand a quick squeeze. "As soon as you guys set a date, let me know, and I'll put in for leave."

The dog tags hanging from the rearview mirror reflect the streetlight. Ben had them made for me when he graduated boot camp. One with his name and one with mine, to remind me that we're in the fight together, no matter the enemy. No matter the distance between us, we're on the same side, even when it doesn't feel like it. Even when it feels like he has deserted me behind enemy lines, which he did that summer nine years ago.

Ben clears his throat as he looks out the passenger window and says, "I was hoping to have a chance to talk to you alone."

"What about?"

"I'm just..." He stops and turns to look at me. "What happened to the Philbrook plan? I thought you were going to tell Dad—"

"Plans changed, Ben." Of all people, he should understand the frailty of plans made and hoped for.

"Kins, look. I'm just saying, you're twenty-four and you haven't even moved out of the house. Your college experience wasn't exactly typical. Don't you want to take some time away from Dad? Get out in the real world? At least taking that job in Tulsa, you could rent a condo or something—"

"A lot has changed since you were home last time."

"Like what? Everything you've dreamed of doing? Has that changed?"

It had been foolish to mention the Philbrook to Ben. Sure, working at the museum would be much closer to the future I want, but it doesn't matter. Someone has to step up and take responsibility for the company's future, and that someone is me.

"What are you talking about?" I try to laugh it off. "This *is* what I wanted. Why do you think I went to business school?"

"Kins, business was never your dream. You always wanted to pursue art. I've seen your paintings—"

"Just undergrad electives, Ben. It's nothing," I lie, staring straight ahead at the paint-chipped hotel doors. If I look at him, the facade will crumble.

"I know you're doing this for Dad. You're doing this for him because *I* didn't."

Resentment trails across my chest, but I say nothing.

"I hoped things would change. I hoped maybe my leaving would wake him up, but it didn't," Ben continues.

"What are you—"

"Just, let me get this out. About a month before high school graduation, I found out Dad was..." He stalls, holding a fist to his mouth as he stares out the passenger window. "Look, he's made a lot of mistakes—no—" He shakes his head. "Not mistakes. Bad decisions—"

"*That's* why you left? Because he made a mistake?" I remember listening to their argument from the hall, their words obscured by the heavy oak doors of my dad's home office. Later, when I found out Ben had enlisted, I asked him why, but all he ever told me was "It's something I have to do." Dad's version: *Ben was being selfish.* And for almost nine years, that's all they've told me about Ben's reason for leaving. Until now.

"No, Kinsley, a mistake is an accident. He *made* these choices, and they've cost the company more than he can ever pay back. He's in too deep."

"It's been nine years. Whatever you found out back then, I'm sure he's—"

"No, Kinsley. He's still in it, and I can't leave without telling you to look out for yourself. You still have a chance to do something with your life. You don't have to get tangled up in his mess."

How can he possibly think there's any other path available? I want to rage at him, to make him understand that he blew up the other paths when he left. But I don't want to end things that way. As much as I try to pretend that he's going away on a business trip or doing research in some faraway land, I'm terrified that the next time he comes home he'll be wrapped in a flag.

"I just want you to know you have a choice, Kins. You don't have to board a sinking ship."

❊ ❊ ❊

It starts as a drizzle, barely sprinkling the windshield with tiny specks. By the time I pull up to Landon's house, it's a full-on downpour. I hurry across the driveway and up the front steps as Landon opens the door and ushers me in, wiping the sticky wet strands of hair from my face.

"Thanks. That came out of nowhere. How was your mom?"

"Same." He shrugs and locks the door behind us. "Wine?"

"Yes, please," I say, walking toward the bedroom. "I'm going to find something dry."

Opening the top drawer of his dresser where I keep a few things, I pull out a pair of track shorts along with one of his old college tees. I strip myself of rain-drenched clothing and dress before crawling into the king-sized bed, bundling myself in the down comforter while the air-conditioner blasts at full force.

"Here, babe," Landon says, handing me a glass and stretching out beside me as the storm announces its arrival with thunder.

I take a sip and then another, hoping to settle the anxiety before it takes root. I hate thunderstorms. It's not living in Tornado Alley, as they call it, that bothers me. Bring on the twister and take me to Oz. At least tornadoes are honest—they come to destroy. Thunderstorms are menacing. Maybe I'll escape with only a broken limb or cracked glass. Maybe lightning will strike and stop my heart. Worst of all, there's almost always a rainbow that follows. Thunderstorms cannot be trusted.

My panic attacks and nightmares started at thirteen, and thunderstorms seemed to be the trigger. Of course, the doctor thought it had something to do with repressed grief over losing my mom, but how could I grieve something I never had? Still, Dad insisted the doctor knew best and encouraged me to take the pills that were prescribed. They help— sometimes. But over the years, nothing has really changed except the new ways I cope with the storm inside.

I finish my wine and swallow my pills as Landon turns off the light. Curled up next to him, I place my hand under his shirt, softly grazing his chest while pressing my body closer to his. He kisses the top of my head and mumbles goodnight, already nearing sleep. Disappointment gathers behind my chest—there will be no celebratory love-making tonight. But it *is* late, and it has been an emotionally draining day. Wrapped in his arms, I close my eyes and wish the wine would hurry up and carry me away on the waves of dreams to some place where thunderstorms and sinking ships can't reach me.

TWO

Twelve years earlier.

I stand inches from the glass, watching raindrops pelt the window as lightning reflects off Lake Thunderbird. There's something beautiful in nature's show of force, as if to say, "Look what I can do. Who could try to stop me?"

If the night had gone as planned, I'd be at Nikki's, sneaking *Teen* magazines and lip gloss from Tammy's room. But Nikki is sick, so I'm stuck at home in a house full of boys. Ben has a few friends sleeping over for his sixteenth birthday. They were at the creek all day and came back smelling awful. They're always gross, but a day's worth of creek water, fish, and dirt make their presence known even if they are two doors down and across the hall. Their stench crawls through the ventilation and invades my room.

Thunder slams the sky, and my windows tremble in fear. When I was little, I would run across the hall to Ben's room and hide under his blanket, clinging to White Rabbit. But now I'm twelve—almost thirteen, so I can't expect Ben to save me.

White Rabbit sits on my nightstand next to a framed photo of me and Ben in a giant teacup. It's my favorite photo. I had summoned all of my preschool courage to board that ride. Even now, when I look at the picture, I can recall the rushing and swirling world around us. We were spinning so fast I thought I would slingshot off the earth and into the clouds, endlessly whirling away. I remember thinking that might not be so bad—maybe I would find my mom out there in the sky.

The boys' cheering and ruckus escape the game room, pulling me from the memory. It will be difficult to fall asleep if they keep it up, but nature tries to drown the disturbance with her sheets of rain and rumbles of thunder. I crawl into bed, tucking myself and White Rabbit under the light blue duvet cover, and open my copy of *Through the Looking Glass*. I pick up reading where heavy eyes forced me to abandon it the night before, with Tweedledee and Tweedledum reciting a ridiculous poem.

* * *

I wake up struggling to breathe as a blanketing weight shoves me into the mattress. Lying on my stomach, I try to push up and fill my lungs to scream, but the force behind me is too heavy, too strong.

"Shhh," he whispers in my ear, and his hand clamps over my mouth —salty and warm. "It's your party favor," he says as he tosses the duvet cover from the bed and hikes up my cotton nightgown. "You'll like it."

I try to free myself, fighting against the body on my back that only seems to grow heavier—stronger. Overcome with terror and the stench of fish and sweat, I draw my legs together to keep him away. But he wins. I'm pinned under him with no escape, vulnerable in the most devastating way. My scream is smothered by his hand. *No one can hear me.* My muffled cries join the pattering rain and now distant thunder.

No one is coming to save me. This is happening.

Anger builds inside me, and I shift my jaw in frantic attempts to bite his hand, but his grip is so tight I only manage to scrape the fleshy folds of his palm before he jerks it away.

"I knew you'd like it rough," he says, moving his hand to cup my throat, just under the jawline.

My mouth is free. I try to scream, but he tightens his hold on my neck—a silent warning that leaves me gasping for air. It feels like my lungs are collapsing into themselves.

I can't breathe. I'm going to die.

Consciousness ebbs as his thumb digs into my jaw and a coolness like metal presses into my collarbone. I surrender the fight, wishing to disappear into the pain.

It could have been minutes, it could have been hours when he lifts from my back. I have full access to air, but I'm too broken to appreciate it. I hear the zipper of his pants and the buckling of his belt. I want to scream, to jump out of my bed and throw something—destroy something like he just destroyed me. But I'm weak and empty.

With the slightest turn of my head, I watch him walk toward my door. I can almost make out a profile, but the room is dark, and my eyes are blurry with tears. *Who?* His voice was familiar, but not distinct. He walks out of my room, shutting the door behind him.

I can breathe.

I didn't die.

Except I did.

I don't move an inch. *What if he comes back?* I lay motionless in the quiet dark for some time. The putrid, fishy air clings to me, and my stomach recoils at the memory of violating pain. I can't hold it back and vomit spills over the bed sheets.

Wiping the bile from my chin, bitter sickness lingers in my mouth and on my lips. I run into the connected bathroom, fearing another spell, but nothing comes. A hollowing pain washes over me like waves beating the shore, taking a piece of me with each retreat.

I turn on the shower and step into the little glass square. Closing the door behind me, I slide down against the cool tile as hot water pelts my nightgown. Tears join the steam clouding the glass wall, and there I stay until my fingers wrinkle.

Stripping myself of the water-soaked nightgown, I step out of the shower. When I peek into the bedroom, it's dark except for the light spilling out from the foggy bathroom. I rip the soiled sheet from my bed and bundle it with my panties that lie on the floor. The cool air conditioning whispers over my bare skin, still warm from the shower. Shivering, I wrap myself up in the blue duvet cover and climb onto the bare mattress where I go back to sleep with the stink of fish and sickness floating around me and the weight of disgust and shame growing within.

The next morning, our housekeeper, Carlita, wakes me to ask if I'm sick. I can only manage a nod. My body hurts in every way—in foreign ways. Carlita cleans up the mess and brings crackers and Gatorade. Later, she convinces me to shower, and after I do, I find my bed made fresh and the room smelling clean as if nothing had happened.

Was it all a bad fever dream? Maybe I'm just sick like Nikki. If it was only a dream, it would explain why no one heard—why Ben didn't save me. It wasn't real. It didn't happen. It was a nightmare—*it had to be.*

THREE

After a week and a half on the road exploring the murals along Route 66 in Nikki's fully remodeled '63 Shasta Scout, I'm back home. It's a testament to our friendship that we can survive ten days together in an eighteen-foot camper.

Nikki likes to refer to it as a *Glamper* instead, and I can't argue with that. When Nikki's parents bought it for her twenty-first birthday, they essentially handed her a blank check to fix it up however she liked, and she really has turned it into so much more than *just a camper.* It might look like the home of a bohemian hippy on the outside, but the inside proves it was funded by the doctor and lawyer power-house couple, Mr. and Mrs. Bolero. Even with the upgrades and top-of-the-line furnishings, I'll never understand why Nikki thinks tiny-house living is a cool idea, but I can't deny the memories we made towing the little pink can of metal up and down the highway.

The trip gave me time to think—not just about what Ben said but also about the wedding. Ten Pinterest boards later, I settled on an early fall ceremony outdoors under a harvest moon. I called, texted, and e-mailed Landon to tell him about my plans, but he was hard to reach—he works full-time for his family's oil company, with most days spent in meetings or out checking on a rig.

It was late when we made it back into town last night, so Nikki dropped me off at home. After dumping my dirty clothes into the laundry room hamper I went upstairs and crashed into bed.

It's morning, and I'm trying to go back to sleep, but my BlackBerry dings with an email notification. It's my dad.

Kinsley,
Please stop by the office today. I need to speak with you ASAP.
–Richard Holland, CEO Charleston Holland Industries

I shoot out of bed like I'm late for class. Because that's how it is with us. He calls, and I come running. I jump through hoops, hoping to prove my worth and earn a place in his world. Maybe I'm trying to fill in the holes Ben left behind, but I know I'll never measure up. I'm nothing like my brother. Ben is smart, ambitious, a born leader, and made for the business world. Maybe that's why he was our dad's favorite for so long. I've been a disappointment from the day I was born. I took the love of his life away from him and all he got in return was a daughter with a knack for messing things up.

* * *

At the end of the driveway, I check the mailbox and find a card from Ben with a return address of the Will Rogers Inn. It's not uncommon for him to send me mail when he's home on leave. If he waits until he gets back to base, it can take weeks. I sit in my car, letting the cool air fill the space as I open the envelope. It's a greeting card with a vintage print of Alice and the Cheshire Cat that reads, *If you don't know where you are going, any road will get you there.* Inside, is a handwritten note:

Kins,
I was looking for a graduation card when I saw this one and had to get it for you. So, congrats on your graduation! And the engagement. I'm happy things worked out for you two.
Please think about what I said. Don't let someone else choose the road for you. If you really want to work with Dad, okay, but make sure it's what you want. But do one thing for me before you make up your mind. Look into CHI's connection to Ouranos Group.
I'll write again when I can,
Love Ben

I wipe a tear pooling in my eye, tuck the card into my purse, and turn onto the road. I can't let emotions wreck my makeup. It's not worth the tears anyway—the decision has been made.

Needing caffeine and carbs to tackle the day, I make a stop at the little bakery downtown before heading to the office. A new message pops up on my phone as I'm getting back into the Jag, coffee in hand.

Did you see my email? I need to meet with you ASAP.

Be there in ten, I type and take a swig of coffee before backing out onto the road.

Shit. I pull up to the lowered crossing bars as the train lays on its horn, announcing its approach. There's no way I'll make it to the office in ten minutes. Even though CHI is just a few miles from the bakery, three railroad tracks lay between them. In this little Oklahoma town, where there are almost as many railroad crossings as there are street lights, you have to plan for at least one stint waiting on a train.

I reach into the bakery bag for my banana-nut muffin and eat my breakfast, mulling over Ben's words as I wait for the train to pass. He accused Dad of making decisions that cost the company, but I can't see it. CHI is doing fine—better than fine. They recently secured two major government contracts, and their workload is backing up to the point that they need to hire more labor. It's far from the sinking ship Ben talked of. And this Ouranos Group—I haven't heard of them before today. Ben means well—I know that, but I always feel like a pawn in their war.

When the train clears the tracks, I push forward through town until turning onto Bone Creek Road. It follows a winding path forged by the waterway and leads to the industrial park on the edge of town. In the center of it all stands a five-story glass-front office building reflecting the morning sun, blinding anyone who dares look it in the eye. I make the mistake of doing just that.

As I blink away the dark stars spotting my vision, I turn into the lot through the main gate and pull up to the front row where there's already a parking space with my name on it. I'm not even on the payroll yet, having only interned during the last semester of business school. Giving me a prime parking spot seems a bit much, but there's no arguing with my dad.

I turn off the ignition and open the door. Stepping out of the car, I wobble to maintain balance in my peep-toe Chanels with my Louis Vuitton in one hand and the brown paper bag in the other.

"Good afternoon, Miss Holland." A familiar voice greets me as I step into the cool air-conditioned lobby.

"Mr. Jeffries." I smile, holding out the brown paper bag. "I was hoping to see you today."

"What's this, dear?" The older man reaches across his security podium with a shaky hand. Mr. Jeffries isn't exactly the security guard you'd expect at Charleston Holland Industries. He isn't quick enough to stop an intruder or young enough to pounce into action. But he's loyal, someone my dad trusts, and trust is everything to him. Growing up, he was someone I could show my elementary school artwork to, someone who'd read Lewis Carroll as many times as I had, and someone who always had butterscotch candy for me.

"It's one of those big banana nut muffins you love from the bakery downtown."

"Oh, you shouldn't have." He tries to hand it back to me. "I can't–"

"Stop it, silly. You know you love them." I raise an eyebrow. "And I know you have a break coming up soon."

"Well…" He chuckles and peeks inside the bag. "It does smell delicious."

I wink at my old friend, then walk across the open lobby, my heels echoing as they click-clack on the polished marble floor. Above me hangs a large-scale model of the company's pride and joy, a B-25 bomber. Charleston Manufacturing, as it was known in 1941, landed a government contract to build the twin-engine warbirds to fight the Axis Powers. My grandfather commissioned the model for the company's seventy-fifth anniversary, just before he retired and Ben was born.

Waiting for the elevator, I check my appearance in the heavy, gilded mirror, smoothing a few rebellious strands of hair back into submission and brushing a piece of lint from my black Valentino dress. He always expects perfection when I visit the office. I'm the face of the company's future after all, and it has to match the projected image. A faint ding interrupts the silence, and the metal doors slide open. *Is this how prisoners felt being led up the gallows?*

When the elevator doors open, I step out into a long quiet hallway with executive suites spaced evenly apart. I take a deep breath and start toward the biggest suite at the end of the hall. CHI employs thousands, though most are skilled laborers in the assembly and manufacturing bays. But here, in the glass building filled with white-collar climbers, the top floor is reserved for a handful—those with the most responsibility, the strongest resolve, and the most to lose. By the end of summer, my name will be chiseled into a placard: Kinsley Holland, Junior VP of something or other—whatever title my dad dreams up for me. The title doesn't matter, my job will remain the same: Follow Daddy's orders and don't ask questions.

I stop in front of a floor-to-ceiling wooden door with deep insets and a bronze scroll handle. With a gentle knock, I open it just enough to enter. A murky gray mural of a mountain scene covers the wall behind him. Sitting at his heavy oak desk, he's Zeus ruling from the top of Olympus. He waves me in, barely glancing up from the papers spread out before him. I close the door behind me and make my way across the suite.

Taking a seat in one of the black velvet chairs opposite the desk, I smooth my dress and turn my gaze to the windows looking down on the world outside. Hundreds of cars fill the parking spots, and this is only one side of the building. Hundreds more fill the lot on the other side and down the road at the maintenance plant. It makes me nervous being so close to the helm of responsibility—one mistake could cost so much.

"Thanks for coming in," he says. Always so formal. As if I were just another employee and not his daughter.

"Why did you want to see me?"

"It's about your start date." He looks up at me, peering over his silver-rimmed glasses. "We're pushing it up a bit. July seventh."

"What happened to starting in August?" I try to stifle my frustration. It's typical of him to change the terms of our deal.

"I had to let Phillips go." The calmness in his voice when he says it makes me uneasy. Phillips has worked with my dad for as long as I can remember. He's almost family.

"What? But he–"

"He was putting the company at risk."

"How?" I ask, wondering if it has anything to do with what Ben mentioned.

"It doesn't matter. I did what I had to do to protect the business–to protect us. Now I just need to fill the position."

My stomach drops. "Me? You mean I would take his place? There has to be someone else."

"No, Kinsley, I need someone I can trust." His eyes tell me there's more to the story, but I won't be invited to hear it. Phillips is—*was*—the company's Chief Financial Officer. Tiny beads of sweat form on my skin at the thought of it.

I've never been a numbers person, and other than a high proficiency in spending it, the only thing I know about money is that anything can be bought. You just have to offer the right price. My recently acquired business degree is proof. Sure, I showed up for class and technically did the work, but I only managed to pass those damn accounting courses with a little help from some friends, specifically Andrew Jackson and Ben Franklin. There's no doubt I'll sink straight to the bottom if I jump into the deep end of managing the company's finances.

"But I... I thought I had more time." A week is too short. I'll have to spend every waking second choking down dry interest rate formulas and tax laws.

"More time for what? To lay around the house and be lazy? To party, wreck cars, and embarrass yourself? We've done enough of that now haven't we?" Every memory I try to forget, the mistakes that haunt me, now tip the scales in his favor. What will he do if he discovers I cheated my way through the classes he paid for? I'm sinking, grasping for anything I can cling to.

"But I just graduated, and I don't have any real experience. How would it look to the others?"

"I don't give a damn how it looks, Kinsley." His tone sharpens. "There's no one else."

I dig my fingers into the velvet armrests. Ben's warning, the news of Phillips, and the idea of filling his shoes swirl in my mind and create a similar effect in my stomach. "Does this have something to do with Ouranos Group?" The words spill out of me.

His eyes flicker up, and he seems to stop himself from speaking. Removing his glasses and pinching the bridge of his nose, he asks, "What do you know about Ouranos Group?"

"Nothing." I shrug because it's true and because the tension between us has doubled since I spoke the words. "It's just something Ben mentioned."

"Ben doesn't know anything about it. He's been out of the mix for years."

"But, he–"

"Kinsley, do you really think he knows a single thing about what's going on here? He's a million miles away playing hero in the desert." His words are venom, and the contempt he holds for Ben all these years later seethes out of him.

"I just think I have the right to know what I'm getting myself into before I–"

"Before you what?" He stares into me.

"Before I become part of something. I think I should know what's going on behind the scenes."

"If you're accusing me of something, Kinsley, you better come out with it."

"I'm not accusing you, Dad. I'm just asking for transparency. You won't tell me what Phillips did to put the company at risk. You're blowing off my question about Ouranos Group. I just want to know why Ben called this a sinking ship."

"A sinking ship?"

I swallow, immediately regretting my words. "What, exactly, did your brother say, Kinsley?" He steps out from behind the desk and now stands directly in front of me.

"He just said that you had made some mistakes…" I choose not to correct the wording as Ben had. "And you couldn't repay what it has cost the company."

His eyes settle on me like he's trying to discern what all I know. "I see," he says, now pacing the floor, arms crossed. "And what did your brother say Ouranos Group had to do with any of this?"

"He didn't say anything exactly, just that I should look into it."

"And did you? Look into it?"

I shake my head. The silence that follows as he processes the exchange is heavy, like waiting for a verdict.

"Alright, look… You know that Ben and I have our issues. He shouldn't be dragging you into them, but there's nothing for you to worry about. Ouranos Group is just one of the companies we use for employee pension funds. And as far as a sinking ship, do you see all this?" He points to the papers covering his desk. "These are contracts and bids. Does it look like the ship is sinking?"

I pause, contemplating my next move. Maybe he's right and Ben had it wrong. Still, whether the ship is sinking or sailing, I don't even have my sea legs yet. I can't be the captain. "I… I can't," I sputter. "I'm sorry, Dad. I can't take Phillips' place–anything else, but not CFO."

"Haven't I given you enough?" He slams his hand down on the desk, startling a jump from me. "Everything money can buy, I've given you. And you can't do this one thing for me? You're just like your brother." He turns away.

Guilt snakes through my gut. After everything I've put him through, I owe it to him, but I can't bring myself to submission this time. The stakes are too high. "I'm sorry," I whisper.

When he turns back to face me, a new resolve burns in his eyes. "Just how far do you think you can get without me? Don't you know I hold the key to every door in this town?"

"Dad, I'm not saying I'm done with you. I just, I can't do *this*."

"Do you have any idea how much I paid for your tuition?" He continues, ignoring my words. "Seventy thousand. And that's including all those little art classes you took in undergrad–don't think I didn't notice those." He stops, and the silence is worse than his ranting. It means he's calculating his next move.

"Seventy-thousand down the drain if I can't even depend on you to do this one thing for me. Is that it? I threw my money away?"

I choke on words, rebuttals lodge in my throat too afraid to meet their foe.

"Take the position or pay me back."

"You can't be serious."

"Oh, I'm serious." He crosses his arms, leaning on his desk with ease. "If you can't pay me back, then I guess the only option is taking the position now isn't it?" Checkmate.

Panic grips my chest and pounds inside my head. The monthly allowance he doles out will never cover it. The air has been sucked from my lungs, and I have to get out of here. "I can't do this." I stand up and start out of the room.

"Running away from your responsibility–just like your brother," he shouts from the door. I pick up speed halfway down the hall, trying to fight back tears.

* * *

Slamming the gear shift into reverse, I jerk the wheel and push the accelerator. Tires squeal as I back out of the parking spot and plow over speed bumps, sending the dog tags hanging from the rearview into a frenzy. Another squeal of the tires, this time louder, longer as I blow through the stop sign at the parking lot's exit. The road opens before me, and I watch the needle rise on the speedometer—an extension of myself.

Running away from your responsibility. You're just like your brother. My dad's bullets ring in my mind. I push the Jag to its limit as the road follows the creek's twists and turns, and when it straightens, I let up on the gas momentarily, just enough to relax my muscles before stabbing the accelerator with renewed force. If I could floor this thing to the moon and never come back I would.

FOUR

Caleb: June 26, 2008

The screen door slams behind me, and not because I'm angry, the screen door always slams. I'm not angry, but I am frustrated—coming so close to the goal just to watch it fade away like a mirage. I pull a worn-out baseball cap from my back pocket and wipe my brow before fitting it to my head.

"Thought you were working in North Field today," Chase says, walking up behind me from the other side of the barn.

"I was about to head over there, but your dad wanted to see me first," I say, climbing up into the tractor.

Chase leans against the fender, arms crossed and looking at the dirt beneath him. "So, he told you, huh? You know, I could co-sign–"

"I'm not letting you help. You've already done enough. Your whole family has."

"Dude, you're like a brother to me. Don't be like that," Chase says.

"I'm not. I just…" I sigh. "I need to do this on my own, alright?"

"Look, I know you were supposed to have another sixteen months to get the money together. Now, you got, what? Five?"

"Four, actually," I say.

"Okay, four months. You can't turn water into wine here, Caleb. You gotta let someone help."

"Just give me a chance to figure it out." I don't want to admit how bad this is. How pissed I am that Marty needs to push up his retirement by a year and a half. But I can't blame him—it's not his fault he needs a hip replacement. I just have to find another way to bridge the gap between what I've already saved and what I need to buy the farm. Even with the loan I discussed with the bank, I'm still $11,000 short. It was going to be a stretch to save that much in sixteen months, but four months—impossible.

"God, you're so stubborn. Just like the day I met you." Chase shakes his head as a wide grin brightens his face. "Guess I didn't give you a good enough ass whooping that day–"

"Oh, please. You didn't give me an ass-whooping. I kicked your ass–"

"Oh, I kicked your ass," Chase mocks.

"Dude, your dad's gonna kick both our asses if I don't get to work." I laugh and start up the engine.

"Alright, I'm just saying." Chase steps away from the tractor, hands up. "Your best friend's about to be a big country star. You should let him help you out."

"Yeah, yeah. Why don't you go work on your confidence some," I tell him and pull forward down the dirt road.

The drive to North Field is just a few minutes by car but a little longer by tractor. At this time of day, the two-lane road is all mine. Early mornings and quitting time are a different story with traffic funneling in and out of the industrial park. The first time I got caught up in the morning rush I was only seventeen. I'd never been honked at, cursed at, and flipped off so much in my life, and it all happened in less than ten minutes.

I pull up to the intersection and turn onto Bone Creek Road. The industrial park sits up ahead on my left, and the entrance to North Field is a bit farther down on my right. Working in North Field is my favorite part of the job. It's set apart from the rest of the farm, so it's quiet and open. Peaceful.

A loud rumble puts me on alert. *Damn engine acting up again.* I lean forward, peering through the glass window, looking for smoke, but instead of sooty clouds pouring out from the green hood, I see a black bullet shot straight from hell speeding toward me. A car straddles the center line and continues at full speed. *What the hell?*

I shift into a lower gear and hug the grass line, but it's not enough. This joker will plow into me if I don't give up the lane. I give it all I can, jerking the wheel to the right, but in my split-second decision-making, I fail to consider the incline that flanks the narrow shoulder. Green grass and blue sky wrestle as the tractor topples on its side. When the world stops spinning, I'm smooshed against a side panel. A searing pain in my right arm makes it challenging to pull myself out of the turned-over Boomer.

"Oh, my god, I'm so sorry. Are you okay?" a voice hollers from the other side of the glass.

"I got it." I snarl, crawling out of the cab and noticing the pink-toed bare feet speckled with dirt and grass.

"Are you hurt? Oh, shit. I'm so sorry," she rambles on.

"Jesus. What's wrong with you?" I hiss, cradling my right arm as I stand up, refusing her help.

"I'm so sorry, I didn't–"

"Look at this mess." I hobble around the tractor, inspecting the scene.

"I know. I'll pay for the damages, I promise."

Squinting in the morning sunlight, I take a full look at her. *Oh, hell. Of course, it's her.* "No shit you'll pay for the damages."

"Let me take you to the hospital to have your arm looked at." She reaches out to me. "And your leg," she adds as I limp toward her, shrugging off her attempt to help.

As I struggle up the incline, I suggest calling the police to report the accident, but she tells me it's not necessary. "It'll be faster if I just take you to the ER now and give you a check for the damages. Besides, you didn't wreck a car–just a tractor."

"Yeah, just a twenty-thousand dollar piece of farm machinery, but whatever."

We cross the empty road to her car, parked without a scratch or dent in sight, and I slide into the leather seat, letting go of my injured arm long enough to reach across and pull the door shut. As soon as she turns the ignition, the speakers blast some god-awful emo-pop song.

"We'll be at the hospital in just a minute," she says, pulling onto the road.

"Do you have a hearing problem?"

"Huh?" She looks over at me, the black smudgy tears dried on her cheeks match the oil stains on my Wranglers. "It's Caleb, right?" she asks, still looking at me as she turns down the dial on the stereo.

"Yeah, and just keep your eyes on the road. I'm familiar with your driving skills."

"Hey, that's not fair. I was distracted."

"Sure. Just distracted, going about what? Eighty in a forty, taking up both lanes on a two-lane road. No wonder you didn't want to call the cops."

She looks toward me again but quickly turns back to face the road as soon as our eyes meet. "I didn't mean to–"

"No one ever does," I mumble.

"It's Kinsley, by the way. Kinsley Holland from school."

"I know who you are," I say. Everyone knows who she is. Sure, it's a small town, but she's the kind of girl who'd be known in any size town.

"Weren't you friends with my brother, Ben, in high school?"

I nod, mouth clenched as she continues. "Yeah, you and Ben and my boyfriend Landon were close. I remember."

"Oh, yeah, best of friends." I close my eyes in pain. She has it half-right. I *was* good friends with her brother, but *not* with Landon. I don't correct her. It's not worth the trouble, and I don't feel like chatting with the girl who just wrecked my day.

"Wow, quite the conversationalist aren't you?"

"You just ran me off the road, and I'm pretty sure my elbow is dislocated, so forgive me for not wanting to reminisce about high school right now."

"Sheesh. I said I was sorry." She turns the stereo back up, blasting my ears. *Just what I need, a migraine.*

* * *

If not for the blinding pain, I would have been more nervous on the ride over. Some people should *not* be given sports cars to drive and Kinsley Holland is one of them. Everyone in town knows how she totaled her Corvette in high school. But when you have as much money as the Hollands do, you can just pay your problems away.

Kinsley slams the Jag into a parking spot near the entrance, adding whiplash to my list of self-diagnosed conditions. I limp across the asphalt, and the automatic doors part before us. She motions for me to take a seat in the waiting room. "Be right back," she says before wobbling away, looking like a train wreck in heels. To her benefit, she does appear to be concerned, but she's probably thinking about her reputation and financial obligations rather than my injuries.

I replay the morning in my head, wishing I had done even one single thing differently that might have kept me from crossing paths with her. *Damn bad luck.*

Since I'm breathing just fine and not bleeding out, I'm not a top priority and spend a good hour in the waiting room thinking of the million other things I should be doing—*would* be doing—if not for her.

"So, you have a farm or something?" she asks. It's not enough to interrupt my work day, now she has to interrupt my brooding too.

"I don't *have* a farm, I work on a farm."

"For how long?"

"I don't know, forever. Since I was a teenager." *Is this a job interview or a speed dating round?*

"Is it hard to drive a tractor?"

I take a deep breath. "Not when people stay in their lane."

"God, I wasn't *trying* to run you off the road, Caleb," she says, folding her arms across her chest and wiggling her dirty high-heeled foot. "Why were you on the road anyway? Aren't you supposed to drive those things in fields?"

"It's street-legal." *Unlike her driving.*

For a moment, she's quiet—maybe she has run out of things to say. But no. She continues for the better part of the hour, asking benign questions and attempting small talk. At one point, for a glorious three minutes, she flits away to the vending machines. But when she returns it's as if she has downloaded a new set of questions to fire off.

"Didn't you have a brother or something? Jimmy... Jason... He was in my class, right?"

"Sure."

"Hey, whatever happened to that curly-haired girl you were dating? I haven't seen her around. Did she move?"

I pan my eyes toward her, my mouth clamped shut.

"Right." She stretches her mouth into a painful frown. "Probably don't want to talk about her?"

Don't want to talk at all.

"Did you get a chance to see Ben when he was home on leave?"

I nod, wishing she would get the hint that I'm not in the mood to shoot the breeze.

"When? What did you guys—"

"We don't have to talk, you know? In fact, you can go. I can get a ride."

"Caleb Lewis," a nurse calls my name, and Kinsley stands up to escort me.

"I got it, thanks." I stop her, needing a break from her prattling as much as I need medication for the pain.

* * *

Almost another hour later, the ER staff releases me with the good news that I haven't broken anything and the bad news that my right arm will be in a sling for four weeks. Other than the dislocated elbow, a few scrapes and bruises, and one completely fucked up day, I'm good to go.

I pass through the double doors to the waiting room where my Nokia has a signal again, and I start to call Chase for a ride when Kinsley hurries to meet me by the discharge desk.

"Hey, I can call a ride—"

"Oh, don't worry about it. I'll drive you home." She offers her arm. "Here, you need help?"

"I'm good, thanks." I let out a defeated sigh and limp past her, through the automatic doors and into the sweltering summer heat.

"So, what did they say?" Kinsley asks as she clicks the key fob, unlocking the car doors.

"Dislocated elbow."

"And..." She gestures, bobbing her head, those big brown eyes bugging out at me.

"And nothing." I slide into the passenger seat. "Just gotta keep it in the sling for four weeks."

"Well, at least it's not broken, right?"

"Yeah, just four weeks as a one-armed farmer. Can't wait."

"Sorry," she says, scrunching up her face and looking toward me as she turns onto the main road. She must have cleaned herself up while I was with the doctor—the smudgy black tears are gone from her face.

"I can give you some money to hire extra help." My head is still pounding, the medication hasn't fully kicked in, and right now, I'd give all the money in the world for her to just stop talking. She takes every turn a little too sharp, and it's obvious that she regards speed limits as suggestions, not mandates. But it's only a short drive home—surely she can't do any more damage in just five minutes, can she?

Kinsley turns onto the winding strip that leads back toward most of the farmland and the site of the accident—the tractor still on its side like roadkill tossed over the embankment. "How are you going to get that out?" she asks as we pass by.

"Flip and tow it," I answer, figuring she doesn't *really* want to know the details. She doesn't care that it will eat up a significant amount of daylight tomorrow. She has no idea what consequences are.

"When will you–"

"I don't know. Tomorrow, I guess. Why do you care?"

"Just making conversation." She shifts her eyes toward me and mouths *rude*. "But, also…" *Here we go.* "It would be better if this stays between us, you know?"

"Between us?"

"I'd appreciate it if my dad didn't know about the accident." She shrugs, staring straight ahead at the road for what may be the first time ever.

"I'm not going to call him up if that's what you're thinking."

"No–I know. I just want to handle this on my own. It's easier that way."

"Sure," I mumble as she finally turns onto my street. The end is in sight, and it has never looked so good.

She pulls up to the older white house Gram left me, the only home I've known since I was twelve. My little sister's bike is gone. Annie must still be at her friend's house—probably for the best. I never know what to expect from a fourteen-year-old full of emotions and opinions. But if she sees me coming home in a Jaguar with a woman, she'll have a rapid fire of questions, I know that much. Gravel crunches beneath the tires as Kinsley parks in front of the house.

"Here, let me help you to the door." She jumps out and wobbles around to the passenger side before I can stop her. I'm reaching across my body to pull the handle when she opens the door.

"I got it, thanks," I say, dodging her attempt to steady me as I climb out of the car. The finish line is in sight, but she follows me up the porch steps like a stray puppy.

"You need me to–"

"No. I'm good."

"Okay, well…" She looks like she's waiting for me to dismiss her. *Haven't I done that already? Like ten times?*

"Oh, shoot. Hold on." She hobbles down the little steps and across the drive to her car. She's half in, half out, and rummaging around. Popping back up, she smooths her black dress and hurries back to me.

"Here's my number," she says, handing me a business card with her name and number on one side and Charleston Holland Industries on the other. I run my thumb over the embossed letters. It feels like treason. "Let me know what you find out about the repairs and hiring help so I can drop off a check."

"Yep, will do." I force a smile and limp through the doorway. Once on the other side, I wait for the sound of the car's engine to know she's truly gone and out of my hair.

FIVE

Kinsley: June 26, 2008

"What's up?" Nikki asks, stepping out of the camper while pulling her long copper hair into a ponytail.

"Worst day ever." I slam the car door and plod across the beaten grass. Inside, I flop myself down on the mini sofa and recount the fight with my dad and the whole tractor mess with Caleb while Nikki pokes around in the retro-style fridge.

"Caleb Lewis?" she asks with surprise, handing me a cold can of Diet Coke, which I eye with disgust.

"Really? Diet Coke?"

"Sorry, I'm fresh out of the good stuff," she says, joining me on the couch. "Man, that sucks. He's already dealing with so much."

"Umm, hello? What about me, Nik?" I pop the top, taking a swig of the soda, wishing I'd find a shot of vodka hidden inside.

"Sorry. Of course, this is about *you* and *your* bad day. It's just, Chase told me Caleb is trying to save up to buy the farm." She shrugs. "It'll probably set him back some."

"He'll be fine. I'm the one who has to pay for the repairs and medical expenses." I take another swig—still no vodka—and slump against the couch. "By the way, I put your address down for the bills. If my dad finds out, he'll go ballistic."

"Yeah, well, he's done that before." Nikki laughs.

"Just more ammo to use against me. To force me to be his CFO."

"So, you're paying back the tuition?"

I shrug. "How can I? I don't have that much in the bank."

Nikki twists her mouth and hums. "What about a loan?"

"My dad pays for everything. I have no credit, no job–not even a work history other than the internship. Face it, I'm screwed."

"Come on." She nudges me "You're not screwed. We'll figure it out. What if you just take the job and–" I stop her with a look because she knows about my less-than-honest methods of passing the finance classes.

"Just let him see how bad you suck and he'll have to let you move to another position," she says.

"And give him more reason to resent me?" I shake my head. *What the hell am I gonna do?*

"I mean, how much worse can it get?"

Nikki's right. There isn't another level to his disdain for me. I hit rock bottom the day I was born, and there really isn't anything I can do to make him love me less. For years, I've tried to climb up, inch a little closer to the surface, where maybe I can prove to him that I'm worthy. Now, the tunnel is shrinking, and the tiny pinprick of light with it.

"Alright, I know what you need." Nikki winks and pops up from the couch. "Buddy's?"

I roll my eyes as a small grin pushes through, and I kick off my poor dirt-caked stilettos. "Fine, but I'm borrowing some clothes."

✽ ✽ ✽

Sitting a little out of the way on the far end of town, Buddy's Bar and Grill quietly promises your sins will stay hidden, but they never do. We find an open booth and slide in. By the time the waitress comes to take our orders, the weathered vinyl is already sticking to the back of my legs. Maybe cut-offs weren't the best choice.

"Be right back." Nikki hops up and dances her way to the jukebox. While she's gone, I pull out my phone to text Landon that I'm grabbing a bite with Nikki. Still no reply from Ben, but that's typical. With the time difference and his responsibilities in combat, I can't expect an instant response. Yesterday's quick web search on Ouranos Group revealed nothing significant. Why can't he just tell me what I need to know?

Right on cue, just seconds after Nikki returns, Martina McBride's "Independence Day" booms over the speakers. "Every time?"

"Traditions." Nikki shrugs.

"Speaking of traditions, are we still set to take the pontoon out next weekend for the Fourth?

"Yeah, Tammy won't be in town though, she has some conference next week she has to prepare for, so you're stuck with the cool sister."

"Well, she'll miss out on my last hurrah then. My dad's either going to disown me or kill me. Either way, I'm toast after the Fourth." Martina belts on about the day of reckoning, and the waitress returns with our drinks. "God, Nik, what am I gonna do?"

"What about Landon, can't you just ask him for the money?"

"Maybe." I sigh, shaking my head at the thought of explaining the whole mess to him. "But he already does so much for me, and I hate to–"

"Just saying, you'll be married soon," Nikki offers in a sing-song tune. Is it a challenge? A test? Nikki isn't Landon's biggest fan, but that's only because I made the mistake of venting to her about our fights. She can't let it go, even though I've already forgiven him. Now, any decision I make regarding Landon is under her microscope.

"Of course, he would do it," I say, skirting past Nikki's test. "But I think I need to handle this myself."

"Oh, I know! A few months back Tammy told me about a charity auction where people donated their designer bags and shoes. They raised a shit-ton of money. You could list your collection of Louis Vuittons on eBay or something."

"Blasphemy!" I gasp, clutching the Neverfull closer to my side in jest. "Besides, do you really think I could raise *that* much in a week?" Our loaded bacon burgers and fries arrive, knocking that conversation off the rails. *Thank god.*

"I picked up *The Other Boleyn Girl* from Redbox, want to stay over and watch it tonight?"

"Do you even have to ask? Wait–" I hold up my free hand, the greasy burger dripping from the other. "I know you're *fresh out of the good stuff,* but do you at least have ice cream?"

"Do *I* have ice cream? Maybe they should have checked *your* head at the hospital."

When I take the last bite of my burger, I see Landon walk through the door. He looks entirely out of place in his khakis and pistachio green button-down. At least he isn't wearing a tie, but still, this is by far the most casual dining in town, and his perfectly styled blonde crew cut and squeaky clean presentation are blinding in the hazy bar.

"Hey Kins, Nik, what's up?" he asks as he sits beside me in the little booth, and I shift my weight to make room for him.

"Dinner. What about you?" Nikki asks. "What are you doing here?"

"Looking for my girl." He puts his arm around my shoulders, pulling me in for a quick peck. "I got your text."

"Yeah, sorry I didn't come over earlier. It's been crazy."

"Don't worry about it, babe." He takes a few fries from the basket Nikki and I are sharing. "Your dad told me."

My dad? Sometimes it feels like they're keeping tabs on me and reporting back to one another. But then again, it's nice that they get along so well. With Ben on my dad's shit list, Landon has become a stand-in son and now soon-to-be son-in-law.

"Well, we were just about to leave," Nikki says, standing up. "You can have the rest of the fries."

I gather my things, inching closer to Landon and the open end of the booth.

"Oh, it's okay, Nik. I'll give Kins a ride home," he says, placing his hand on my thigh under the table, sliding it closer to the frayed hem of my shorts. "I haven't seen you all week, babe. We have some catching up to do." He winks and flashes a grin that melts me every time.

Nikki rolls her eyes, waiting for me to make the final call—her or Landon. But the choice has already been made. I offer Nikki an apologetic smile. "Raincheck on the ice cream and movie?" Nikki's opinion isn't hidden from her face as she forces a grin.

"Yeah, Nik," Landon says. "You two can have all the ice cream and chick-flicks you want next week. Someone has to take care of her while I'm in Dallas."

"You're going to Dallas?" This is news to me.

"Some meetings with investors down there." He waves it off, popping a few more fries in his mouth.

"Cool." Nikki clicks her tongue. "Well, I guess I'll see you next week." She turns to leave, her long ponytail whipping around her.

"Still not a fan, huh?" Landon chuckles. "After all these years, you'd think she'd find a way to get that stick out of her ass by now."

"Landon, please." I grab his hand. "She's—"

"Here we go. I know, I know. She's your best friend, like a sister to you. Just try to get along." He pulls out his wallet, leaving cash on the table for the tip, then winks and kisses my head. "Ready?"

*　*　*

Filling my lungs with the soft night air, I enjoy the quiet chirp of summer nocturnes as Landon punches in the code at the security gate. It isn't stifling yet, still being June. The real summer heat—the one that doesn't let up even in the dark—is coming and there's no stopping it, like the trains that roll through town, blowing their horns.

The ornate metal barriers part, allowing Landon's Viper to pass before locking back into place behind us. We drive through the quiet neighborhood of beautiful designer homes on spacious lots that allow privacy and discretion. Though it isn't home yet, I feel relief at the sight of his house.

Once inside, I drop my purse on the coffee table. "I'm going to take a bath."

"Sure babe," he says from the kitchen as he pulls down two wine glasses.

"You read my mind." I kick off the sandals I borrowed from Nikki and walk into the bedroom.

An oversized bathroom sits behind frosted double doors, which I slide to each side, revealing a large whirlpool tub in the corner. I walk over and turn the faucet knob. The pooling water is soothing white noise, something that would comfort a baby back to sleep. I wiggle out of the cut-offs and lift the black tank top over my head, letting it fall to the floor. The Carrara marble is cold beneath my feet but not unwelcome. Opening the cabinet on the right side of the vanity I find a jar of bath salts Landon gave me. Anniversary? Birthday? Apology?

When the tub is nearly full, I pour a scoop-full of the magnolia-scented crystals. The aroma fills the air as I remove my bra and panties and climb into the warm, welcoming waters. I turn the knob, stopping the flow, and for a moment, the room is silent but for the small pops of effervescing salts. Uncomfortably silent. The kind of silence where I can't help but hear the voice inside. The one I try all day to tune out and all night to forget. I push the button to turn on the jets, letting the bubbles and flow of water massage my body and drown my thoughts.

"You make it look so inviting." Landon tilts his head as he carries two glasses of red wine and sits on the edge of the tub, handing me one.

"Thanks," I murmur, taking a long sip and sinking back into the waters. He places his glass on the edge of the tub and unbuttons his shirt. *God, it has been too long.* I watch Michelangelo's *David* disrobe before me, his tall, fit frame tapers down to narrow hips and a tight ass I love to hold onto when he buries himself inside me. The tub is big enough for two, but he takes up most of it, sitting across from me with my feet resting on his thighs.

"Did you see the email I sent? About the wedding theme?" I pour another long draw of wine down my throat before setting it aside.

"Yeah, something outside, right?" he says, wine glass in one hand and drawing little circles on my leg with the other.

"I was thinking next year. In the fall? We could–"

"Next year?" He places his wine glass on the built-in shelf and rubs his hands across his face in frustration. "I thought this was what you wanted."

"It is… I just don't see how I could pull it together for *this* fall. There's so much to do, plus making sure Ben can–"

"Babe, that's what a wedding planner is for." He smiles and I watch it fade as a familiar streak of pain shadows his face. "It would mean a lot to me to have my mom there."

His face reminds me of a sculpture I studied in college—some hero of Greek mythology, strong but wounded, brows drawn and softened with pain. The last year has been a whirlwind of promising treatments, renewed hope, and twice as many setbacks. The doctors aren't optimistic, six months to a year at most. A sinking weight threatens to pull me down under the bubbling magnolia waters. *So selfish, Kinsley. So inconsiderate.* Of course, we have to plan the wedding sooner. Still, what about Ben? My heart aches at the thought of getting married without him there, and I doubt he can take leave again so soon.

Everyone wants more and more from me, and they want it *now*—my dad's ultimatum, rushing the wedding. Every alarm is ringing, muted behind a veil of obligation and wine. A small, salty tear rolls down my cheek without emotional fanfare and I slide forward, close enough to take his face into my hands. I smooth my thumbs over his cheeks, then move my hands behind his neck and gently pull my fingers through his blonde hair, damp with bath water.

"Okay," I breathe, and the air is gone from my lungs like the time I fell off the swing in the backyard and landed on my back. Breathing had always been so easy, so natural. Not after that fall. Filling my lungs with air again—it hurt. Maybe that's why babies cry when they take their first breath. Living hurts, but we get used to it. Until we're reminded again.

❉ ❉ ❉

A soft tickle on my neck wakes me. "I'm heading to the office," Landon says and kisses my ear, smoothing a mess of hair away from my face. I flop onto my back and shield my eyes from the morning sun slicing through the shutters.

"You know, Kins." He stands up and walks to the large mirror hanging above the dresser and preens his hair. "You really should give your dad a call—work things out with him. It's not that big of a deal."

"CFO isn't that big of a deal?" I laugh at the absurdity.

"Kins." He returns to the bed and sits next to me. "This is what you went to school for. It's not like he's asking you to fly the airplanes, just manage the cost of making them." Attempting a solo flight would be preferable at this point. I squeeze his hand. He's only trying to be supportive. It's not like I ever told him about the special arrangements I made to pass my finance classes, and I have no intention of telling him now.

He checks his watch and leans forward to kiss my temple. "Gotta go. We'll talk later and nail down a date for the wedding." Then he's on his way out of the room.

"Bye," I mumble from a hazy cloud, pulling the covers tighter in his absence. A minute later, the alarm chirps as the front door shuts. The house is silent. Impossibly silent. I can't go back to sleep, so I pull Landon's bathrobe over my naked body and shuffle to the kitchen to make a cup of coffee. Waiting for the brew, I flip through the recordings on the DVR and land on a *Grey's Anatomy* rerun.

The fridge is stocked with my favorites and his. His housekeeper, Aileen, takes care of the shopping too. Landon even gave Aileen a list of toiletries to keep on hand for me. He wants it to feel like home when I stay over, and it usually does. I considered moving in about a year ago, but it was deferred by a rough patch—misunderstanding and uncommunicated expectations, the typical drama.

After breakfast, I find a pair of sweatpants I left here a while back and one of Landon's tee shirts. I carry them into the bathroom where wine glasses still sit on the edge of the tub, and turn on the waterfall shower head in the mosaic alcove.

Wishing the hot water would dissolve me like sugar, I stay in the shower until steam clouds the bathroom. When I step out, the air is thick, challenging my lungs to fight for oxygen. I flip on the vent and turn to wipe the mirror when I see it. *Sierra heart Landon.* The message appears like magic ink on the foggy glass, waking every nerve in my body.

It could be old, I tell myself, attempting to settle the anxiety spreading across my chest. But I know Aileen cleans the mirrors weekly. Standing there, exposed and sucker-punched, I try to rationalize, but possible explanations cease. Except the one I don't want to face. It's not the first time he has done this sort of thing, but each fight, suspicion, and moment of self-doubt has been followed by Landon's sweet, convincing declarations that turn my thoughts upside down over and over again. And when I finally land, I really believe it will never happen again.

With the wedding and his mom's cancer, I want to keep the peace, but I can't sit here and stew all day while he's at work. The message will taunt me and I'll spend hours looking for proof I don't want to find. I dress and watch as the fog clears the bathroom, taking the message with it. Since my car is still at Nikki's, I text her for a ride, reminding her of the gate code.

Be there in ten, she replies.

As I wait for Nikki, I sit on the sofa and slide the ring he gave me off my finger, turning it over in my hand and noticing its weight. I've been on this ride with him for as long as I can remember. He was my first kiss, my first love—my *only* love. Through all the ups and downs and twists and turns, he's *still* here. But is he still mine and mine alone? If there's a perfectly good explanation and I confront him, it could ruin everything—I could lose him, and I'm not sure I can find someone else to love me like he has. Nikki's horn beeps, startling me as I lock the ring back into place behind my knuckle.

"Thanks for the ride," I say as I climb into the Range Rover. "Sorry about last night."

Nikki shrugs. "It's fine." But I know it isn't. I've bailed on Nikki more times than I want to admit, and each time Landon was the reason for it.

SIX

Kinsley: June 27, 2008

I picked up my car from Nikki's and drove home, music blaring, hoping to lose myself in something louder—stronger—than my problems. Music does that, but other things do too. I consider losing myself in one or two of those other things, but it's still early and Nikki will be over soon for a swim. If she finds me self-medicating before nightfall, there'll be an intervention. So, instead, I slip into my new powder blue bikini, grab my iPod, and head out to the pool.

As I wait for Nikki, I stretch out on a pool lounger, my back to the sun, and shuffle my playlist—a little Kid Rock, some Taylor Swift, and a sprinkling of Motown oldies. I've been told my taste is eclectic.

After six songs, I flip over to tan my front and listen to six more. I'm dying. The sun, while I love her for the UVs, is a bitch and might be trying to burn me alive. I pull out my earbuds, grab my sunglasses, and splash into the deep end. The cool water is heaven. Still no sign of Nikki, and it has been at least an hour. I hang off the side of the pool, listening to the world—birds squawking, someone mowing, a train horn bellowing in the distance. There's *always* a train. Maybe that's why Nikki's late—she's waiting on a train.

Allowing myself to fall back and float, I clench my eyes shut behind the sunglasses. I'm weightless. The world is muted by water filling my ears. All I hear is the sound of my breathing and the subtle movement of the water that carries my body. In this moment, life is bearable—my mind is quiet. I want to stay here until my skin prunes. I imagine I'm on gentle, rolling waves in the middle of a sea where no one can find me. But a disturbance in the water alerts me, and I raise my head to see Nikki kicking off her shoes as a big grinning alligator floats toward me.

"Thought you stood me up," I say, swimming over to the side of the pool.

"Sorry. I stopped by the farm to see Chase. He has a show in Stillwater tonight and won't be back until Sunday."

"Oh, I see how it is."

"Like you have room to talk," Nikki says, lowering herself into the pool and smacking the water to splash me. I drop back under, allowing my body to float to the surface at nature's will. Nikki's only teasing, but it's another reminder of how much I suck—putting Landon before our friendship when he can't even put me before some *Sierra*.

"I know. Sorry," I say when my head is above water. "I'm just under pressure about the money and my dad." I don't mention the writing on the mirror. Not yet anyway.

She pulls the alligator's tail, spinning it around toward her and rests her elbows across its back. "I was thinking about that on the way over. What if you hire someone to do the work for you?"

"Oh, sure, like my dad won't notice that."

"No. Look, you could say they're your *assistant*," she adds with air quotes.

"I don't know, Nik. I mean, maybe…" I think about Ben's warning. If my dad *is* up to something and I bring an outsider into the fold who might blow the whistle, it could destroy the company. It could destroy my dad. Even me. "God, I wish I could just pay him back and take a VP role like we agreed."

Nikki laughs. "If you pay him back, why wouldn't you do something you love instead, like that job at the Philbrook?" I haven't allowed myself to think about that. Not really. Long ago, I resigned my dreams to the life my dad envisioned for me, and any time my pesky little passions attempt to take root and grow, I stomp them out.

"That *is* what I want to do, Nik," I say, but Nikki doesn't argue or accept. She just offers a slight nod and changes the subject.

"Let's talk wedding. Did Landon like your ideas?"

"Small change of plans. It's going to be summer, not fall."

"Still outdoors though?"

"God, no, it's too hot."

"Well, maybe if you have it in early June?"

I shake my head. "Too late. We're doing it this summer—"

"Whoa. What's the rush?"

"His mom's prognosis."

"Oh." Nikki lays her head down on the alligator and floats. It's quiet —no trains. Just the deafening reminder of how selfish I am for not considering Landon's mom. "How long does she have?" Nikki asks.

"Six months to a year, but they think it'll be closer to six months. So, the sooner we do it, the better."

Nikki looks at me with a sad smile before climbing out of the pool. "Where are you going?" I ask.

"You said there are tubs of your parents' wedding stuff in storage. Maybe we can find her dress. You were thinking about using it, weren't you?" She grabs two towels from the cabana and walks back to the pool. "Come on, Buttercup, let's go."

* * *

Wrapped in beach towels, we ascend the stairs to the third floor. It's essentially a large storage room with dormer windows. I flip on the light, taking in the open space. The walls are lined with all sizes of tubs and boxes stacked neatly on shelves. *This could take all day.*

After just twenty minutes, the floor is covered with open boxes and remnants of life lived—from my high school graduation cap and gown to Ben's collection of honor roll certificates and a little pink box full of my baby teeth. Our nannies and housekeepers archived the mile markers of growing up.

"Awww, look, Kins." Nikki holds up a high school yearbook. "I don't even know where mine are." She laughs and stacks it plus three more on the floor beside her. I reach into a large gray tub, and my fingers graze a thick envelope. I can tell by its size and bulk that it holds photographs, and I pull it out. They are mostly pictures of Ben and his first car, a '68 Plymouth Roadrunner in near-mint condition. He loved that car, but my dad sold it the day after Ben left for boot camp.

The roll of film must have been from Ben's sixteenth birthday when my dad gave him the car. There's a photo of Ben standing by the shiny blue hot rod with a huge silver bow on the hood. I flip through a series of blurry candid pictures of Ben and his friends in the game room. There's even one of Ben standing by his cake with his friends. Landon is there too and looks so young. That was still a couple of years before we started dating. He was hardly a blip on my radar then, but two years later, he was the only thing that mattered.

I keep the photo of the boys by the cake and return the rest to the tub. Sitting cross-legged on the floor, I scoot over to the large wooden trunk against the wall, unhook the latches, and raise the lid.

"Find it?" Nikki asks, sitting down next to me.

"Looks like my dad's old stuff or something," I say, judging by the waft of stale air and cedarwood as I pull out a large leatherbound photo album. Inside, there is a photo of my mother. She looks like me, with chestnut brown hair, large and expressive brown eyes, and a narrow chin. The pages that follow are filled with wedding photos.

"Wow, your dad looks happy." Nikki points to another photo. He *does* look happy. Of course, he's younger in the photo but also softer—hopeful—not the shadow I live with now. Nikki abandons the photo album and pokes around in the cedar trunk. "We're getting closer. From her bouquet maybe?" She hands me a small collection of dried roses, and I set them aside. I'm still flipping through the photo album, distracted by the smiling faces of a past I never knew.

"Kins, here it is!" A large box covers Nikki's lap and I see the folds of lace and chiffon nestled within. I reach for the box. It's the closest I've ever been to something of my mom's since the day I was born. All of her belongings were either given away or stored somewhere unknown to me. Growing up, I only had photographs and my grandparents' fairy tales to piece together this mythical creature I longed to know.

I run my fingers along the fabric that once laid across my mother's skin. How would it feel to step inside—to be swaddled by her gown? I decide to try it on, and I pull it out from the box as I stand up. Holding the dress at arm's length and allowing it to unfold, I notice something tumble out of the layers of fabric. Nikki reaches for it. "It has your name on it," she says, holding out a cream-colored envelope. I take the envelope and examine the delicate handwriting that forms my name, tracing my fingers over the letters. Returning to the floor beside Nikki, I carefully return the gown to the box and open the envelope.

July 2, 1983

Dearest Kinsley, I'm writing this letter as I sit in your nursery. I've made sure everything is ready for your arrival just in case you're an early-bird like me and decide to join the world sooner than the doctor thinks you will. Either way, next month, I'll be sitting right here, holding you in my arms instead of my womb.

I'll give you this letter on your wedding day, but I'm writing it now because that's what early-bird mamas do I suppose. And over the last few months, I've had time to reflect on my life. There are things I wish I knew on my wedding day. Like it's okay to eat a donut or burger before the wedding. Your dress will still fit. And don't let the stress of the day ruin the memories you're making.

More than that, there are things I wish I knew after the wedding. I'm going to be honest with you. Marriage will be challenging at times, even breaking your heart. But it can turn out beautifully like your heart has found its home.

As a woman, wife, and someday a mother, there will be times when you don't think you'll make it. But you can, and you will. You must hold onto what you know is true. Truth will guide you in any storm.

I hope that by the time you read this I have helped you grow into a strong woman who knows she's worthy, capable, and loved. Regardless of what she feels in each fleeting moment.

I'm sure that over the years I will tell you this story many times, but here it is again. When I was young and dating, my mother always made sure I had a few dollars in my handbag in case I needed to call home or hire a taxi. "Mad Money," she called it. In case something went wrong on the date or my suitor was less than gentlemanly. I want you to have the same safety net, something to catch you if you fall. This is my wedding gift to you, and perhaps peace of mind to myself that no matter what, you'll have a little "Mad Money" if you need it.

Love Mom

I set the letter aside, revealing a declaration of trust, naming me as the beneficiary of $100,000 upon marriage. *Holy cow.*

SEVEN

Kinsley: June 28, 2008

I tossed and turned all night, weighing my options. No, I don't want to get married without Ben here, and maybe I have been questioning things since I saw the writing on the mirror, but what other choice do I have? This is the lesser of two evils. And marrying Landon has always been part of the future I imagined. It's just going to happen a little sooner than I planned.

I can't possibly pay for Caleb's medical bills and tractor repairs without a job, but I cannot be CFO. If I refuse both the job and the payback, my dad will probably cut me out of his life entirely. I want to ask him why he never mentioned the trust fund but figure it's best to leave it alone—at least until after I talk to Landon. We can pull together a small ceremony in no time. His mom can attend and I'll collect the trust, take care of Caleb's expenses, pay my dad back, and make everyone happy in one move. Surely there's someone else in the company to take over Phillips' role. There *has* to be.

It's nearly noon and I'm planning to meet with Nikki later, so I decide to pick up the clothes I borrowed from her—they're still at Landon's. I can't remember when he said he was leaving for Dallas. Or if he even said at all. I text him to see if he's home, and while I wait for a reply I walk over to the arched window near my desk. Pulling the semi-sheer white curtains to the side, I take in the view. Below the rocky cliff, Lake Thunderbird glistens with little ripples of golden white dancing under the noonday sun as a siege of herons flies over. Minutes pass without a response from Landon. If he's still in town he's probably playing golf with the guys, but I can use the code to get in through the garage. I let the curtains drop back into place, grab my keys, and slip on my Gucci flip-flops.

* * *

I park on Landon's circular drive and walk over to the security pad to punch in the code. When the door rolls back, I'm surprised to see the metallic red convertible in the garage. Maybe he just came back from the club. Maybe he left his phone at home. The alarm system chirps as I open the door to the utility room. The house lights are off, but I notice what looks like a wine glass or two in the sink as I pass through the kitchen. *When did Aileen clean last?*

"Landon?" I call out but hear no response. I make my way through the open living room and down the hall. My heart catches in my throat. His bedroom door is shut, but light peeks out from under it. The mirror message flashes in my mind. *Is he in there with someone? With Sierra?* I listen but hear nothing—only the pulse thumping in my ears. Terrified of what lay beyond the door, I consider retreat, but it's too late. The door opens.

"What are you doing here, babe?" Landon's voice is sweet, surprised—*genuine.* He places his hands on my waist and pulls me into a hug.

"I came by to pick up the clothes I left." I attempt to peek around his embrace. "They're Nikki's."

He looks over his shoulder without letting me go. "I don't see them. I bet Aileen picked them up. I'll check the laundry room." A quick peck lands on top of my head before he releases me and walks away. I tentatively step into the room as if something or *someone* might appear. Taking a deep breath and slowly releasing it from my lungs, my nerves begin to subside. I'm alone in the room.

It's tidy and I don't see Nikki's clothes anywhere, so I drop down on my knees to look under the bed, and stretch my arm out, groping the plush carpet in every direction. When my fingertips brush across something lacey, I hook it like an arcade claw machine and pull it out. *What the hell?* I drop the burgundy thong. It's not mine.

"Here, babe," Landon says from just beyond the open doorway. I jump up to see him entering the room with Nikki's neatly folded top and denim shorts. "Aileen washed them." Sweat trickles down my back as if I'm the one caught. "You okay?" He tilts his head and draws me into his arms.

"I thought you were going to Dallas."

"I am. Jet leaves at four," he says. I nod, pulling away and avoiding his face.

"What's wrong?" He places a hand under my chin, tilting it up so I meet his eyes. The fork in the road—I never pass this test. Even when I think I've chosen the safe path, somehow I always end up regretting it.

"Nothing," I lie, and he studies my eyes for a moment before pulling me into a kiss. I accept it, but I don't engage, so he jerks back.

"You're lying to me."

I shake my head to deny it, but he continues. "Why did you kiss me like that?"

"I didn't–"

"You didn't *want* to."

"No–I…" But he's right. How could I with a mystery thong under the bed and *Sierra hearts Landon* hiding in the mirror?

"I know when you're lying." His eyes narrow on me.

"I'm not lying. I'm sorry–"

"I don't believe you." He turns away, raking his fingers through his hair. And though I didn't want him to hold me before, somehow in the absence of his touch I'm hollow—cold.

Landon sits down on the bed and drops his head into his hands. "Why are you doing this to me? Why do you treat me like this?" His voice is weak, and he suddenly seems so much smaller than the man I know he is. I've broken him—again. It's almost always a misunderstanding or my overreaction that does it. After all that I've put him through, it's a wonder he still loves me.

"I'm sorry–" I reach for his hand, but he snaps it back and stands up just inches from me.

"Is this what I should expect for the rest of our lives? You whipping me back and forth, giving me love, and taking it away without reason?"

"Without reason?" I say and instantly regret it.

"Am I missing something?"

I scramble to the other side of the bed and reach for the evidence. "What's this?" I ask, dangling the dark red lace from my index finger.

"Looks like your panties."

"No, Landon. Not mine." I shake my head and march back to him with the proof.

"What are you saying, Kinsley?"

"Don't play dumb."

"Oh, I'm dumb now?"

"I said don't play–"

"Did you put it there? Huh? Just to start a fight?" He snatches the thong from my hand and flings it across the room. "You found it a little too quickly, don't you think?"

"I found it when I was looking for Nikki's clothes," I say.

"*Okay,*" he says, tilting his head condescendingly. I hate it when he looks at me like I'm a stupid child who knows nothing.

"I didn't put it there, and I didn't write Sierra hearts Landon on the bathroom mirror either." The words shoot out of my mouth like a bullet, and the look on his face tells me I hit the target.

"You know, Kins..." he says in a tone far too calm for the accusation I just fired. "The way you're acting and accusing me of things..." He brushes his hand along my arm and leans in, kissing my ear. "It's making me...FUCKING MAD," he shouts, sending rings of pain through my head. Instinctively, I reach for my ear, but he grabs my wrist.

"Do you know how many women would trade places with you in an instant?" I don't, but I'm guessing Sierra or someone missing a burgundy thong is on the list. "And after all you've put me through–after all your fuck-ups, I'm still here. You think anyone else is ever going to love you like me?"

I shake my head, clenching my eyes shut as memories bubble to the surface and flood me with waves of guilt. He relaxes his hold on my wrist and leads me to the bathroom. "This is what you're all worked up about?" He points to the mirror. *Of course, it's clear now.*

"It was there when I got out of the shower, Landon. I swear."

"Aileen cleans every week. I wonder how she missed it."

"It was there," I say, but it's hardly more than a whisper.

"Or maybe it's all in your head, Kins. You've been under a lot of pressure lately." He pulls me into his embrace and smooths my hair. "Have you been taking your pills? You know they can mess with your head. Maybe you dreamed it."

It's true—I have been taking my pills more often with the stress of graduation and my dad's demands. I suppose it *could* have been a dream. It's not like that sort of thing hasn't happened before. Sometimes my dreams are so vivid I can't tell them apart from reality.

"Look at me." He pulls back and tilts my head toward him, softly brushing my tears aside. "Do you know how crazy you sound? Accusing me of being with someone else. Why would I propose if I didn't want to be with you?" His eyes cut into my soul. But this doesn't make sense. If he loves me, then who is Sierra? Why did I just find another woman's thong under my fiancé's bed?

He drops his hands from my face and walks back into the bedroom. I'm alone in the bathroom with only my reflection in the mirror. No Sierra. No message. No Landon.

He's done with me. I'm losing him. I can't lose him.

"I'm sorry," I say through tears as I go after him. When I catch up, I have to stand on my tippy toes to reach, but I guide his head toward mine, placing my lips on his and begging him to forgive me. I kiss him again, and again, but he doesn't respond.

He's giving me a taste of my own medicine—he wants me to know how I made him feel. I deserve this.

"I'm sorry," I whisper, leaning my head against his chest. I need him —and not just for the trust fund. I need to feel loved and forgiven, to be accepted by him once again. I can't let him leave for Dallas like this. "Please, Landon." I reach for his belt buckle, sliding the smooth leather strap out of the hook. "I trust you," I say as I unbutton his khakis and tug the zipper down. My heart pounds as I look up at him.

"Prove it," he says, and in one swift motion, he pulls me into a kiss and walks me backwards until we bump into the bed. As we tumble onto the mattress, I hold onto him, grabbing his hair, his shirt—whatever I can—to bring him closer. I can't lose him.

He flips me onto my stomach and yanks down my shorts. My chest tightens and I turn my head, trying to see his face over my shoulder. I don't like it when I can't see him during sex, and each time he has tried to fuck me from behind it ended with me having a panic attack and sucking him off because I was too upset to try again.

"Landon, not like this, please," I beg him.

"I thought you trusted me," he says. "I thought you were going to prove it."

"I do–I am… It's just…" I struggle to protest because my breath is shorter, quicker as the panic sets in.

"You'll like it, babe. Trust me," he whispers in my ear. I squeeze my eyes shut and try to focus on my breathing, but I can't stop the anxiety that rips through my body. He starts slow and gentle, but he becomes careless and rough, seeming to feed on our argument, the accusations, and hurt. Between my panicked breaths and his weight pressing my lungs into the mattress, I feel like I might pass out and try to signal to him, raising my hand and smacking the pillow beside me.

"You have to trust me." He grabs my hand in his, pinning it to the bed with a grip so strong it crushes my knuckles. He continues as if to prove the power of his love. Landon has shown me two sides of love. This isn't the love he trapped me with all those years ago. This one grows quietly in the shadows, feeding on jealousy and misunderstandings, disappointments and mistakes. But it never stays. It retreats to the darkness almost as quickly as it appears.

When he releases my hand and rolls off my body, I flip onto my back and fill my lungs. The ceiling spins above me as he pulls my aching hand to his lips, kissing it and offering a repertoire of praises: *You're so beautiful. No one gets me like you do. You're the only one for me.* He tells me everything a girl wants to hear, every syllable dripping with sickly sweet lies that I want to believe, and it takes all of my willpower to push back tears.

He dresses and I kiss him goodbye in the bedroom. I listen for the alarm chirp to signal his departure, and once he's gone, I allow the tears to consume me. The fear I pushed down as he pushed me into the mattress now rushes back to claim its due. It's the kind of crying that involves the entire body, not just the eyes or the heart. I don't know what to believe. What is true? I don't know if I can trust him, but I'm conditioned to. It hurts to love him, but *not* loving him might hurt more.

Close to an hour later, I dry my eyes and dress, then grab Nikki's clothes as I leave the room. But on my way to the garage, I stop at the kitchen sink and lift one of the two wine glasses I saw earlier. Holding it up, I examine the lip prints along the rim. Dark plum—a color I don't own.

Fucking bastard! I slam it back into the sink, splinters of glass exploding onto the granite countertop, and get the hell out of there.

✽ ✽ ✽

"Where have you been? I've called you like fifty ti– Oh, god. What happened?" Nikki steps back inside the camper, letting me pass.

"I can't do it. I can't do it, Nik. I can't–" It's becoming harder to achieve a full breath. "I can't–" My head is a balloon and an anchor at the same time as sweat beads form on my clammy cold skin.

"Shhh, sit down," Nikki says, leading me to the little sofa. "Breathe with me, Kins." I feel her hand making circular motions on my back. I try to model her breathing and drop my head forward between my legs to even the keel. When the world stops spinning, I collapse into Nikki's arms. I blubber and sob and writhe in heartache and desperation. Nikki doesn't ask why. She doesn't tell me to calm down. She just holds me and cries with me. And when I finally tell her I can't marry Landon, Nikki says, "I know."

EIGHT

Kinsley: June 29, 2008

The camper door shuts softly as I stir in Nikki's queen-sized bed. It's luxuriously plush with the right balance of cloud and control, but sharing it with Nikki almost makes the little sofa seem preferable. Nikki is active in all she does, even sleep. After sharing the bed on our recent road trip, it's a wonder I didn't come back with bruises.

"Oh, you're up." The bed gives slightly as Nikki sits down. "Iced vanilla latte?"

"You're a saint." I sit up and take the sweaty cup. "What time is it?"

"About noonish. Why?"

"I've gotta dig out my old accounting books and finally crack the spine." I gulp down the latte like it's water.

"You're giving up that easily?"

"Nik, I told you I can't marry–"

"Oh, god, Kins, I know. And I wouldn't let you. Not *now.*"

"Right..." What did I say last night? I thought it was all incomprehensible blubber and squeaks—did Nikki decipher it? "So I have to take the job, that's it."

"No, you can still pay him back–"

"Not without marrying Lan–" But I stop, recognizing the look on her face. I call it Nikki's *Lucy and Ethel* face. I'm going to need more coffee. Nikki jumps up, pulls a top and a pair of shorts from the built-in cabinet above the bed and tosses them to me. "Get dressed, Buttercup. We have work to do."

I dress in the less-than-closet-sized bathroom and join Nikki outside. "So what are we doing, Lucy?"

"Oh, *I'm* Lucy?" Nikki clicks the key fob to unlock her Range Rover. "I always thought I was the more sensible Ethel. You know, saving Lucy's ass and all."

I climb into the passenger seat and fish through my bag for sunglasses, coming across the little black velvet box instead. I remember ripping the ring off my finger last night, ready to chuck it out the door when Nikki stopped me and tucked it safely in its velvet cocoon. If I open it, what will escape? And could I ever put it back in?

* * *

Nikki leads me up the stairs of my own house, past my bedroom, and to the storage room that gave me so much hope the other day. "What are we doing, Nik? You think we're going to find a husband in storage too?"

"Gotta start somewhere," she says, as she walks with a mission to one particular tub on the middle shelf near the window and pulls out the stack of high school yearbooks. She has the memory of an elephant.

"Seriously? This will never work."

Nikki ignores me, criss crossing her legs and lowering herself to the floor in one quick motion, already scanning the pages. "Oh, what about Oliver Bishop?"

"Are you kidding me?" I plop down beside her.

"What? It's not like it's a *real* marriage."

"Yeah, but still. Your sloppy seconds?"

"Oh, my god, Kins. It was sixth grade, and all we did was kiss. *One time.*"

I slide a yearbook from the stack and open it—my freshman year. Flipping through the black and white photo-filled pages, I recognize faces and names. I turn to my own class picture. It's hard to miss—Nikki surrounded it with a hot pink heart the day she signed my yearbook.

I'm struck by how young I look. My shoulder-length brown hair is smooth and straight and a small smile tries to hide the confusion and sadness I was overcome with that year. I didn't know then and barely understood now, why Ben changed his mind overnight. In all of the fighting and tears that summer, Landon came to be more than my big brother's best friend. At first, he would commiserate with me, sharing my frustration and confusion over Ben's choices. Then it quickly evolved into something more.

I turn to the senior class pictures and find Landon's from that year. *Bastard.* I want to take a sharpie and black out every trace of him. But when I flip the page, I'm confronted with memories that still pinch my heart: wavy-haired girls with big smiles hanging off the arms of senior studs, Landon included. Senior-only parties and prom, events I couldn't attend, but he did. I close the book—I'm over this trip down Memory Lane. "This is dumb, Nik. I don't want to marry anyone. People suck."

"Hey, now." Nikki feigns offense.

"Except you. Can I marry you?"

"Funny you'd ask. It's not legal here—"

"So, we'll go to Cali or wherever."

"Right, but the thing is since the trust is set up in Oklahoma, my mom said it would be a long court battle to—"

"You told your mom?"

"Calm down. She doesn't know I was talking about you. I didn't mention names. Anyway, you wouldn't see the money any time soon if we went that route."

"Why couldn't you have a brother?" I groan.

Nikki laughs. "My dad wonders the same thing."

"This is crazy." I toss the yearbook on the pile. "How am I going to convince some guy to do this anyway?"

"Money talks," Nikki says. "How much do you have to work with?"

"Seventy goes to my dad for tuition, and the running bill with Caleb right now is about ten-thousand, so I should have around twenty left. How much do husbands cost these days?"

"Google it. Oh, hey, speaking of Tractor Boy." Nikki points to a picture of Caleb with a lopsided grin and scraggly brown hair. She freezes before turning to face me. *I know this look. This isn't good.*

"What about Caleb?"

"Please, Nikki, you're out of your mind—"

"No, hear me out. We know he's not a creep, and you already owe him money. Plus, with Chase's dad retiring early, he's running out of time to get the rest of his funding together for the farm. It's perfect. Just offer a few extra thousand on top for his troubles."

He was such an ass when I tried to help him after the accident. He'll say no. More likely, *hell no.* "There's no way he'll go for it," I tell her.

"Come on, let's go." Nikki jumps up, abandoning the yearbook and reaching for my hands.

"What? Where?"

"To ask him. We can't waste any time–"

"He's not gonna go for it, Nik."

"Better to find out tonight than tomorrow," she says, pulling me to my feet.

* * *

Nikki parks the car next to an old red truck in front of the little white house, and I feel a nervous sickness coming on. "What do I even say?"

"Be honest. Tell him about the trust fund. That's how you're covering the expenses." Nikki shrugs and reaches for her phone that's ringing. I don't think it will be enough to convince Caleb, but Nikki's right, I don't have time to waste.

As I walk across the drive, little bits of gravel slide into the space between my feet and my Gucci flip-flops. I climb the concrete-chipped steps to the landing and shake the gravel out of my shoes. Looking over my shoulder, I see Nikki holding the phone with one hand and gesturing wildly with the other. This has to be one of the dumbest ideas Nikki has ever come up with. I turn back and knock on the door. When it opens, I'm face-to-face with Caleb's annoyed expression.

"Hi," I say.

"Hi?"

"So, umm…about the money I owe you. There's a little situation." I fumble with my hands. His slow blink and raised eyebrows make it harder to push out the words. He rolls his hand for me to go on.

"Right…so the thing is, I have the money in a trust fund, but I can't access it until I get married." I look down at my dust-covered Guccis before rushing through the ask. "So, basically if you marry me, I can pay you back."

It's quiet except for the Range Rover humming behind me and the locusts coming out to sing. *Did I actually say it out loud? Maybe I just thought I did.*

"Is this a joke?"

Okay, definitely said it out loud.

"Are you crazy? I'm not marrying you. You ran me off the road."

"But I apologized–"

"And now you want me to trust you with my life, in my home, with my baby sister?"

"I'm not asking to move in with you or be married for real. We just need a marriage certificate for the trust."

"Why can't you get the money from your dad? He's loaded."

"It's complicated." I look down at my toes that desperately need a fresh pedi. "Please, Caleb."

"Ain't gonna happen," he says, turning into the house.

I stop the door with my hand. "We just have to sign the papers. Once we get the money, we'll file for a divorce and go our separate ways."

"If it's that simple, get some other guy to sign your papers. Hell, ask your boyfriend to do it, Kinsley."

"I can't. It's complicated…" I'm losing ground.

"Yeah, seems to be a theme with you. Not really a selling point when you're trying to convince someone to marry you by the way."

"Caleb, come on. You need the money, don't you?"

"Of course I do."

"Then this is the *only* way–"

He shakes his head. "Nah, you can marry any poor sucker. Doesn't have to be me."

"Caleb," I say, but it comes out like a whine and I loathe myself for the desperation I hear in my own voice.

"You'll figure something out," he says, closing the door in my face. Disappointment and failed plans settle on my shoulders as I walk back to the car.

"I knew it wouldn't work." I huff, slinging the passenger door open and crawling inside. "Now what am I going to do?"

"He wouldn't go for it?"

"Just like I told you he wouldn't."

"Don't worry. We'll figure something out," Nikki says, as we back out of the drive. "Is there anyone from undergrad you can think of? What about that guy that wouldn't stop hitting on you in that one class, what was it? Philosophy of Art or something?"

"Art *Theory*." I groan into my hands. "And that's a pass. He was way too clingy. It would be impossible to shake him off in the end."

"I wonder if my cousin in Missouri would do it..." Nikki pulls up to the stop sign and grabs her phone, tapping out a message, but I'm not holding my breath. It was a stupid plan to begin with. It was stupid to think I could break free or choose my own path. Someone else is calling the moves in this game, and I'm simply the pawn.

NINE

Caleb: June 29, 2008

Fucking lunatic. I shut the front door and wait for the sound of tires rolling on gravel before returning to the little laundry room in the back of the house. Pulling the warm towels and clothing from the dryer, I drop them into the laundry basket.

I don't know Kinsley well—even though I was friends with her brother growing up. I was a year ahead of her in school and we didn't run with the same crowd. Sure, I've always thought of her as wild and reckless, but I didn't see this coming. I transfer the wet clothes to the dryer and start another load in the washer, scowling at the bizarre proposal. I one-handedly pick up the basket of clean laundry and carry it to the little wooden table that's covered with newspaper.

I've been browsing the classifieds for part-time work to bring in extra money. Of course, finding the time to devote to a second job will be another challenge. As it is, the farm consumes my daylight hours, and I still don't feel comfortable leaving Annie home alone overnight. Graveyard shifts are out. I'll have to pick up a weekend gig, and that means asking Annie to step up and fill in for me around the house. I try to keep things balanced, helping her learn responsibility without stealing her youth. I want her adolescence to be better than mine was.

I move the sheets of newspaper and clear a spot to fold and sort, mostly towels with a few work shirts and rogue socks. Annie is pretty good about keeping up with her own laundry, but occasionally a stray item or two ends up in mine. I can't complain. She does *most* of the chores I ask her to, and for a fourteen-year-old that's saying something. I carry a small stack of laundry into her room, a disaster of clothing, shoes, magazines, and a few stuffed animals yet to be retired.

Cleaning her room is *not* a priority for Annie, and she had quite convincingly laid out her argument that it's none of my business if she wants to live like a slob as long as she keeps her door shut and I don't have to see it. She'll probably become a lawyer one day.

I shuffle through the room, trying not to step on or break anything strewn across the carpeted minefield. With my one usable arm, I clear a bit of surface area to place her clothing on the dresser, and a small avalanche tumbles to the floor. I kneel down to pick up my mess, not that Annie will notice it. I'm not even sure which items fell and which were already there, but I gather the gel pens, a bottle of pink nail polish, and a small notebook that lies open and stand up.

Large colorful letters across the top of the page catch my eye. I'm not trying to snoop but it's impossible to ignore the words *OMG I'm in LOVE!!!* I drop the nail polish and pens on the already cluttered dresser and follow the bubbly handwriting as it continues down the page.

Eric Birmingham is absolutely the hottest guy in the world. He's literally perfect. And he might even like me too! I saw him today at the rec center and he freaking smiled right at me. I almost died. Not even kidding. I asked Brittany if I imagined it. But no, she saw it too!!! He was playing basketball with her brother, so she's gonna find out if he likes me too. OMG I might get a boyfriend this summer!

A queasy knot forms in my gut. Maybe because I'm crossing an invisible line of privacy, but also because Annie is growing up and I can't stop it. Sure, I've seen her eyes follow a boy or two when they walk by, but she isn't old enough to be *in love.* Her "all or nothing" view of life doesn't pair well with fickle teenage emotions, and I can see the train wreck heading straight toward us. I turn the page to the latest entry.

Brittany asked her brother if Eric likes me, and he said "maybe." Then I heard he was hanging out with Sadie. Like I even stand a chance. She's gorgeous and obviously knows how to make a guy like her. She has already had a million boyfriends. There's no way I can compete with her.

This is so stupid. I'm so stupid. And I don't even have anyone to help me with it. Sure, I have Brittany, but she's just as clueless as me! If Jessica was still around I could ask her. She would know exactly what to do. She would help me get Eric to notice me and LIKE me. But Jess is gone. Caleb's the moron who won't bring her back. And I'm a loser with no boyfriend. Forever. The end. Life sucks.

I let out a long, slow puff of air. The emotional pendulum I was worried about is already in full swing. And of course, she's still stuck on Jess and mad at me for how things ended. Jessica had become like a big sister to Annie, and it broke my heart when she left—not just because I loved her but because Annie did too. Still, I couldn't *make* her stay with us. I tried to help Annie understand, but I can't tell her the whole story—it would break her heart, and in her short life, she has already endured too much of that.

✳ ✳ ✳

October 19, 1995: Thirteen years earlier.

"Where's she going?" I ask my dad. He's slumped into the couch and doesn't answer me. From the living room window, I see headlights backing out of the driveway, then a red haze of tail lights as the car drives away. It's October and it's already dark outside. We haven't even had supper yet. Maybe she's going to pick up a pizza, I hope, but I know she isn't.

"Dad," I try again. "Dad, where's she going?" No words still, but for a second, I catch my father's bloodshot eyes before he sinks his head into his hands. I look around the room. Piles of laundry here and there, a few dirty dishes on the coffee table, a box of baby wipes and a stack of Annie's diapers on the floor near the fireplace. *Annie.*

Nervousness prickles my neck as I walk down the dim hall to my parents' room. Peeking in, I see dresser drawers hanging open, almost off their tracks. An unmatched sock, a broken necklace, a half-empty bottle of hand lotion are scattered across the floor. Unnecessary things remain—she only took the essentials. Kicking a pink fuzzy slipper out of my path, I walk over to the port-a-crib. *Please, please don't be there*. But my heart is crushed when I look down and see Annie sleeping peacefully, her little chubby fingers curled, her cheeks a rosy hue from the cool dry air of fall.

How could she do this? How could she leave Annie? I knew she might leave me, and James, and Dad because sometimes she would talk about it when she was angry. But Annie? She's helpless. Only a monster leaves a defenseless baby behind. It's not fair, and it's not right. I hate my mom even more than I already did.

I quietly close the door behind me, shuffling across the hall to the room I share with James. The room is cold with biting October air creeping in through the open window. James doesn't even bother to shut it anymore. He has become lazy in his sneaking out. I don't know why he doesn't walk out the front door—like Mom just did. Whose attention is James trying to get when he acts out? Doesn't he know our dad is too distracted by his own pain to see ours? Does he really think our mom gives a damn about us? She packed up and left us—*all* of us. Even Annie.

I leave my bedroom door cracked to listen for Annie's cries, and for once, the house sleeps quietly. No battles rage in the next room. It feels empty without the war. Is this peace? It doesn't feel like it. Maybe the absence of war isn't peace. I let my mind drift in the new, unexplored quiet of the night until I find rest in the nothingness of dreamless sleep.

* * *

June 30, 2008

Some days, I want to scream *fuck it*—to hell with my plans, my dreams, my hopes. To hell with it all. I should stop busting my ass because it doesn't make a shit bit of difference. Today is one of those days. The portable dishwasher, the one I saved up to buy for Gram's sixty-eighth birthday, crapped out. Right after the extended warranty expired. *Of course.* Call it the proverbial straw that broke the camel's back. Call it bad luck. Call it life. I'm ready to call it quits. Before leaving for work, I roll it into the garage and scribble a note to Annie that we're going old-school again. I leave the note and plastic drying rack on the counter and head to work.

In the silence of the field, preparing the soil for seeding, I breathe in the fresh country air. It washes through me, helping to clear my head and settle my frustration. I'm not one to rush into decisions, and whatever happens with the farm and my foolish dream of buying it, I have to keep going for Annie. We might have been dealt a shitty hand in life, but I'm determined to change the outcome for her. I thought buying the farm would offer some security and stability, but I need to do it on my terms—alone. I learned at a young age that people can't be trusted to keep their word. It's best to handle it myself if it's something that truly matters. But between the accident and Marty's early retirement, the goalpost is moving farther and farther away. Maybe it's time to give up—take a job driving a forklift or welding. It wouldn't be bad work, but it's hard to bury a dream.

By noon, the sun is high in the sky, and I make my way back to the main barn where I parked the truck. I've been taking my lunch breaks at home, a convenience of living right around the corner from the farm. Plus, I save a ton of money by eating homemade sandwiches or leftovers each day instead of picking something up from the diner or convenience store. I've been counting every penny. Not that it matters now.

If I hadn't lent James money last month, I might have been able to pull it together in time. But it's a joke to think my brother will ever repay me. A few years ago, I mistakenly told him about my plan to buy the farm and the savings I started for it. Ever since that day, James throws the savings in my face whenever he needs help.

He's just eleven months younger than me—Irish twins they called us, but we couldn't be more different. When we were kids and things were bad at home, I tried to comfort and distract Annie from the screaming, objects shattering against the walls, and slamming doors. But James would sneak out the window, gin and cigarettes under his coat. When the dust settled, I cleaned up the broken pieces as James went on his own rampage, leaving an echoing disaster in his wake. From being picked up by the cops for underage drinking and public intoxication to assault and attempted robbery at the EZ-Mart, James took the pain and fears our parents dumped on his shoulders and spewed them all around town. I carried those same burdens in silence. Someone had to think about Annie.

When I make it to the barn, I see Nikki walking toward me. "You here for Chase?" I ask, stepping out of the farm UTV.

"No. You, actually."

"What's up?" I follow her inside the shade of the barn, removing my hat and enjoying the light breeze blowing through.

"Look, I know what Kinsley asked sounds a little crazy–"

"A *little* crazy?"

"Just think of it as a mutually beneficial business arrangement."

"More like mutually assured destruction."

She waves her hand and continues, ignoring my quip. "How much do you need to make up for Marty's early retirement?"

"Eleven thousand." *I'll never crawl out of this massive living grave.*

Nikki looks around, but no one else is in the barn. "What if Kinsley pays you an extra ten on top of what she owes you?"

"Why would she do that?" I ask, but I have an idea of where she's going with this.

"Because she needs someone to marry her before Saturday."

"Before Saturday?" I whistle as my mind adjusts to a new level of crazy.

"Come on, think of it as a part-time job, Caleb."

Ha. Being married to her won't be a part-time job.

"She wouldn't be living with you or coming around to bother you. You'd only see her to get the check and sign the divorce papers."

"What's her boyfriend gonna say about it? Think Landon will be cool with some *not real* marriage?"

"Don't worry about Landon. They're not even together anymore. Look, Caleb this could be the answer for you…the farm, Marty's retirement…"

Ten thousand. It's hard to ignore the offer. I've been working day and night for this, dreaming of it for so long, and now, the carrot is dangling right in front of me. All I have to do is reach out and take it.

"What if people find out?" I shake my head, I can't believe I'm even considering it. "I don't want Annie getting attached, getting hurt like she did with Jessica."

"I get that, but no one will find out. I'll take care of it. We'll go out of town where no one knows you guys."

I catch my reflection in the glass of the little office window behind Nikki. *How did you let it come to this? Everything was on track and now…*

Nothing to do now but wait for the vultures to finish you off. I don't want to marry Kinsley. I don't want to marry anyone—whether for real or on paper, but it might be the easiest way to get the money in time. Disappointment lodges in my throat as I weigh my options.

"Do we have a deal?" Nikki asks.

TEN

Landon: July 2, 2008

Dallas, Texas

"Good afternoon, Mr. Hawk. Your uncle is ready to see you," a petite blonde in a tight-fitting white dress tells me as she walks across the lobby. I stand up, running my eyes along her curves as her cheeks flush. The fabric hugs every asset and she knows it. Her lashes flutter when my gaze stops on her face.

"Right this way," she stammers. I pick up the cardboard tube that leans against the chair and follow her through the frosted glass door and down the hall, observing the way her little round ass moves with each step. I imagine that ass moving on me and have to look away before I walk into my uncle's office with a hard-on. She stops, turns to face me, and motions to the open door on my right.

"Landon, how you been, son?" Uncle Malcolm booms from his desk, Stetson still on his head. "Come on in, take a load off. Thirsty?"

I hand Malcolm the cardboard tube and take a seat in the tall leatherback armchair across from him. "Bourbon, if you have it."

"Make that two." Malcolm tells the blonde. "Stopped by the ranch yet?"

"No, just came from the hotel."

"Well, you better get over there and let Aunt Ruby lay eyes on you before you run outta town again or I won't hear the end of it."

The curvy blonde leans forward, offering me a bourbon and a shot of cleavage. "Thank you, Miss…" I say, pulling my eyes from her chest in no great hurry.

"Mandy," she says, blushing and practically melting into a puddle at my feet.

"Thank you, Mandy. That will be all," Malcolm dismisses her. "Alright. Down to business. Are these the surveys?" he asks, opening the tube and sliding the rolls of paper onto his desk.

"Yeah, they checked out. Shale, just like we thought."

Malcolm unrolls the sheets, pinning the curled edges down with horseshoe-shaped paperweights and looks over the drawings. "And you've secured it?"

"Essentially. I should have full control before the end of summer." I swish the woodsy amber liquid around my mouth, savoring the hint of honey and the cinnamon that chases it.

"*Essentially?*"

"Joint property. The mineral rights are family owned, and I'll be family before August." I point to my ring finger.

Malcolm smacks his palms together. "Hot damn, son. Congratulations! I have to say, didn't see you as the type to settle down so quickly."

"Yeah, well…when it's the right one…" *And they're sitting on a gold mine.*

"What about the others? Are they on board?"

"They will be. Kinsley's clueless and her dad owes me."

"Enough to let you run point?"

"Oh, yeah, trust me. He's so deep in my pocket, he'll never see the light of day–not after that cleanup job a few years back. You remember?"

"With the truck?"

I nod, taking another sip. "Trust me, he won't risk the truth coming out on that one."

Malcolm leans back in his chair, scratching his neck beneath the collar of his shirt. "Alright. Sounds like you've got it squared away on that end. How about your dad? He come around yet?"

"No, but we don't need him–"

"Landon, son, it's quite an undertaking."

"I can do it," I say, leaning forward for emphasis. "*We* can do it. You and me. We just have to get it started–prove him wrong. Once he sees the product, he'll want in and have no choice but to let me lead the new division. You know how he is–"

"Of course, I know how Devon is. He's my brother. But if he doesn't—"

"Then I'll pay you back. We'll lease to Chesapeake or Maverick." I settle back in the chair and have another sip of bourbon.

"You'd take it to his competition? Damn, son. Didn't know you were that cutthroat."

"I doubt it will come to that, but if it does, it'll be his fault." I finish off my drink and stand up, extending my arm to shake his hand. "We gotta look out for ourselves, no one else will. Isn't that what you always tell me?"

"Damn straight," Malcolm says, clasping his hands around mine. "I'll let my guys know and call you with the ETA."

"Perfect." I start for the door with other business in mind.

"And Landon, don't forget to stop by the ranch."

"Will do, Uncle Malcolm. Thanks for seeing me."

Mandy meets me at the end of the hall, her back pressed against the frosted glass door so that I have to face her to pass through.

"Mandy, was it?"

She nods with wide-eyed anticipation.

"You wouldn't happen to be free tonight, would you? I'm in town for the week and really hate eating alone."

ELEVEN

Caleb: July 3, 2008

"I now pronounce you husband and wife," the reverend says with a wink. "You may kiss the bride." Heat crawls up the back of my neck. *Just get it over with.* I lean in, giving her a quick peck—it hardly qualifies as a kiss. The organ bleats out the ceremonial tune, signaling the completion of our phony vows. I grab Kinsley's hand and lead her out to the lobby, where she immediately drops my hand and steps away.

"Congrats, lovers!" Nikki hooks her arms through each of ours, tugging us toward the exit. "Should we go celebrate?" I start to protest, but Kinsley whips her head and glares at Nikki. "Right. Home it is," she says with a laugh.

The drive to the wedding chapel was long, but it's nothing compared to the ride back home. Nikki continues to force her "wedding day" playlist on us. How many times can a person endure "Chapel of Love" and "I Swear?" Not to mention she put "Amazed" on the rotation. If I never hear that song again I'll sleep just fine. It was my song with Jessica. We spent our five-year anniversary at Country Fever, and when Lonestar came on stage, playing *our* song, we danced in the crowded field of sweaty, drunken fans. That was the moment I decided to start saving for a ring. A year later she crushed my heart and dreams like the crushed beer cans we danced around. Even now, nearly two years after the breakup, the song still gets under my skin.

"You got anything else on that iPod of yours, Nikki?" I ask when the song comes on *again.*

"Yeah, please, Nikki. Give it a rest already," Kinsley says.

"Fine, party poopers. There's a Fourth of July playlist I started for this weekend. Will that work?" She hands the iPod to Kinsley in the passenger seat. "So, Caleb. Have any big plans for your first holiday as a married man?" Nikki asks, giving me a wink in the rearview mirror.

"Funny. No, just taking Annie to the Expo to watch the fireworks. You going down to Liberty Fest to watch Chase play?"

"No, Kins and I have standing plans. We spend every Fourth on my parents' pontoon. It's tradition."

"Think the certificate will come by the time we get back from the lake?" Kinsley asks, turning the volume down on the car's stereo.

"I doubt it. They said something like four to six weeks."

"What the hell, Nikki? You never told me that. I can't wait four to six weeks."

"You don't really have a choice, Kins." Nikki glances at her apologetically before looking back to the road.

"I just need mine before October, so four to six weeks isn't a problem," I tell her.

"It might not be a problem for you, but it *is* for me." She slumps, jarring the seatback in front of me.

The Range Rover is packed with awkward tension, but Nikki's mix of country patriotism, classic rock hits, and a stray summer pop song here and there fill the remainder of the drive, keeping the conversation minimal. In the distance, I watch oil wells pumping like those birds they sell at gift shops, bobbing up and down to drink from a glass. The sun's warmth through the window settles on me as the lull of highway driving nearly rocks me to sleep. By the time we pull up to Cunningham Farm, it's almost three and Chase meets us on the dirt path where Nikki stops the car to let me out.

"Thanks for covering for me, man," I say as I crawl out of the backseat.

"Anything for my best bud on his wedding day." Chase grins, draping an arm around my shoulder razzing me.

"Yeah, yeah." I step out from under his arm. "I gotta change and get back to work. Catch ya later."

TWELVE

Kinsley: July 7, 2008

That extra shot of espresso was a bad call. Caffeine buzzes through my veins as I drop my head forward, placing my palms flat against the cool stone countertop of the first-floor women's restroom. I inhale deeply and try to visualize the breath floating around the knotted tension inside my core and carrying it out with my exhale. Raising my head to face the mirror, I look myself in the eye. *No turning back now.* Another deep breath, a quick lint check of my black slacks, and a minor adjustment to my white chiffon blouse. I'm stalling, but I'm out of time.

The elevator takes me up to the mountaintop where I'll face God. Convincing my dad to wait a few weeks won't be easy—I thought I would come in this morning with money in hand. The doors slide open and I make my way down the quiet hall to my dad's office. I knock, take one last deep breath, and enter the room.

"Ah, Kinsley," he says, looking up from his desk. "I knew you would make the right choice. You've always been someone I can depend on. Now, today I need you to–"

"Wait." I hold up a hand as I make my way to stand in front of his desk. "I can't take Phillips' place. I'll do any other job, but I can't be CFO–"

"Kinsley…" he starts as he stands up to meet me face-to-face. The four-inch Louboutins were the right choice, putting me on an even playing field heightwise if nothing else.

"I have the tuition money. Like you said–CFO or pay it back. That was the deal right?"

He tilts his head just so, brows drawn together as if trying to comprehend. "Kinsley," he finally says. "Please sit down." He motions to the black velvet chairs next to me and shifts his weight to lean on the desk. I obey, ever the dutiful one.

"How, might I ask, did you get your hands on $70,000?"

I wrestle with whether to tell him or not. It's none of his business, but I know he won't let it go. "I found a letter from Mom…" I start strong, but lose confidence along the way, finishing with a mumble. "About a trust she set up for me."

"Excuse me?"

"A trust fund. I'll have access to the money soon. By the end of the month. I'm just waiting on some paperwork." I try to sound nonchalant as if everything is above par.

"What are the terms?" he asks, his voice steady. He doesn't seem surprised by the mention of it. He must know about it. Of course, he does. He knows *everything*.

"I just have to be married." I spit it out because he already knows and there's no point playing games with him now.

"Mm-hmm." He nods, mouth pursed. "Am I to understand that you and Landon will be marrying within the month?"

I look down at my hands, rolling the smooth black fabric of my pant leg between my fingers. "Well, actually…I'm already married."

"I see. An elopement. When did this all take place?"

"Thursday," I say and peek up to see him reaching for the day planner on his desk, tapping his index finger on the open page.

"Hmm. I met with Landon in Dallas on Thursday. He didn't mention you were there."

"I wasn't." It's hardly more than a whisper but it fills the space between us.

"Kinsley?"

I focus on my polished toenails peeking out from under black patent sandal straps. "Who did you marry, Kinsley?"

His eyes narrow on me and I rip the bandaid off. "Caleb Lewis."

"Why did you do that?" He nearly growls.

"Because I needed the money."

"Why wouldn't you just marry Landon?"

"I don't know if I want to marry him."

"But you wanted to marry Caleb?" He throws his hands in the air.

"No–I… It's just to get the marriage certificate. It's not real."

"Oh, it's not real, is it? You think Landon will accept that answer? Or did you forget *he's* planning to marry you?"

"No, I–"

"You have no idea what you've done, do you, Kinsley?" He stands up and begins pacing, hands on his hips.

"What do you mean? I did what you asked."

"I did *not* ask for this."

"What does it matter who I marry as long as you get the money back?"

He comes to a stop in front of me. "Kinsley, you need to get the marriage annulled immediately and hope Landon doesn't find out about it."

"Why? Why does it matter if Landon finds out?" I know why it matters to me, but why does *he* care?

"It matters because marrying Landon is the only way to fix this." He gestures wildly to the room. *What the hell is he talking about?* He turns away, but I can see red heat creeping up the back of his neck. "You've ruined everything." His voice is measured. The weight of every syllable, every letter crushes my heart.

"Dad, I'm sorry. I was just–"

"Why couldn't you just do what I asked?" He turns back to me, the red of his face nearly purple now. "Is that so hard? After I gave you everything?"

"I'm sorry." Tears sting my eyes and I know I can't hold it together anymore.

"Sorry cannot fix this, Kinsley. You've ruined it. I had a plan. Everything was under control until you had to go and act like a spoiled, ungrateful little bitch."

His words don't pierce my heart, they shatter my soul. "Dad," I sob. "I'm sorry, I'm so–"

"Shut up! Stop saying you're sorry. That won't fix it." He resumes his pacing, putting more distance between us. "The only way you can fix this is by annulling the marriage and taking the position. Now can you do that?"

I've never seen him so angry—not even when Ben told him he had enlisted. How can *this* be worse? The only thing I understand in this moment is that I've somehow fucked everything up, *again.* Blinking out a tear, I slowly shake my head. Our eyes meet and I notice a speck of fear behind his anger.

"It's ruined." He sinks into his office chair, throwing his head back and closing his eyes. "The company, *me*. Everything's ruined because of *you*. First your mother, and now this? You've destroyed everything that matters, Kinsley." His words are venomous, seeping into the wreckage of my soul and paralyzing me.

"Dad–I... I don't understand." He doesn't speak, and in the echoes of his rage, the silence stings. "Dad–"

"Don't be home when I get there. You don't live there anymore," he says, refusing to look me in the eye.

The words wrap themselves around my heart, around my throat, squeezing, constricting, breaking me. "Daddy, please," I sob, but he rolls his office chair around, turning his back to me. The conversation is over.

Empty inside like someone cut me in half and carved out my being, my body functions on autopilot as I walk to my car and drive home. No— not *home* anymore. I call Nikki, sobbing, and a few minutes later, she's at the door, helping me pack and load both of our cars with as much as we can. When we make it to Nikki's camper, I just want to crawl into bed and go to sleep, which I do as Nikki sits next to me, brushing her fingers through my hair.

THIRTEEN

Kinsley: July 8, 2008

"What am I going to do, Nik?" I groan as Nikki peruses the menu. We came to Buddy's for lunch, though I have far too much on my mind to concern myself with food.

"About your dad or Landon?"

"My dad. I can't even think about Landon right now."

Nikki looks at me like I've missed something obvious. "Kins, you're married and your fiancé has no idea. You're going to have to deal with this eventually."

"Right, but not today. I have bigger problems." *And I'm sure Sierra will keep my fiancé busy while I deal with my dad.*

"I still don't understand why he's so mad at me. He won't even answer my calls or emails."

"It does seem like he's overreacting," Nikki says.

"Do you think if I give him a few days, maybe he'll come around? Reconsider the Junior VP role?"

"Why are you willing to work with him after how he talked to you, Kins?"

"He's still my dad, Nik. Just because we're arguing doesn't mean I don't love him. He's under a lot of pressure with work and–"

"Stop making excuses for him. He can't treat you like that." She shakes her head. "My dad would never–"

"It's not the same, Nikki. Your dad didn't bury his wife."

"That doesn't give someone a free pass to be an asshole to his kids."

I shrug, hoping to drop it. There's truth in her words, but still, Nikki doesn't know what it's like. She doesn't see how much my dad depends on me with Ben out of the picture. I'm the only family he has left, and all of his dreams for the future of CHI rest on my shoulders.

The waitress delivers our meals, and I look over to see Landon walking toward us. *Shit.* What appetite I conjured up instantly scampers away.

"There's my girl. If I didn't know better, I'd think you were avoiding me." He slides into the booth next to me. "I've called. Sent texts. I missed you while I was in Dallas. Thought my fiancé would be happy to see me." He squeezes my thigh a little too hard and I try to hide the pain from my face.

"She's not your fiancé," Nikki says.

Oh, shit, Nikki. Shut up!

He snaps his head toward her. "Excuse me?"

Nikki doesn't blink an eye, she just stares right into the dragon's mouth and laughs. Landon turns and brushes his knuckles along my cheek. So gentle. So sincere. "Why don't you stay at my place tonight, babe? I'll take the day off tomorrow and we'll look at wedding venues."

"Actually…" I stall and look at Nikki. "I already have plans tomorrow. Dress shopping." I wait to see if the lie floats. Landon stares into me. Does he know I'm lying? He always seemed to before.

"Fine," he says. "The day after tomorrow. You two don't have plans then, do you?" I shake my head. "Don't fuck with me, Kinsley," he whispers in my ear as he slips his arm around me.

I meet Nikki's eyes with a silent plea to keep her mouth shut when Landon takes hold of my chin, turns my face to his, and claims a kiss that just last week would have left me dizzy and wanting more.

"Thursday," he says, standing up from the booth. As he saunters away, I catch three female diners falling prey to his pretty boy looks. They're practically salivating, and not for the hand-battered onion rings. I once reveled in it—knowing that I had something so special and shiny. Something the other girls wanted. But shiny things can be stolen. And when I realized what I had wasn't mine alone, it didn't feel so special anymore.

When the door closes behind him, I can breathe again. "What the hell, Kinsley," Nikki says. "What's going to happen Thursday when he expects you to go look at wedding venues?"

"I don't know," I stammer, trying to clear my head. "I just needed time."

"Kins, you're out of time. You're *married*."

"Shhh!" My eyes shift to the patrons nearby—no one I know, thank god. I just have to keep things quiet and get the money. Then I can figure out what to do about Landon.

* * *

"Hey, Kins," Nikki says as she fluffs her pillow. "I've been meaning to talk to you about this weekend."

"This weekend…" I crawl under my blanket and try to find a comfortable position on Nikki's mini sofa. It's not possible. And if I share her bed, I'll wake up with bruises. That woman has a *very* active dream life. *God bless Chase.* "What's this weekend?"

"I thought I told you. Chase has a show in Broken Arrow. We were planning to take the camper and spend the weekend at the campgrounds. Oh, and from the twelfth to the seventeenth we'll be down in Norman for the music festival."

"Oh…" *Fuuuuck.*

"I mean, of course you can come with us, Kins. It's totally fine. I just wanted to let you know so you could…" *Just plug my ears and bury my head in a pillow over here while you and Chase rock the camper all night?*

"No, are you kidding? I'm not going third-wheel on–"

"Stop it. You wouldn't be a third-wheel."

I stare at the moonlit sky through the camper's little window. I'm drowning. I could sleep in my car. Maybe Buddy's would let me crash in a booth. "Your parents done with the renovations yet?" I ask with a half-hearted laugh.

"Lord, no. They have another three months of it, but I'm sure they'd be happy to pay for a room–"

"No, Nikki. I don't want anyone else to know about the drama with my dad. It'll just cause another fight between us. Besides, I should have the money soon. Maybe tomorrow, even. I'll swing by Caleb's and…" The camper is dark and quiet. I can't see Nikki's face, but I know *exactly* what it looks like right now. And I know exactly what she's thinking. Because I'm thinking it too. *Shit. Caleb.*

FOURTEEN

Kinsley: July 9, 2008

Nikki is here for moral support, and maybe to throw her weight around a bit since she's dating Caleb's best friend. I mean, come on, we're practically friends-in-law. But I doubt Caleb will see it that way.

As we approach the little porch steps, Nikki's phone rings. It's Chase. *Of course.* "I'll be right here," she says. "You got this."

Her obscure chatter and flirtatious giggles sprinkle the air behind me as I climb the steps and knock. A moment later, Caleb opens the door, dishrag in hand.

"It's not here yet," he says.

"Umm, no. Actually, I need a favor–"

"*Another* favor?"

"I know, and if there was any other way…but there isn't." I look over my shoulder for Nikki. *Backup! I need backup!*

He folds his uninjured arm across his chest and leans on the door frame. "Well, get on with it."

"I need a place to stay." I cringe. This isn't going to end well.

"Stay? Like here?"

"Please, Caleb. It's only temporary. Just until we get the marriage certificate. My dad kicked me out when I told him we got married and–"

"*Married?*" A young teenage girl pops around from behind the door. "You got married? When? Why didn't you tell me, Caleb?" Her eyes are as wild as the wavy auburn hair framing her face.

"Annie, give us a minute," he says, jaw clenched as he pulls the door shut behind him. He steps off the porch and begins pacing back and forth on the small patch of dirt between shade grass and gravel. His eyes are fixed on something, or nothing, in the distance as he blows out a long, slow breath that's almost a whistle.

"Caleb–"

"I didn't want Annie to know about this," he says.

"Sorry. I didn't mean to…" I look back to see Nikki *still* chattering away on her phone. "It's just for a week or two–maybe less. Then–"

"Then what? What am I supposed to tell Annie?"

I shrug. "Just tell her–"

"You don't get it, Kinsley. She's gonna get attached to you. Don't you see how excited she is already? *This* is what I was trying to avoid."

"Can't you just tell her the truth? I'm sure she's old enough to understand."

"Hey, what did I miss?" Nikki joins us. *Finally.*

"Annie overheard Kinsley say we got married."

"Oh, shit." Nikki grimaces.

"Caleb, look, I'm sorry she overheard me, but the cat's out of the bag. She knows we're married, and she's going to have questions either way. What's she going to think if I *don't* move in with you?"

"Was this part of your plan?" He glowers at me.

"My plan? I don't have a plan–"

"You think if Annie finds out, well then I'll *have* to let you move in. Nice, Kinsley, real nice."

"How was I supposed to know she would hear me–or even that she was here?"

"Come on, Caleb, she didn't know," Nikki says, reaching a hand out in the space between us as if we're about to throw down.

Caleb stews, muttering something I can't make out. *As if I would ever plan to move into this hole.* I look at the house and catch sight of Annie peeking out the front window. "She's watching us."

"What?"

"Your sister. She's watching from the window." I smile and give a little wave.

"Damn it, Kinsley."

"So…can I?"

He closes his eyes, dropping his head back toward the sky, and exhales. "Guess I don't really have a choice, do I?"

"Thank you, Caleb." I hold my hands together like a pathetic beggar because, let's face it, that's what I've become.

"Just don't say anything about the money, alright? I gotta figure some things out." He goes back into the house, letting the screen door slam behind him.

* * *

"Where should I put this, Caleb? Is there an extra bedroom or closet?" I ask, an hour later when I walk into the house with a backpack slung over my shoulder and a large cardboard box in my arms.

"Just over there in the corner, I guess." He points to the back wall of the living room where a bookcase stands.

"Great." I click my tongue and lug my things across the room.

"Can I help?" Annie asks, nearly pouncing on me.

"Yeah, thanks." I smile and glance over at Caleb who's shaking his head. Annie and I make a few trips to Nikki's car and back before she asks Caleb why he isn't helping us unload. I have to look away to hide my stifled laughter—the look on his face is priceless. But I tell Annie I don't want him to hurt his arm that's still healing in the sling.

"I have so many questions! When did it happen? What did your dress look like?" Annie asks as we carry another round into the house.

"Umm, simple sundress. And last week."

"Why are you just now moving in?"

"Oh... I had to take care of some packing and family stuff."

"Why didn't you let me come, Caleb? I should have been there."

"It wasn't planned." I try to cover for him, hoping to win a few brownie points of forgiveness for everything that has happened. "It was just like a heat of the moment kind of thing, you know?"

"So romantic." Annie pretends to swoon, then snaps her head toward her brother. "You didn't even tell me you were dating anyone. *Rude*."

"I don't have to tell you everything, Annie."

Not wanting to interrupt their little tiff, I motion to the door and whisper, "We're going to go pick up the rest."

"There's more?" Caleb asks, looking around the living room full of bags, boxes, and tubs. "Where are you going to put it?"

"Your room." Annie shrugs. "Duh!"

I back out the front door as Caleb gives me a look I'm becoming familiar with.

* * *

I drive the Jag, packed to the brim, back to Caleb's, and when I pull up in front of the house, Annie comes running out. "Oh, my gosh, your car is so cool! Can I ride in it?"

"Of course! Anytime." At least *someone's* happy to have me here.

After the last bag, box, and tub are unloaded, Nikki leaves and I look around the living room, overwhelmed by the mass of belongings in such a small space.

"Want help unpacking?" Annie asks.

"Okay." I smile and accept her offer. I won't be here long, but I still need to access the basics. "Where am I going to put all of this?"

"Well, your clothes can go in your room. Here I'll carry them." Annie picks up a box of clothing overflowing on the couch. Before I can stop her, she's already dropping the box in a little bedroom off the kitchen. It's small and tidy with minimal furniture and a worn armchair in the corner.

Annie opens the sliding closet door on the wall to my right. "Just push his stuff over to make room for yours." She smiles and leaves me alone in the room. On the far side of the bed is a little wooden nightstand holding a lamp, alarm clock, and a stack of books. I feel like I'm snooping somewhere I don't belong. A person's bedroom should be their sanctuary, and I'm desecrating this holy ground in Gucci flip-flops.

Back in the living room, I overhear Annie and Caleb bickering as I sort through boxes, trying to find my makeup and anything else I can stash in the bathroom. Gathering what I can into a box half full of clothes, I walk back into the bedroom and find Caleb clearing out a dresser drawer.

"Annie said you need a drawer," he mumbles as he relocates the contents from one drawer to another.

"Oh…thanks." I set the box down near the closet. "Is this?" I point to a slightly open door along the same wall.

"Bathroom."

Once inside the little bathroom, I open what I expect is a closet. But it's a door to the hallway. *Just one bathroom? This will be fun.* I turn around and face the mirrored front of a small medicine cabinet hanging above the pedestal sink. Inside the little cabinet, I find a razor, shaving cream, deodorant, cologne, and a comb—bare minimum compared to Landon's collection of grooming essentials. Good thing he's low-maintenance because I fill every available inch in the cabinet with my toiletries. The older faucet is flanked on one side by a green bar of soap and on the other by a glass cup holding a tube of Crest toothpaste and a dark blue toothbrush. I add mine to the glass with a clink.

"Oooh, this is so cool! Can I borrow it?" Annie walks into the bathroom holding up a floral skirt.

"Sure." I shrug. She's cute, and her excitement makes me feel like less of an intruder. I open a small cabinet full of feminine hygiene products. *Looks like Annie's already claimed this spot.* But I manage to squeeze a few of my own into the space. Walking back into the bedroom with an empty box, I see Caleb closing a dresser drawer.

He gestures to an open drawer on his left. "Here ya go."

I rummage through my bags for pajamas and underwear. After shoving as much as I can into the drawer and hanging the rest in the closet, I take the empty boxes to the living room and add them to the stack. I'm exhausted and need a break, so I grab my phone and kick off my sandals. Three missed calls from Landon and zero from my dad. *As expected.* I stretch out on the couch. Just for a few minutes. Then I'll deal with this mess.

FIFTEEN

Caleb: July 10, 2008

The alarm clock wakes me at five in the morning, and I shuffle into the bathroom where I flip on the light. Squinting, I allow my eyes to adjust, but I'm seeing double when I reach for my toothbrush and find two. Oh yeah—it wasn't just a nightmare. As I go about my morning routine, I open the medicine cabinet for my deodorant and an avalanche of bottles, jars, and tubes tumble out. *Damn it, Kinsley.* I shove what I can fit back into the cabinet and leave the rest on the ledge of the sink.

When I've dressed for work, I have a quick breakfast and clean up my mess. Heading to the front door, I pass through the disaster that is my living room. Kinsley is asleep on the couch, and even though she's unconscious it still annoys the hell out of me that she's here. *Ten-thousand dollars. I can put up with her for ten-thousand dollars.* I grab my hat and keys and leave for work.

Mr. Cunningham greets me as I step out of the truck. "Mornin', how's the arm?"

"It's getting there," I say with a nod, but the truth is I'm so damn frustrated. You don't realize how much you depend on something until you have to live without it. But I have an appointment with the physical therapist next week, and I'm hoping to lose the sling soon.

After a full morning of mucking pens, tending to livestock, weeding, and planting, I head home for my lunch break. A welcome breeze blows through the windows of the old '89 Ford I inherited from Gramp. It's not fancy, but it's dependable.

When I pull up to the front of my house, the peace I achieved on the short drive fades away. *What the hell?* Two sun-kissed bodies wearing barely enough material to make a toddler's swimsuit are lounging on lawn chairs. A Bluetooth speaker blasts music, and magazines cover a makeshift table of crates that once resided in my garage.

"What are you two doing out here? This ain't a beach–or a pool," I holler as I step out of the truck and slam the door. "Put some clothes on, would ya?"

"We're tanning, Caleb. Clothes interfere with that," Kinsley says.

"Then take it to the backyard. What are the neighbors gonna think when they drive by and see you two like this?"

"They'll probably think it's their lucky day." Nikki laughs, and Kinsley says the backyard is too shady.

What the hell did I get myself into?

Inside, I open the olive-green fridge, take out the deli meat and cheese, and grab a loaf of bread from the cabinet. "Annie," I holler, as I make my lunch. "You here?" No answer.

Sitting down on a bar stool at the little counter that divides the kitchen from the combination dining-living room, I eat my sandwich and sort through a stack of mail, hoping to see the marriage certificate. No luck. Just bills.

The quiet, cool stillness of the house offers a reprieve from the sun that has blasted me all morning. But it's interrupted when I hear the screen door squeak and slam. Kinsley walks around the corner and into the kitchen, barefoot and nearly bare-bodied, humming a tune. I try to preoccupy myself with the stack of mail as she opens the fridge and bends down to peek inside. I hear her place something on the counter and shut the fridge.

"Hey, you know where Annie is?" I ask, eyes glued to my plate. *Don't do it. Do not go there.*

"Yeah, she said she was going to her friend's house–Brittany?"

It sounds like she's struggling with something, and I make the mistake of looking up. She's facing the cabinet on my right, giving me a full view of her profile. Gram always said it's not polite to stare, but how can I ignore this suntanned body with curves in all the right places, walking through my house in a flimsy little bikini? *Damn it, Kinsley.*

"You almost done?" I ask, pulling my eyes away for a split second before they gravitate right back. She's on her tippy toes, reaching for a pitcher on the top shelf.

"Yeah, I just can't reach this…"

And now she's jumping, trying to reach the pitcher. I should have eaten in the bedroom. "Please don't do that."

She whips around to face me. "What am I supposed to do, Caleb? I can't just grow taller."

My better judgment has zero say in my body's response and I'm pushing the bar stool back and walking over to her. "Here." I take it from the top shelf and hand it to her.

"Thanks." She takes it and peeks inside. Standing beside her, I smell the coconut tanning lotion on her skin. I'm close enough to notice a freckle on the side of her neck, and the curve of her lips. I take a step back. *Pull yourself together, man.*

"Is this your plan for the day, then?" I ask and pick up my plate from the bar, carrying it to the sink.

"Excuse me?" She's pouring and mixing god knows what in the pitcher.

"You're just gonna lie around tanning and waste the day? Don't you have a job or something to do like a real adult?" I scrub the plate with soapy water and a little extra force, as if I could somehow scrub the image of her body from my mind.

"It's summer." She scoffs like that explains everything.

Placing the clean dish in the drying rack, I steal a peek over my shoulder. *Damn it, Kinsley.* I brace myself, my free hand flat on the countertop, and with my eyes closed, I take a deep, coconut-scented breath.

"Well, at least clean up your mess," I tell her when I walk back to the counter bar and grab my hat and keys. Then I admire the view for a few seconds longer than I want to admit.

On my way back to the farm, I struggle with the gear shift—still haven't mastered driving a standard without the use of my right arm. When I look down at the light blue sling lying across my chest, I notice it's nearly the same shade of blue as that little bikini. *Aww, hell. It's gonna be a long-ass day.*

SIXTEEN

Kinsley: July 10, 2008

He's an ass. A rude, judgmental ass giving me crap about not being a "real adult." I open the freezer where I remember seeing a small bottle of vodka buried in the back. It's not full but it isn't empty either. Yet. I unscrew the lid, pour the contents into the pitcher, and toss the empty bottle in the trash, making a mental note to replace it with a full bottle later.

"Whatcha got there?" Nikki asks, peeking over her sunglasses when I rejoin her in the front yard.

"Oh, just something I whipped up." I fill two cups with the bright green liquid.

"Whoa, Kins–" Nikki coughs. "What did you put in this? It tastes like straight-up nail polish remover and lime."

Taking a sip, I smack my lips and try to swallow down the sharp, fruity concoction. "Yeah, well I was a little distracted."

"Oh, yeah?" Nikki raises an eyebrow.

"Pfft, not like that. He was nagging me about tanning and said I wasn't a *real* adult or whatever just because I don't have a job. He has no idea what I'm going through. I need time to process everything."

"Sure, I get that, Kins, but you should probably think about doing *something*. You'll run out of money eventually unless you decide to take the CFO position after all."

I let out something between a groan and a whine before downing what's left in my cup and flinging myself back on the lawn chair. "I thought this would fix things, but I just made everything worse. He hasn't called or anything."

"Who, Landon?"

"No, my dad. Landon won't stop calling. He's expecting me to meet him today to talk about wedding venues."

"Yeah, what about that?"

"I don't want to deal with it."

"Obviously. Kinsley, that's part of the problem."

"I know, alright, but he doesn't know I'm staying here so it's not like he's going to hunt me down and drag me off to tour ballrooms and country clubs."

"You can't keep putting him off, Kins."

Why didn't I think to raid my dad's wet bar when I packed? I pull the sunglasses down over my eyes and welcome the sun's rays melting into my skin.

A while later, a soft breeze blows across my face, and I open my eyes to see a fireball of red floating by. Annie hops off her bike, laughing. "What are you doing out here?"

"Working on our tans," I tell her. "Have fun at Brittany's?"

"Yeah, but she has to babysit her cousins." She shrugs, walking her bike to the side of the little house.

"We're going to the mall in a bit, wanna come?"

"Really?" She turns around with the biggest grin.

✳ ✳ ✳

About an hour later, we pull up to the mall. Annie begged to ride in my car, which I agreed to, but Nikki insisted on driving it. I relented even though I knew I could do it. I didn't have *that* much to drink, plus the faint buzz I achieved had already worn off.

We show Annie all of our favorite shops, and I'm shocked that she doesn't have the store map memorized already. The mall was my playground at her age.

In my rushed packing, I only grabbed enough underwear for a few days. But I have a Macy's gift card—one of my dad's associates gave it to me as a graduation gift. So, instead of buying trendy decor for my nonexistent office, I'm restocking the panty drawer. When I ask Annie if she needs anything while we're out, she blushes and hugs her arms across her chest.

"I picked up a sports bra when we were getting groceries at Walmart one time, but I think I got the wrong size. It's a little baggy," she says.

Nikki and I help Annie pick out three bras in the *right* size and a few other things, just because. She tells us about her Gram—the only mom she has known, and how close she was with Jessica before she and Caleb broke up, but it has been a couple of years if I follow her timeline correctly. This poor girl has navigated thirteen and fourteen without much help.

It's clear Annie doesn't feel comfortable talking to Caleb about "girl stuff," and I don't blame her. If it hadn't been for Tammy, Nikki's big sister, taking me under her wing, I would have been the same way—blindly traversing the world of bras, tampons, and liquid eyeliner.

We deplete the Macy's gift card and stop by the food court for a quick bite. "This is the ultimate after-shopping meal," I tell Annie across the table and hold up a slice of pizza so big it requires both hands. "It's like a mandatory stop before going home."

"It's a tradition," Nikki agrees.

"Mmm, it's good," Annie says after a bite. "So, when did you and Caleb meet? He never tells me anything."

Oh, boy. We're doing this. I take another bite to buy myself time before answering. "Actually we met when we were just kids. He was friends with my big brother."

"Did you guys start dating after Jessica left?"

"No…we bumped into each other–"

"Let me guess, love at first sight?" Annie sighs, and Nikki nearly chokes on her food.

"Something like that." I attempt to steer the conversation away from Caleb and the myriad of questions that might follow. "You like magazines? *Teen, Vogue, Style?*"

Annie nods. "Brittany lets me borrow hers since Caleb doesn't want to waste money on a subscription."

"Well, I have a stack in my camper. They're yours if you want them," Nikki tells her.

"Really? Thanks, Nikki." Her eyes light up as a grin spreads across her face. "And you too, Kinsley. Thanks for letting me come with you guys…and for the bras and stuff."

"Of course, any time," I say through a mouth full of pizza. "I know what it's like growing up without a mom around."

"You do?"

I nod and say, "My mom died when I was a baby, so it was just my dad, my brother, and me."

"Oh..." She presses her lips together and looks down at her food. "Maybe that's why you and Caleb are perfect for each other. Because you're also the perfect sister for me."

Nikki glances at me, eyebrows raised. "You're probably right," I say because how do I respond to *that?* I want to be honest with her, but I can't crush her little heart right here in the food court. *Thanks, Caleb.*

* * *

Nikki deems me fit to drive and tosses me the keys in the parking lot. She even lets Annie ride shotgun on the way back to the house. When we step out of the car onto the gravel drive, Caleb is on the front porch steps, scowling. *What's wrong with him now?*

"Bye, Annie," Nikki says, tossing her bags into the passenger seat of the Range Rover. "Good luck." She shoots me a wink. "I'll text you after the show tonight."

"Tell Chase I said break a leg...or whatever musicians do."

"Where have you two been?" Caleb barks, and I follow Annie up the steps, forcing him into the house so we can pass. Annie scurries off to her room with arms full of shopping bags and I drop mine on the couch, kicking off my shoes and ignoring Caleb's obvious irritation.

"I took Annie shopping for some...*girl stuff* she needed." I sit down at the little wooden table in the kitchen and flip through a new issue of *Vogue.*

"You didn't ask if you could take her out." His voice is so parental—like we broke curfew or something.

"I didn't think I needed your permission. It's not like I took her to get a tattoo or piercing."

"What if something had happened to her?"

"Nikki and I were with her the whole time. She was perfectly safe."

"In your car? With you driving?"

"Whoa, hold on." I abandon the magazine. "I'm not a bad driver."

"You totaled a car–"

"That was a long time ago, Caleb. High school, ancient history."

"Alright, well in more recent history." He points to his arm in the sling.

"Oh, my god, I was upset. It was a bad day, would you let it go already?"

"Kinsley, you may have gotten over it, but my arm is still fucked and the tractor is still out of commission."

"I'm sorry, alright. I can't do anything until I get the marriage certificate and the money." His eyes grow wide, and he holds a finger up to his lips.

"Sorry," I say through clenched teeth. He's delaying the inevitable, but I guess I know a thing or two about that. "Look, she's back home in one piece, not a scratch on her."

"What did you buy her anyway? She doesn't need that much stuff."

"Yes, Caleb, she does. She's fourteen years old and she needs… undergarments and things. Trust me."

"Trust you?"

Eyes locked on his, I stand up and shove the chair back into the table with a bang. Then I march into the living room, snatch up my shopping bags, and stride past him again with a death glare. In the bedroom, I toss my new purchases in the dirty hamper to be washed and fume. This is how he responds when I do something nice for his sister? He's a grade A asshole.

The house is too small, and whichever room I'm in, I feel Caleb's irritation seeping through the walls. So I take my sketchbook outside and sit on the front porch step, enjoying the breeze. A cool front has come in, bringing the temperature down to 82°F, but the sky is gray with the coming storm.

* * *

Sprinkles of rain finally break through, and I return inside where piles of my belongings remain scattered throughout the living room. I find my pillow and blanket and start making my bed on the couch when Annie walks in.

"Why are you sleeping out here?" she asks.

"Oh…you know, Caleb has to get up early for work and…"

"And?"

"Well, I actually like the couch. It's pretty comfy."

"That's a lie." Her ability to cut through the crap is surprising and impressive. "Are you guys fighting already?" She lets her shoulders drop. "Is it because we spent too much money at the mall? We can take the stuff back."

"What? No–no, we're not fighting."

"Then why are you sleeping on the couch?" She places her hands on her hips, looking me square in the eye.

Shit. I've got nothing, so I holler for Caleb. "Can you come out here for a second?"

A moment later, his door opens, and he joins us in the living room. "What?"

"Why is she sleeping on the couch?" Annie cocks her head. "Are you guys mad at each other?"

Caleb looks at me for help, but I shrug—I already tried and failed. "Okay," he says. "Yeah, we were upset, but we're not now. We made up, so…" He motions awkwardly to me. "You don't have to sleep on the couch."

Am I supposed to play along?

"Oh, okay…" I gather my bedding and walk toward him cautiously.

"See?" he says. "Everything's fine. Alright?" He pats my shoulder like someone would pet a mangy dog, but Annie doesn't look convinced.

"Okay. I'm just going to get a glass of water," she tells us and walks toward the kitchen, keeping us in her view as long as possible.

"Com'on," he grumbles and I follow. Once we're in his room with the door shut, I offer to sleep on the floor. He hesitates then says that's ridiculous.

"Do you have an air mattress or anything?"

He shakes his head. "When Gram was alive, I had a fold-away cot and slept in the living room, but that thing was a safety hazard. Pitched it a while back. You can have that side." He points to the side nearest to me and walks around the bed. I toss my pillow down and get in, covering myself with my own blanket. It's a much smaller bed than I'm used to, especially with another person in it.

"What is this? A full?" I struggle to get comfortable without bumping into him.

"Yep," he says with his back to me. I flip and squirm as I reposition. "Are you done?"

I huff and close my eyes, thinking how much more comfortable I would be *alone* on the couch. But *someone* won't tell his sister the truth. This has to be the most pathetic way of getting a girl into bed—nice Caleb, well played.

It's hard to find sleep because I'm self-conscious about disturbing him, and I don't feel like being barked at again. Plus, the thunderstorm has finally rolled in. Lighting strikes light up the room, and thunder shakes the old window panes as I fall asleep, cocooned in my blanket.

SEVENTEEN

Kinsley: July 11, 2008

"Hey, Annie, do you know when Caleb's coming home?" I holler from the living room, where I stare into a cardboard box full of art supplies.

"He just said he'd be late tonight. Probably working until the sun sets. He didn't tell you?" Annie's voice carries down the short hall from her bedroom.

"Oh…I just couldn't remember what he said. I was hardly awake." I want to use my free time to work on some art, but everything is still boxed up and I need a place to unpack.

"Think he'll mind if I make room for my art stuff on this bookshelf?"

"Nah, I'm sure it's fine. It's your house too," Annie says as she walks over to the couch and plops down. *Good enough for me.*

I rearrange books, making new stacks on top of the neatly lined rows. With one and a half shelves cleared, I unpack bottles of paint, brushes, canvases, sketchbooks, and pencils.

"I don't know why he has so many books. That's what libraries are for," Annie says and turns the TV on with the remote.

"Whatcha watching?"

"Gossip Girl."

"Love that show." I join her on the couch and take out my phone. The last message from Ben was vague and short: *You'll make the right choice. I believe in you. Love ya, Sis.* But that was in response to the text I sent last week. I haven't told him what I did yet. How can I drop a bomb like that over text? I put my phone away, allowing myself to get wrapped up in someone else's drama for a while.

Two episodes later, I'm in the kitchen assessing our dinner options when Annie calls out from the living room. "Hey, who drives a red convertible?" Anxiety ripples through me, and I stand on my tiptoes to peek out the window above the sink. Landon's Dodge Viper is parked in front of the house. *Fuck.*

"Oh...umm, that's an old friend." I hurry back to the living room. "I'll see what he wants. Stay here."

I step outside, and Annie watches from the window. Nerves twist my core as I cross the gravel drive to meet him in the street. "What are you doing here, Landon?"

"Excuse me? What are *you* doing here, Kinsley?"

"I'm just hanging out with a friend."

"Hanging out or living here?"

How does he know?

"It's just temporary, okay? I'm only staying here for a week or two."

"And why is that?" He cocks his head.

"My dad and I got into a fight and he kicked me out." *He must know all of this already. Why else would he be here?*

"Hmm," he says, scratching his chin as he slowly approaches. "That's the only reason?"

I nod. "And Nikki's out of town."

"Interesting." He stops as if to ponder the idea. I've seen this act before. "Don't you think people will find it curious that you're staying with Caleb Lewis instead of your fiancé?" He steps closer and tucks a piece of hair behind my ear.

"Someone's watching, Landon."

"So?"

"It's Caleb's little sister." I look over at the front window where Annie keeps watch.

"Why do you care?"

"Because. I don't want her to worry or think we're fighting."

He bends down to whisper in my ear. "Are we fighting?" I scrunch up my shoulder at his breath on my skin and take a step back.

"What are you doing here Kinsley? Why are you shacking up with Caleb Lewis? Screwing him to get back at me? Typical."

"No, I–"

"Really, Kinsley. This is a new low, even for you. Slumming it with white trash Lewis. Hope you've had your shots."

"I told you, I just need a place to stay, and Nikki's out of town."

He throws his arms up. "I'm not an idiot, Kinsley. Your dad told me everything."

"Listen, Landon, I wasn't trying to hurt you–"

"Hurt me?" He scoffs. "You didn't hurt me, Kinsley, but you sure as hell have pissed me off."

"I just needed the tuition money. That's all–"

"I would have given it to you and you know it."

I meet his eyes, full of heartache and nearly a decade's worth of memories. Fuck, it hurts to pull away from the soul yours has been stitched to for so long. I look down, blinking back tears.

"You know what I think this is really about?" He cranes his neck so that we're face to face again. "I think you're just trying to make me jealous after that little fit you threw over those panties last week."

He's angry, but maybe he's angry because he loves me. Like I was angry when I saw the mirror—and the panties. Hell, I'm his fiancé, and I'm living with another man—another man I *married*. "No, Landon–"

"You went too far this time, Kinsley. Biggest fucking mess you've ever made."

"It's fine, my dad will calm down in a few days. When I get the money from the trust fund, I'll pay him back, get divorced, and everything will be fine." *Who am I trying to convince?*

He shakes his head. "I guarantee that your dad will not calm down in a few days. This is so much bigger than you know."

"It's just a job, Landon. He'll get someone else to do it."

"Not if he wants to keep the company."

Anxiety clouds my chest and my mind races, scanning for any missing piece I overlooked that would help me make sense of this. "I–I don't understand…"

"Aww, Kins." He cups my face in his hands. "God, you're still so naive. How will you make it when everything falls apart, huh? You've fucked me over by marrying Caleb. Your dad's going to lose everything if the board replaces Phillips before he can. Ben's gone." He looks down into my eyes. "You'll have no one. And *nothing*."

"But my dad—"

"Think about it, Kins. You've let him down over and over again. Since the day you were born, isn't that what you always tell me?"

I nod as guilt eclipses my heart and tears sting my eyes.

"There's no coming back from this," he whispers in my ear and plants a soft kiss just below it.

* * *

Shell-shocked, I walk back into the house, shut the door behind me, and continue to the couch in a daze. I bury my head in my hands to keep Annie from seeing my tears, but a light hand touches my shoulder.

"Kinsley," Annie speaks cautiously. "Who was that guy? Why was he mad at you?"

"It's just an old friend," I say, attempting to steady my voice. "It's fine."

"It didn't look fine... *You* don't look fine."

I try to pull myself together, forcing a smile and wiping my cheeks. "Will you be alright here if I leave? I need to check on something for Nikki." Annie nods, but there's worry in her hazel eyes.

I lied. I don't have to check on something for Nikki. But Annie doesn't need to know that. I don't understand how my decision *not* to step in as CFO could ruin everything. I'm fairly confident that I'd ruin everything if I *did* take the job. What am I missing? How could he lose the company?

Ben's concern amounted to nothing. My dad said Phillips *was* putting the company at risk, but he's not now since he's out of the picture. Why can't any of them just come out and tell me the truth?

My dad usually stays at the office until eight, and sure enough, I spot his Audi in the parking lot. I hurry through the lobby and catch the elevator, and when I step out into the dim hallway, I see light peeking from beneath his office door. Without knocking, I open it and find both Landon and my dad looking over a mess of papers on the desk.

"Kinsley?" my dad asks and turns to Landon with confusion.

"Tell me what's going on, Dad." I march over to him. "Landon said you could lose the company. What is he talking about?"

"Kinsley, sit down." He gestures to the large velvet chairs and I obey. "The reason I need you to take the CFO position is that Phillips was...well, less than honest in his recordkeeping. If you would just take his spot–even temporarily, it would buy me some time to get things in order. But if you don't, the board will find someone else, and when they look at the books, they're going to have questions, and I won't have the answers. It could destroy everything–all I've worked for."

Landon was telling the truth.

"I...I'm sorry, dad. I didn't mean to. Can't you explain to the new CFO–"

"What–explain how thousands of dollars went missing?"

"Okay...my trust fund. You can use that to–"

"Sweetie, your little trust fund wouldn't make a dent." Landon says, taking a seat beside me. I blow out a breath, struggling to process the severity of it all.

A hundred thousand dollars won't make a dent? Holy shit, how bad is this?

"Then, just tell the new CFO. Tell them it was Phillips. You–you can't lose the company over something he did."

"It's not that simple," my dad says. "The company's finances are failing. If word gets out, we'll lose our contracts, the banks will call in our loans. Everything will collapse." He sinks into his chair, eyes set on the desk before him. He's broken, wearing the face he does every year on my birthday. Guilt sucks the air from my lungs.

"There is a way to fix this," Landon says, breaking the painful silence. "I've been working with my father to see if one of his companies could afford to merge with CHI. It might not be ideal, but it could be handled discreetly and avoid the financial fallout."

"Okay...that–that sounds perfect. Let's do that." I study my dad and Landon because they don't respond with enthusiasm. They don't respond at all, and I'm clearly missing something—*again*. Landon reaches across the side of the chair, taking my hand and gently running his thumb over my knuckles.

"Kinsley..." my dad says, shifting in his seat. "I think...well, I–"

"You need to annul the marriage," Landon finishes for him.

"I am. Well– I'll get the divorce after the trust fund money."

"An annulment would be much cleaner. Quicker," Landon says. I try to pull my hand back, but his grip tightens.

"Why does it need to be quick? What does this have to do with a merger?"

"Kinsley, Landon told me about your little meltdown, and I think the best thing for everyone would be to clean up this mess you made with Caleb, continue with the original plan for you and Landon to marry this summer, and look into some therapy or something for your...personal insecurities."

My little meltdown? Personal insecurities? I cannot believe he told my dad about that. "Are you..." I turn to Landon and tug my hand again without success. "Are you saying you'll only do the merger if I marry you?"

"Kins, sweetheart, we were always going to get married. That never changed–"

"Yes it did. It changed when I... When I..."

When I realized that *he* is never going to change. I love my dad, and I don't want to be the reason he loses everything. I love Landon, but he will be the reason I lose everything. I can't speak—I can hardly breathe.

"When you what?" Landon says, tilting his head. I jerk my hand back and manage to run out of the office and down the hall without pursuit.

Adrenaline pumps furiously as I step into the elevator and hold my breath, waiting for the doors to close. I'm a pawn. That's all I am to them. I exhale sharply once metal touches metal, and as the adrenaline dissipates, my heart rate steadies. A couple of seconds pass, but the elevator doesn't move. I push the lobby button again, but it doesn't stay lit. Instead, the doors open, allowing Landon to step inside.

"We're not finished," he says as the doors close behind him.

"Please, Landon. I'm tired."

"Aww, babe." He steps closer, tucking a piece of hair back into place behind my ear. "You're tired?" He nuzzles my neck and slips his arms past my waist to grab hold of the railing behind me. "You have no idea what it has been like for me, Kinsley." He works his way up my neck with soft kisses. I try to resist the way it feels to be in his arms, under his kiss—this man I have loved and trusted with my heart and body since I was just a teenager.

I don't want this. *God, I want this.* No—I can't keep playing this game with him. I'm tired of losing. *I'm tired of losing him.*

"No, Landon…" I say, but it's weak and not even half-hearted. He reaches one arm to my right, and the elevator bounces to a halt. "Landon…" I manage to speak with more conviction, but he brings his free arm back and wraps it around my waist, tugging the hem of my shirt upward.

"Stop, Landon." I place my palms against his chest and try to push him back—he's too strong, or maybe I'm not really trying. I lean away from him as best I can, but I'm still pinned between his arms.

He stops, his body tense against mine. "Did you forget who you're talking to?" His eyes cut into my soul, and choppy bits and pieces of a memory flash in my mind like a picture book's pages being flipped too fast. I'm caught like prey, suspended in the middle of a cold, concrete tower, choking on tears because I know the meaning in his eyes, and I know I'm not getting out of here without losing a piece of myself.

"Shhh." He wipes my cheek. "No one will ever love you like me."

EIGHTEEN

Kinsley: July 11, 2008

The elevator lunges into motion again, and I grip the railing as Landon buttons his dress shirt and tucks it in. I look down at my own clothing. Fly buttoned and everything in place—as if nothing happened. As if he didn't twist my emotions and thoughts, making me doubt my own will and ability to act on it.

When the elevator doors open, he steps aside, holding his arm out so I can pass. "Lady's first," he says, but I can't look at him. We walk through the empty lobby to the main doors, which he also holds open for me.

With shaky hands, I push the button on my key fob and unlock the car. Landon slips his arm around my waist, sending a shudder through me that I can't hide. "Love you, babe." He pulls me closer and kisses me tenderly. I'm too numb to fight back, and it's dizzying—the constant shifts. I hate him right now, so why does my heart flutter when he kisses me like that? And when was the last time he told me he loved me?

I drive to Nikki's instinctively and remember she's gone when I'm about halfway down the winding road of her parents' property. Slamming on the brakes as dirt clouds kick up in the rear view, I take out my phone and send her a text: *U free? I need to talk. It's bad.*

While I wait for a response, I try to find the musical festival's lineup on my phone's browser. I can't remember which town they're in tonight so I give up my search and text Ben, but he doesn't answer—it's the middle of the night for him. *Damn it.* I should have gone with Nikki and Chase and slept in the backseat of her car. I could drive there now if I remembered where the hell she said they were going. Or if she would just text me back. *Come on, Nikki!*

I send another text and call her twice with no luck. I need advice. I need comforting. I need my best friend. And the longer I wait, the more I need to pacify the growing ache inside so that it doesn't consume me entirely. I turn the car around and head to the only other place I know to go.

❊ ❊ ❊

Buddy's is packed with unfamiliar faces in town for the rodeo. *Better for hiding.* I slip into a spot at the bar and wave to get the bartender's attention. "Hey there, flying solo tonight?" Jim asks. He's used to seeing Nikki by my side. "Need a menu?"

"Shot of tequila, Patrón Silver if you have it."

"You got it," he says and fills a shot glass in front of me. "Bad day?"

"Never worse," I say and take the shot before checking my phone—still no response from Nikki. I think about calling her again, but if she hears the bar in the background, she'll lose her shit, call the main line, and tell them to cut me off. She has done it before. I turn off the phone and drop it back into my purse.

Across the room, a vaguely familiar face shoots me a wink. *Not interested.* I avoid eye contact, but apparently that means "come talk to me," and within minutes, the scruffy John Doe joins me at the bar.

"Hey there, party girl. Remember me?"

Unfortunately, I do. He's some poor sucker who got caught up in my drama with Landon. I'm not proud of it, but yeah, I've hooked up with a guy or three to get Landon's attention, to make him jealous, to hurt him back. But it always ends up hurting me more.

"Sorry–think you're confusing me with someone else," I tell him and scan the bar for Jim.

"No way, baby. I'd remember you anywhere. You showed me a real nice time after the Bluegrass Festival. Come on, you remember." He leans in, whispering reminders in my ear that make me want to hurl. His breath is sour and his scent is repulsive. *Tell me he did not smell like this when we hooked up.* His grimy arms snake around my waist, and I shove him away.

"Wrong girl, asshole."

I need another round, or ten, but Jim is busy with other customers, so I wait. And wait. And wait. I could probably drive to Mexico and get it myself as long as this is taking.

The rodeo crowd voices their disapproval when "Wonderwall" comes on the speakers, interrupting the constant flow of boot scootin' boogies. I welcome the change until the lyrics sink into me. *You're gonna be the one that saves me.* Over and over again. It's like my dad has possessed the jukebox.

I finally snag Jim's attention and another round as two girls I remember from high school step up to the bar. *Will there be no end to the Ghosts of Kinsley Past?*

We exchange pleasantries, if you want to call it that, but their fake smiles and judgy eyes tell me I'll be the topic of conversation when they leave. *Yes, yes—it's me. Kinsley Holland, grade A fuck up, alone in a bar, ruining my father's life and business, married but running from my fiancé who has likely fucked you both. Nice to see you.*

Country hits overtake the jukebox again, and my fake besties move to open stools on the other side of the bar. Two shots in and we're starting to get somewhere, but not fast enough. What the hell am I gonna do? Take the CFO job and hope my dad can come up with the missing money before we all crash and burn—or walk away? I have no other options because I *am not* going to marry Landon like chattel so he'll do the damn merger.

I should have asked for a double because it has been at least ten minutes since I last saw Jim. When a hand touches my shoulder, I assume it's John Doe back for another try, but I turn to see Nikki hopping onto the barstool beside me, adjusting her Prada crossbody bag. I stare at her, mouth agape.

"Figured I'd find you here. What's going on?" she asks.

"How are you here?"

"You're lucky the festival is less than an hour away."

"Ahh, there's your partner in crime," Jim says, walking over to us and I motion for two this time. "Need a menu?" he asks Nikki and pours my shots.

"Burger and fries, and put hers on my tab," Nikki tells him. "Did you order, Kins?"

I down the tequila. "I'm not hungry," I say as the alcohol seeps in, softening the edges of my barbed-wire heart. Nikki looks at me disapprovingly. "What? I'm not hungry. I'm too upset to eat."

"But not too upset to drink?"

"Obviously." I take the other shot, and it spreads through my body like warm honey.

"Okay, slow down, tiger. How many of these have you had?" she asks, placing her hand on my forearm. "Let's talk about it."

"I don't wanna talk," I say, shifting my arm so that Nikki's hand drops off. I want the curtain to fall and blanket my world in darkness.

"Place is packed tonight, huh?" Nikki tries again.

I ignore her attempt at conversation. Talking time was an hour ago —or two—and she wasn't available. Now, I want to forget. I want to escape. I want to disappear.

"Kins, are you upset with me?"

I stare at my sad, empty shot glasses and think maybe I'm a sad, empty shot glass too.

"Look, I'm sorry I didn't pick up when you called. I couldn't hear my phone over the band, but I'm here now." She leans forward on the bar, craning her neck to meet my eyes.

"It's fine. Whatever."

"Well, I can tell it's not fine. Why don't you just tell me what's going on? What happened earlier?"

I catch sight of Jim and raise three fingers. Nikki tries to shut it down, but I pull out a fifty from my purse and wave it at her. "Chill. I got it."

"Kinsley, put your money away–"

"No. You're all freaking out over here like I'm gonna bankrupt you."

"It's not about the money," Nikki says, taking the bill and putting it in her jeans pocket. "I'm worried about you. This is like–"

"Like what? Like a few months ago? Like high school? Yeah, I'm a fuck up, everyone knows." My head is a bowling ball wobbling on a twig. Jim delivers Nikki's meal and fills three little glasses. "Drink me," I coo, picking up one glass and downing it.

"Kins…"

"What? It was good enough for Alice," I say and take the second shot.

"Kinsley, slow down." Nikki tries to block my reach for the third shot. "Don't you think you've had enough?"

"Am I still here?" My head bobbles as I look at Nikki with very wide eyes. "Then, no." I finish the last shot and wave for Jim.

"Another round?" he asks.

"No. She's done." Nikki slides her credit card across the bar and points to her food. "Can I get this to go?"

"Rude." I huff and spin my barstool around in circles.

Jim returns Nikki's card and hands her a white styrofoam container. She transfers her meal to the box quickly before taking my arm. "Come on, let's go." She steadies me as I stumble out the door.

* * *

After a bumpy car ride to Caleb's house, she leads me to the front porch steps and asks if I have a house key. *Hell if I know.* I shrug and stumble as the ground turns to waves under my feet. Nikki grabs my arm and helps me sit down on the bottom porch step.

"Oooh, look." I gasp, looking up at the night sky.

"Mm-hmm," Nikki mumbles as she searches my purse for keys.

"It's so swirly. See, Nik?" I lean back, enamored with the dark sky and the dancing stars that spill out in every direction.

"Finally." Nikki huffs, keys jingling in her hands. "Let's see if any of these work."

"It's so pretty, Nik. It's like man-go."

"Mm-hmm, yeah mango."

"Not mango," I burst out laughing and correct her. "*Man*-go."

"Yeah, I see it, Kins. Oh, shit."

"Oh, shit," I repeat after her.

"Someone's coming," Nikki hushes me.

"Nooooo." Then an upside-down Caleb opens the front door.

"Hey," Nikki says. "Sorry to wake you. We couldn't find the key."

"Is she drunk?"

"Nope," I say, making the sound of a popping bubble at the end, but Nikki rats me out.

"Damn it, Kinsley."

"Come on, Kins, let's go inside." Nikki helps me into the house. "Alright, let's put you right here on the couch." I allow gravity to take me and land with a soft thud. "Where's her blanket?" Nikki asks.

"It's on my bed. I'll get it," Caleb tells her, and walks away.

Nikki's eyes widen. "Umm, what?"

"Oh, yeah, we're sleeping together now. Don't tell Landon." I giggle as Caleb comes back into the room carrying my lavender comforter.

"*Only* sleeping," he says. "It's a long story."

"You didn't tell me about this little arrangement." Nikki raises an eyebrow at me and takes the blanket from Caleb.

"Shhh." I put a finger up to my lips and laugh.

"Hey, keep it down," Caleb barks. "I don't want Annie to wake up and see you like this."

Nikki covers me with the blanket, tucking me into the couch. "Let's try to sleep it off, okay?" She brushes the hair back from my clammy forehead. "You want me to stay over, Kins?"

"Mm-hmm." I close my eyes, entering the spinning darkness.

"Is that okay?" Nikki asks Caleb.

"Yeah sure, just keep her quiet. I gotta get up in a few hours."

"Goodnight husband," I whisper. I can practically feel him rolling his eyes as the floor creaks under light footsteps.

NINETEEN

Kinsley: July 12, 2008

I spend a good portion of the morning getting to know Caleb's toilet and bathroom tiles. Nikki says she'll take me to pick up my car from Buddy's this afternoon when I'm feeling better. I've showered and nibbled on toast and bananas. So far, everything is staying down, but my head is foggy and pounding. I shuffle into the kitchen and see Caleb. "Hi," I say, avoiding eye contact.

"Rough morning?" he asks, smoothing mayo on the piece of bread in his hand. I take a seat at the table and pick up the now less-than-hot coffee Nikki made for me.

"So, about last night…"

"Ugh, I don't want to talk about it, Caleb."

"Kinsley, we have to talk about it. If you're going to go out and get shitfaced, don't bring it back here."

"Fine, sorry," I say, burying my head under my arms on the table and wishing he would shut the fuck up because my head is about to explode from pain.

"I don't want Annie involved in any of that." He sits down across from me with his lunch. I catch a whiff of bologna and it almost sends me back to the bathroom.

"Okay. Leave me alone."

"Does this have anything to do with a red convertible coming by the house yesterday?"

"What? How do you know about that?"

"Annie told me an *old friend* came by in a red convertible and you two argued. She was really worried about you."

"She was?" I ask, raising my head.

"Keep your drama away from my house. Annie doesn't need to get mixed up in it."

"I didn't ask him to come over–"

"Whatever, just fight with your boyfriend at his place next time."

"He's not my boyfriend." I groan and lay my head back down.

"Whatever he is, just take your drama somewhere else, alright?"

I mumble a nonsense response against the tabletop and give him a thumbs up.

* * *

Shortly after Caleb leaves, Annie returns home from Brittany's. "Are you feeling better?" she asks.

"Yeah, thanks. Rough morning."

"Think you're pregnant?"

"No! Oh, no, no, no–probably just something I ate." I laugh and instantly regret it because my stomach muscles are still dying. "Hey, I'm sorry for worrying you last night," I tell her.

"I'm just glad you're okay," she says and hugs me. A car horn outside startles her. "Is that your friend again?" she asks and looks over her shoulder toward the window.

"I think it's Nikki. She's taking me to pick up my car." I step out of her embrace and look out the window to confirm. Annie slumps down on the couch as I slip on my shoes and grab my purse. She looks disappointed and I'm pretty sure it has to do with me.

"Hey, you wanna ride with us?" I ask and she looks up at me. "I have a gift certificate to the nail salon. We can get pedicures after." *Lord knows I need some pampering after this morning.*

Annie perks up and agrees, and we ride with Nikki to pick up my car from Buddy's.

"Are you sure you'll be okay?" Nikki asks, pulling into the parking lot and looking over at me with doubt.

"I'm sure," I tell her. *Again.* She offered to skip out on the five-day festival with Chase, but I told her I would behave. Apparently she needs convincing because this is the fourth time I've told her.

"Promise me there won't be an encore of last night?"

"I promise," I say and reach across the center console to hug her. "Have fun at the festival. Thanks for saving my ass."

* * *

Annie and I enjoy an hour of girl talk, coddled in the massage chairs and soaking our feet in the warm, bubbling basins. We talk about our favorite movies and ice cream flavors, what she's looking forward to about starting high school, and every topic she offers that isn't Caleb-related. When our toes are perfectly polished, I present the gift certificate to pay for the pedicures and find the fifty I waved at Nikki last night. It's tucked into my wallet with a post-it note reading "NOT for tequila!"

"Pizza?" Annie asks.

"You're a quick learner."

I'm halfway down the escalator when cheesy, greasy deliciousness hits my nose and makes my mouth water. I've had coffee, toast, and bananas all day, and I'm ready to live again.

We're in line, waiting for our lunch when Annie grabs my arm and squeals. "Oh, my god. He's here!"

"Who?"

"Eric," she says, blushing. "OMG. He's *right* there. Don't look!"

I chuckle and pay for our food, then lead her to a nearby table. Annie looks over at Eric, then away, then back again—she continues on a loop. I can understand the appeal. He's not too bad for a teenager. His face is fairly clear, he dresses well, and his hair looks like he actually cares.

With boys that age any two out of three is good, and the real cherry on top is someone who practices personal and dental hygiene.

"So that's Eric, huh?" I ask, eyeballing the boy who looks a smidge older than Annie. Sending surfer-boy vibes, he casually leans against a food court table, running a hand through his medium-length sandy blonde hair and laughing. The life of the party, I can tell.

Annie stares in a dreamy haze. "Yeah. Eric Birmingham."

"Birmingham? Is he related to the Birminghams with the Chevy dealership?"

She nods. "His dad and uncle."

The Birminghams are Landon's cousins on his mom's side. I met them, of course, at family events with Landon, but I don't know much about them.

"Is he in your grade?" I ask, taking a bite of pizza.

"No, he's a year older."

"Oh, so sophomore this fall?"

"Mm-hmm, and he turns sixteen next month."

"Oh, yeah?"

"He already rides though. It's so cool," Annie gushes.

"Rides?"

"Yeah, a bright green Ninja."

"You mean, like a motorcycle?" I dip my head.

"Mm-hmm." Annie finally pulls her attention away from Eric long enough to take a little bite of pepperoni pizza. "You only have to be fourteen to get a motorcycle license."

Why would anyone think that's a good idea?

"Oh, god. He just saw me looking at him." Annie blushes and turns to hide her face.

"Are you sure?" I look around. "The place is packed. Maybe he—" But Eric's approach stops me.

"Hey Annie, what's up?" he asks, taking a seat in the empty chair next to her.

"Oh, ya know. Just hanging out." It's painfully obvious to me how *cool* Annie is trying to sound. For her sake, I hope it's not obvious to Eric too.

"Cool, cool. Who's this?" He gestures to me. Luckily, I haven't seen the Birminghams in a few years, and if I ever met Eric, he would have been a little kid at the time.

"Oh, this is my sister, Kinsley."

"Sister?" Eric looks at both of us as if searching for a family resemblance. "I thought you only had two brothers."

"Sister-in-law," Annie explains. "Caleb just got married."

"And I wasn't your date to the wedding?" He pretends to be hurt, and Annie blushes. Again. *Was I this transparent at fourteen? Probably.*

"No." She laughs, twisting a strand of hair between her fingers. "They eloped."

"Ahh, okay. Well, I guess I can forgive you then." He winks at her. "But the next wedding," he says, wagging his finger. "I better be your date."

"Okay," she gushes like a sappy little loon. *Good lord, she has lost her mind over this boy.* But after sitting there talking with him for a while, I can see why. He's a charmer—must be a family trait.

"So, Annie, you going to the carnival Friday?" Eric asks.

"Maybe." She looks at me and answers with a hopeful shrug. "Are you?"

"For sure, wouldn't miss it." He offers her a flirtatious little grin, and she turns as red as the pizza sauce. I have to get this kid some high coverage foundation.

"Well, hey." He nudges her. "I gotta go, but I'll see ya at the carnival. I'll save ya a seat on the Ferris wheel." He stands up, flashing some killer dimples, and walks across the food court to his friends. As he rides up the escalator, he looks back over his shoulder to give Annie a little wave. She melts right here in front of me like the cheese on her pizza.

"He's so hot," Annie says in a daze.

I chuckle and check my phone. "Oh, shoot, it's getting late. We should probably get back before Caleb gets home. He'll have search parties out looking for you."

❋ ❋ ❋

July 13, 2008

It has been a lazy Sunday morning with Caleb out of the house running errands or fishing or something. He returned a short time ago, grumbled about laundry, and went puttering on about his day. I'm at the counter bar, drawing in my sketchbook and trying to ignore the grumpy vibes that accompany his presence.

"Kinsley," Annie calls from the bathroom. "Will you show me how to use this liquid eyeliner?"

"Sure, be right there." I hop off the barstool and join Annie in front of the mirror. After a few tries, she almost has it—a nice smooth line, but she jumps at Caleb's voice shouting my name from the laundry room.

"Sorry." I grimace and give her a piece of tissue paper to clean up the smudge. *What did I do this time?*

"You don't have to shout, the house isn't that big," I tell him as I walk into the little laundry room.

"Kinsley, this is exactly why I didn't want you taking Annie out shopping. I can't believe you would get these for her. It's totally unacceptable, she's entirely too young, and she has no business wearing anything like this."

His tirade is out of control, and I can't imagine what he's mad about. I didn't let Annie buy anything inappropriate. In fact, I steered her away from a pair of hipster panties that looked a little too cheeky for her age. I did purchase them for myself though. Super cute.

"What the hell are you talking about?"

"These," he says, glaring at me as he holds up a pair of peachy pink lace panties. "She's too young for these, Kinsley. A fourteen-year-old does not need a pair of sexy panties."

"Caleb–" I try to interrupt him, but he continues his rant, smoke practically steaming from his ears and froth forming in his mouth like an angry dog.

"Caleb," I say again, raising my voice and managing to finally shut him up long enough to say, "Those aren't Annie's. They're mine." I grab them from his hand as his face develops an instant sunburn. Stuffing the panties in the back pocket of my cutoffs, I return to the bathroom to find Annie beaming with pride and perfectly lined eyes.

✻ ✻ ✻

After dinner, I ask Annie if she wants to join me for a *Princess Diaries* marathon. Of course she does, so we settle on the couch for a nearly four-hour stretch of feel-good chick flicks. By the happily ever after, Annie is asleep. I carefully slip out from under the quilt we were sharing, cover her freshly polished toes, and turn off the television before going to bed myself.

I try to move quietly through the house—don't want to wake the beast. But a small avalanche occurs in the bathroom when I pull my makeup remover out of the cram-packed medicine cabinet. Cringing, I wait for the clanging and ringing of scattered toiletries to stop. After a moment of silence, I pick up the mess and prepare for bed.

As soon as I open the bathroom door, I flip off the light and tiptoe across the room. My eyes haven't adjusted to the darkness, and I trip over a pair of shoes, falling to the floor with a thump. "Shit!" A cloud moves lazily across the sky, allowing a sliver of moonlight through the window on Caleb's side of the bed. As I scramble to my feet, the hint of light reveals the bed and one scowling man. "Sorry," I whisper, climbing under the covers.

"Can you please try to be quiet? I have to get up for work in a few hours." The words are polite, but the tone, not so much.

"I said I was sorry. I didn't mean to wake you up. I tripped over my shoes." I grab my pillow and flip it over, slamming it down on the mattress.

"Maybe they don't belong in the middle of the floor." The bed jerks as he repositions. "And what was that in the bathroom? You trying to wake the dead?"

"Again," I say through clenched teeth. "I didn't mean to. It was an accident." My words are sharp and defined.

"Fine."

"Fine." I send it right back at him in a matching tone.

"Shhh."

"You shhh."

"Do you have to have the last word? Is that what this is?"

"No," I say with a huff.

TWENTY

Caleb: July 14, 2008

I pull up to the front of the house around noon, checking the mail for the marriage certificate—nothing but bills. Piles of boxes, stacks of magazines, and heaps of clothing seem to have exploded in the living room while I was gone. *Are you kidding me?* I walk through the disaster to the bedroom, where I find more of the same. "Damn it, Kinsley," I say, stumbling over a backpack on the floor, nearly falling on my already injured arm. "Kinsley," I holler. "We gotta talk. The house is a wreck. I've seen livestock pens cleaner than this."

Back in the living room, I find her. "You gotta clean up your mess. You've left piles of junk everywhere."

"It's not junk, Caleb—it's my stuff. Where am I supposed to put it? There's no room."

"Maybe you don't need it then. Do you *need* sixty-two pairs of shoes?"

"I did not bring sixty-two pairs of shoes."

"Damn close," I mumble. "You gotta learn to clean up after yourself, no one else is gonna do it for you here." I motion to a stash of dirty dishes on the table as I walk toward the kitchen. "Like this."

She comes over, picks them up, and places them in the sink. "Okay? There." She starts to walk away, but I step in front of her.

"No, not *there*. You gotta wash your dishes when you're done."

"Fine." She stomps back toward the sink. "Where's the dishwasher?"

It's like dealing with eleven-year-old Annie all over again. I pick up a hand mirror *someone* left on the table and hold it up in front of her.

"You're lookin' at it. And this," I say, wiggling the mirror, "Doesn't belong in the kitchen."

"Fine, I'll take it to the bathroom." She snatches it from my hand and stomps past me.

"And while you're there," I holler, "pick up the towels and laundry you left on the floor."

I look around at the kitchen—sink full of dishes and food left out on the counters. Guess I should be happy she even remembered to close the refrigerator door. I warm up a container of leftovers in the microwave, then slide junk out of the way so I can sit down at the table and eat.

When I finish my meal, I manage to wash out the container in the crowded sink, placing it and the fork in the drying rack. If I can do it one-handed, she has no excuse. What peace I found in the uninterrupted meal dissipates when I turn to the mountain of trash overflowing from the can and see that Kinsley has returned with a pile of laundry in her arms.

"Oh, and by the way, when the trash can is full, like this," I gesture and continue, "We take it out."

"I just–"

"What? Haven't you noticed it piled up like this?"

"Yeah, but then the next time I saw it, it was empty again."

"What did you think, Kinsley, that little trash fairies came and took it out when you weren't looking?"

"No. I– I don't know. I just didn't think anything of it I guess."

"That's the problem. Look around. You don't think about any of this." I lift the trash bag out of the can and carry it out of the kitchen. "Be back later. House better be clean," I holler.

"Okay, Dad," she mocks just before the screen door slams behind me. I toss the trash into the dumpster and drive back to the farm to finish my workday. It's like driving away from a tornado's path. She has blown in and made a mess of everything.

* * *

After putting in another six hours, I return home, afraid of what I'll find. But when I walk through the front door, I'm surprised to see the living room in better shape than when I left it—except for the wall of stink that accosts me. It smells of burnt food. *What the hell did she do now?*

Stepping into the smoky kitchen, I wave my hand to clear the air with no result and walk over to crack the window above the sink. "What are you doing?"

"Making dinner."

"No. You're not making dinner, you're *ruining* dinner."

She whips around to face me. "I didn't mean to–"

"You should get that tattooed somewhere."

She huffs. "I was trying to make pancakes and bacon."

I pick up a hard blackened disc. "This is supposed to be a pancake?"

Kinsley turns away from the stove, leaving the bacon unattended behind her. "Hey! At least I tried, okay? It's my first time."

"No kidding."

"You're such an ass, Caleb." She waves a spatula at me. "I'm trying to do something nice and you can't even say thank you."

"I'm supposed to thank you for this?" I look around with disgust. "I'm opening another damn window. I can't breathe in here."

I open a window in the living room and return to the kitchen where Kinsley is about to pour water over the flaming pan on the stove. Adrenaline rushes through me and I shout at her, then pull a bag of flour from the cabinet and dump it out to kill the fire. Blowing out long, heavy breaths, I try to slow my heartbeat.

"I'm sorry," Kinsley starts again, tears welling in her big brown eyes. "I was just trying to make up for earlier…trying to be responsible."

"By burning the house down?"

"No. I didn't mean–"

"Look, lesson number one if you're ever going to cook in this house again. Do *not* pour water on a grease fire."

"Geeze, fine." She wipes her cheek. "How was I supposed to know?"

I close my eyes and pinch my lips together. *You were supposed to know because you're a grown adult.*

"Aww, man. Look at this mess. And I just cleaned the kitchen."

Yeah, that must suck for you. I want to walk away, let her deal with this on her own—it's her mess after all, but I'm afraid of what the kitchen will look like if I do. Instead, I grab the broom from the corner behind me, and when I turn back to sweep up the flour, Kinsley is about to pour grease down the sink. I immediately drop the broom and grab the pan from her. "You can't pour grease down the drain, Kinsley," I yell.

I shouldn't have yelled because now she's crying again. But how the hell does she not know these things? "Just let the grease sit. Once it's cool we can scoop it out and throw it away," I say and retrieve the broom from the floor.

"Oh, my god," Annie says, coughing as she walks into the kitchen. "What happened?"

"Kinsley tried to cook," I mumble and turn to Annie, who's giving me *the look* and gesturing for me to console Kinsley. She's standing in the corner of the kitchen, quietly wiping tears and staring at the linoleum floor.

"I'll clean it up," Kinsley says and sounds genuinely sorry.

Damn it, Kinsley. I set the broom aside and tell them we're going to the diner. "This mess will be here when we get back."

Kinsley attempts a peace offering on the way out the door. "Wanna drive my car?" she asks, holding out her keys.

"Sure, thanks," I say with a tight-lipped grin. Lord knows I don't want any more waterworks tonight.

* * *

The diner isn't terribly busy, being a Monday night, so our orders arrive quickly. As usual, Annie orders chicken strips, fries, and a Dr. Pepper. "Thanks," I say, taking the plate of meatloaf and potatoes from the waitress.

"Were you in Home-Ec? That where you learned to cook?" Kinsley asks, taking a bite of her BLT sandwich.

"Probably in one of his dusty old dead guy books," Annie quips.

Kinsley laughs and looks at Annie. "What's a dusty old dead guy book?"

"Oh, you know. He's got a bookcase full of them. Dusty old books written by a bunch of boring old dead guys."

"They're not boring, Annie," I say before taking another bite.

"If you say so."

"Annie doesn't understand why I still read books when I'm no longer in school."

"No," she says. "I understand why. You're a boring hermit."

"Anyway," I ignore her and continue. "Our Gram taught me how to cook and *not* burn the house down."

"Right," Kinsley says. "Gram raised you guys."

"And Gramps," Annie adds and the mood shifts.

Gram and Gramps are the only parents Annie has known. It wasn't long after my mom left that something had to change. My dad was in shambles. Between the depression and alcohol, there might be one day a week when he was coherent and sober enough to be useful. I worried about Annie while I was at school—who was taking care of her? Gram and Gramps didn't know their daughter had left her family—her baby—to chase a new life with someone better. So one day, I rode my bike over to their house and told them, and that was the day we had parents again.

Losing them both has been hard on Annie. In the past four years, we've not only buried our grandparents, but James left and Jessica walked out of our lives. Annie doesn't need to lose anyone else she cares about, which is why I didn't want her to know about Kinsley. *Good job, Caleb.*

"So, you know the carnival is this weekend," Kinsley offers, breaking the heavy silence.

"Can we go?" Annie asks, looking at me.

Kinsley nudges her. "Annie's actually planning to meet a friend there."

"What friend?" I ask, chewing slowly.

"Mmm, I think she said it was Eric," Kinsley mumbles, avoiding my eyes.

"Eric?" I repeat, remembering the name from the diary. Annie's face matches the red vinyl booth we're sitting in. "You're too young to date, Annie."

"It's not a date," Kinsley says. "Plus I'd be there."

Not a selling point.

"And you could be too."

"I have things to do." I shake my head, returning to my meal.

"That you could do Saturday instead. Caleb, please. She's really looking forward to this." Kinsley puts her arm around Annie's shoulder, pulling her close. "Can't you just do this for her?"

Annie's big hopeful eyes find mine. *Damn it.* I'd do anything for that kid. "Fine, I'll think about the carnival. But don't nag me."

* * *

The jingle bells on the door ring as we walk out into the setting sun. "Hey, Kinsley," Annie says. "There's your friend who was so mad the other day." I turn to see Landon strolling toward us with a menacing grin. *Well, shit.*

"If it isn't the newlyweds out for a little family dinner."

"We're leaving," Kinsley says, walking toward the car.

"Oh, come on, surely you have a minute to catch up with an old friend." He looks at Annie. "I bet you didn't know the three of us go way back, Middle school, wasn't it Caleb?" Landon shifts his eyes to me, then Kinsley. "And I've known Kinsley since she was just a kid. In fact, I thought she was going to marry me until your brother here snagged her right out from under my nose."

"That's not what happened," Kinsley says.

Annie screws up her face. "What?"

"Oh, Kinsley didn't tell you?" Landon feigns shock. "I proposed to her just last month. Gave her a gorgeous ring and everything."

"Let's go to the car, Annie," I say, pushing the key fob.

"Bye, Annie." Landon exaggerates sweetness, and I glare at him as we climb into the Jaguar.

"Who is that guy?" Annie asks, leaning over the driver's seat and watching.

"Landon," I say without emotion.

"He's your friend?"

"No."

"But he said–"

"We've known each other since we were kids. We were never friends."

"Did you know he proposed too?" Annie and her endless questions, she should become a journalist.

"No... I didn't." I watch as Landon puts his hand on Kinsley's shoulder and leans in as if to whisper. I can't understand what she sees in him. He pulls her in for a hug, and she holds her arms firmly across her chest. The silence in the little car is uncomfortable as we watch, waiting for the lingering hug to end.

"Does she love him?" Annie asks, breaking the silence but not the tension.

"What?"

"Kinsley–does she love that guy?"

"Oh, I don't know. How should I know?"

"Because she's your wife, Caleb. Wake up." Annie playfully smacks me.

"Oh, yeah," I backpedal, "I mean–no she doesn't love him now, but I don't know, maybe she did before."

"You're so confusing."

"Back at ya," I say, watching Kinsley approach the car.

"Sorry, guys. Let's go home." She rests her chin on her hand and stares out the window as I back out of the parking spot.

"Are you okay, Kinsley?" Annie asks from the backseat.

"Yeah." She sniffles. "I'm fine, Annie. Thanks."

"Guess he's still pissed you dumped him, huh?"

Kinsley chuckles, wiping her cheek. "Yeah, I guess so."

We ride home in silence with Kinsley staring out the window and Annie giving me death stares in the rearview mirror. I know what they mean—my level of concern for my "wife" doesn't meet her approval. So, to appease her, I gently pat Kinsley's warm suntanned shoulder while we wait at a red light, checking the rearview mirror after. *Happy now?*

When I pull up to the house, I put the car in park and turn off the engine. "Go on inside, Annie." I hand her the house keys. "We'll be there in a minute." She takes the keys and lets herself in as I walk around to the passenger side of the car where Kinsley is standing, arms holding herself and looking down.

"Why didn't you tell me he proposed?" I ask once the front door closes. "You could have married him–"

She throws her arms up. "Why does it matter Caleb?"

"It matters because I didn't have to do this."

"I couldn't marry him–"

"It sounds like you could have."

She crosses her arms again and looks away. "Fine. I didn't *want* to marry him."

"What? How do you date someone for a decade and not want to marry them?"

"It wasn't a decade."

"Just about," I mumble, shaking my head. "I'm just trying to understand how we ended up here. Like this."

"It's just… He's…"

"What? An asshole? Yeah." I nod. "Took you this long to figure it out?"

"You weren't there, Caleb, you don't know."

"Look, I don't like being lied to–or tricked. And with Annie a part of it too…" *How the hell did I let this happen?*

"I didn't trick you… And I didn't lie. You never asked if he proposed."

"It's called lying by omission, Kinsley."

"Okay, fine. Yes, he proposed, but look, you're getting the money for the farm–"

"Shhh!" I scan the yard for signs of Annie.

"Oh, my god, Caleb. She's going to find out at some point."

"Yeah, well not today, she isn't. Besides, I could have found another way to get the money. I didn't need to get involved in this mess."

"I know, okay. I mess up everything." Holding herself and rocking back on her heels, she stares at the crushed gravel beneath us. "I just…" She starts to cry. Again. Does she have zero control over her tears?

Fuck it. "Come on," I say. "I'll help you clean up that mess in the kitchen."

TWENTY-ONE

Kinsley: July 15, 2008

My sleep is interrupted by grumbling and dresser drawers opening and closing with force. The alarm clock reads 5:03 like a constellation dotting the dark room. "Shhh." I pull the covers over my head.

"Kinsley," Caleb whispers.

"Hmm?" I mumble, wishing the noise would stop.

"Have you seen my socks? I can't find a single pair."

"Nuh-uh."

"Kinsley," he says again, this time louder.

"What?" I jerk the covers back from my cocoon.

"My socks," he continues. "Have. You. Seen. Any?"

"No. I. Haven't," I return in his same tone.

"I can't understand where they went. Are you sure you didn't see any when you did your laundry?"

I laugh. "I'm sure I didn't. I haven't done laundry since I moved in." I can feel his glare even though it's shrouded in early morning darkness. He pulls the covers off the bed like a magician performing the tablecloth trick. "Hey! I'm cold," I say, bringing my knees up to my chest as goosebumps form on my legs.

"What are these?" he asks, taking my right foot in his hand.

"Socks, obviously."

"Kinsley, these are *my* socks!"

"Well my feet were cold." I whine, pulling my foot back and tucking it into the ball I've made of myself.

"Your feet are always cold."

"They are not."

"Why can't you wear your own socks?"

"I didn't have any that were clean. You weren't using them anyway."

"I would be using them *today*."

"Fine. Take 'em." I slide the socks off my feet.

"No! I'm not wearing them now."

"Why? Do I have cooties? My god, Caleb. You sleep right next to me every night."

"Yeah, not by choice," he grumbles. "Forget it. I'm late for work, and I gotta find some socks." Rummaging through the dirty laundry basket, he huffs and puffs, and I wonder if he'll blow the house down.

"Stop wearing my socks," he barks and leaves the room.

* * *

When I wake up again, it's around 10:30. I leave a messy bed and abandoned socks behind as I enter the kitchen, where Annie is already up and eating breakfast. "Morning," I tell her as I shuffle by, still clearing sleep from my eyes. I pour cereal and milk in a bowl and join her at the table. "So, what are you up to today?"

"Nothing much. I might go to Brittany's later when she's done babysitting her cousins. What about you?"

"Laundry, *apparently*. Caleb shit bricks this morning because I was wearing his socks."

Annie contorts her face. "Why would he care if you wear his socks? You're married."

A jolt of nerves slams into me and I try to downplay my slip up. "Oh… I think it's just part of adjusting to married life, you know?"

When I finish my cereal, I place my bowl in the sink and start to walk away when I remember Caleb's meltdown over the sink full of dishes and begrudgingly turn back to wash the damn bowl *and spoon*. When I've placed them in the drying rack on the counter, the box of cereal I left out catches my eye, so I snatch it up and cram it back into the cupboard.

"Well, here I go," I tell Annie. "Let's see what kind of trouble I get into this time."

"It's just laundry, how much damage can you do?"

"About to find out. It's like every time I try something new around here I screw it up."

"Wait–new? You mean you've never done laundry before? How is that possible? Do you just buy new clothes when they're dirty?"

"No." I laugh. "Our domestic assistant always took care of it for me."

"Your what?"

"Domestic assistant. You know, someone who manages the house, laundry, errands…"

"Like a maid?"

"No–well, maybe… I think a maid just cleans. Carlita does so much more."

"Okay…"

"Anyway, now that my dad's ki–," I stop and correct myself. "Now that I don't live with my dad anymore, I guess laundry is my job."

Annie looks bemused. "I started doing my own laundry a few years ago."

"Really?"

"Sure. It's easy. The machines do most of the work for you."

I gather my dirty clothes and haul an overflowing hamper past Annie on my way to the laundry room. The basket drops with a thud, and I read the worn out print around the knobs and buttons. Opening the washer's lid, I peek inside and find it empty. Then I hoist the hamper up and release a landslide of laundry into the drum, pushing the load down so that everything will fit. I pick up the bottle of laundry soap and pour it over the clothes like syrup on pancakes. Then, I close the lid, turn the rigid dial with a click-click-click, and pull the knob. A moment later, the machine begins to fill with water. *Not too bad.*

It hasn't even been twenty minutes when Annie hollers for me. "Hey Kinsley, I think we have a problem."

What did I do now? I meet her in the hall and see what she's talking about. The laundry room floor puddles with soapy water, leaking from the top of the washer.

"Oh, shit."

"What did you do?" she asks.

"Laundry?" I take a step forward into the hall and my toes squish into soapy wet carpet. *He is straight up going to kill me.* I turn to Annie, whose eyes are wide and worried. "I'm in so much trouble."

"It's alright," she says. "Umm, we can just clean it up before Caleb comes home. No biggie."

"No biggie?"

"It's okay. Look, just turn off the washer and I'll get some towels to soak up the water," she says, hurrying away down the hall.

I gingerly step over the wet soapy puddles in front of the washer. *Where's the off button?* When I hear Annie's approach, I turn to ask her, but it's not Annie. Caleb stands a few feet away from me, shaking his head and pursing his mouth closed.

"I got the towels," Annie says, returning with arms full and slamming to a halt when she sees Caleb.

"Umm I... I..."

He holds up his hand. "No, let me guess. You didn't mean to?"

"I'm sorry, Caleb. I was just trying to do laundry like you said. I didn't mean–I didn't..." I give up trying to explain.

He steps forward, and when his boot squishes on the wet carpet, he goes from irritated to fuming. "The carpet is soaked, Kinsley! What did you do?" He brushes past me and opens the lid. "Is this everything you own?"

"It's just my dirty laundry–"

"Since the day you were born?"

"I, umm...." There's nothing I can say to fix this.

"Kinsley, this is too much. You can't overload the machine like this. It's old and won't drain."

"How was I supposed to know that? I've never done this before."

He stops, dropping his head and bracing himself on the edge of the washer. "You've never done laundry before? How is that even–"

"Our domestic assistant."

"Your what?" He looks at me and it's a mix of disbelief and disappointment.

"Domestic assistant. She always did the laundry and–"

"Maid. Your maid?"

"No, like I was telling Annie, a maid only–"

"Kinsley!"

"Sorry," I say quietly, stepping back an inch and rolling the frayed hem of my shorts between my fingers.

"I don't care what you call your maid."

"Domest—"

He raises a hand to stop me and looks over his shoulder, asking Annie to toss him a couple of towels. Catching them as they fly through the air from just outside the little laundry room, he puts them underfoot and they darken in color, absorbing the puddles.

"Give me that empty hamper," he says, pointing behind me. I pull it around between us and watch as he reaches into the washer, pulling out sopping wet pieces of clothing, and dropping them into the hamper. Each one lands with a thud and releases little droplets of soapy water.

"First," he says, "put all the wet clothes in this basket. Then I'll drain the machine. I'm going to find more towels." He walks out of the laundry room, boots squishing on the soggy carpet. I reach into the machine and pull out water-heavy pieces of clothing, dropping them into the hamper.

"You get it?" Caleb asks when he returns, and I nod, staying quiet and trying not to piss him off. He shuts the lid of the washer, turns some knobs on the machine, and pushes a button. Water drains and he picks up the hamper full of wet clothing, carrying it out of the laundry room. I follow him down the hall. The carpet is covered in bath towels and looks like the beach on spring break. The hamper thuds when it lands on the bathroom floor and I watch from the doorway.

"You have to wring the extra water out of these before you wash them again. Like this." He reaches in and grabs a piece of clothing, wringing it out against the wall of the tub. "I gotta grab lunch and head back to work," he says as he walks past.

"Annie," he hollers from the kitchen.

"Yeah," she says, coming around the corner.

"When the washer's drained and she's done wringing out the clothes, show her how to load the washer and get it going."

"Okay."

"And," he adds, "The dryer. I don't want the house going up in flames while I'm gone."

I stand in the hall, observing their interaction. Everyone else seems to know how to get through life without making a mess of everything. *Why can't I?* Kneeling by the tub in the bathroom, I wring the laundry out piece by piece. Warm, soapy water flows down the drain along with my quiet tears.

July 16, 2008

There's a knock on the bedroom door and Annie's voice is muffled until she pushes it open and peeks her head inside. "Can you give me a ride? My bike chain is messed up again."

"Sure," I say through a yawn. "Be there in a minute."

Stretching as I walk to the bathroom, I bump into the hamper near the door and remember my disastrous attempt at laundry. Like the opposite of Midas, everything I touch falls apart. *Why am I such a helpless fuck up?* I stare into the mirror, searching for an answer, but there's no use. I've tried searching before—the missing piece isn't hiding on the other side of the glass.

As soon as I drop Annie off at Brittany's house, the low fuel alarm dings, so I pull into the gas station down the street, park at the first pump, and step out into the morning heat. I swipe my credit card, but the screen at the pump reads *Card declined. Please see cashier.* I try three more cards with no luck. Damn technology.

I push the call button to ask the attendant if their computers are down, but the voice coming through the crackling speaker says, "It's not us, it's you." Sitting down in the driver's seat, I pull out my phone to check the account balance and see the message: *Account closed.*

What the hell? Did he really close the account? I know I messed things up big time, but how can he just cut me off like that? Scouring through my purse, I find a stray twenty-dollar bill, which I use to pay for gas and drive back to Caleb's house, silently willing the marriage certificate to be in the mailbox.

The mail has come, but not the certificate. *Damn it.* I slam the mailbox shut and slump inside. Dumping the contents of my purse out on the kitchen table, I sort through loose change, cash, and gift cards from graduation. My assets total to a free large coffee, twelve dollars and ninety-three cents, and two Redbox movie rental codes. *Winning.*

After scooping my life savings back into my purse, I open the newspaper to the jobs section. Even a temporary or part-time job would be okay. I have to do something until I can withdraw the trust fund. The RV dealership is hiring, but I don't have five years' work experience. The diner needs a cook. I laugh. Welder, mechanic, nurse—nothing. I scan the listings. "Secretary/Receptionist. College degree or minimum two years' experience required. $12 hourly."

Yes! Perfect. I turn the page to continue reading the ad. "Apply in person at Charleston Holland Industries." *Of course.* All but two of the remaining ads on the page belong to CHI. They're the largest employer in town. More than that, really—they employ over half of the neighboring town as well.

The screen door squeaks and slams. "Hey," Caleb says, walking past me into the kitchen. "Catching up on current events?" I don't respond, the voice inside of me is too loud, telling me what a failure I am.

"You okay?" he asks and walks over. "What's this? Oh, job listings." He sits down beside me. "Anything good?"

How will I make it without my dad's money? Without Landon's money? Without the trust fund? I'm helpless. Fucking pathetic and helpless.

"Kinsley," Caleb says, nudging me. "What's going on with you? You always have a million things to say."

"My dad closed my accounts, so I'm shit out of luck until we get the trust fund money."

"Oh," he says after a moment and clears his throat. "Well, I don't know if you'd be interested, but I could use some help on the farm while Justin's away at church camp."

I snort. "Me? Work on the farm?"

"No pressure," he says as he stands and walks back to the kitchen counter to resume his lunch prep, and I notice his arm is no longer in the sling. "It would just be for next week while he's gone, but if you're interested you can do a test run tomorrow."

It might be the only option I have, and it couldn't be *that* bad—could it? "You don't think I'll mess everything up? Like yesterday?"

"Yeah, about that." He looks down, sucking air through his teeth. "I need to apologize. I might have been a little hard on you. I didn't know it was your first time. I guess I just thought…" He chuckles, replacing the lid on the mayonnaise. "Anyway, I'm sorry. You didn't know, and it was an honest mistake. I acted like an ass."

"It's okay," I tell him with a half smile. "You didn't mean to."

"Nice." He smirks and returns to the table to eat his sandwich. "So, you wanna give it a try?"

I nod. *What else am I gonna do?*

TWENTY-TWO

Landon: July 16, 2008

"Oh, Landon. Come in. I'm so glad you could stop by. What's the latest?" Richard says, ushering me into his office.

"I saw her Monday night, and we spoke briefly, but she was about the same."

Richard pulls his brows together, and age lines on his skin appear like cracked leather. "Don't tell me that's it. You're giving up?"

"No, of course not, but I'm at a loss at how to get through to her. She's really being difficult this time."

He walks around the desk, shoulders hunched forward a bit, and sits down, motioning for me to do the same. "I don't understand. You two have had your arguments before and you were always able to win her back. Surely, you have some trick up your sleeve."

"I'm working on it, but it might be helpful if I had a little more to throw at her. You know, to help her understand just how badly you need her."

"What else is there to know? I explained it to her last week. You were here."

"Right, you told her about Phillips' involvement, but what about yours, Richard?" I ask, holding his gaze.

"Excuse me? Are you insinuating that I had something to do with it?"

"I'm not insinuating anything. I'm reminding you that I was there with Ben the day he found out about Ouranos Group—about the pensions your were stealing—"

"Borrowing."

"Borrowing, huh? So that's all been paid back?"

"Well, umm," he stammers and looks away.

"Look, Richard, I want to help you. I really do, but I can't sell my dad on the merger if I don't know exactly what we're dealing with."

He doesn't respond but tidies the papers on his desk with shaky hands. I lift my wrist to check the time on my watch. If Richard isn't willing to talk, there's no reason to waste anymore time here, so I stand up to leave.

"Wait," he says and I sit back down. "I... Look, you can't tell anyone about this. Not even your dad." His face is almost white with terror.

I lean forward. "Richard, if I wanted to ruin you, I have more than enough information already. I could have turned you in years ago. Hell, I could have taken both you and Kinsley down in one move when Gabe died."

His face regains color and reddens with anger. "It was your truck, Landon–"

"But it was *her* mess, I had nothing to do with it. My dad pitched in on the clean up because I asked him to. For Kinsley." I watch as Richard's face softens and his color returns to normal.

"Now, can you be honest with me and tell me what we're dealing with?"

Richard leans forward on his desk, his elbows like paperweights pressing down on the documents. "Ouranos Group is still in the hole, and Phillips was getting antsy. I figured out a way to bridge the gap. Temporarily. But he wouldn't go along with it. All of a sudden he grew a conscience. So I let him go, paid him off, and made sure he'd keep his mouth shut."

"What was the plan? The thing Phillips wouldn't go along with?"

"I started moving some money around. Just temporarily..." He hesitates, looking down at his desk. "But I'm going to put it back before the end of the year. I just–"

"What money, Richard? Where did you pull it from?"

He shifts his eyes away, drawing his mouth tight like he's fighting a battle with himself to let the words out. "Employee tax withholding," he says.

Fuck. I run my hands back and forth over my face. "That's...that's worse than I expected, honestly."

"But I have it under control, Landon. I'll have it cleaned up before the end of the year."

"How do you know you can? Where's this miracle money coming from?"

"The bids we have out right now. I know for a fact we'll win at least two of the three. I just need Kinsley to stand in for Phillips until I can put the money back. She could be the interim CFO–it wouldn't have to be permanent. Or…" Richard pauses.

"Or what?"

"If you can convince your dad to do the merger, we could set it all right even sooner. We wouldn't have to wait for the contracts."

I shift in the chair, and press my fingers together like a church steeple. "It's a pretty tall ask. A lot of risk."

"But you said–"

"I *did.* And I'm still willing to talk to him, but I'd feel better about doing it as a favor to my wife and father-in-law."

"Of course." He nods emphatically. "So, you've got to convince her."

"And what are you doing to help the cause?"

"I closed her accounts. She's bound to run out of money soon and she'll come to one of us for help."

"Not if she gains access to her trust. We need to talk to Caleb and convince him to get the annulment. I'm not sure why he's playing along with her scheme, but everyone has a price, and we just have to offer him more than Kinsley has."

TWENTY-THREE

Kinsley: July 17, 2008

I set an alarm for the first time since graduation. Caleb told me he'd pick me up for a test run on the farm when he comes home on his lunch break, and I don't want to risk oversleeping. I brush my teeth, dress, and make a bowl of cereal before returning to bed to chill.

My phone dings with a text notification. It's Landon. *Kins, we need to talk. I miss you. Please give me a chance to win you back. You're everything to me.*

What changed since his little performance outside the diner? He certainly wasn't trying to win me back that night, reminding me of all the times I messed up and embarrassed him. If I'm that much of a train wreck, why would he even want to be with me? *Why would anyone?* I don't reply and put my phone away just as Annie comes into the room.

"Has Caleb said anything about the carnival?" She flops down on the bed beside me.

"Not yet, but I'm sure he'll come around. I mean, it's just a carnival and I'll be with you. How can he say no?"

"Do you even know the man you're married to? He's like the fun police. Always shutting things down before I can do anything cool."

"Well, there's a new sheriff in town." I laugh and nudge her. "And I'm going to make sure you ride that Ferris wheel with Eric."

Annie reaches down and squeezes my hand as we lie, staring at the popcorn ceiling. "I'm so nervous, Kinsley. I just really want him to like me."

Rolling toward her, I prop myself up on one elbow. "I don't think you have to worry about that Annie. He seemed pretty interested at the mall."

"Really? Do you think he might try to kiss me?"

"I mean…it's possible. Is that what you want?" Annie's face blooms red in response. "Oh, boy. Would it be your first?"

"God, I'm such a loser."

"Please, you're not a loser. I was about your age when I first kissed a boy."

"What was it like?"

I close my eyes, letting my mind wander back to that day in the game room. It was the summer Ben was at boot camp and Landon kept coming around to commiserate with me. At first it was mutual confusion over Ben's leaving, both seeking answers that neither of us had. Then it became movies on the couch and a teasing flirtation I had never experienced before. He made me feel special and grown up and wanted. I fell so hard, so fast.

"It was pretty great, actually," I say. "It's not like that for everyone. Nikki's was practically a horror story, but mine was everything I could have hoped for."

"How did it happen?" Annie flips on her side, mirroring me.

"We were watching a movie at my house. No one else was home. And when it was over, I started to get up to change out the DVD, but he grabbed my hand and pulled me onto his lap. My heart was beating so fast I thought I would die. Then he tucked a piece of hair behind my ear and pulled my face so close to his." My pulse picks up at the retelling and I take an unsteady breath before continuing. "I closed my eyes—it was like looking at the sun. Then he kissed me and everything just melted into the best feeling. It was everything."

"What was everything?" Nikki's voice breaks through the hazy memory.

"Kinsley's first kiss." Annie says.

"Oh, yeah? You should hear the story of her first kiss with Caleb. Even better."

"You're back!" I sit up so quickly my head goes light. "And you just barge into people's houses these days?"

"Yes, actually when the front door is open and I haven't seen my best friend all week. Wanna grab lunch?"

I look at the alarm clock on Caleb's nightstand. "I can't. Caleb's picking me up to go work on the farm soon."

Nikki bursts out laughing. "I'm sorry. What did I miss?"

"I'm filling in for some kid while he's at camp. I need the money."

"Right, but *you* doing farm work? God, I wish I could stick around and watch."

"Why can't you?"

"I'm running down to the library this afternoon to do some research. I sweet-talked the editor into letting me write an article for the paper."

"The editor is your uncle."

"And I pitched a stellar idea–along with his favorite brownies."

"What's it about? Tiny house living off-grid? Ten ways to live like a bohemian hippy in 2008?"

"You're hilarious. No, I'm writing about when they found Gabe. That case is still unsolved, you know."

Yes, I know, and it gives me anxiety to think about it.

"Kinsley, you awake?" Caleb hollers as the screen door shuts. I've never been so happy to hear that grumpy ass call my name. I slip on my shoes, grab my phone, and scramble to the kitchen.

"Oh, hey," he says. "Get dressed, we're leaving after I finish."

"I am dressed."

He looks me up and down, eyebrow raised. I'm not dressed up—just cut off jean shorts, a tank top, and flip-flops. "What's wrong with what I'm wearing?"

* * *

"Okay, you can start by cleaning out the chicken coop." Caleb picks up a shovel and walks toward me. "Get all the chicken poop and mess out of the pen, put some new pine down, make sure the nesting boxes are clean and have fresh pine too." Not entirely sure what all of that means, but not wanting to blow it on my first task, I smile and take the shovel. "I'm going out to the fields to check on the corn," Caleb hollers as he walks away.

I cautiously approach the chicken pen and begin scooping out the stinky mulch, bits of it falling on my exposed feet beneath the tiny rubber straps of my flip-flops. *Nasty!* I shake my foot, trying to rid it and my shoe of the droppings and repeat the action a few more times before giving up on the idea of keeping my feet clean. The sun is high overhead, mocking me and sending a trickle of sweat starting on my neck and running down the center of my back. I pause my task for a moment to wipe the sweat from my forehead and look around at the rest of the work waiting for me. *Chickens must be full of shit.*

Once the mess is removed from the pen, I grab a metal dustpan and peer into the little wooden hen house from the opening near a tiny ramp. The small enclosed space suffocates me with a hot mucky odor. I pull my head out quickly, coughing and trying not to gag.

Taking a deep breath, I prepare to dive back in, metal dustpan first and head following. Struggling to reach the mess inside the little house, I scoop and sweep what I can into a pile near the opening now blocked by my chest. My left arm braces the little doorway as my body hangs out of the coop, flip-flops abandoned. After gathering all I can possibly reach I shimmy backwards, pulling the top portion of my body out. I stand up straight and cough out the stink I inhaled.

I hear laughter through the breaks in my coughing and turn to see Caleb watching from the other side of the fence. "What's so funny?"

"What are you doing?" He's smiling. I didn't know it was possible.

"I'm cleaning it out like you said."

Caleb walks through the fence gate and past me to the back of the little wooden house. There's some banging and I follow the noise to see what he's doing. He lifts almost the entire back wall of the chicken coop and attaches a hook to keep the hinged door from falling back into place. I twist my mouth. *Well, shit.* "That would have made things easier."

"Thought you knew," he says as he walks past me and out of the fenced area.

When I finish cleaning the coop, I sprinkle fresh pine shavings and lean the shovel against the fence. The worst is over. Maybe he'll have me water some plants or pick some carrots now that I've proven myself capable of dirty work.

"Now what?" I ask him when I walk into the barn, where he's messing with something under the hood of a small rusty tractor. He stops what he's doing, resting his palms on the machine. Muscles form under his white cotton tee shirt and I'm deliciously distracted. *Where did these come from? No. Stop it! Don't look at those.*

"Now the compost," he says.

"Huh?" I drag my eyes back up to his face.

"The shit you just shoveled." He points to the pile. "Fill that wheelbarrow. Then come find me."

I can literally feel the blisters forming on my palms when I pick up the shovel. I should have asked for gloves. When the wheelbarrow is full, I holler for Caleb. He comes out of the barn, wiping his hands on a stained red rag and points to a pile about a hundred feet away. "See that big pile over there?"

I groan, pick up the wooden handles, and start walking. The salty sweat and dirt sting my newly formed blisters and my feet slip in sweaty flip-flops. After three round trips, I've cleared the pile. But the work doesn't stop there. I pull weeds, sweep the barn, pick berries, and sort and label inventory for the farmer's market.

By six o'clock every limb is rubbery and useless. Collapsing next to the barn, resting my back against the warm metal siding, I pick at a few pine shavings and god knows what else that's stuck to my chest. My suntanned legs have temporarily taken on a darker shade from the dirt and dust. I kick off my flip-flops, revealing dark lines of dirt where the rubber straps had been.

Caleb walks out from the barn, looking down at me where I sit. "You done?" he asks.

I nod and stand up slowly—painfully. "That was stupid."

"Aww. Pretty little rich girl can't handle the farm life." Caleb laughs and walks toward the truck.

"You think I'm pretty?"

He stops and turns around. "What? No. That's, no–I didn't say that."

"Yes, you did." I tilt my head with a teasing grin. "You called me a pretty little rich girl."

"Have you looked in a mirror?" he asks with a chuckle and turns back toward the truck. I follow and bend down to check my reflection in the side mirror. *Not my finest moment.*

"Anyway, if you think you're up for the job, you can start Monday morning at six." Caleb hands me two twenty-dollar bills as payment.

It's hard work. Gross, dirty, sweaty work, but I need the money to hold me over until we get our hands on the trust fund. "Alright," I say. "I'll take it."

TWENTY-FOUR

Caleb: July 17, 2008

Back at the house, I sort through mail as Kinsley makes a beeline for the shower. "Leave some hot water for the rest of us," I holler, tossing junk advertisements and extended warranty offers in the trash. No marriage certificate.

"Can we please order pizza or something good for dinner, Caleb?" Annie whines and plops down at the table.

"We have food here."

"Not *good* food."

"It's already been paid for, so it's good enough for me. Besides if you really want to go to the carnival tomorrow night–"

"I do!" Annie straightens up.

"Alright, then we should save the money for that. Unless you'd rather have pizza…" I would rather order pizza than go to the carnival, especially since Annie plans to meet up with Eric, the punk she's "in love with" according to her diary.

"No, I'm good. No pizza. I'll eat whatever you make. It'll be delicious. Can I help?"

* * *

I turn off the stove and take out three plates. "Annie, go tell Kinsley the food's ready, would ya?" She still hasn't come back from the shower. There won't be a drop of hot water left. Annie calls her name as she walks out of the kitchen while I grab a carton of farm-fresh strawberries from the counter, rinsing them in the sink and pouring them into a vintage Pyrex bowl with daisies that match the olive fridge.

Annie returns, stealing a berry and taking a bite. "She's asleep."

"What? It's only–" I look at the clock on the oven that reads 7:32. She didn't even work a half day *and* I took it easy on her. *How the hell is she gonna make it a full day?*

Annie and I eat our chicken and gravy, just like Gram used to make —crisp and buttery, smothered with creamy peppered goodness and a side of green beans. The room is unusually quiet. I guess I've become used to Kinsley's meal-time chatter. When she and Annie get going, it's like I'm in the high school cafeteria again.

Over the past week I've been tempted to revisit the diary, to find out more about Eric and what Annie expects to happen at the carnival, but I'm worried about the fallout if she ever discovers my snooping. Still, I know nothing about him except that Annie thinks he's the hottest guy in the world. I wrestle with bringing up the conversation but take the plunge and hope I don't regret it. "So, tell me about this guy you're seeing tomorrow. Eric, right?"

Her cheeks flush strawberry red and she answers without looking up from her plate. "Mm-hmm, Eric Birmingham. I know him from school. He's a nice guy."

A nice guy. Ha. There's no such thing at that age. Just horny little devils with far too much gumption. I press my lips together, searching for a safe response.

"It's not a date. We're just meeting up with some other friends. So you don't need to freak out or anything," she says.

"I'm not freaking out." Though I am, in fact, freaking out just a little.

"Riiiight."

"Like you said, it's not a date. Nothing to freak out about. Just friends." I lock eyes on her with my best parental warning stare. Obviously *she* considers it a date. I'm not dumb. I know how she feels about the kid, and I'm going to watch them like a hawk, never letting them out of my sight. I'll make sure they have no chance to turn it into a date.

❋ ❋ ❋

July 18, 2008

It's four o'clock when I cut off work early and head home. The girls are chattering and laughing in Annie's room. *Doing makeup,* they said. I don't see the point. It's just a carnival, and they'll be outside sweating it off anyway. But Annie seems happy and that's hard to interrupt. Giggles and squeals carry through the wall separating Annie's room from the living room where I sit, reading to pass the time. When her door opens with a creak, I look up to see Annie wearing a short little yellow sundress.

"Oh, hell no." I stand up, fingers between the pages of my book to mark my place.

"I told you he'd freak out," Annie says, turning to Kinsley who followed her out.

"Caleb, it's just a dress," Kinsley says.

"It's *hardly* a dress. Where are the straps?"

"Right there." She loops her finger under a tiny strip of fabric resting on Annie's shoulder. "They're just tiny."

"We're not leaving until you change, Annie." I sit back down and return to my book, though stomping feet and a slamming door challenge my concentration.

"Really, Caleb, it's not that bad." Kinsley sits down on the couch across from me.

"It *is* that bad. It's too short."

Kinsley lets out an exasperated sight. "It's summer, and it's hot outside."

"It's too mature."

"She's fourteen."

"Exactly!" I give up trying to read and fling the book on the coffee table between us.

Throwing her head back in laughter, Kinsley says, "My god, it's just a sundress, Caleb, not a negligee. I wore dresses like that when I was her age."

"And how'd that work out for you?"

"What the hell is that supposed to mean?" She sits forward, palms on her bare thighs.

But before I can answer and shove my foot further in my mouth a door slams in the hall and Annie comes back into the living room wearing jean shorts and a light blue blouse. "Will this work *father*," she asks, arms crossed and hip popped out.

"That's better, thank you." I ignore the jab.

"I look stupid, but whatever." Annie marches past me and out the front door.

We join her at the truck, and Kinsley slides into the middle seat, serving as a barrier between us. "I think you look really nice, Annie," she says as I start the engine.

When we arrive at the expo grounds, the carnival is in full swing with crowds pouring in and lines forming near the tilt-a-whirl and the scrambler. The sun is still high in the sky with at least another hour of blazing daylight left.

I purchase ride wristbands and game tickets for each of us. Twenty a pop for the wristbands alone—*this is going on Kinsley's tab.* As we walk past the concession stands, the sweet smell of funnel cakes and cotton candy floats heavy in the air.

With an hour to kill before Annie meets her friends, we hit the midway where Annie kicks our butts at the water gun game. My losing streak continues at bottle toss. My arm, though recently out of the sling, isn't quite up to pitching baseballs. Kinsley knocks down all but one of her bottles, and I make a mental note not to be on the receiving end of whatever she finds to throw.

Ridiculously overpriced corn dogs, funnel cakes, and lemonades make up our dinner. The cacophony of carnival games, roaring thrill rides, and talkative crowds make any discussion over dinner impossible, and by the time we finish eating, my ears are nearly numb from the commotion. I gather the trash from our table, tossing it in a nearby bin, and return to find Kinsley primping Annie's hair and straightening her blouse.

"So, I guess your friends are here now?"

"Yeah, they're just over there." She gestures to a group of teens not far behind her.

I shove my hands in my pockets and rock on the heels of my boots because I'm not entirely sure how to handle this new territory. "Alright, well…" I clear my throat. "Have fun. I'll be keeping an eye on you."

As Annie walks over and joins her friends, one boy seems to pay her a little more attention than the others. *So that's Eric.* Something about the kid reminds me of Landon, and my distrust of the little punk doubles.

The group pushes through the crowded midway toward the rides, and we follow. When Annie and the others join a line for the bumper cars, I stand by the safety fence rather than participating. I'll be able to keep a better watch this way.

"You know, you don't have to watch her every move, Caleb. Nothing's going to happen," Kinsley says, joining me at the fence.

"You don't know that." I keep my eyes locked on Annie, but I can feel Kinsley's judgment boring into me.

"Yeah, Caleb, I do. They're driving bumper cars. What could possibly happen? Just relax for a minute."

She has no idea what it's like to be responsible for another being. She's hardly responsible for herself. I watch the bumper cars bouncing off one another, eliciting laughter from drivers and passengers. Maybe some people—people like Kinsley—are born with bumper rings around them. No matter who or what they slam into, they bounce right back, unharmed, and continue on their merry way.

The bumper cars conclude without incident, not that I would admit it to Kinsley. We follow the kids through the sweaty crowds, stopping at the zephyr swings, circling like a mechanical lasso overhead. "You riding this one?" Kinsley asks. I shake my head. Just looking at the ride makes me anxious. I've never been a fan of thrill rides or roller coasters, the loss of control doesn't appeal to me.

"Not my favorite either." She looks up at the ride, face contorted. "I'm going to get dessert. Want some?"

Funnel cake wasn't dessert? She has the diet of a ten-year-old. "Nah, I'm good."

She walks toward the concession stands, and I turn back to the ride, searching for Annie as the last passengers take their seats. The sun has melted like rainbow sherbert into a candy-colored sky, and the glowing mechanical disc starts to turn, picking up speed as the lights flash a dizzying pattern. Soon it's nothing but a blur of motion and lights.

Kinsley returns with a pink mass of cotton candy bigger than her head, and when the swings come to a stop, Annie has the biggest grin, her wavy hair all a mess from the ride. I start for the exit, but Kinsley reaches for my arm. "Give her some space, stalker," she says.

Wishing she'd put more cotton candy in her mouth and shut up, I shake her off of my arm.

Annie and her friends head toward the fun house, and my anxiety spikes. There's no way they're going in there alone. I pick up pace, but just as I'm gaining on them, Kinsley reaches out and grabs me. *Again.*

"Slow down. They're fine."

"No way. I'm going in there with them."

"Please, Caleb, you'll embarrass her."

"So what? Who knows what he'll do to her in there." My mind maps out the worst possibilities.

"It's not like he's taking her to a motel room on prom night," she says, dropping her hand from my arm and tearing a bit of cotton candy with her fingers. "Want some?"

I shake my head and look over as Annie and her friends join the line. Kinsley has no idea what she's talking about. I know what it's like to be a teenage boy—she *does not.* But here I am, watching Annie walk into the unknown with some guy, and I'm not there to protect her. My life has been hijacked by this annoying, cotton-candy-fingered adult child.

I move to an open bench in view of the fun house, where I sit, eyes glued to the exit.

"Didn't you ever come to the carnival when you were her age?" Kinsley asks, joining me on the bench and popping clouds of sugar in her mouth.

"I guess. Maybe once or twice." *This woman never stops talking.*

"And look, you survived, didn't you?"

"It's different. I wasn't all hyped up on the idea of being in love."

"In love? Really, Caleb. That's a tad dramatic."

"Her words, not mine." *Shit. I did not just say that.*

Kinsley shifts on the bench to face me. "She told you she was in love?"

"No– Not exactly… Never mind that, okay? It's still different. She's an innocent fourteen-year-old girl in there with–"

"With an innocent teenage boy," Kinsley says with a laugh.

"Ha! Boys aren't innocent. Not at that age."

"Oh, come on."

"You're just like her. Gullible, naive, walking right into the mouth of the lion with a stupid smile on your face."

"And you don't trust anyone." She leans back on the bench, stretching her sun-kissed legs out in front of her. "That's gotta be lonely."

"Whatever," I mumble. "What's taking them so long?" My mind races through every possible answer and none of them are good.

"Just breathe, Caleb. It'll be okay."

When Annie and her friends trickle out of the fun house, I nearly jump off the bench with relief. Her smile is bigger than ever, which Kinsley uses to support her *I told you so* claim. Their next stop is the Ferris wheel, and when Kinsley asks if I want to ride, I agree. After losing sight of Annie in the fun house, I'm willing to ride any attraction just to keep a closer watch.

The swinging gondolas fill up, one couple at a time, and I watch Annie and Eric climb into their seats. After what feels like an eternity, it's our turn. I crane my neck to find Annie, but all I can see is a sliver of their pink basket.

"Relax," Kinsley says, as the ride attendant sends our gondola up one rung. "She's fine."

"This was a bad idea. If I had stayed down there, I might have been able to see her better."

"And what would you have done?" She turns, her face now just inches from mine.

"I... What?" I'm suddenly hit with a blast of cotton candy sweetness in the air.

"What are you afraid of anyway? Do you think they're going to start making out or something?"

"I don't know…yeah, maybe or he might, you know, try something."

Kinsley laughs. "Caleb, there's no way he could try much up here. There's hardly room to move. The most they could possibly do is hold hands or maybe kiss. It's no big deal."

"It is a big deal. She's too young to be doing any of that."

"She's fourteen!"

"Exactly! She's too young."

"I was her age when I had my first kiss." She brushes a piece of stray hair out of her eyes.

"That doesn't make me feel any better." I look away, trying to create distance between us, which is nearly impossible.

"Okay, Caleb. I get it. You don't want Annie turning out like me, but there are plenty of girls who kissed boys at fourteen and turned out just fine. You need to give her some room to grow up. If you don't, it'll be worse."

It's true, I worry about Annie becoming wild and reckless, but I also worry that she'll end up with some jerk like Landon.

"I'm just trying to protect her," I say as the ride begins its slow steady roll.

"You can't protect her from everything."

"I don't want her to get hurt. So many people have walked out of her life already. If she gets attached to this boy and he breaks her heart, I don't know how she'll take it. I can't stand to think of her hurting like that."

"She'll have her heart broken someday." Kinsley looks down at the crowd and adds, "It's part of growing up."

Even so, I want to delay that growing pain as long as possible.

"Look, the first star," Kinsley says, pointing to a small speck of light in the dimming sky.

"Actually that's Venus."

"Hmm… Goddess of love. It's beautiful."

"What, the planet or the myth?" I scoff.

"Umm, both. You don't agree?"

"I wouldn't call the planet beautiful. It's kind of a nightmare–covered with thick clouds of carbon dioxide and sulfuric acid that make it impossible to see straight. It's hot enough to melt your skin off, and the atmospheric pressure is so high it'd basically crush you. Aptly named though, definitely sounds like love to me."

"Whoa. That's what you think love is? My god, what did Jessica do to you?"

I focus my eyes on the growing light in the sky. "It wasn't just Jessica. I've seen love wreck an entire family." It sickens me—the thought of my dad dissolving into nothingness, loving a woman who went off chasing new, better love.

Kinsley puts her hand on mine. I don't flinch, but my stomach drops. *It's the heights.* "I don't think that was love," she says.

"What do you know about love, Kinsley?" I turn and we're face to face. My stomach sinks further, and I notice her big brown eyes seem to hold sadness behind their sparkle.

"I guess...I don't really know much about it," she says softly as the cotton candy air blasts me again. The ride jerks into motion and she squeezes my hand in response before pulling away and apologizing.

My heart is racing and my head is light. *Damn heights.* I turn away, scanning the crowd below for Annie and filling my lungs with cotton candy-free air.

When the Ferris wheel returns us to earth, I hurry to catch up with Annie and her friends. Her hair blows in the evening wind as I track her through the crowd. Kinsley catches up with me as the teens come to a stop in front of the balloon pop game. The crowd clears enough for me to see Annie holding Eric's hand. *What the hell?* I start toward them instinctively, but Kinsley stops me, grabbing my hand.

"Caleb, don't. It'll be okay."

It doesn't feel okay. It feels like the first time Annie tried to ride her bike without training wheels. I thought I prepared her for it, but she fell and scraped her knee. The cut was so deep she still has a scar. I felt like shit watching her fall, listening to her cry—I should have done better. I look down—Kinsley's still holding my hand. Am I that much of a flight risk?

"You want to find some place to sit? Where we can still see her," she asks, dropping my hand. I look back at Annie as she walks through the midway, a colorful explosion of flashing lights, bells, and chatter.

"Fine," I say and follow her to a nearby bench.

"So how do you know all that stuff about Venus," she asks, obviously trying to distract me. I will not let her become a distraction.

"Just reading I guess. What do you even know about this punk?"

"Eric?" She laughs. "Let's see, his dad owns the Chevy dealership in town, he's a sophomore, about to turn sixteen–"

"Sixteen! No. Not happening." I try to stand, but Kinsley puts her hand on my knee to stop me. It's not that she's strong, it's just that the world is off balance somehow and I'm still here, sitting on the damn bench.

"Caleb, calm down–"

"He's sixteen and she's a child."

"He's *almost* sixteen, and she's not a child."

"You know what sixteen means, right? Driving."

How did I let it get so out of control? *Kinsley. This never would have happened before her.* I run my hands over my face and lean forward, almost taking on a sprinter's stance. I *need* to protect Annie, but a cotton-candy haze fills my head and I can't think straight.

"You're freaking out for nothing."

"You don't get it. I'm the only one looking out for her."

"That's not true. I'm looking out for her too, Caleb."

How can she possibly look out for Annie when her track record proves she can't even look out for herself. Turning my attention back to the midway, I search for Annie through the flashing lights and frenzied crowd. I finally spot her, by the ticket booth—*kissing* Eric. *Oh, hell no.*

I jump up and start toward them, but before I make it halfway, Kinsley is standing in front of me, placing her hands on my chest. She looks up at me and my breath catches in my throat. My heart is beating like crazy, but it's only my concern for Annie. It's nerves, anxiety, adrenaline. That's all.

"Come on, it's her first kiss. Don't ruin it," she says, trying to draw me back from the attack—her hands haven't moved from my shirt. "Don't you remember your first kiss? It's kind of magical."

"You're kind of delusional."

She laughs and I notice the way it settles into a smile on her lips. "I'm not delusional, Caleb. I just remember what it's like to be a teenage girl with a crush."

"Oh, yeah, Landon right?"

Her smile fades and she steps back, dropping her hands. Annie is walking toward us with a red face and nervous smile. "Ready to go?" she asks, hooking her arm around Kinsley's.

* * *

The windows are down, filling the cab with the sound of cricket songs and the soft beating of tires on the road. Kinsley sits between the us again, though her placement as a buffer doesn't do much to lessen the tension. My focus is jarred each time I move the gear shift and my knuckles graze her knee.

When we arrive home, Kinsley and Annie scurry into the house, but I stay behind, leaning against the hood of the truck. A pearl-white moon owns the night sky. I'm not ready for this. For Annie to grow up. Kiss boys. Have her heart broken. I'm in way over my head, and now that it has started, I don't think I can stop it.

When I step inside, the house is quiet. Annie's door is shut and the lights are off. I grab pajamas and change in the bathroom, then slide under the covers, trying not to disturb Kinsley. As I settle in and close my eyes, a hint of cotton candy sweetness drifts in the dark. This time, I breathe it in deeply, longing for more.

TWENTY-FIVE

Kinsley: July 19, 2008

"Come in," Annie hollers over the radio blasting Taylor Swift. I enter and plop down on the twin bed that's covered with a purple polka-dotted comforter. Annie turns the radio down. "What's up?"

"Umm, hello." I hold out my hands. "Tell me all about last night with Eric." I hug a heart-shaped throw pillow as Annie climbs onto the bed, blush painting her cheeks.

"It was amazing. I was totally freaking out at first, but then he held my hand and it was like… Well, I was still freaking out, but in a good way." Annie giggles and folds herself forward, squealing.

"You should have seen Caleb's face. He about lost it when he saw you holding hands."

"I legit thought he would drag my butt right out of the carnival."

"He almost did when he saw you two kissing. I literally had to hold him back."

"Oh, my god, that would have been so embarrassing. *Thank you.*" Annie throws her arms around me, squeezing tight.

"So are you guys dating now? Like a couple?"

"I don't know." She fumbles with a beaded bracelet on her wrist. "Should I call him or wait for him to call me?"

Relationship advice is not my expertise, so I try to imagine what Nikki would say. "Let's see… Is there anywhere you might casually run into him?"

"He likes to hang out with his friends at the rec center and play basketball. I could ask Brittany if her brother knows when he'll be there. They're friends."

"There you go. Then you don't have to stress over calling or waiting for him to call."

"You're brilliant!" Annie runs out of the bedroom to call Brittany. Minutes later, squeals and running feet hurry back toward the room. "Score! He'll be there at three, now what am I going to wear?"

* * *

"Kinsley, does this look okay?" Annie comes out of her room about an hour later wearing a little black halter top that ties behind the neck and a pair of cutoff jean shorts.

"Is that my top?" I cock my head.

Annie blushes. "Is that okay?"

"It's fine with me, but Caleb might shit a brick." Annie's eyes light up, and she bursts out laughing. "And let's not tell him I said that."

Annie grins. "Deal. What about my makeup? I tried the liquid eyeliner again. How'd I do?"

I step closer to inspect the smooth black lines hugging butterfly lashes. "Nice job, Annie. I think you've got the hang of it." A familiar scent hangs in the air. "Are you wearing my perfume?"

"Umm." Annie looks down, fumbling with her hands.

"It's okay if you are." I laugh, patting her on the shoulder. "I told you to help yourself to my makeup and clothes–perfume too."

"One more thing… Can you drop me off at the rec center? I could ride my bike, but I don't want to get all sweaty, and I definitely don't want to ask Caleb to take me."

"Sure, just let me get my shoes and keys." I slip on my sandals and grab my keys before meeting Annie at the front door.

"Can we listen to your Taylor Swift CD on the way?" she asks.

"Obviously!"

* * *

I drop Annie off at the rec center with a little cash in case she needs anything and tell her to call if she wants a ride home. Blasting Taylor's "Picture to Burn" and singing every word, I drive to Nikki's.

When I step inside the camper, Nikki looks up from her laptop. "What's up?"

"Nothing, just dropped Annie off at the rec center. Caleb's working, so the house is empty and boring."

"Aww, sweet little domesticated Kinsley."

"Oh, please, it's not like that," I say, and my cheeks warm. Nikki needs a fan in here.

"If you say so. It's cute you guys got all snuggled up at the carnival."

"What are you talking about? We just took Annie to meet her friends–"

"A little bird told me you two looked pretty cozy last night."

Cozy? Okay, maybe there *was* a moment on the Ferris wheel, but it was only because his cologne or soap or whatever the hell he uses smells so damn good and those pesky muscles of his kept showing up whenever he clenched his fists, worrying about Annie. *Fucking muscles.*

"Whatever, can we talk about something else?" I plop down on the mini sofa.

"Alright, how's Landon?"

"Try again."

"Talked to your dad lately?"

"Man, I'm so glad I stopped by to see you."

"Me too!" Nikki closes her laptop and climbs off the bed. "I have to take some pics for work. You can come with, and since I gotta make a stop downtown, we can grab coffee."

From her tiny house living blog to writing about community events for the town's website and freelancing for the newspaper, Nikki has many side hustles. But her main source of income is managing the website of her mom's law firm, and for that little job she is compensated *very well.*

With an added promise not to discuss Caleb, Landon, or my dad, Nikki convinces me to tag along. Our little expedition includes a stop to take updated photos of her mom's law office since they had a new outdoor sign installed. Then, she takes interior pics and interviews the owner of the new antique shop downtown. After a stop to make good on the promise of coffee, we visit the Belvidere Mansion and Tea Room. The Belvidere, which is supposedly haunted, is hosting a ghost tour as part of a film documentary. Nikki's covering the story for the town's website and asks the manager if she can come back at dusk and take exterior pics.

"One more stop," Nikki says as we pull away from the three-story Victorian-style mansion. Three Carrie Underwood songs later, we come to a stop on the side of the road.

Nikki grabs her camera and steps out, so I follow. Walking through the brush in my flip-flops, I brace myself, placing a hand on the coarse bark of a tree. I take a moment to enjoy the shade it provides, but when I look over to Nikki, standing by a little white cross, I'm suddenly nauseous. This is where the search party found Gabe after an apparent hit and run.

Obscure moments from that night flash in my mind. I've tried for eight years to forget it, to just accept what Landon told me, but I can't make the pieces fit together. The party. The fight. The next morning. The memories are jagged bits of a mosaic that don't work, no matter how I rearrange them.

"You okay?" Nikki asks. "You're looking kind of pale. Maybe you should get back in the AC."

"Umm, yeah." I crawl back into the car and kick up the AC to full blast, adjusting the vents toward my face. The icy air causes my eyes to water and nearly freezes my cheeks, but at least it numbs some of the thoughts stirring in my mind.

"Girl, you're going to have fun on the farm." Nikki laughs when she climbs back into the car. "Might need to tell Caleb to have the paramedics on standby in case you can't take the heat." I attempt a laugh and wipe the cold sweat from my forehead.

❊ ❊ ❊

Annie is still at the rec center when I return to the house, and Caleb is in the kitchen, puttering around. A hint of clean, soapiness teases the air as I walk past him to pick up a magazine lying on the counter.

"Hey, where's Annie?" he asks over his shoulder.

"She's at the rec center with Brittany. I dropped her off earlier." I sit down at the table and open the issue of *Vogue*. "Mail come?"

"Yeah, but it's not here yet. Know when she'll be back?"

"No, she didn't say. I told her to call if she needs a ride. I gave her some cash, too."

He's opening and closing cabinets, and rattling cooking utensils. "Want some help with dinner?" I ask. Then I hear laughter.

"No, I'd prefer dinner unburnt and the house fire-free."

I smack the magazine down. "I'm just trying to be helpful. You don't have to be an ass about it."

"This is above your skill set. It's not heating up a frozen pizza or warming up food someone else prepared for you."

"Hey, I can cook."

"Really? What can you cook, huh?" He turns to face me, leaning back on the counter, with a stupid little smirk on his face.

I hurry to come up with an honest answer. "Toast… And salad."

"You don't *cook* a salad, Kinsley."

"Whatever–just trying to act like a *real adult*." I roll my eyes and return to my magazine. *Asshole.*

"Fine," he says a few seconds later. "You can help me make spaghetti." I stare at him for a moment. Is this a joke? "Come on, it's easy." He motions for me to join him.

"Okay…" I say and cautiously approach the counter like I'm sneaking up on skittish prey.

"We need to cook the beef and boil water for the noodles," he says, holding out a large stainless steel pot.

"I know how to boil water, Caleb."

"Jello shots?"

"Shut up."

He sets the pot aside and hands me a package of ground beef. "This one?" I ask, gesturing to the frying pan on the counter. He nods as he fills the pot with water, and I open the package, dumping the wavy pink loaf into the pan with a thud. Then he gives me a spatula and sets the pot of water on the stove, accidentally bumping into my arm, mumbling an apology.

Caleb steps aside, giving me elbow room as I push the meat around in the pan. It starts to sizzle and pop, filling the kitchen with savory goodness. "Once the meat is all brown, we'll drain the grease–"

"*Not* in the sink," I add. The corner of his mouth twitches as he side-eyes me. The water starts to bubble, and I pour the noodles out of the box, then drain the grease. Caleb stands by, quiet as a mouse, as I spoon out crushed tomatoes and sprinkle seasoning into the beef. He's probably choking on the foot in his mouth. Here I am, cooking and *not* burning the house down. Thank you very much.

"Sorry, just preheating," he says when he brushes against my arm, reaching for the knob that controls the oven temperature. "Now, stir the sauce, but watch out because it can bubble up and splatter on you." The smell of tomato, oregano, garlic, and beef is coming together nicely.

"Did Annie have fun last night?" he asks, wrapping a loaf of french bread in aluminum foil. "I didn't see her when I came home for lunch."

"She said it was *amazing.*"

"Humph." He leans with his back against the counter, arms crossed, and I notice those muscles peeking out from under the sleeves of his tee shirt. *I told you not to look at those!* The spaghetti sauce pops and splatters like a paintball, marking the counter and wall.

"Shit. Sorry." I grab the spoon and stir the sauce as Caleb grabs a rag and wets it at the sink. He steps behind me, reaching his arm past my waist to wipe up the mess I made. The little kitchen is getting hot. The summer sun in the window, the stove, the oven, the muscles. *Shit. No. Not the muscles.* I take a half-step back and bump into him.

"Sorry, it's just easier to clean it up before it cools," he says and then takes a step back, tossing the rag in the sink. "Oven's probably ready now." He picks up the foil bundle, and I step out of the way so he can open the door, sliding it on the rack as the heat blasts my legs.

"What's Nikki gonna think of all this? Becoming a *real adult* and such," he asks after the oven door bounces back into place.

"Hilarious. She's too busy with her article right now."

"Article?"

"Remember Gabe White?"

"Of course. That was terrible." Caleb leans back against the counter across from me.

"She's writing about what happened to him."

"They never figured out who hit him, did they?"

I shake my head and wipe my palms on my denim shorts. "Were you there that night? At the party?"

"Nah, Jess and I didn't hang with that crowd. Were you?"

"Mm-hmm. I might have been the last person he talked to before the accident. Kinda freaky to think about it." I hate thinking about Gabe because I feel guilty. If I had just gone after him, tried to talk to him, maybe things would have turned out differently.

"I think the noodles are done," he says and turns off the stove. "Did you see it? When he was hit?"

"No. The last time I saw him was when he was leaving the party. That's when we talked."

"So, what did he say?"

Anxiety gnaws at my core, and I place my arms across my waist. *Yeah, right. Like that will stop it.* "Umm… I don't really remember. Too long ago."

The thrum of an idle motorcycle engine carries through the window, and my brain makes the connection a split second before Caleb storms out of the kitchen. I follow, rounding the corner just in time to see the front door smack against the wall and hear Caleb mutter, "What the hell?" I peek around him to look out the screen door. Annie and Eric stand lip-locked in front of the motorcycle. *Oh, shit.*

"Annie Pauline Lewis," Caleb shouts as he busts out onto the front porch.

"Caleb!" I try to stop him from embarrassing Annie, but it's too late for that. Annie walks toward the house, red-faced and shooting a death glare at her brother. Once she's inside, Caleb slams the door and turns to her. His face matches hers, glare for glare.

"What do you think you're doing?"

Annie stands next to me like a baby chick with a mother hen. "I was at the rec center and he gave me a ride home." Her tone is calm and casual. This kid is either a great actress or she cannot read the room.

"I did not give you permission to ride on that boy's bike. Do you have any idea what could have happened?"

"But it didn't."

"Still, I didn't give you permission."

"You're not my parent, Caleb!"

"I'm your guardian, Annie. That means–"

"That means you get to ruin my life and embarrass me. Cool, thanks." She drops onto the couch dramatically and starts to cry, so I sit down beside her and pat her back.

"Annie," I say, attempting to mediate. "I don't think Caleb was trying to embarrass you or ruin your life." Receiving no response, I continue. "Maybe he overreacted a little–"

"Overreacted?" Caleb shouts and I raise my hand, pleading for him to shut up for just a second.

"Like I was saying…" I glare at Caleb. "It's only because he loves you and doesn't want anything bad to happen to you." Annie finally looks up at me, *not* Caleb, wiping her eyes, mascara and liner now running down her cheeks.

"Makeup, kissing, motorcycles? Really, Annie?" Caleb starts up again, pacing the floor, and Annie throws herself into my arms, waterworks flowing. "Where did you get that–that…*thing* you're wearing?"

Annie doesn't speak, she just convulses and shutters—a ball of emotion in my arms. "Are you talking about the shirt?" I ask.

"That's hardly a shirt. It looks like she took a napkin and tied it around her chest. Did you buy her that?"

"No, it's mine."

"You said I could wear it," Annie pipes in. *Nice timing, kid.*

"Yes, I did," I say through gritted teeth. "And I believe I also said your brother would freak out."

"And you still let her go out in public like that? With a boy?" Caleb rubs his forehead with one hand and clinches the other into a fist, all the while beating a path into the old carpet beneath his feet.

"I don't think there's anything wrong with it, Caleb. It's just a halter top. It's summer for god's sake."

"Of course you wouldn't think there's anything wrong with it."

"What's that supposed to mean?" I glare at him, but he just shakes his head, and ignores the question. "No, Caleb. I'm tired of these insinuations that I'm some kind of bad influence."

Annie pulls away from me, and worry flashes in her eyes as she wrinkles her nose. "What's burning?"

"Damn it," Caleb and I say at the same time.

"Annie, you need to get changed and clean up for dinner," Caleb barks, heading to the kitchen.

Annie stands, wiping her eyes and quietly leaves the room. A moment later, the oven door squeaks then bangs shut. Caleb comes back into the room and sits down in the chair on the other side of the coffee table.

"Kinsley," he says and clears his throat. "I'm…that's not what I meant… Every–"

"Forget it." I refuse to look at the asshole.

"I was only thinking that you saw her as a friend. An equal—not a little sister who needs to be looked after. I wasn't making a dig at you. I swear."

He sounds sincere, but it's hard to know for sure. I've learned from Landon that words can be twisted and a person's sincerity can't be taken at face value. I nod at Caleb, just wanting to put it behind me. Annie's door opens, and she comes down the hall.

"Dinner's ready," Caleb says, standing up and walking into the kitchen, but I'm not hungry. I want to be alone—anywhere but here. I can't run off though. It would upset Annie, and she has already been through enough tonight, so I join them at the table and pretend to be okay.

TWENTY-SIX

Kinsley: July 20, 2008

Gritty concrete burns the back of my thighs as I sit down in the shade of the roof's awning. I flip through my sketchbook and land on a drawing I started before graduation. It's a woman facing a mirror, but I haven't drawn her reflection yet. I'm not sure what I want hers to say. Do mirrors ever lie? Sometimes I hope they do.

I pick up where I left off, allowing last night's tension to pour out through the graphite. Annie *did* go too far riding Eric's bike, but everything else? The clothes, makeup, and kissing—what's the big deal? Shame laces through my chest because I know what Caleb is worried about. He doesn't want Annie to turn it like me. I don't exactly blame him—sometimes I wish I could go back and turn out differently. Be someone else. Someone better. But I don't think clothes, makeup, and kissing are responsible for who I've become. It would be convenient to blame it on those things—things so tangible and easy to name. It would be convenient, but it wouldn't be true.

The thrum of an engine grows louder as it approaches, and I look up in the direction of the noise. A moment later, Landon's Viper screeches to a halt in front of me. *Shit.* At least Annie and Caleb aren't home. I close my sketchbook and stand up, dusting the grit and dirt off my butt.

"Why are you here, Landon?"

"We need to talk and you won't answer my calls," he says, crossing the yard.

"What is there to talk about?"

"I'm trying to help you, Kinsley. Why are you being so difficult?"

"If you want to help me, just do the merger."

"It's not that simple. Your dad hasn't told you everything."

"Exactly!" I fling my arms out. "Because neither of you will tell me the truth. You only give me crumbs of information and expect me to go along with whatever you want. You think I can't handle it? That I won't understand?"

"No, we're trying to–"

"Protect me. I know." Crossing my arms, I take a step back. "Maybe I don't need your protection."

"I was only doing what Ben asked. He didn't want you to know."

"What are you talking about? Ben tried to warn me about this. He said something about Ouranos Group–is that connected to Phillips?"

"What did he tell you?"

"That my dad made bad decisions and they hurt the company. That I should look into Ouranos Group before boarding a sinking ship. And I did, but nothing came of it. Why can't any of you tell me the truth–*all* of it, not bits and pieces."

He reaches a hand to the back of his neck, rubbing it as he looks past me. "Alright, can we go somewhere and talk? It's not a quick answer."

I look around the yard, weighing my options. I don't want to go anywhere with him, but I don't want Caleb or Annie to come back and find him here either. "Fine. Buddy's. But I'm taking my own car."

❊ ❊ ❊

We find a booth, order drinks, and resume our conversation. "Start at the beginning, Landon. And tell me *all* of it this time."

He leans forward with his hands clasped in front of him, speaking low. "The bookkeeping your dad told you about–it wasn't just Phillips. He was in on it too." *My dad?* Sure, he's manipulative sometimes—even cutthroat, but not corrupt.

"Ouranos Group is a shell. Together, they've been siphoning pension funds for years. When Ben found out, he wanted your dad to come clean, to make things right, but he wasn't up for that and they got into a big fight. Ben even threatened to turn him in, but your dad told him it would be stupid to do that. How could he go to college and take over CHI if the company was gone and your dad was in prison?"

I'm certain my jaw is on the dirty bar floor. *Siphoning pension funds. Ben found out. Prison?* I feel like I'm going to be sick. Landon reaches for my hands and I let him.

"What would have happened to you if he went to prison? And with no money to live on? The public shame. Ben didn't want that for you, so he enlisted."

"So he thought *leaving* was the answer?"

"He didn't know what else to do, Kins–"

"He could have been honest with me." The anger and resentment I've carried all this time echoes in my chest.

"Your dad backed him into a corner. Ben didn't want to be a part of the cover up. I don't know, maybe he was trying to balance the scales in some way by doing something good."

That sounds like Ben. He never would have gone along with Dad's schemes, but he wouldn't have done anything to hurt me either. Except his leaving did hurt. I've been looking for the answers since the day Ben told me he was joining the army, and for years—*years*—they had them hidden away. I pull my hands out from under Landon's. "You knew all this time and never told me?"

"He made me promise–"

"You saw how upset I was when he left. I felt like he'd abandoned me. You sat there while I cried. You could have at least told me why."

"Come on babe, don't be mad at me. We were just kids." He reaches across the table, brushing my hair away from my face. Familiarity calls to me, and something seems to slip past my defenses, burrow deep in my heart, and take root.

"There's more," he says, taking my hands again. I squeeze my eyes shut, afraid of what skeleton he'll reveal next. "Your dad had a plan to pay back the pension funds, but Phillips wasn't on board. That's why he had to let him go."

"But why wouldn't Phillips want to pay–"

"It was risky. Phillips got scared, but your dad… Well, he went ahead with it."

Every answer leads to another question. Will I ever get to the bottom of it? Do I even want to? I take a deep breath and forge on down the rabbit trail where the truth lies buried deep. "What did he do, Landon?"

He surveys the space around our booth before answering. "He's been taking it from the employee tax withholding."

My lungs forget how to work. Even with my limited knowledge of accounting and finance, I know this is bad. It hits me like a brick wall—my dad could go to prison. He could lose everything. And so could I. *Fuck.* Why didn't they lay out all the pieces up front? They always hold something back—no wonder I always make the wrong move.

"But if you do the merger, like you said…" I look into his eyes, begging him to save my dad, to save me.

"Listen, I suggested the merger when I found out about Phillips–when you were off running around the state with Nikki. It's one thing to take a hit that big when you're doing it for family–for your wife and father-in-law. You don't do it for just anybody."

My heart sinks to my stomach. "But I didn't know. I just…"

"Kins, I care about you–and your dad. I don't want this to destroy either of you, but you have to see that I'm the only one who can help you." He runs his thumb over my knuckles. "You need me. Your dad needs me."

"Everything okay over here? Can I refill your drinks?" The waitress approaches us with a smile.

"Just the check, please," Landon says.

He walks me to my car and draws me into his embrace. He hasn't been cocky or mean or threatening once. How can this be the same man who has broken my heart over and over again? I've fallen for it every other time, and I hate myself for it. But this time it's different. This isn't about my feelings or insecurities. This is about keeping my dad out of prison and protecting the company.

"Maybe you should talk to your dad," Landon says and kisses my temple before releasing me from his arms.

If I had any money to my name I would walk right back into Buddy's and lose myself in whiskey, tequila, anything. But I'm broke, and as loyal a customer as I've been, I doubt they'll extend a line of credit to fund my binge. I consider going to Nikki's, but the last thing I need right now is to hear about the article. I have enough demons to fight today—I don't need another one popping back up, and I'm not ready to face Caleb after yesterday's drama. So I drive to the lake and sketch until the moon returns to the sky.

TWENTY-SEVEN

Caleb: July 20, 2008

I park the truck in front of the house and notice Annie's bike isn't in its usual spot. Kinsley's car is gone too, so wherever Annie is, she's not with Kinsley. A week ago that would have given me peace, but today, with the image of Eric and his motorcycle fresh in my mind, I would prefer Annie to be riding around town with Kinsley. I knew that Eric kid would be trouble.

I carry bags of groceries into the house, and under a magnet on the fridge is a note from Annie.

Going to the rec center with Brittany. On my bike. NOT Eric's. Be back for dinner. —A.

Some time back, we discussed adding a line to my cell phone plan, but the bill would nearly double, and our note system works just fine. I never had reason to question her honesty before. Now, though, it would be nice to call and check on her. Maybe after the money comes in from the trust fund I'll get her a phone.

After putting away the groceries, I start a load in the washer and check the dryer, finding a mix of Annie's and Kinsley's laundry. I'll empty it if I absolutely have to but hope it doesn't come to that. I do *not* need any more material for my overactive imagination. It hasn't been this bad since high school. Every once in a while, I'll think of how I raved and ranted at Kinsley over those sexy little panties. Each time the scene replays in my mind, heat crawls up my neck as if it's happening all over again. I can't forget it. Worse, I can't stop myself from picturing her in them. Not after my brain filed away every visible inch of her suntanned body the day she pranced around in her bikini. *Fuck.* I'm thinking about it now.

I walk down the hall and stop at Annie's bedroom, grabbing the doorknob. I'm tempted, *so tempted*, to take a peek in her diary. Only to see if she went too far with Eric. It's not that I want to know those personal details about my baby sister, but the last thing we need right now is a teen pregnancy, and the combination of Annie's immaturity and excitability terrifies me. I drop my hand from the doorknob. Maybe I can find out enough from Kinsley to put my mind at ease. Or, if not, at least warrant an invasion of privacy.

In the living room, I search the bookshelves for *Plato's Symposium*, an old favorite—or a *dusty old dead guy book* according to Annie. It's not where I left it. In fact, the entire shelf is out of order with books stacked and shoved in a chaotic mess. The shelf above holds a collection of paints and brushes. Kinsley has invaded every inch of my life—and my house. Even my bathroom has become Kinsley-occupied territory, smelling like a vanilla flower garden with a coconut breeze. It's impossible. It's wonderful.

The front door opens and I look over my shoulder to find Annie. "Hey, have fun at the rec?"

"Yeah. Did Kinsley tell you about the game night?"

I give up my hunt for the book and walk around the couch to meet her. "She might have mentioned something about it." Kinsley and Annie concocted the idea of a game night at home. It sounded innocent enough until I heard Eric would be in attendance. It's their way of getting me to agree to a *date*. With supervision.

"So… Is that a yes?"

I rub my hands over my face and exhale. "It's a *maybe*." A smile tugs at the corners of her mouth, and she starts to walk away. "Hey, you've got laundry in the dryer."

"On it," she hollers from the hall.

* * *

Sunday is "leftovers night," so I have a sliver of time to relax. Hence the book I was looking for. I resume my search in the bedroom, scanning the top of the dresser and the nightstand without luck. A few loose sheets of paper are scattered on the bed. Gathering them into a neat stack, I notice a sketch of what looks like a chrysalis, its transparent skin revealing a woman curled up inside. I sit down on the side of the bed, admiring the work. *Kinsley drew this?* Somehow, she has captured the sheen and delicate crevices in the fibers of nature. How, with only paper and lead, did she create textures that I can almost feel?

"Oh, I…um. Sorry," Kinsley says as she walks into the room, kicking off her shoes. "I didn't know you were in here." She stops and her eyes come to rest on the drawings I'm holding. "Are those…"

I feel like I've stolen a glimpse of something intimate. I feel like I did when I read Annie's diary. "Sorry. I wasn't snooping. They were on the bed and…" I stand up, holding them out to her. Brows drawn, she takes the stack of drawings from me and looks down at the braided rug beneath her feet.

I can't tell if she's mad or embarrassed or something else, but she doesn't speak or even look up at me. She reminds me of a wild animal, frozen at the sight of a predator. I clear my throat. "Alright, well… Early mornin' tomorrow." I scoot past her but stop at the doorway. "You're really talented, Kinsley."

"Thanks," she whispers.

❋ ❋ ❋

July 21, 2008

"You know the work day started three hours ago?" I tell Kinsley as she walks into the barn at 9:04 a.m., two iced coffees in hand and wearing one of *my* flannel shirts and baseball caps. Somehow she managed to find her own cutoffs and boots.

"Sorry, I had to buy farm shoes. Here, for you." She holds out a sweaty plastic cup.

"Umm, thanks." I take the cup and then a sip. Not bad considering the ice has all but melted in the heat. "They're called work boots. Is that my shirt…and my hat? Socks weren't enough for you, huh?"

"I don't have farm–work clothes."

Shocking. "Where'd you get the boots?"

"Atwoods. Annie helped me pick them out," she says, showing them off. "That's why I'm just now getting here."

"It took three hours to pick out boots?"

"No, just one, but I had to track down Nikki to borrow money for the boots and get ready and do my hair and–"

"I got it. We start at six tomorrow, so plan ahead. And maybe go to bed earlier. I tried to wake you up at five. You were dead to the world."

"As one should be at five in the morning." She takes a sip of her coffee and looks around the barn. "So, whatcha got for me, boss?"

"Remember the chicken coop?"

"Yeah… Clean it again? I just did the other day."

"They've pooped since then. You know what to do," I tell her as I walk away. "And don't forget the door on the backside of the coop this time," I say and can't help but laugh at the memory.

❋ ❋ ❋

The morning sun is heating up and I have a full day of work ahead of me. A half hour passes and I return to the tractor barn, where Kinsley isn't as bright and shiny as she was when I left her. "Looking good," I say, and she raises an eyebrow. "The coop, I mean. *It's* looking good. When you're done you can feed them."

"The chickens?"

"Yeah, then you can dump the compost."

"Freaking chickens." She wipes her forehead, leaving a trace of dirt behind.

I hook up the disc mower and I'm about to climb into the tractor when Kinsley tells me she finished cleaning the coop. "The feed's over here." I motion to the shed right off the barn and lead her inside where a line of bins stand. Pulling out a plastic bucket, I fill it with tiny brown pellets. "And the mealworms."

"Mealworms?" She cringes.

I hand her the bucket of feed and grab a container from the shelf. "They're not alive, don't freak out. Chickens love them. You'll be their new best friend." I scoop a handful to show her.

"Oh, god, they smell awful," she says with a cough.

"Well, there's a lot of that here, you'll get used to it." I walk out of the shed and through the gate where I sprinkle mealworms on the ground. A hoard of chickens rushes me, waddling and pecking the ground like crazy. "Here you go." I give her the bag. "Your turn."

She reaches into the bag and scoops a handful, flinging them almost instantly. "Gross." She shudders, little bits and pieces of the freeze-dried insects sticking to the sweat on her hand. "Are we done?"

"Nope, still gotta feed them." I motion to the bucket she's holding. "Don't forget to dump the compost," I holler over my shoulder as I walk away.

Not long after walking into the barn, I hear screaming and rush back out to find Kinsley running around the chicken yard, arms up in fright as the little black rooster chases her, kicking his spurs up whenever he gets close enough.

"This thing is trying to kill me!" she yells, looking at me wide-eyed.

"He knows you're afraid. You can't let him think you are."

"But I am!" She shouts as she runs past. This could go on for a while. I grab a shovel and the bag of mealworms and enter the yard, making kissy noises to get the bird's attention. Once I sprinkle mealworms on the ground, the rooster loses interest in Kinsley and saunters toward me.

"I got him, go on out," I tell her as the bird inspects the offering, then turns and runs full speed at Kinsley as she hurries to the gate.

"Caleb!" she yells, but I'm already running over, shovel in hand, to ward off the attack.

"I got him." I hold the shovel out between Kinsley and the bird so she can exit the yard. Once she's on the other side, the rooster lowers its hackles and pecks the ground for treats.

"What did you do to piss him off?" I ask, joining her on the other side of the fence.

"Nothing. I was just petting the big white one and he started attacking me."

"Oh. Yeah, he didn't want you messing with his lady bird. He's a little possessive–"

"More like asshole." She crosses her arms with a huff.

"He's just doing his job," I say and try not to laugh. "He doesn't know you. It takes time."

She sends the rooster a dirty look. "I don't like him."

"He's probably thinking the same about you right now. Back to work, compost is waiting. After that, check the list in the barn."

* * *

I maneuver the tractor into the gently rolling farmland, a blanket of green covering the earth. Simple. Peaceful—for about forty-five minutes, until Kinsley comes flying toward me in the green and yellow farm UTV. *What the hell?* "Who said you could drive the Gator?"

"Mr. Cunningham," she hollers over the motors. "Where do you keep the goat feed?"

"I told you. In the feed shed." I toss my arms up, wondering if she simply ignored me earlier or if she's really that absentminded.

"No, you didn't."

"*All* the feed is in the feed shed."

"But which one is for the goats?"

"The blue bin," I say through gritted teeth. She glares at me, giving the Gator a sharp turn and speeding off. "Slow down!" I yell, but she doesn't hear me. I yank off my dirty baseball cap and wipe perspiration from my forehead. In the distance, the Gator bounces over the terrain, growing smaller and smaller. *What the hell was I thinking?*

I manage to finish the field without any additional stops and start to wonder if she got lost or wrecked the Gator—or both. But when I make it back to the main barn, my cotton shirt thick with sweat from the morning sun, I find the Gator in one piece. Kinsley too.

"Heading to the house for lunch," I say, climbing down from the tractor.

"What about me?" she asks, hurrying up behind me.

"You can take a lunch break too. Be back by 1:15."

"Can't I just go with you?"

"Sure," I say, without looking back. "But I'm leaving now. Don't have time to wait around."

* * *

Annie is home, painting her fingernails and reading magazines on the couch. "How was it?" she asks Kinsley when we walk through the door.

"Okay, I guess. Lots of animal poop."

"Yep." She laughs. "You'll get used to the smell."

"I doubt it."

I make a sandwich and sit down to eat at the table. Kinsley follows suit, putting the perishables away when she finishes. "Hey, you're learning," I joke, pointing to the clean countertop.

She smirks and joins me at the table, and for once, food seems to take precedence over talking. But Annie fills in for her, she won't let a captive audience go to waste.

"So… About game night?" Annie says, fluttering her eyes at me. "I'll make sure the house is clean and the dishes are done. You won't have to do any extra work. And Kinsley said she'd make spaghetti." Kinsley shifts her eyes to me, her mouth, though preoccupied with chewing, wears a grin.

"This Friday?" I ask, attempting to stall the inevitable.

Annie nods. "And Kinsley said we could ask Nikki and Chase to come too."

I still don't like the idea of Annie having a boyfriend or dating, but this is preferable. At least they would be here, where I can keep an eye on them. *It could be worse.*

"I guess that'll be alright." I take another bite of my sandwich as Annie squeals and stomps her feet under the table. "But he's outta here by ten, got it?"

Annie jumps up and runs around the table to hug me before bouncing over to hug Kinsley, who has somehow mustered the energy to join the squealing celebration. It sounds like a pig pen at feeding time.

* * *

Back at the farm, I remind Kinsley where to find the items she'll need to complete her tasks, hoping I can get through my work without interruption this time. And I do—for about an hour. Then the Gator shows up again.

"What do I do with the eggs I collected?"

"You seriously rode out here to ask me where to put the eggs?"

"I've never done this before, Caleb. I don't want to mess it up."

"Take them to Ms. Mary. She's in the small barn." I point to the little red structure in the distance with a rusted metal windmill spinning lazily beside it. The faint breeze can't contend with the afternoon heat that's burning through my patience.

"But what about—"

"Just take care of the items on the list, Kinsley. Don't come riding out here every time you have a question. Just figure it out. It ain't that hard."

"Well, *sorry*. I didn't know."

"Now you do," I say, getting back to task.

"Wait—"

"Kinsley, I can't hold your hand through this."

"I didn't ask you to hold my hand, Caleb." She glares at me.

"It's an expression." I drop my head in exhaustion, waiting for her to scamper away, which she does, but not without taking her aggression out on the Gator. "And be careful driving that thing!" *One speed—that's all she knows.*

Quitting time finally arrives. Kinsley hasn't bothered me in a while. A miracle. When I walk into the barn, she's hunched over a folding table with a box fan blowing in her face.

"You finish that list?"

She nods, looking instead like the list finished her. "Alright, you're free to go. I have a couple things to take care of. You can tell Annie I'll be there in a bit."

* * *

The sun is setting when I get to the house, and when I walk through the door, I see Kinsley asleep out on the couch. The dirty flannel she borrowed is balled up on the floor beside her. By the looks of it, she barely made it in the house before passing out. One forearm drapes over her eyes, shielding her from the overhead light. One foot is on the floor, and the other hangs off the side of the couch. *Amateur.*

I carefully remove her muddy work boots, revealing *my* socks on her feet. *No surprise there.* Then I lift her legs, placing them both on the couch and she stirs but doesn't wake. One of Gram's quilts is folded on the top of the sofa, so I pull it down to cover her body. Her hair is a mess and there's still a trace of dirt on her forehead. She's beautiful. I flip the light switch and the room darkens. *What the hell was I thinking?*

TWENTY-EIGHT

Kinsley: July 23, 2008

The first couple of days working on the farm are rough. The July sun threatens to melt my skin right off as my body cries buckets of sweat. By the time I make it back to the house at the end of the day, I hardly have the energy to shower or eat. And in the mornings, muscles even my long-lost personal trainer never challenged raise their protest. It's not getting any easier, but now I know what to expect and how to better prepare: Sleep. Water. Sleep.

I sit down with a plate of leftovers. Annie is out, and Caleb had to stay back on the farm to meet with Mr. Cunningham. The house is quiet and cool, and it's no small struggle to keep my butt glued to the wooden chair when the bed is just within reach—literally *feet* away. I peel my eyes open and look at my phone. The message inbox is full—a consequence of being too exhausted to function. Landon has texted me twelve times since Sunday, and while the messages start with a pleasant tone, his hostility increases. I nearly choke on my lunch when reading his most recent text. *Daddy can't save you from prison.*

I know I'm running out of time and I'll have to confront my dad soon, but I wish I could talk to Ben. There has to be a way to make things work with Landon that doesn't require marriage. I just can't think of anything, and the last thing I want is to confront my dad without a plan. I type out a message to Nikki. *Hey Lucy, it's Ethel. Come by the farm this afternoon?*

Back at the farm, I work my way through Caleb's list. I label the goat milk soap and tie price tags on the cans of jelly with ribbon—new tasks added in preparation for the farmer's market. I tuck the crates neatly on the shelf and look over my shoulder to check the sun-yellowed clock on the wall, and when I do, I see Nikki. "Hey!" I spin around to greet her.

"I got your text, Lucy. What's up? We stompin' grapes?"

"I wish. Come on." I climb into the dusty green Gator. It looks like an adult-sized Power Wheels jeep.

"Well, look at you. Kinsley Holland, professional farmhand. Can't believe Tractor Boy gave you permission to drive," she says, climbing into the UTV.

"He didn't. Mr. Cunningham did. I might have mentioned that I was best friends with his one-day-daughter-in-law."

"You did not." Nikki's eyes nearly fall out of her head and I laugh. I turn the ignition and drive around the side of the barn, following the dusty earthen path past the vegetable garden and the goat yard. I point out the corn fields in the distance that I helped harvest, and we come upon Caleb in a grazing field bailing hay.

"I learned how to do that yesterday," I tell her.

"Oh, really?" Nikki raises an eyebrow.

"Don't sound so surprised. I'm not completely incapable... Okay, I had some help."

Nikki laughs. "I don't think you're incapable, it's just a different side of you. Getting your hands dirty out here doing real work. It's kinda bizarre."

"I know, right? I mean I don't know if I could do this every day of my life, but it's not as terrible as I expected."

"I'm speechless."

"That's a first."

I pull over to the hay shed and turn off the engine. "Follow me." I climb the stacked bales like a kid on a playground and plop down when I reach the top. Nikki joins me, pushing her sunglasses on top of her head.

"We're not stomping grapes, so what are we doing?"

"It's about my dad. I know why he wanted me to take over for Phillips, why he got so angry with me." I pause, taking in the sweet country air. "Look, you can't tell anyone–not even your mom."

"I swear–"

"Not even *hypothetically,* Nik," I add with air quotes.

"I promise."

I tell her the important parts—Ouranos Group, Ben finding out, my dad's disagreement with Phillips, and the tax withholding. Nikki's naturally optimistic expression washes away. "Kins..."

"I know. It's bad. But Landon offered a merger with one of his dad's companies. He just doesn't want to do it if we're not married–"

"Are you kidding me?" Nikki throws her hands up and smacks them down on her thighs. "You cannot seriously be thinking–"

"No, no–I'm not. But that's what I need your help with. There has to be another way to convince him."

"Kins, it's Landon we're talking about. He's... Well, you know how he is. Have you ever been able to change his mind? Like *really*?"

I close my eyes. It's hopeless. "I'll think on it," Nikki finally says. "But I don't know how much help I'll be. Can you call Ben?"

"I tried Sunday night, but I couldn't get through. I'll keep trying..." I have an idea of what his advice will be: *Walk away. Let Dad get what he deserves.* But where would that leave me? Alone. The last piece of family I have, the piece I've tried so hard to secure, destroyed by my own hand. "What if he goes to prison, Nik? He's the only family I have."

"That's not true. You still have Ben. And you have me." Nikki drapes her arm around my shoulders. "*If* that happens, you'll move in with me–" I stop her with a look and we both laugh, knowing exactly how that would turn out. "Alright, I'll get a bigger camper, *then* you'll move in with me. You'll sell your art, I'll write, and we'll grow old and get into all kinds of good trouble like Lucy and Ethel." I wipe a rogue tear from my sun-warmed cheeks, filling my lungs with a shaky breath.

"But you really should talk to your dad, Kins."

"I know. I am–tomorrow," I say as I twist a piece of hay between my thumb and index finger. "Oh, one more thing.... Are you doing anything Friday night?"

"Umm, no. Why? Need me to babysit for a date night?" She winks and gives me a teasing nudge.

"Sort of..." I rub my lips together, playing along. "I'm pretty excited about it actually."

"Ooh la la." Nikki fans herself.

"It really all started at the carnival..."

"I knew it!"

"We just can't resist it anymore. Caleb put up a good fight, but..." I bounce my knees in excitement, gripping my hands together, and drop the bomb. "Annie's having Eric over for a game night."

Nikki's excitement fizzles. "You..."

"Sorry, Nik. I couldn't help myself." I nudge her side as a wry smile touches her face.

"Uh-huh... I see how it is."

"Anyway..." I take a deep breath to clear the laughter. "I thought maybe you and Chase could come, help break up the tension. It's the closest we could get to a date with Caleb's approval." I roll my eyes at the last part. *He's so unreasonable.*

"Chase has a show, but I'll be there. Just tell me when."

"Thanks, Nik. Caleb is just so freaking..."

"Hot?" Nikki asks as she nods her head toward the clearing outside the shed's open side.

"Seriously, Nik? We're doing this..." But I lose my train of thought when I see what Nikki's looking at. Caleb has pulled the tractor over to the side of the shed, it must be acting up again because he has taken off his tee shirt and is using it to twist open a cap on the side of the machine. His bare muscles flex as he works, glistening in the sunlight. *Fuck.*

"Damn, you're telling me you're sleeping next to that every night and nothing is going on?" My words and breath catch in my throat, and a hunger I've neglected for too long unfurls. Nikki shakes her head, clicking her tongue. "If I was single and he wasn't your *husband*..."

"Oh, please," I say with a nervous chuckle. But I let my eyes rest on Caleb, his slightly tanned back—solid and strong, his hips snug in his work jeans, stained with a day's worth of dirt already. He rummages for something in the tractor's cab, then pulls out his flannel. Putting it on, he hooks a few buttons and walks to the other side of the building and out of view. The shade of the hay barn has suddenly lost its cooling effect. "We should probably get back," I tell Nikki. "I still have to check the chickens' food and water and collect the eggs before it gets too late."

"Mmm, mmm, mmm." Nikki flutters her eyelashes at me.

"Oh, stop it." I laugh as summer heat flashes across my face.

* * *

I chug my water bottle as the air conditioning tries to combat the heat. Even with parking in the shade of the cottonwood tree, the car's leather seats sting the back of my shoulders. Draining the bottle empty, I toss it on the passenger's side floorboard. The heat index puts us at 113°F, so Caleb let me and the other farmhands leave early. Since it's as hot as Satan's asshole, I figure it's the perfect day to endure hell and confront my dad about his lies. I adjust my messy ponytail and wipe the sweat from my neck before backing out.

The AC roars to life as I pick up speed, water towers and grain mills dotting the distance between the farm and CHI. A pebble of hope escapes reason and whispers *maybe what Landon said isn't true.* Either way, I'm confronting my dad and giving him a chance to explain—a chance to make things right.

❋ ❋ ❋

"Were you ever going to tell me about Ben?" I storm into the office, startling my dad. "Or is that another piece of the story you don't think I can handle?"

"Kinsley, what are you— Did anyone see you like this?" He hurries to shut the door behind me, to shield any passerby from my unkempt appearance that isn't in line with the company image.

"You made Ben leave." I cross my arms as he approaches.

"No. He chose to leave us."

"He wanted you to come clean, Dad. He would have stayed if you did."

He stops midstep, straightens his back and asks, "What do you think would have happened to me if I did? And you—who would have taken care of you? You'd have ended up in foster care, Kinsley."

"Maybe. Or maybe Nikki's parents would have taken me in. Plus Ben would have been here. He could have taken care of me."

"Don't be foolish, Kinsley. Ben couldn't have cared for you–"

"That's not the point. I don't understand why you did it. You already had money."

The look on his face almost knocks me to the ground. Vulnerability? Fear? Remorse? I've never seen it on him—like a kid showing up for a test he forgot to study for. He walks around the desk, putting it between us, and sits down.

"It was only supposed to be temporary," he says. "Until I could settle things and pay it back. Then we lost a few contract bids and hit some hard times, but we were managing." He rubs his forehead, his wedding ring glares back at me, shooting arrows at my heart. "Your brother had no reason to freak out. Everything was under control."

"Obviously not because you're using the tax withholdings now."

"Lower your voice," he says, eyes shifting to the office door.

"You could go to prison, Dad. You could lose everything."

"You think I don't know that, Kinsley? Why do you think I was so upset when you wouldn't cooperate?" His face reddens.

"That's not fair. I didn't know anything about it–"

"Well now I've told you."

"No, you didn't tell me. I had to find out from Landon and confront you. If you had been honest from the beginning I would have given you my trust fund to help. I had no idea–"

"That's why you should have trusted me and done what I asked instead of making a mess with your own choices."

"Do you hear yourself? You can't pin this all on me."

"But if you had just–"

"Continued to be a submissive little pawn in your game?" Adrenaline and courage mix, practically sending my heart through my chest. "No. This time it isn't *my* mess we're cleaning up–it's yours."

I place my farm-dirty palms on his desk. "Look, I don't need a big house or expensive car. Hell, you've already closed my accounts, and I've survived. You have to make this right. Sell your assets, downsize wherever you can. Just pay the money back–"

"How would that look, Kinsley? We'd never come back from that– the company would never come back from that."

"How's it going to look if you go to prison, Dad? You think the company will bounce back from that?" I throw my hands up and begin to pace.

"There are other solutions," he reminds me, his tone too familiar.

"Right. The merger with Devon. But Landon's holding out on you."

"No, Kinsley. I believe you're holding out on Landon."

"Really, Dad?" I stop and face him, hands on my hips. "There has to be some other way to convince Landon to do it. Can't you offer him a stake in the company? Something? Anything other than *me* you could give him to make it happen?"

"Kinsley, this is important for both of our families–for CHI and Devon's companies too."

"My god, this isn't the Tudor Dynasty you're trying to save, Dad." I throw my arms up again in exasperation. We're getting nowhere. "I'm leaving. Call me when you come to your senses."

TWENTY-NINE

Kinsley: July 25, 2008

I wrap up my last day of work on the farm and hurry back to the house to take a quick shower. With hard-earned money stuffed into my Prada wallet, I run to the grocery store and return with everything I need to make dinner. Nikki is here early. She doesn't want to miss a minute of "Kinsley in the Kitchen."

"It's got a nice ring to it. You should think about a vlog," Nikki says.

"I can make one dish, Nik. You're a little ahead of yourself–"

"Fails bring in a ton of views. Either way, you'd get hits."

"I'll keep that in mind." I say and shoo her out of the kitchen so I can work.

In less than an hour, spaghetti is served. No one dies, and the house is still standing. After dinner, I prepare to wash the dishes, but Caleb tells me not to worry about it.

"Really?" I ask, wondering if I accidentally used magic mushrooms in the sauce.

"Yeah, they'll be here after Eric leaves. It's fine." Hallucinogenic or not, I don't need persuading and drop the rag on the counter before walking away.

The night starts off innocently enough with a game of Trivial Pursuit, but it's abandoned when Caleb collects his fourth token while the rest of us struggle to claim one. We play a few rounds of Pictionary, boys versus girls, but it's a shutout with the girls winning each time. When Annie complains of boredom from the easy wins and suggests Twister, Caleb says he doesn't think it's a good idea.

"Why not? It's a game and this is *game* night." Annie challenges him.

"There's not enough room, and who would do the spinner?"

"I can," Nikki pipes in, earning herself a look of annoyance that I thought Caleb only sent my way.

"There's still not enough room," he argues.

"Yes there is. We just have to move stuff around." Annie walks over to the couch and coffee table. Pushing and pulling furniture out of the way, she reveals a large open square of carpet.

With that, Caleb's argument dies, Annie lays the game mat in place, and Nikki sits cross-legged on the couch with the spin board in her lap. "Ready?"

Everyone confirms but Caleb. The plastic spinner whirls, and a moment later, Nikki begins calling out our moves. We shuffle and slide our hands and feet to the correct dots as the game progresses, with Nikki teasing and cheering us on. When I peek under my arm, looking behind me, I see Annie and Eric sharing a blue dot with their hands, fingers mingling. Turning a blind eye to their rule breaking, I look back to Nikki. "Spin, spin! Please," I beg, my arm muscles trembling from a week of manual labor.

"Muhahaha." Nikki fakes a menacing laugh before spinning the board and calling the move. Just one round later, we're so tangled up that I can feel Caleb's breath on my back. By this point, I can't even look around to see what kind of figuration Annie and Eric have worked themselves into. I can look straight ahead toward Nikki or down to my right where Caleb's hand sustains his weight. His hand is *strong*. And large. How did I not notice this before? His tendons flex as he shifts his weight and my eyes follow the subtle movements under his skin as his forearm supports his body. And now I'm staring at his muscles again. *Stop it, woman!*

"Kinsley," Nikki hollers. "Hello? Left foot on red. Keep up." Blood rushes to my head, and when I attempt to swing my leg around to the dot, I collapse, taking Caleb down, then Annie and Eric like dominoes. Pained laughter fills the room, and when I roll over, I'm inches away from Caleb's face.

"Oh, umm, sorry." I push myself up on my elbows and scramble to my feet.

Annie and Eric go for snacks in the kitchen, and Caleb lurks behind them while Nikki and I pack up the game. "Anyone up for Truth or Dare," Nikki asks, wiggling her eyebrows. *Oh, boy. This won't go over well.*

And right on cue, Caleb objects. "I don't think so. How about something like UNO or Mousetrap?"

"Mousetrap?" Annie and I repeat in unison.

"What? It's a fun game," he says. Caleb's eyes follow Annie as she takes Eric by the hand and leads him back to the open carpet by the couch.

"Come on, Caleb. It's not like she suggested spin the bottle," I whisper. We've outnumbered him again, and I almost feel bad for the guy, but then again, he really is overreacting. Twister turned out just fine—no one left the game pregnant, and Truth or Dare will be just as chaste.

I join Nikki on the couch, and Caleb follows, taking a seat beside me. "Okay… Who's my first victim?" Nikki asks, strumming her fingers like an evil mastermind. "Oh, my BFF of course," she says. "Kinsley, truth or dare?"

"Truth."

"Oh, you're such a scaredy cat… Fine." She pauses to think. "Okay, what do you love most about your husband?" *Really, Nikki?*

"Don't you think that's a little personal?"

Nikki shrugs. "That's the point of the game."

I take a deep breath and look over at Caleb—he's less than amused. "I love how much he cares about his family. About Annie."

"Well isn't that the sweetest thing," Nikki says with a teasing grin. "What about you Caleb, what do you love most about your wife?"

"Okay, my turn," I cut in. "Annie, truth or dare?" She's wide-eyed, mouth twisting in contemplation and finally picks truth. "What do you find most attractive about your current crush?"

She smiles, looking down at the carpet. "His eyes."

"Same, girl," Nikki offers with a wink. "Your turn to pick a victim." I expect Annie to pick Eric, but she asks Caleb instead.

"Truth," he answers without emotion as if to remind us of his objection to the game.

"Tell me about your first date with Kinsley."

Annie's ask is innocent, genuine, and my heart cracks at the oncoming lie. Caleb seems to be thinking, his eyes are focused on the armrest of the couch where he rolls a snagged upholstery thread between his fingertips.

"It was at the hospital–" I start, trying to cover with at least a half-truth.

"No," Caleb says. "It was back in middle school."

Huh? My face hides nothing, and I know it.

"Yeah, remember Kins?"

He never calls me that.

"We were at the skating rink for a Valentine's party, and you were wearing bright pink roller skates."

Lucky guess on the pink skates.

"Nikki was crushing hard on Andy Parker and was glued to him the entire time," he continues. "Kinsley was sitting by herself, looking kind of lonely, so I rolled up to her and asked what was wrong. She said she didn't have anyone to skate with, and I told her I'd skate with her."

Did this really happen?

"We got out on the rink and started skating. She seemed to cheer up a bit, but we were only on our second lap around when they announced couples only skate. I could see she was disappointed, and I just wanted her to smile again." Caleb turns and looks at me. "So I grabbed her hand and we kept skating."

It's coming back to me now. I remember *someone* skating with me that day, but I only remember it being one of the older boys—a seventh or eighth grader. I forgot it was Caleb. How can he recall it with such clarity?

"That's the sweetest thing I've ever heard Caleb. Why haven't you told me that story before?" Annie asks.

He shrugs and looks down. "It just never came up." A quiet mix of recovered memories and present expectations fills the room.

"Your turn to ask," Nikki reminds Caleb, breaking the silence.

He clears his throat. "Fine. Nikki, truth or dare?"

"Dare. Y'all are turning this into a game of Truth or Truth. Gotta shake it up."

Caleb thinks for a minute. "I dare you to wash the dishes."

"No, Caleb, that'll take forever," Annie whines.

"Fine, clean the toilet."

"Challenge accepted, Tractor Boy." Nikki scoots off to the bathroom.

"That's so lame, dude." Annie shoots Caleb a look of disgust. "Haven't you ever played the game? You should have dared her to chug milk or drink hot sauce."

"And waste groceries?" he asks.

"Hot sauce wouldn't work. She likes spicy stuff…" I trail, my head still cloudy with middle school memories.

Within minutes, Nikki returns, plopping down on the couch. "Done. My turn now. Kins, truth or dare?"

"Me again? Nik, you asked me last time–"

"Right, and you picked truth, so by *our* rules, you have to pick…"

"Dare." I roll my eyes. *Nikki and her rules.*

"I dare you to kiss your husband," Nikki says, but her eyes challenge Caleb—not me.

"What?" Blush whispers across my chest.

"What's the big deal," Annie asks. "You guys are married. You kiss all the time."

"Oh, really?" Nikki turns her gaze to me as heat creeps northward to my cheeks.

"You know what," Annie says. "Now that I think about it, I've never actually seen them kiss."

"Wow." Nikki shakes her head slowly as if she's disappointed. I shoot her a look of daggers, but Nikki just shrugs. "Go on." She waves her hand. "Kiss your man."

He's beside me, elbows on his knees, looking down at his hands. "Caleb," I whisper. Hunched forward like he'll bolt if I move too suddenly, he looks at me over his shoulder. I lean in closer, inches from his face, breathing in the fresh soapy mix of his shampoo and deodorant. I wipe my palms on my knees. It has to look natural and easy or Annie will have questions.

With eyes closed, I gently place my lips on his. They're soft and warm and taste like cinnamon gum. *When did he do that?* I don't expect anything in return, but he doesn't pull away. He gives back to me, and a warm tingling sensation blooms, sending a blush all over my body.

Nikki clears her throat and I open my eyes, pulling away from Caleb as I attempt to regulate my pulse and breath. "Your turn," Nikki reminds me.

"And don't forget Eric," Annie adds. "He hasn't had a turn yet."

My head is fog, and I glance at Annie. "Umm, okay. Eric, truth or dare?"

"Truth." He grins, turning to Annie.

"Is Annie your girlfriend?" A low grumble comes from Caleb and Annie looks like she might be sick. *Oh, shit. What if he says no?*

"Um… Yeah." Eric squeezes Annie's hand and looks at her. "I mean, I hope she is." Annie makes a full and instant recovery with pink cheeks to boot. I don't turn to check on Caleb's status. I can't look him in the eye yet.

"This seems like a good place to end the game," he says, standing up from the couch. "There's a chance for rain, and Eric's on his bike, so…"

He's trying, I'll give him that, but his weather report won't cut through the romantic charge buzzing in the room. This is a big deal for Annie–to have confirmation, *finally,* that they're a couple. I've never seen her this happy.

"We have dishes to do." I motion for him to follow me to the kitchen, which he does with a wary eye. A moment later, Nikki joins us, holding out her cell phone.

"Caleb, phone for you–it's Chase."

"Wha–" he asks as Nikki shoves the phone in his hand and nudges him toward the hall.

I plug one side of the double sink and let the hot water run. The buzz of young love has followed me into the kitchen, and I can still feel Caleb's kiss on my lips. It was nothing like the quick peck we shared at the wedding chapel.

"That was intense." Nikki stands beside me at the sink, handing me a dish.

"I know. I can't believe I forgot it was him at the skating rink."

"Wait, so that actually happened?"

"Mm-hmm." I smile, reliving it *all* again.

"That explains *a lot*." Nikki turns around and leans against the counter so she's facing me. "Like why that kiss was so hot."

"Please, it was just a dare," I tell her, hoping my own words aren't true. The hot water steams from the sink, warming my chest and face.

"That was *not* just a dare, that was– I'll take the trash out." Nikki hurries away.

What the... I look over my shoulder to see Nikki disappear while Caleb walks toward me. He steps up to the sink and grabs a dish, sliding his hands—his big, strong, fucking hot hands—into the soapy water. He scrubs, I rinse, and we complete the task without speaking.

"Thanks," I say quietly, like my voice has forgotten how to do its job.

Nikki pops her head around the corner. "Hey, Kins. I'm gonna head out. Thanks for dinner." I scoot past Caleb and hug Nikki goodbye. A moment later, the screen door squeaks and is followed by muffled voices and quiet giggles. Caleb looks in the direction of the noise and follows it to the living room, where Annie and Eric are cozied up on the couch, holding hands and talking close.

He clears his throat. "It's getting late, Annie. I think you two should say goodnight." Annie looks part irritated, part bummed, but proceeds to walk Eric to the door. It's obvious Caleb has no intention of giving them privacy, so I brush his hand with mine, giving it a little tug as I step behind the wall that divides the kitchen and living room. He follows but stands close to the wall's end and tries to peek around the corner. I grab a handful of his tee shirt and pull him back. When he looks down at me, I expect to find irritation in his eyes as I so often do when I intervene, but instead, his eyes are soft and seem to be searching mine for something. All I can think of is that kiss.

The front door shuts, and Caleb takes a step back as Annie bounces into the kitchen with the goofiest grin. "Thanks, Kinsley. It was perfect." She throws her arms around me, hugging me tight before scurrying off to her bedroom. A moment later, the motorcycle engine revs to life and sputters into the night. Even in the absence of young love, the quiet house hums with nervous energy.

"I'm going to lock up," Caleb says and walks into the living room. I don't want to move—to disturb whatever might have been forming between us. The house grows darker with each lamp and light switch he turns off. Will it be lost in the dark? Whatever *it* is?

Caleb returns to the kitchen and flips the switch beside me. As my eyes adjust to the near blackout, I feel his hand on my back, guiding me past the table and to the bedroom door. Nothing ever happens on that side of the door but sleep. I stop, unwilling to turn the knob, wishing he would whisper in my ear, put his arms around me, say my name—anything—to let me know he feels the same way.

He reaches past me and opens the door. It's dark except for the lamplight casting a warm haze that doesn't reach the corners of the room. I take two heavy steps inside, each one like heartbreak. When Caleb closes the door, I turn to face him, silently begging him to see in my eyes what I want from him. What I *need* from him. He leans back against the door, closing his eyes and taking a deep breath.

"Caleb," I whisper and step closer. When he opens his eyes, it's a reflection of everything I feel. He leans forward and brushes a strand of hair away from my face. His thumb follows my cheekbone down to my lips, tracing their curves—his touch tugs at something deep inside. I part my lips, just enough to draw in the air between us, and he's kissing me, picking up where the last kiss left off as he explores my mouth with his own. He wraps his arms around me, pulling me closer.

I break the kiss only to lift my tank top over my head, exposing a peachy pink lace bra. I reach for the hem of his cotton tee shirt, tugging it upward as I moan into his perfect lips. He pulls away, lifting his shirt over his head while I plant a trail of kisses on his chest. I look up at him and his breath catches as I wiggle out of my jean shorts. Standing before him in those peachy pink panties he was so mad about, he rests his forehead on mine and whispers, "You're killin' me, Kinsley." I find his lips again, wrapping my arms around his neck as he runs his hands up and down my back and over the lacy fabric. A moment later, he picks me up, startling a small laugh from me as I wrap my legs around him, and he carries me to the bed.

THIRTY

Caleb: July 25, 2008

Her long, tan legs wrap around my body as I lift her into my arms and carry her to the bed. I nuzzle her neck and inhale the intoxicating scent that's been driving me insane for weeks. When I lay her down on the bed, I pause to appreciate just how fucking beautiful she is. She draws her brows and props herself up on her elbows.

"What's wrong?"

"Not a thing," I say and lower myself onto the bed, kissing her lips, her neck, her shoulder. I want all of her, and her body tells me she wants that too. I reach behind her, to unhook her bra and when I do, she flings it away. The bikini left little to the imagination, and my mind has been working overtime since that day, but here—in my bed, under my hands, against my lips—my imagination did not prepare me for this.

I sprinkle my kisses over her body, from her collarbone to her ribcage. She's arching her back beneath me, raising her hips in response, but I skip over those sexy little panties. I've spent too many hours thinking about how they would look on her curvy little hips, and my reveries don't compare to what I'm seeing now. I sit back on my knees, bringing her left ankle to my lips, and kiss my way up to her knee, her thigh, and finally stop at the promised land. She's begging me with her movements, her voice, and her scent. I can't play this game of wonderful torture any longer.

I kick off my jeans and boxers, my eyes don't leave hers once. She's so damn beautiful, so sexy. How is this even possible? She pulls her eyes from mine, and I watch as they make a trail downward—I can *feel* her gaze. She smiles at me, and I'm above her again, kissing her, tasting her sighs and moans. She reaches down between us to pull off her panties and I stop her, pulling her hand to my mouth and kissing it before I crawl down to do the job myself. I rest my cheek on her stomach and lace scratches my chin. I plant a kiss by her hip bone, then just under top of her panties. She's grabbing my hair and wiggling beneath me. And she smells So. Fucking. Good. *Damn it, Kinsley.*

With one hand on each side of her hips, I slide the panties down her legs and dive back in. I need to be inside her, but I want to taste her too. I slide my tongue between the soft folds of skin as she tugs on my hair and moans my name. *Fuck it.* I return to her lips, kissing her hard, and take a condom from the nightstand. I look down at her one more time before I tear the package. It would be pure hell to turn back now, but I need to know she's certain. As if she can read my mind, she takes the wrapper from my hand and opens it herself, then reaches down to put it on me. And I'm burying myself inside her, she clings to me, squeezing her legs around my waist, kissing my neck and breathing little whimpers in my ear that are literally killing me dead. It's been so long since I've been with a woman, and *this?* God, this is ending me. I want to keep going for her, to keep hearing her sighs of pleasure, but it's too much. I come, and by the sounds of it, so does she. *Thank god.*

When I roll off her, I pull her to my side and kiss her again, this time soft and tender. She grazes her fingers across my chest and breathes a contented sight.

* * *

Waking with Kinsley in my arms feels natural. I don't know if it's just the familiarity of sleeping beside her every night or something more. I slip out of bed, careful not to disturb her. I hate to leave, but I have a list of projects to tackle and I need coffee. As the percolating brew and morning songbirds mingle with the quiet, I close my eyes, revisiting last night—the sweetness of her kiss, the way she looked at me with a need I haven't seen before, how her body fit mine like a puzzle piece, and the passion we found together in the dark. When Jessica left, I locked a part of myself away, and last night, it broke free, took the wheel, and sped straight toward the flames.

But as I stand at the sink, peering out the window and sipping my coffee, I can't ignore the truth of our situation. This was never real—never meant to last. Sure, maybe I had a soft spot for her when we were kids, but she was Ben's little sister and lived in a world beyond my reach. Then, when she started dating Landon, it was the train wreck that would never end. I heard of countless breakups only to see them back together as if nothing had happened. How Kinsley could forgive Landon or turn a blind eye to his cheating I could never understand. Now, here I am tangled up in one of their breakups. It's only a matter of time before she runs back to him, and this time, it's not just me, but Annie that will bear the fallout.

For weeks, I've spent every waking moment resisting my own nature, protecting my heart, calling painful memories to the forefront of my mind. *She'll leave you and break your heart. She'll run back to Landon like she always does. Think about Annie.* The little white postal truck stops at my mailbox, and a phantom fist slams into my gut. *The marriage certificate.* Its arrival will mark the beginning of the end. Nerve-sick, I check the rusty old box by the curb and return to the kitchen with only Valpak coupons and a utility bill.

I busy myself with every little project I've put off for lack of time. It's a helpful distraction but not enough to silence the regret. I should have lied when Annie asked about our first date. I should have made something up instead of sharing the long-held memory. The truth is out there now, released from Pandora's box, and nothing can put it back in. Then, the kiss. What was I thinking? I saw it coming like a twister, and I just stood there, letting it take me. And later, after Eric left and Annie went to bed, I was frozen as sensibility and desire battled for control. She pulled me in, holding on so tight—needing me. I couldn't pull myself away from her, and in the dark of night, I silenced the fears and better judgment racing through my mind.

I've been kicking my own ass all morning for allowing things to go too far last night. Nothing good ever comes from stupid party games. When Annie bounces past me on her way out the door to Brittany's, I know I have to talk to Kinsley.

THIRTY-ONE

Kinsley: July 26, 2008

I wake to an empty room and empty bed, but it's not alarming. Caleb is always up and at 'em early, even on weekends. I let the memories of last night wash over me. I didn't know sex could be like that. Sure, there were good times with Landon, but there was always a hint of distrust lurking in the back of my mind that made it hard to give myself completely —to embrace him completely. But last night was different—I felt safe. I trusted Caleb. How is it possible to trust a man I hardly know more than the man I've dated for almost a decade?

I roll over and breathe in the scent of his pillow, closing my eyes and embracing this new feeling. When the door opens, I turn to see Caleb walking into the room. My body reacts, ready for an encore of last night.

"Oh, you're up," he says. "I was hoping I could talk to you while Annie's out." I sit up and try to push down the apprehension stirring behind my navel. I don't know if it's the tone of his voice or simply the daylight shining on this new territory we've crossed into, but I'm terrified of what he'll say next.

"It's, well…" He sits down on the edge of the bed, eyes forward to the wall. "It's about last night." *Fuck. This isn't good.* Waiting for him to speak, I forget how to breathe.

"I just don't want to complicate things," he says, and I die. Under the weight of those seven words, a crack forms in my chest, threatening to release the flood waters, but I choke them back.

"Annie's going to be devastated when this is over." He leans forward over his knees, hands clasped in front of him and eyes on the old beaten rug. The fibers of my heart rip one by one each second that he doesn't speak. "Don't want to make it any harder," he says.

"Mm-hmm." I have no words, only heartbreak, and the silence that follows is suffocating.

"So...um." He looks over his shoulder at me, a near echo of the way he did before our kiss. "Sorry for letting myself get carried away." He clears his throat, his eyes darting away before one last glance. "We good?"

I nod because that's all I can do. If I try to speak, I'll lose it. If I try to breathe, I'll lose it. If I look him in the eyes, I'll lose it.

Just leave, I beg him silently. And when he does, a shaky breath fills my lungs but does nothing to ease the hurt. For the next hour, I hide under my blanket, listening for the sound of the front door closing to know it's safe to come out. It was stupid to think this could be something real. When did I start believing the lie?

The front door shuts, releasing me from my self-imposed prison. My stomach is busy flipping and twisting with humiliation and hurt, so food isn't an option, but caffeine is. As I sit in silence, sipping my coffee, I attempt distraction with an issue of *Vogue*. The Valentino skirts and Gucci bags try their best, but they lose the fight when Caleb comes back inside carrying his tools. "Fixing that leak under the sink." He motions as he walks by.

Every Saturday since I moved in, he has gone off to the farm or fishing, but of course, *this* Saturday he's a homebody. I take my sketchbook and move to the front porch steps, which brings privacy but not reprieve. And within thirty minutes, privacy is ripped from me too.

Caleb is mowing the grass. The roar of the motor is a welcome buffer to my thoughts, but it's not loud enough to drown my pain. With every pass he makes through the yard that damn white tee shirt dampens in the summer heat and collects speckles of green like confetti. The game of hide and seek is getting old, and I'm running out of places to hide. Nikki should be home, and what is a best friend for if not to distract you from the heartache of developing feelings for your husband?

On the drive, I try to drown my thoughts with music, but every damn song makes me think of him. His stupid smile, his perfect kiss, his annoying smirk, and the way he worshiped my body just hours ago. Worse than the beautiful memories, there exists under the shattering pain a small ember of hope burning for another chance.

* * *

"So, tell me all about it." Nikki claps her hands together and joins me on the sofa.

"What do you mean?" I shrug. "You were there."

"No, after I left. When you went to bed." She wiggles her eyebrows.

"Nothing happened," I lie as the crack in my heart develops a new branch like pond ice in the sun.

"Oh, please. There was so much heat–"

"I'm serious, nothing happened."

"Oh." The silence is heavy, and I avoid Nikki's eyes. "But you *wanted* something to happen, didn't you?" I don't respond but feel the summer heat returning to my face. "Oh, my god." Nikki squeals.

"You're such a child."

"Kinsley and Caleb sitting in a tree–"

"No– No tree."

"But you–"

"It doesn't matter what I want." I fight the wave of emotion advancing in my chest. "He's not interested."

"That's a lie." Nikki laughs, running her hand through her hair.

"He said he doesn't want to complicate things."

"What's complicated about it? You're married."

"Come on, Nik, you know it's not real."

"Okay, but if nothing happened, how could it complicate things?" Nikki's eyes light up.

"I don't want to talk about it, Nik," I whisper.

She must finally get it because she places her hand on mine and apologizes. "Sorry, I thought you came here to dish."

"I came here to be distracted." *Why isn't there a pill to induce memory loss?*

"Noted." Nikki reaches for her laptop on the built-in shelf to her left. "Want to read my draft? I just have a few little things to finish up." Reliving the night Gabe died isn't exactly what I had in mind when I asked for a distraction, but it's important to Nikki, so I read the draft, and while it interrupts my thoughts of Caleb, it releases fragments of a memory I buried long ago.

Gabe White was friends with Ben and Landon, and his death made tidal waves in our little community. Eight years have passed and unanswered questions still haunt the town. The last time I saw Gabe, before everything happened, was at Lainey Evan's lake house. It was the summer after freshman year, and Landon was home from college. The party, a reunion of sorts, drew recent graduates and current students. There are missing pieces from my memory of that night, and the ones that remain torment me. For so long, instinct pushed me to search for answers—to make sense of everything, but I could never form a complete picture. The frustration of lost memories is maddening, so I've tried to forget it altogether.

Nikki's draft is good—too good. Ready for a change of scenery, hoping to shove the demons from my past back into the closet of my mind, I petition for an impromptu road trip—anywhere but here. Nikki, ever the responsible one, can't drop everything and run away with me, but she counters with an afternoon at Redbud Spa. Negotiations reach an agreement only after I up the ante to include a girls' night at the rodeo club in Tulsa we used to frequent.

* * *

By late afternoon, I've slipped into a plush Turkish cotton robe, and I recline in a massage chair while the Redbud Spa estheticians perform miracles on my cuticles and recently acquired farm calluses. Nikki spares no expense when it comes to cheering me up, adding nearly every treatment and upgrade to the bill.

A low, rumbling thunder overtakes the pan flute melody as I nibble on a cranberry orange muffin and sip jasmine tea. Outside the window, a gray mask chokes the afternoon sun. When the massage therapists call our names, we follow them to our respective rooms. I disrobe and lay on the table, face in the cushioned opening with a cool sheet covering my backside.

The rain is coming in, just like the weather predicted. Just like Caleb talked about when he explained the need to bale the hay before the weekend —too much moisture in the bale can lead to a fire. Why does every word he has ever spoken cling to the shadows of my mind? I'm supposed to be relaxing, not thinking about him and all the stupid things he has told me and all the wonderful ways he has made me feel. The massage helps some, but it doesn't erase the hurt or embarrassment that stains my heart.

Leaving the spa, Nikki asks if I want to stop by the house and pick up an outfit or shoes for tonight. "I'll just borrow something of yours," I tell her. "Can't have a run-in with Caleb undoing all the therapy you just paid for."

"Guess that means you'd rather not ride with me to the farm, huh? I was going to stop by and see Chase for a minute."

"Why don't you drop me off at your place first. I'll order the pizza, and by the time you get back from seeing Chase, it'll be there. Besides, that gives me time to raid your closet."

* * *

Back at the camper, I call in the pizza order and help myself to Nikki's clothes. And when my phone rings, that stupid little seed of hope springs to life. *Caleb?* But no—it's Landon. I decline the call and power off my phone as if that will shield me from future disappointment.

I need a distraction, something to draw me away from myself so rejection can't rip my heart to shreds with its razor-sharp claws. Nikki's mini fridge offers no poison or cure, so I take the little orange bottle from my purse, twist the lid, and pop a pill.

After pizza and primping, we embark on the half-hour drive to the club. The eerie dusk of a rain-soaked sunset creates a sepia world where the neon lights seem to glow brighter than usual.

"We're not doing seven shots of tequila tonight, got it?" Nikki says as she parks the car.

"I know," I tell her. "Two max, promise."

The club is dark and loud with blinding flashes of light and a deep thumping base that sends vibrations through my chest. I'm ready to lose myself in the music, in the dark sea of people, where I can be no one to nobody. Where I can disappear and maybe the pain won't find me.

THIRTY-TWO

Caleb: July 26, 2008

My phone rings and it's Nikki. I saved her number to my phone a while back when Chase had car trouble and they called for help. "Where's he broken down this time?" I ask.

"Caleb, you need to come get Kinsley."

"Wha–"

"She's out of control, and I don't want her to do something she'll regret."

I tense with concern but cloak it in lies. "Not my problem," I say and hate myself for it.

"Yes, it is," Nikki says, and I hear music thumping in the background. She's at a club. *Damn it, Kinsley.*

"I told you not to involve me next time she got shitfaced."

"She's not though. She only had one drink."

"Sure," I say, and apparently Nikki hears my eye roll through the phone.

"I'm serious Caleb, she's upset… It's *you*." The brokenness on her face this morning nearly killed me. And I hate that I'm the one who put it there.

"Hello? Caleb? It's either you or Landon. If you don't come help me, I'll have to call–"

"No. Where are you?"

* * *

The club is dark, but flashing lights sync with the music that threatens to bust my eardrums, and I spot her in the crowd. Little black dress hugging her curves—the ones I held onto and showered with kisses last night. The ones that fit my body so perfectly. *Damn it, Kinsley.* She's dancing without a care in the world while some creep of a rodeo wannabe gropes her like she belongs to him. The jerk holds onto Kinsley's hips, guiding her against him as he nuzzles her neck. Heat spreads across my chest, longing and fury stir up a storm, and I'm ready to tear him off her.

"Kinsley," I shout over the music and push my way through the sea of sweaty, rhythmic bodies. "Kinsley," I try again, now closer. This time her eyes find mine, the flashing lights reveal momentary glimpses of sadness and humiliation.

"Come on, we're getting out of here." I reach for her arm and she snaps it back.

"Easy," Rhinestone Cowboy says, stepping between us as if Kinsley needs protection.

I sidestep him and reach for her arm again. "Kinsley, I'm serious. Let's go."

"Come on man, she don't wanna go with you." Rhinestone places his hand on my shoulder. He's asking me to sock him, and I'm genuinely considering it.

"Yeah, she's partying with us tonight." Rhinestone's near twin comes up behind Kinsley, slipping his arms around her waist. My eyes shift from the creep's hands on her body to Kinsley's face. I could never misinterpret the look she's giving me—not after last night. A vulnerable pleading to pull her out of the darkness, to love her like she deserves. I push past Rhinestone and take Kinsley's hand, this time without her resistance.

"Leave the girl alone," Rhinestone number two says. I'm not here to fight, but if it comes down to it, I'll gladly go a round with the little asswipe.

"She's not a *girl.* She's my wife."

"Whoa, dude, sorry." He backs away, arms up. "She didn't say nothin' about being married."

Kinsley glares at me, and I lead her out to the truck where Nikki catches up with us. "Thanks, Nik. I got it from here," I tell her.

"You called him?" Kinsley hisses, snapping her head to face Nikki as I open the passenger door.

"Thanks, I'll check on her tomorrow," Nikki says, climbing into her car.

It's a long ride home filled with quiet tension. The slightly open windows let a rain-scented breeze blow in, tossing Kinsley's hair and sending traces of her perfume my way. I reach for the radio dial to combat the awkward silence, but Kinsley whips her head to face me. "Why did you do that?" she asks.

"What? Stop you from getting into trouble?"

"I was fine, Caleb. I can handle myself."

"Didn't look that way," I say and turn my eyes back to the road.

"What does it matter to you anyway? I'm not really your wife. What the hell was that about?" I don't answer. I can't—not without confronting the truth of how I feel. "You're an ass, you know that?"

"That's what you tell me." She's quiet for a moment. Am I really getting off that easy?

"You know…" she starts. *There it is.* "You shouldn't worry about Annie hooking up with some asshole who'll break her heart. You should just make your peace with it now because *every* guy is an asshole. It's like a requirement when you grow a dick."

She's fired up and we still have twenty minutes left on the road. I need to diffuse the bomb. "Whoa. C'mon, that's a bit of a generalization."

"No, it's not. Every guy I've ever known has been an asshole."

"Even your brother?"

"Yeah, even Ben. He left without telling me why. That's an asshole thing to do." I'm not prepared for that jab and I'm lost on what to say next.

"I'm such an idiot," she says, her voice breaking, and it kills me.

"No, you're not." I look over at her, but she's staring out the passenger window.

"Yes, I am. I never learn. It's the same every time. You guys take what you want and walk away. You get bored or scared and you just walk away. Like it's so easy for you. Like you never cared at all. And I keep playing the game even though I lose every damn time."

I want to defend myself, tell her I'm not like the other guys—like Landon, but what can I say? After last night and this morning, I look like every other asshole out there. I can't tell her that this is killing me, that it broke my heart to break hers this morning. She wouldn't believe me anyway.

When we get home I consider sleeping on the couch, but that will only hurt her more and invite questions from Annie. So I lie beside her in the bed, on sheets that still smell of last night, and close my eyes, but I know I won't sleep. As she sniffles and quietly cries into her pillow, I don't allow myself to hold her, comfort her, kiss her tears, and it's the hardest thing I've ever done.

THIRTY-THREE

Kinsley: July 27, 2008

I didn't sleep well. How could I with Caleb right next to me in that stupid little bed? With the memory of his kiss still on my lips. The memory of his body holding mine, and the humiliation still burning inside. I'm such an idiot. I reach for my phone and type out a message to Nikki.

Thanks for ratting me out last night to Caleb. Super fun ride back home. Ur the best. :x

While I wait for a reply, I brush my teeth and stare at my pathetic reflection. You stupid, hopeless fuck up. Look at you—stuck in this pressure cooker of a house until the damn certificate arrives. No resolution with your dad or Landon. No plan for what you're going to do after the trust fund. And now, you've stunk up the one place in the world that was beginning to feel like home.

Why did I let myself believe Caleb could actually care about me? And where the hell is Nikki? I pick up my phone and send another text. *Hello? U alive?*

Sorry. Finishing up Gabe article. Tight deadline. Work things out with your husband. xo

I toss the phone onto the foot of the bed. *Gabe* and *husband*—two words I'd like to ban from Nikki's vocabulary.

* * *

I've had the house to myself most of the morning, with Annie riding off to the rec center and Caleb nowhere to be found. Annie has only been gone for half an hour, so I'm surprised when the front door opens. "Back already?" I ask from the kitchen where I'm washing out a coffee mug.

"Lunch break," Caleb says, walking into the room. I gather my strength, ignore the breaking of my heart, and walk past him into the bedroom. "Hold up, Kins. Are you okay?"

Don't act like you care about me.

"I'm fine," I say as emotions threaten to pull me in every direction at once. "Working on a Sunday?"

He follows me to the dresser where I open my drawer and rummage around mindlessly. "Filling in for one of the weekend guys today and next week," he says.

I slam the drawer shut and turn to face him. "You look tired. Probably shouldn't have been out so late last night."

"Kinsley."

"Why did you do it?" I wrap my arms around myself, taking a step back.

"Nikki called and said–"

"No, why did you tell those guys I was your wife? You had no right to do that, Caleb."

"I… I was just looking out for you." His voice is calm, sincere, believable. *Don't fall for it. They all know how to sound like that.*

"I don't need you to play the hero and save my ass. I would have been fine. In fact, I would have been *great*." I glare at him, challenging him to know my meaning and feel even an ounce of the pain and regret that I do.

"No, I don't think so. I think you would have woken up feeling like shit and ashamed in some stranger's bed."

"Yeah, well I did this morning in yours." The cannons are loaded, bring on the war.

"Kins, please." He reaches one arm behind him, rubbing his neck as if it's pained.

"Why do you keep calling me that?"

"It's your name–"

"No. It's a nickname, and you never call me that."

"I do…sometimes." His eyes shift away from mine.

"Yeah, game night. That was a mistake." *The best mistake of my fucking life.*

"I wouldn't call game night a mistake," he says.

"Right, but everything that happened *after* it sure was." I turn my back to him, arms crossed like I can shield my heart when it's already full and breaking at once.

"Kins," he says, stepping up behind me. I want to play cold, hide behind a wall of anger and hurt, but the enemy is in my head, in my heart, disarming me with hazel eyes and stupid cotton tee shirts.

"Kins, look at me." He places a hand on my shoulder with a gentle nudge. I turn and look up at him, heart pounding in my chest.

"I was wrong... When I pushed you away, when I didn't pull the truck over on the way home last night and tell you how I really feel. When I let you cry yourself to sleep, knowing I could have stopped it... I thought I was doing the right thing, but I was wrong."

God, I want to believe him. My heart aches with yesterday's wounds, but here I am, opening it up to him again. "Don't play games with me, Caleb," I whisper.

He leans down, forehead resting on mine. "Kins, you were right. I got scared—of my feelings, of this whole thing exploding and breaking Annie's heart. If you run back to Landon—"

"No." I close my eyes, shaking my head, never losing contact with him. "I want *you*. I want *this.*" Then, his hand reaches around to the small of my back, pulling me closer as he brushes my cheek, smoothing away a tear and bringing me to his lips. I grip his cotton tee shirt and kiss him as my heart explodes.

❊ ❊ ❊

His lunch break ends too soon and he's out the door with a sandwich to eat on the drive back. I want to text Nikki, but she's working on her article—tight deadline and all—so I'll have to tell her later.

I'm in the kitchen, sorting laundry, and I hear the front door open. I look over and see Annie running down the hall in tears. "Annie? Annie, what's wrong?"

Her bedroom door slams, shaking the old house. "Annie." I approach the door but hear no response, so I knock. "Can I come in?" Still nothing. I try the knob and peek inside to find Annie, face buried in her pillow, crying.

"Hey," I whisper as I enter the room and close the door behind me. "What's wrong?" I sit down on the side of the bed, rubbing Annie's back, her cotton top damp and warm from the bike ride home. Annie lifts her head off the pillow just long enough to sob Eric's name.

Oh, shit. "What happened?"

"He doesn't like me anymore. I saw him flirting with Jenny." Annie collapses into a sob.

"Oh, babe." Looking at Annie, I see myself at her age. I know the ache of betrayal too well, and it still hurts, even now, to think about his lies and how he humiliated me. It was one thing to know that Landon had been hooking up with other girls, but everyone else knowing? That was a twist of the knife already lodged in my back.

Annie has exhausted herself with tears, so I creep out of the bedroom and find my sketchbook. The reminiscent heartache mixed with culpability for encouraging Annie's relationship kills me. But, how could we have known Eric would treat her that way? *Caleb knew.* He was so worried about Annie getting hurt, and here she is brokenhearted. *He knew.* And he'll blame me, at least in part. But what does it matter if he blames me for some or all of it? Guilt isn't measured in degrees. It's black and white.

THIRTY-FOUR

Kinsley: July 29, 2000

Eight years earlier.

Lainey Evans' lake house is the prime party location. Nestled in the woods near the lake, it's off the radar and neighbor-free, which means the cops are hardly ever called. With Landon home for summer break, I intend to soak up every minute with him, and when he mentioned the party, I persuaded Nikki to reschedule our movie night and meet me at Lainey's instead.

I've been here for about thirty minutes and the room is starting to spin. Jell-O shots will do that. Landon is out back, catching up with other recent graduates that have boomeranged back for the summer. Graduates like Kyndra and Heather—two of his "girl friends," *not* "girlfriends," that I'm still not sure I can trust.

I'm in the kitchen looking for something to replace the pain. I get that he wants to see his friends, but I've missed him too—doesn't he want to spend time with me? I swallow another Jell-O shot because it's familiar and tasty, then pick up a clear glass bottle with lemons on it.

"You don't want that," I hear someone say and turn around to see Gabe mixing a drink at the kitchen island.

"I don't?"

"No. Well, not by itself." He extends his arm. "Here, let me see it." I give him the bottle and watch as he pours a dash into the plastic cup he has been working on. After a quick stir, he hands it to me. "Try it."

It smells like cola and a hint of lemon-lime, and when I take a sip, I can hardly taste the alcohol. It's not bad. "Thanks," I say and take another sip.

"No problem. You here with Landon?" I nod and swallow a bigger gulp this time. Gabe looks around and laughs. "Are you sure?"

Through the glass doors, I see Landon sitting on a patio chair, Kyndra on his lap and his arm around her waist. I chug the rest of the drink and toss the cup on the counter. Liquid courage and all, I'm ready to claim what's mine, but Gabe stops me.

"Don't. The best thing you can do is act like you don't care. He's not going to want you if you go over there and bitch him out. Stay here and hang out with me. Then he'll care." I look past him, Landon and Kyndra are laughing and have their hands all over each other. Just a "girl friend," my ass.

So I stay in the kitchen with Gabe and obsessively check on Landon through the glass doors. But soon, my tipsy spin becomes more of a wobble, like trying to walk through a funhouse with uneven floors. I can't see Landon from the kitchen anymore and the ground gives way. I'm on my ass, my back against the oven door.

Now Gabe is helping me stand and I stumble down the hall. The room flips and I'm on my back, staring at a ceiling fan, spinning, spinning. Heavy blinks like guillotines shutter out sound and light, and soon blackness swallows my eyes.

* * *

I open my eyes and the ceiling fan is still spinning. The house seems louder than before. I sit up, my head heavy with alcohol, and push myself off the bed. My steps are disjointed and weak, but I manage to make it to the living room. Landon sits like a king on his throne with three bimbos fawning over him, one holding a bag of ice to his cheek.

"What the hell?" I say, but no one hears me over the party noise. When Landon sees me, he jumps up, shaking off the blonde nearest him.

"You're up." He steadies me as I touch the freezer-cold bruise that's pinking his cheek.

"What happened?"

"Nothing, babe. Don't worry about it. Just some jackass."

"I don't… I need to sit down."

Landon leads me to the armchair and offers me a drink. I sip as reality comes back into focus. *Lainey Evans' lake house. Party. Drinking. Landon. Nikki. Where's Nikki?*

"Want something to eat? There's pizza in the kitchen."

I shake my head. "Where's Nikki?"

"Haven't seen her yet," he says, high-fiving some dude with a painted face that walks by.

"How long was I asleep?"

"I don't know. An hour or two?"

"Lando!" A guy calls from the bar, and Landon leans down to kiss my head.

"Be back in a minute, babe."

I sip my drink, but I need water. I'm nauseous and my eyes are still heavy. I don't want to sleep through the whole party.

"Hey." Nikki walks up beside me. "I heard about the fight."

"What? When did you…"

"Landon and Gabe," Nikki says.

"Gabe?" *Why didn't he tell me it was Gabe? They're best friends.*

"I was asleep. What was the fight about?"

"Asleep? Kins…" Nikki steps back and examines me. "You feeling okay?"

"Yeah. Just tired. What happened?"

"I just got here, but Lainey said Gabe punched Landon and a bunch of guys had to break up the fight. They destroyed a bookcase."

Gabe punched him? That was a mistake. My head is pounding, and the drink Landon gave me is making it worse. "Nik, can you find some water for me?"

"Sure, sit tight."

Nikki returns with a bottle of water and I take a drink. Then another.

"Oh, shit, there's Gabe." Nikki laughs. "Round two? Ding, ding, ding."

Gabe is a mess, his shirt is torn at the neck, and his lip is busted. His eyes burn a hole into me. *What the hell did I do?* He walks with purpose straight toward me and leans down to whisper in my ear. "Kinky little slut. You like being raped don't you?"

What? His words scramble in my head and don't make sense. I think I might vomit. "Gabe!" I jump up to go after him, to ask him what the hell he's talking about, but he's already out the front door.

"What was that about?" Nikki asks.

"I have no idea." My heart is racing and I look around for Landon.

"What did he say?"

Ignoring Nikki's question, I walk into the kitchen and find him. "Hey, can I talk to you?"

"What's up babe?" He wraps his arms around me.

"Why were you fighting with Gabe?"

He laughs. "Because he was being a jackass. Don't worry about it."

"He just said something really strange... What the hell is he talking about, Landon?"

"You know Gabe, he's probably high. Just ignore him." He leans down and kisses me, but I pull back from his aggressive, whisky-soaked lips.

"But he was asking–"

"Kins, just drop it. He has issues."

I can't *just drop it.* I've lost two hours of the party and can't even remember falling asleep. Then Gabe says I *like* being raped? *Raped?* I've never been raped. My stomach sinks at the thought of it—and the hours I can't remember.

"Whatever. If you won't tell me, he will." I turn to leave, but Landon grabs my wrist, and I squirm at the pain.

"Don't make a scene," he says through his teeth as he nuzzles against my neck.

"Let me go."

"We're leaving together, Kinsley."

"Fine, let's go–"

"I'm not ready."

"Well, I am." I glare at him.

"I don't care. Stop acting like a baby."

I try to get away but he's too strong, pulling me close and pinning me against him. It's hard to breathe. I can feel his keys in his front pocket, so I relax, look up at him, and apologize. His hold softens as I kiss him. I wrap my arms around his body, the blue polo coarse under my fingertips as

I pull my arms back to his chest, kissing him still and trailing my hands down to rest on his belt. He walks me backwards until I bump into the wall, and while his tongue is searching for more, I slip the keys out of his front pocket and dart away.

My heart pounds a rhythm of adrenaline and excitement as I run outside to the truck. The field is dark under a waning moon, and the muffled sounds of the party recede behind me. I scramble into the truck and start to drive away down the gravel path when the passenger door opens and Landon jumps in.

"What the hell, Kinsley?"

"I told you I wanted to go."

"And I told you I wasn't ready. You can't just steal my truck."

"I'm not stealing it." The cab swerves, my jittery nerves are no match for a souped-up 5.3.

"Stop the truck, Kinsley."

"No!" I accelerate, kicking up a cloud of gravel dust as I turn onto the dark country road. "I want to know what Gabe was talking about."

"It's nothing, he was just talking out of his ass."

"What happened when I was sleeping?" I turn to face him, demanding an answer. His eyes are dark with rage and flicker to the windshield.

"Kinsley, watch out!" He grabs the wheel and jerks it. A heavy thump hits the truck and I slam on the brakes.

"Oh, my god. What was that?" The headlights illuminate a scene of dancing insects and nothing more. "Why did you do that?"

"There was a deer, Kinsley. I told you to watch out."

"You grabbed the wheel!"

"I was trying to keep you from hitting it."

"But we *did* hit it."

"It might have just bumped us and ran off."

I look out the passenger window to the wooded darkness, heart thumping in my ears. "We should call someone–" I reach for the phone in his pocket, but he grabs my hand.

"No, it's just a deer. It's fine."

"What if it's hurt?"

"Come on, Kinsley. It happens all the time." I'm sucker-punched by the mix of adrenaline, fear, and alcohol as tears well in my eyes. "Calm down." He snaps at me and runs his hands over his face. He does that when he's in trouble. *This is bad.*

My breath is quick and shallow and my head goes light. "Oh, my god. I killed a deer. I'm a monster!" I break down into sobs.

"First of all, you didn't kill it. It's probably off running in that field already. And you're not a monster. Come here." He pulls me to him, wiping away my tears and kissing my head. "You're a mess, and you shouldn't even be driving. Slide over." He opens the passenger door and walks around the truck to the driver's side as I scoot across the bench seat.

"Did you see any blood?" I ask through shaky breaths.

"What?" He climbs up into the cab. "No, it's fine."

THIRTY-FIVE

Caleb: July 28, 2008

The sun is still asleep, only the fading moon lights the room as I watch her dream, hair messy around her face, those perfect lips. I kiss the freckle on her neck, inhaling the sweet, familiar scent of her skin. "Kinsley," I whisper and she murmurs into the pillow. "Wanna go fishing with me?"

She rolls over and smiles, blinking her eyes awake. "What about work?"

"I'm off today and tomorrow, remember. I picked up Jason's weekend shifts. Wanna go?" She nods and looks over to the alarm clock. "Get dressed," I say and plant a kiss on her forehead. "I'm gonna get the gear."

The waking sun barely lights the sky and the crickets continue their night song as Kinsley comes down the front porch steps wearing flip-flops, cutoff jean shorts, and one of my flannel shirts. I hand her a pair of muck boots. "Wear these, the ground's all wet with dew."

"Oh, I need socks." She starts back toward the house, but I catch her hand and pull out a pair of mine.

"You're letting me wear your socks, huh?" She looks at me with teasing in her eyes and the most inviting smile on her lips.

"I've never been able to stop you." I tuck her under my arm and lean down to kiss her. *Fuck.* Now I'm reconsidering the fishing trip. I want to carry her back to bed and make love to her, kissing every perfect curve and losing myself in her little whimpers and sighs as she responds to my touch. Without leaving her lips, I take a step toward the house, tugging her along with me, but she breaks our kiss.

With a wry smile, she shakes her head and says, "We're going fishing."

I rest my forehead on hers and groan. "You're killin' me, Kinsley."

❈ ❈ ❈

We stop at the bait shop and grab coffee and a package of mini donuts. "Whoa, this is strong." Kinsley sips from the little white cup and coughs as we walk back to the truck.

"Yeah, it's not the best, but it'll wake you up."

We climb in, and I start the engine. "Here, you're gonna want this when the sun comes up," I say, handing her a baseball hat from the dashboard. She fits it to her head and smiles at me.

"Shirt, socks, hat–you're just all over me aren't you, Caleb?"

Damn it, Kinsley. I can't focus on the road, I can hardly keep my eyes *on* the road. So I choke down a swig of coffee to kill the fire that's building inside—except, I don't want to kill it, I want to feed it and fan those flames until it consumes us both.

Somehow, I manage to drive to the creek on the far side of the farm, where Ben and I used to go fishing. I grab the fishing rods from the truck bed and lead her to the edge of the water. "Oh, god." She coughs. "Does it always smell like this?"

"It's not always this bad, but it does leave an impression. Figured you'd be used to it by now, working at the farm and all," I say with a laugh.

"Guess not." She waves her hand in front of her nose.

"Ben and I used to come out here and fish sometimes."

"I remember he talked about fishing at the creek. This is it, huh?" She sits down on a large rock nearby.

"One time a bunch of us came out here together. It was pretty bad that day too. Ben was so worried we'd stink up his new car. In his defense, we *were* wading for trout." I laugh at the memory. "Probably smelled like a load of manure pulling up to your house."

"You came back to my house after?"

"Yeah it was some low-key birthday thing for Ben," I say, kneeling down and shuffling through my tackle box. "Maybe sixteen or seventeen? When your dad gave him that Roadrunner."

"Oh, yeah… Sixteen," she says as I hold out a worm so she can bait the line. "Ewww, it's alive." She scrunches up her face and pulls away.

"Yeah, that's the point."

"Nu-uh. It was bad enough grabbing a handful of dried worms for the chickens."

"Kinsley, it's just a worm. It won't bite."

"It's wiggling." She shakes her head in disgust.

"Fine." I laugh. I'd do just about anything for her right now.

We cast our lines, watching them disappear into the water, and I sit down on a large rock, enjoying the peaceful stillness of the morning.

"How long does it take?" she asks. Her fidgeting and antsy movements tell me this isn't happening fast enough for her.

"Could be a while. You might want to sit down."

She joins me on the rock, yawning. "Why so early?"

"That's when the fish bite."

"I don't think they're awake yet, Caleb."

I chuckle. "Maybe not."

"Don't you ever sleep in? You get up at the butt-crack of dawn even on your days off. That's just self-inflicted misery." She yawns again, jiggling the fishing rod like it'll speed things up. The sunrise kisses her sleepy face and misery doesn't look so bad from where I'm sitting.

"Oh! Something's happening." She jumps up. "What is that? Is it a fish?" Her line bobs and tugs in the water.

I stand next to her. "Looks like you caught something. Just reel it in, nice and slow." I do the same as she pulls it out of the creek, flipping and twisting on the end of the line as its greenish-gray scales glisten in the morning sun.

"Oh, wow. I can't believe I caught one."

"See, patience pays off." I nudge her and start to remove the sunfish from the line. "Hey, would you get that cooler from the truck?"

"Sure, thirsty?" she asks as she walks to the tailgate.

"Huh? Oh, no it's for the fish." I hold it by the head with one hand and remove the hook from its gills with the other.

"What?" She sets the ice chest on the ground next to me, opening it to reveal nothing but ice.

"To keep it fresh until we get back home," I tell her.

"Why are we taking it home?"

"That's the point of fishing. Dinner."

Her face is pitiful. "No, Caleb. I don't want to kill it."

"Kins," I laugh, shaking my head. "You've already hooked it."

"I can't. Please don't make me." She holds onto my arm, those big brown eyes pleading with me. How can I tell her no? I toss it back in the water. It's just like a woman to hook a man, put him through the struggle, then toss him back into the water. Just put us out of our misery, why don't you?

"You gonna try for another?" I ask her, preparing to bait the line.

"I think I'd rather draw if that's okay. I brought my sketchbook."

"Sure, go for it. What are you drawing today?" I ask, casting my line back into the creek.

"Maybe you."

I look over at her with a playful grin. "Me, huh?"

"Maybe. If I'm feeling inspired." She winks.

"Oh, yeah?" I recognize the look in her eyes. It slayed me last night. *Oh, man, I'm a goner.* I lean over, kissing her softly, sliding my tongue between her lips and finding hers. I pull back and look at her. "How's your inspiration now?"

"A little better." She smiles, daring me to do it again. Who am I to back down from a dare? I join her on the rock and inspire her a little longer. She hooks a leg over mine, letting her sketchbook fall to the ground as she slides a hand under my shirt, running her fingers over my chest and abs. My free arm wraps around her waist, and I pull her closer. I think about taking her in the bed of the truck, and now I'm growing hard. *Damn it, Kinsley.* She trails her hand down to my jeans, adding friction where I don't need it, but fuck, it feels good.

I haven't been paying attention to the line I cast—how the hell could I—but when it tugs, I nearly drop the pole. "Shit, I caught something," I say and she laughs, unhooking her leg from mine and reaching for the sketchbook. I stand to reel it in, blowing out a breath and trying to calm my arousal. I glance over my shoulder—Kinsley is sketching. The fish squirms in my hands and I remove the hook. "It's your lucky day, bastard," I whisper and toss it back into the water.

I spend the rest of the morning using crap bait and don't catch anything. If I want to bring home dinner next time, I'll have to go solo. When we pack up and drive home, she asks if I caught anything. "Nah, fish weren't biting today."

* * *

The house is quiet—it's only nine, and Annie is still asleep. Kinsley kicks off the muck boots and lays down in bed. "Are you going back to sleep?" I laugh, but I'm not surprised.

"Yeah, I'm tired, and that coffee was stupid."

"Okay, sweet dreams," I say, flipping the light switch.

"What are you doing now?" she asks, peeking out from the bundle she has made of herself.

"I have some errands to run."

"Oh, okay," she murmurs, closing her eyes.

I close the door behind me and go to grab my keys from the kitchen table. I have a shit-ton of things I need to do today, but damn it, I can't stop thinking about her. Not after our little episode at the creek. Just the thought of it gets me going again, and it's decided. We have to finish what we started.

THIRTY-SIX

Kinsley: July 28, 2008

I'm curled up in the blanket alone because Caleb has errands to run. I miss him, but I settle for a daydream of how things could have gone at the creek. I imagine Caleb dropping the fishing pole and pulling me onto his lap, then unbuttoning the flannel and tugging my bra down, exposing my nipples to the morning air before taking one into his mouth and covering it with his warm tongue, while running his thumb over the other, cupping my entire breast in his hand as I arch my back and press myself against him, hard with arousal.

The door opens and I'm startled, my breathing is already short and my body wet with longing. I pop my head out of the bundle I've made, hoping to god it's not Annie because I *have* to finish this.

It's not Annie.

"I thought you were running errands," I say and send a silent prayer that he hasn't come back in for his keys or wallet. I don't think I can let him walk out that door again. Not *now*.

"Errands can wait." He smiles, closing the door behind him.

He doesn't waste time. He's undressing and god, he's beautiful. I've spent hours and hours touching his body, wrapping myself around it, becoming one *with it*. But lying here, taking in a full view of him, every muscle and sinew exposed, I'm convinced *this* is the body that inspired Bandinelli's *Hercules*. Hours of farm work have refined muscles I've only seen in art. *And he. Is. Art.*

I wiggle out of the blanket. I'm just in my panties and a tank top because I had planned to take care of myself while he was out, but fuck, this is going to be so much better than anything I could have imagined. I lift my tank top over my head and he covers me, taking my breasts in his hands and lowering his mouth to cover one nipple. It's just like my daydream, but *better*. I buck beneath him, I'm so turned on already. Hell, I was ready to jump him at the creek, and I would have if I thought he was up for it, but he cooled down after he caught a fish. *Damn fish.*

I run my fingers over his shoulders, tracing the dips and curves of his muscles, then I work my hands into his hair and he moans into my breast. I hold him against me as he sucks and tugs on my nipple. He pulls away, and looks up at me, his hazel eyes full of desire. *Me too, baby.*

He slides down my body, and brings me closer to the edge with each kiss he lays on me. I squirm, begging him to slide into me and put me out of my glorious misery. He removes my panties and slips a finger inside. "You been thinking about me?" he asks, and I can't speak, but my body tells him that I have. I'm writhing with desire and I need more than a finger. *Come on, Caleb. Fuck me!*

With his finger still inside, he kisses my thigh, then the other. He's so close, I can feel his breath on me and it's driving me fucking crazy. I reach down and grab handfuls of his hair, guiding him toward me. His tongue slides back and forth as the stubble on his chin creates the most pleasurable friction. I can't take it anymore and I roll my hips against his face, faster and faster until I'm gone—somewhere else entirely, every nerve in my body consumed by pleasure.

He removes his finger, as little jerks take over my body—every inch of me is alive. But before he leaves, he plunges his tongue inside, like he can't get enough of me—of my arousal. I cry out and shove my hand over my mouth so I don't wake Annie. He laughs and the vibration against my body nearly kills me. *Again.* He sits back on his knees and reaches for the drawer on the nightstand. "You ready?" he asks with a crooked grin and I nod. *I've been ready all damn morning.*

He reaches for my hand and pulls me to his lap. I lower myself onto him. He fills every inch of me. *Every. Inch.* I'm already rocking against him, gliding up and down as his tuft of hair tickles my clit. *Holy fuck.* His hands are on my hips, guiding me, squeezing me. He lowers his mouth to my breast, taking in a nipple, and that's when I lose it. *Again.* Thank god this man is strong because I can't hold up my body. I collapse into the pleasure he's bringing me, and he pulls his mouth up to take mine, kissing me deeply as he finishes. *Holy fuck, that was better than I imagined.*

It's almost noon, and I roll over to kiss Caleb's chest. He stirs in his sleep and I wonder if he's dreaming. The blankets are on the floor and the bedsheet only comes up to his hips. I spend a moment admiring this gorgeous man who makes me feel sexy, and protected, and loved.

Loved?

Maybe.

Isn't this love? With Caleb, I feel safe and valuable and *equal*—both in bed and out. All things I struggled to hold onto with Landon. But maybe things will change with Caleb too. It's still early. Maybe it's foolish hope, but something inside tells me I can trust him. And I have no reason to believe he's hiding anything from me or holding back bits of the truth like Landon—my dad—even Ben. I kiss his shoulder softly before crawling out of bed to shower.

When I return, he's waking up. "Hey, where are you off to?" he asks as I sit on the end of the bed to put on my shoes.

"To see Nikki. She's gonna die when she finds out her matchmaking worked." I smile over my shoulder at him. He crawls up behind me, wrapping his arms around my waist and kisses my neck.

"Mmm, you smell good." His stubble tickles my shower-fresh skin.

"You smell like the creek." I laugh, but the scent stirs up a nightmare I've tried to forget. My stomach churns, and I pull away from his embrace, squeezing my eyes to shut it out.

"You alright?" he asks.

"Yeah, sorry, just…the fishy creek smell got me again." I blow out an uneven breath and hope the queasiness passes soon.

He kisses my shoulder. "I'll shower while you're gone."

As I pass through the kitchen, I see Annie sitting at the table with a catatonic stare aimed at the magazine in front of her. I walk around to read over her shoulder. *Will Your Summer Flame Fizzle?* I don't have to ask if she took the quiz or what results she received. It's written all over her face.

"Hey, you busy?"

Annie barely shakes her head in response. "Go on, get your shoes. We're going out," I tell her and watch as Annie shuffles hopelessly to her room. While I wait for her to return, I crack open the bedroom door, popping my head in to let Caleb know Annie is riding with me.

✳ ✳ ✳

We stop by Nikki's camper, but she isn't home, so I text her with an invite to join us if she's free. At the little old-fashioned ice cream shop downtown, we sit on tall vinyl-topped stools at the red and white speckled soda bar and cool off with triple scoop sundaes.

"Ready to talk about it?" I ask, peeking at her.

Annie shrugs. "I guess so." After a heavy sigh, she continues. "I went to the rec center yesterday to surprise him. Brittany told me he was going to play ball with her brother, but when I got there, he was sitting on the bleachers with Jenny, and they were laughing and flirting. He had his arm around her, and he…" Annie's face reddens and tears pool in her eyes.

I place a hand on her back, rubbing little circles. "It's okay, Annie. We don't have to talk about it if you don't want to. I just wanted you to know I'm here if you need to talk or cry…or throw darts at his picture, we can do that too."

Annie laughs and wipes her cheeks. "Thanks, Kinsley. I just feel so freaking stupid. Of course, he wouldn't like me. I mean, look at me, I'm–"

"You're beautiful, Annie. Don't let some jackass make you feel bad about yourself. You deserve better than that."

Annie stares into her melting ice cream. "I just really, really like him, Kinsley."

"I know, babe." I put my arm around her shoulder, pulling her to me. "I know."

THIRTY-SEVEN

Caleb: July 28, 2008

The front door opens as I walk out of the laundry room with a basket full of folded clothes in my arms.

"Pizza night?" Annie asks. "You feeling okay, bro?"

"Just thought it'd be nice to take the night off."

Kinsley follows me into the bedroom, closing the door behind her. "Hey," I say, setting the basket down and taking her into my arms.

"Hey to you too." A rosy smile blooms on her face before she takes a step back. "I need to talk to you about something. It's Annie and Eric. I think he broke up with her." I sit down in the armchair by the window, waiting for the roulette ball to land. Is this good news or bad?

"I'm sorry, Caleb. I know you didn't want her to date, and I pushed it, and now she's–"

"Stop." I look up at her, taking her hands. "It's not your fault that kid's a little asswipe."

"But I–"

"Kins, I'm not upset with you." I pull her onto my lap. "You were right, back at the carnival when you said I couldn't stop her from having her heart broken." Tears build behind my eyes and I swallow back the emotion. "It sucks, but it's like learning to walk. She's gonna fall, and it's gonna hurt."

Kinsley nods and I lean in, kissing her forehead as a burst of vanilla coconut sweetness hits the air. I always thought I'd be relieved to hear that they broke up, but instead, it's a fist to my gut, sharing a sliver of Annie's heartbreak. "Damn it, this hurts."

* * *

"You know what we haven't done in forever?" Annie asks as she clears the plates and pizza boxes from the table.

"Gone to bed early?" I say and watch heat creep across Kinsley's face.

"God, you're such an old man," Annie scoffs. "Monopoly night. Can we? Please." She brings her hands together to beg. "We haven't had one since Kinsley moved in."

I look at Kinsley to confirm what I already know. It's going to be the longest game of Monopoly ever.

We play badly, trying to lose and put an end to the game. It's a wonder Annie doesn't call us out for overspending and driving our finances straight into bankruptcy. That damn paycheck won't stop coming around and keeping us afloat. "Man, y'all really suck tonight," Annie says, *more than once*. Every glance across the table to meet Kinsley's eyes makes it harder to concentrate, and I love it.

It has been *hours*, and we've finally bankrupted. Kinsley stands up, stretching and forcing a yawn. "I'm beat, guys." She adds another yawn for good measure before leaning over Annie's chair to give her a hug.

"It's only ten." Annie rolls her eyes. "Y'all are boring."

"Yeah, and it's your night to do dishes," I remind her.

"Come on, Caleb, I'm emotionally distraught right now." She pouts, and Kinsley tilts her head from the bedroom doorway, an encouragement to go easy on Annie.

"Alright, I'll do it, but you owe me." I wink at her and watch as she hurries off to her room with maybe a little more spunk than she had before.

It doesn't take long to wash the dishes, but the bedroom is empty when I enter. The bathroom door is shut, and I hear Kinsley humming on the other side. After changing into my pajamas, I flip off the light and settle into bed.

Kinsley opens the bathroom door and walks over to me. She's wearing one of my flannel work shirts, the hem hitting the top of her bare thighs—thighs I sank my fingers into as I held her tight against my body this morning. "You just can't stay out of my clothes can you?" I ask.

"Do you want me out of your clothes?"

"I don't know." I tilt my head. "You got any more of my clothes on under there?" She shakes her head and crawls toward me on the bed. "Why are you doing this to me?" I groan.

"Doing what?" She asks as she positions herself on my lap, face to face, with those thighs hugging each side of me.

"You know exactly what I'm talking about." I reach behind her, slipping my hands under the flannel, grazing her soft, warm skin and confirming that she, indeed, does not have any more of my clothing on. "You're driving me crazy," I breathe, pulling her closer.

"Mmm… I am?" She arches her back, pressing her bare skin hard against my palms. She's playing with me. It's tortuous and I want more.

"You've been doing it since you moved in."

"Really?" She feigns ignorance and leans into me, raking her fingers through my hair.

"Mm-hmm, you know what I'm talking about."

"Nuh-uh," she mumbles, kissing my neck as a coconut-vanilla scent overwhelms me. I pull her closer, running my hands up and down her bare back under the shirt.

"Tanning," I say. "That damn bikini." I try to steady her rocking movements, but she doesn't stop.

"Just a bikini."

"When I found your panties."

"You were so mad," she whispers and kisses the other side of my neck. My hands rub her back feverishly as a growing need clouds my brain.

"The carnival." My breath catches as she lifts my tee shirt over my head.

"Carnival?" She asks in a near whisper, placing her hands on my bare chest and trailing them up and over my shoulders.

"You kept touching me." I run my hands, never leaving her skin, from her back to her knees, slowly following the curves along the way. "You smelled like cotton candy."

"It tasted good too," she says so close to my lips it's a dare. I take the challenge, kissing her with passion as I work my hands up her thighs and grab her ass, pressing her body against mine.

She pulls away just enough to look me in the eye. "Am I driving you crazy now?"

"Like you don't know." I flip her off my lap and onto the bed, her hair splayed across the pillow and her face full of laughter. "It's my turn to drive you crazy."

THIRTY-EIGHT

Kinsley: July 29, 2008

I wake to the sun piercing through the miniblinds and shuffle out of the bedroom, clearing my eyes as I yawn.

"Why are you up so early?" Caleb asks, pouring himself a cup of coffee and taking another mug from the cabinet. I join him at the counter and shrug.

"I guess I'm used to it. That today's paper?" I point to the counter bar.

"Yeah." He hands me a mug full of goodness. "Job hunting again?"

"Nikki's article," I say and sit down at the table with my coffee.

"Oh, I didn't read it yet. Front page story caught my eye though."

"Why's that?"

"Reminded me of what happened to my dad when I was a kid." He sits down beside me, and I scan the front page headlines.

"He won first place in the goat show?"

"No," Caleb says with a half-hearted laugh. "When he was laid off." He points to the headline reading *Marquest Manufacturing to Close Doors: Hundreds out of Work.*

Marquest isn't too far from here, about a half-hour drive or so, and it's a much smaller company than CHI. In the article, a dock worker is interviewed and shares the shock he felt when the news came out. Like the rug was pulled out from under him, he says. And with the state of the economy and unemployment levels, he's worried about how he'll provide for his family.

"Your dad worked at Marquest?" I ask, taking a sip of coffee.

"No, CHI."

How did I not know this? "Oh, I...and he was laid off?"

"Yeah. When I was in first grade. I remember coming home after school one day and my dad was already there. He never got home from work before dinner, so I knew right away something was wrong."

"I'm so sorry, Caleb." I reach for his hand. "I had no idea."

"Don't apologize. It has nothing to do with you, Kins."

"Yeah, but it was my dad…"

"It was business. It happens." He shrugs as if it's nothing, but his eyes are clouded with pain.

"What happened? I mean, after he was laid off? Did he…"

"Did he find another job?" Caleb's blank stare is set on the newspaper. "Here and there, yeah. Little odd jobs and temp work. Nothing substantial. But he played a part in it too, don't go blaming your dad's company for all of it."

I appreciate how level-headed Caleb can be, but he doesn't know everything. He doesn't know the shit moves my dad made that likely contributed to the layoffs. "Is that how you ended up here, with your grandparents?" I ask.

"Not immediately, but yeah. It was a domino effect." He offers a vacant smile.

"I'm sorry. We don't have to talk about it. I didn't mean to pry."

"It's fine." His smile transforms into something real. "Long story short? When Dad couldn't find steady work, he became a steady drunk. Mom couldn't stand it. She wanted more out of life than what he could give her. So, she found someone else who offered her a better life and she left us. Dad couldn't cope, and thank god for grandparents." He squeezes my hand and smiles, but it doesn't reach his eyes. I see heartache instead.

"I'm sor–"

He stops me with a kiss. "Don't. It wasn't your fault." I wrap my arms around his neck, bringing him close enough to breathe in his soapy freshness, this time with a hint of clove from shaving. "Gotta run a few errands. I'll be back in a couple hours," he says and stands up, taking his coffee mug to the sink.

"Okay, I might be out when you get back. I have a few errands to run, myself." I flip the newspaper to Nikki's article, taking a deep breath and a gulp full of coffee before reading.

Eight-Year Anniversary, Still No Leads In Town's 2000 Unsolved Crime

By Nikole Bolero: July 29, 2008

Eight years have passed since the untimely death of Gabe White, a record-setting running back and '99 graduate of Thunderbird High. In the early hours of July 30, 2000, White's family contacted the police when he did not return home from a local party.

Community members joined the search efforts, which were ultimately called off when Detective Ott located a body lying in the brush off South 5100 Road near the Lakeside Overpass. Paramedics arrived on the scene and transported White to Mulhall Regional Hospital, where he underwent multiple surgeries to combat the extensive brain damage that he suffered. Within a week's time, however, it was evident to doctors and White's family that he would not make a full recovery, and at 11:03 a.m., Saturday, August 5, 2000, Gabe White passed away in the presence of his family and friends.

In response to the tragic passing, the Gabe P. White Fund was set up in cooperation with Charleston Holland Industries (CHI) and Hawk-Reynolds Corporation of Tulsa. Mr. Zachary White, Gabe's father, was employed by CHI at the time of the incident. The fund, which received a total of $498,657.00 in donations, was established to ease the family's financial burden related to medical and funeral expenses. The White family has extended their heartfelt gratitude to both CHI and Hawk-Reynolds Corp. for their generous donations, without which the fund would not have met $100,000.

In the weeks following the incident, police launched a comprehensive investigation, interviewing hundreds of community members, and performing a city-wide search for the vehicle involved. Chief Birmingham expressed his deep remorse over the loss of such a young, talented member of the community, calling it a "senseless death." Though law enforcement meticulously tracked every lead, the case remains unsolved.

Chief Sanders, who replaced Birmingham upon retirement last year, said that he hasn't given up on solving the case: "The missing piece of the puzzle is out there. Someone knows something." As today marks exactly eight years since the hit-and-run that took the eighteen-year-old's life, local law enforcement and the White family hope that someone will bring that missing piece forward, providing closure and a chance to heal. Citizens are asked to call the anonymous tip line or stop by the police department if they have any information related to the incident.

That damn article. I send Nikki a congratulatory text, but something in the details lodges itself in my mind, and I can't shake it. It's the money given to Gabe's family for his medical expenses and funeral. If everything Landon and my dad told me is true, at that time, CHI would have been in no place to make such a sizable donation. What the hell was my dad thinking?

It feels like moral compensation—like he was trying to balance the scales of guilt and redemption. But Landon and I didn't have anything to do with the accident. And it had nothing to do with the fight at the party. Landon drilled that into me a million times in the weeks following Gabe's death. But the more I uncover about my dad's business deals, the more questions I have, and each answer alters my perception of reality. I have to know if there's more to this story too.

* * *

When I reach my dad's office door, I offer the obligatory knock but let myself in, and once the door shuts behind me, I hold nothing back. "Why did you donate so much to Gabe's fund?"

My dad looks up from his desk in apparent shock. "What?" he stammers. "You know why. He was Ben's friend. His father worked for CHI. It was the least we could do."

"But why so much? If CHI was already struggling, why would you–"

"Is this an audit?" His tone—his words, they confirm the little nudges in my conscience.

"Look, I know you haven't been honest with me about…well, anything, really, but I need to know the truth about Gabe's accident, Dad."

"What are you talking about, Kinsley? You know what happened. It was a hit and run."

"But that was a lot of money–"

"Because his medical care was extensive, and then the funeral costs…" He removes his glasses and pinches the bridge of his nose.

"But why so much from CHI? You didn't have the extra funds to throw around at the time, it's almost like–"

"Almost like what?" His eyes cut into me like I'm the one being interrogated.

"Like you were trying to pay off the guilt."

"That's nonsense."

"Is it?" I hold his glare. "I don't remember everything from that night, but I know I hit–"

"A deer, Kinsley." He stands up, planting his hands on his desk with a bang. "You hit a deer."

I weigh the sincerity in his voice, the conviction in his eyes. Something doesn't measure up. I've never been good at reading people, but I've learned to pick up on my dad's bullshit when he talks business, and this is an echo of his country-club schmoozing.

"Right, a deer." I turn to leave, disappointed that even now, he's still holding back some part of the truth.

"Where are we at with the merger, Kinsley?" He shouts from his desk.

"I don't know. Talk to Landon," I holler back, not giving a damn if anyone else hears.

❉ ❉ ❉

Stepping out of my car onto the perfectly manicured lawn, I look around for any sign that Landon is home. I pound on the door, and for half a second, I worry who might answer. A Sierra perhaps? But why should it bother me now? My heart doesn't belong to him anymore.

"Well, look who it is." Landon smiles as the door opens. "I missed you, babe, come in." I step inside as he closes the door behind me. "I knew you'd come back."

"That's not what this is."

"Kinda looks like it." He puts his hands on my waist, pulling me in, but I resist.

"What do you know about my dad's contribution to Gabe's fund?"

"That's random, Kins." He takes a step back.

"No, it's not. My dad wouldn't tell me anything–just like before with Ouranos Group and the tax withholding. What isn't he telling me, Landon?"

"Hell if I know." He shrugs and walks through the foyer to the living room, and I follow close behind.

"I just don't see why my dad would contribute so much when the company was already struggling financially unless…"

"Unless what? What are you getting at?"

"It feels like he was trying to clear a guilty conscience. After what happened that night and then to find Gabe the next day on the side of the *same* road. And a hit-and-run? Then the money–"

"What does it matter at this point?" He turns abruptly so that I'm standing inches away from his chest.

"Are you saying–"

"I'm asking," he pauses to look down at me. "What would it matter? It wouldn't change anything for Gabe or his family, but it *would* make things worse for your dad." Landon moves to sit down on the deep blue Chesterfield sofa beside us, strumming his fingers on the armrest. "And you. Have you even thought about how these accusations would affect your life, Kinsley?"

I start to speak but my words tangle up in fractured memories held together by a thread of shame.

"See this is a perfect example of why you need me." Something about his smile, the self-satisfied arrogance of it—I used to see drive, intelligence, and charisma in it, but now I want to slap it clear off his face.

"I need you for what exactly?"

"Seriously, Kinsley?" He reaches for my hand. "You're so naive, so gullible."

I'm scrambling to put the puzzle together, to get every piece in just the right place so that it all makes sense for once, but the picture forming isn't one I want to see. "You told me I hit a deer, Landon!"

He doesn't respond and my heart is pounding in my head. "Landon!" I jerk my hand back from his.

"What?" he shouts—his tone is sharp, dangerous.

"Tell me the truth." I sit down next to him. "Did I hit Gabe?"

"Come on, Kinsley. Don't act like you don't remember that night," he says, confirming all I've tried to hide from and push to the recesses of my mind.

It wasn't a deer.

Panic fills my chest, catching in my throat.

I killed him. I killed Gabe.

I can't breathe, I think I might pass out or be sick. It's a lot to process—the knowledge that I killed someone. *Killed* someone. But Landon is calm. He's calm because he has already processed it. He has known for years. Rage burns through every other emotion vying for control.

"Why did you lie to me?" I scream, balling my hands into fists. "Why didn't you–"

"Because I knew what would happen, Kinsley." He grabs my wrists so I can't hit him. "You were *fifteen*. You shouldn't have been driving, plus you were wasted. And with the fighting, how would it have looked?"

I weaken under his grip and he lets go. Listening to him recall details of the night is like a surgeon removing my insides while I'm awake —no anesthetic.

"What do you think would have happened to you? To me, our dads' companies if it came out?" Landon lets out an exasperated sigh. "You go around making messes and have no idea the consequences you'd face if it weren't for us cleaning up after you."

Messes. That's all I'm good for. But how could I clean it up if I didn't even know about it? I've fought so hard to pull the truth out of my dad and Landon this summer, I'm not going to lock it away now that it's out. "Landon, it's not right I have to tell–"

"No, Kinsley. You're not telling anyone anything because if you do it will ruin us. You could go to prison. Did you even think about that? And what about me and my dad? We'd lose everything. Is that what you want? You would do that to my mom?"

Guilt and heartache rip through me as I search his eyes, finding remnants of truth and logic. His mom is already suffering, and it would be heartless to dump this on her now. The police would investigate my dad and the company—*everything* would come out. The company would go under, my dad would go to prison. I would too.

Annie? Caleb? What would it do to them and our relationship? I try to reason with myself, playing Landon's axioms over and over. Speaking up now won't bring Gabe back. It will only cause more problems for me and everyone I care about. He was drunk, walking down a dark country road in the middle of the night. *Anyone* could have hit him. It just happened to be me. And when he died, we did the only thing anyone could do to help ease his parents' grief.

Landon brings me into his arms. "I'm only trying to protect you, Kinsley. That's all I've ever tried to do."

I'm numb. Swallowing a secret like this will do that.

"Why don't I pour you some wine? You look like you need it. Maybe a bath too?"

"No, I'm not staying." I stand on unsteady legs, and he grabs my arm, pulling me back down to the couch.

"I'm done playing games, Kinsley."

"I'm not–"

"Where are we at with the annulment?"

"Same as before. It's not happening, Landon." I jerk my arm from his grip.

"Kinsley, this is stupid. You're willing to send your dad to prison just to prove some little point?"

"No, *you're* willing to send him to prison over something I can't comprehend. Why do you insist on marrying me, Landon? You don't even love me."

"Babe," he starts, smoothing my hair. "You know I–"

I smack his hand away. "I know you've cheated on me too many times to count."

"Like you never did anything to make me jealous?" He cocks his head, challenging me with his eyes.

"I never started it, Landon. It was only to get back at you for cheating on me first." I hate myself for playing his stupid games—I always lost. "I'm done with it. I've moved on–"

"You can't seriously think…" A smug grin appears on his face. "Are you… You know you're only *playing* house with Caleb. It's not real, Kinsley." He laughs, raking his fingers through his hair. "You always do this–you go off and fuck around with some loser to get my attention, then it's over and you come back to me. You know, you'll have to give him half of everything when you divorce, right? He's just using you for money. It's like you're a reverse hooker–"

"Fuck you!" My palm smarts. I've never slapped him *that* hard before. I jump up and hurry out of the house before he has a chance to react.

*　*　*

The sun slowly fades as gray spreads across the sky. I park next to the old farm truck, stepping out into the thick July air sprinkled with honeysuckle and cut grass and make my way inside.

As I enter the bedroom and walk past the laundry hamper, a hint of creek water floats in the air. *It's your party favor*—a whisper of a dream haunts me. Of all the things I can't remember from the night of Gabe's accident, how can one dream I had at twelve still be so clear?

"What's up?" Caleb asks from the bed as I take pajamas from the drawer.

"Nothing, why?"

"Seems like something's on your mind." He raises an eyebrow closing his book.

I change into my pajamas and sit down at the foot of the bed. "Have you ever had a dream so real that you wondered if it was even a dream at all?"

"No. But I'm guessing you have?"

"It was one of those crazy fever dreams when you're sick, you know?" I shift my body and turn to face him.

"What was it?"

I've never told anyone about it, not even the doctor my dad sent me to see the summer I started having nightmares. Not even Nikki. A dream *that* disturbing, wouldn't it mean there's something wrong with me?

Carefully selecting my words, I tell Caleb about the dream that has tormented me for twelve years. "I was lying on my stomach and it was like someone was pinning me down. It was hard to breathe, and they smelled awful–like rotten fish." My face contorts in disgust at the memory. "I couldn't move or scream, and when I tried to get away, they grabbed my throat. I could hardly breathe."

I gloss over the details, claiming it was more a feeling than anything concrete, but that's a lie. "It was a long time ago, but sometimes it'll just come back to me, you know? I think that nasty creek water triggered the memory." I look down at the bedspread beneath me, tracing the faded thread lines with my fingers.

"You want to talk about it?"

I shake my head. "I just wish I could forget it."

"Maybe I can help with that."

I look up at Caleb. His crooked little grin feels like home. He reaches out his hand, and I take it, curling up beside him. The memories, the nightmare, the guilt—they won't be silenced. Maybe I can forget, at least for a moment, but it won't last. Tucked under his arm, I let the beat of his heart, his soapy freshness, and the warmth of his embrace quiet the voices in my mind until the sun comes up, shining light on all that refuses to stay hidden.

THIRTY-NINE

Kinsley: July 30, 2008

With Caleb back at work and Annie nursing a heartbreak, the morning creeps by slowly. I sit cross-legged on the couch, sipping my coffee as every stupid choice I've made since graduation runs on a loop through my mind. I've only made things worse and haven't moved any further down the chessboard. Flipping through channels, I search for a distraction, but the choices are slim. I look around the room, blowing out a slow puff of air, when my eyes land on a photo album. I pull it from the side table and open it to reveal age-yellowed sheets of memories not my own.

A few pages in, I find a baby picture with Caleb's name written in cursive beneath. Below that is a photo of Caleb and his brother. Caleb must have been about four or five, standing just a smidge taller than James, with a lopsided grin, his brown hair curling at the tips. The pictorial timeline progresses to class photos, where I watch Caleb transform from a child to a young man before my eyes. But something stands out to me—a familiarity. I set the album aside and rummage through my purse, pulling out the photo from Ben's sixteenth birthday. I return to the album and compare the boys in the photo to Caleb's class picture for confirmation. It's him.

Caleb stands on one side of Ben while Landon is on the other. Anxiety creeps across my chest—but why? When we were fishing, he told me he was at Ben's party, so why does this feel like more than an echo of something I already know? I'm probably just paranoid and anxious from my conversation with Landon yesterday. Now I'm looking under every rock for hidden sins. *Let it go.* Slipping the photo back into my bag, I take another swig of coffee and push the concern to the back of my mind.

At the end of the album I find a picture of Caleb's parents. He has his father's smile and his mother's eyes. They look young and happy. The date below the photograph is 1982. How would their lives have turned out if it wasn't for the layoff? I trace my fingers along the edges of the photo and think of Caleb growing up too soon and of Annie growing up without a mother. I look around at the little home they've made and wonder what could have been.

Guilt weighs heavy on my heart, knowing that everything fell apart for Caleb's family when my dad knocked over that first domino in the line. If I can stop that from happening to another family, shouldn't I? What will happen to the employees at CHI if my dad goes to prison and the company goes bankrupt? There's no room for more guilt—not after facing the truth about what happened to Gabe. Maybe working for my dad, even if it means being CFO, is the right thing to do. I might be able to fix things, or at least keep my dad from making things worse. He has, after all, cleaned up all of my messes before. Still, will it be enough? Without Landon and the merger, can we even make it?

FORTY

Caleb: July 30, 2008

My phone rings just as I start the truck. It's the same number that has been calling me all week. At first, I thought it might be James needing bail again, so I let it go to voicemail. I can't take another hit to my dream, not now that it seems like I might actually cross the finish line. Turns out it wasn't James, but I let it ring anyway.

When I get back to the house on my lunch break, Annie is holed up in her room. One day she seems better, and the next day, the world is over. Kinsley says it's normal, part of the process—just give her time to heal. It's a comfort to know that she has Kinsley to talk to. She can relate to Annie better than I ever could.

Kinsley joins me at the table while I eat my lunch, but she's distracted and less chatty than usual. "You got something on your mind?"

"Always." She offers a fake smile and lets out a sigh. "I think I need to go ahead and take the job."

"With your dad?"

She nods. "I owe him, and it's the right thing to do."

I think about what this means for her. I don't know all the details, but I know this is something she's been running from all summer. "Will it make you happy?" I ask, but I already know the answer. She's not quick to reply and leans in to kiss me instead. When she pulls away, with a hint of worry in her eyes, she says, "You make me happy."

Before I leave the driveway, I take out my phone and listen to the latest voicemail. It's almost a word-for-word copy of the previous seven. I punch in the number, and anticipation spreads across my chest as the line trills three times.

"Hello, this is Caleb Lewis. I'm returning your call." I fidget with the tattered threading of the steering wheel and listen to the voice on the other end of the line. "Tomorrow? Yeah, I can do that. Around noon?" I wait for confirmation before I end the call and head back to work.

* * *

I put the last clean dish away and the house phone rings. It's Brittany calling for Annie. "Just a sec," I tell her and carry the receiver to the front porch where she and Kinsley are watching the lightning in the distance.

"Phone's for you, Annie." I hold it out and she takes it, scurrying inside, the screen door banging shut behind her. I sit down beside Kinsley, reaching for her hand and fitting it inside mine. "Storm's coming this way."

She closes her eyes, taking a deep breath. "I can smell it." The mineral-tinged earthy breeze floats in and mosquitoes come out to hunt their prey.

"Annie seems better tonight," I say.

"You never told me why you and Jessica broke up."

"Alright…" I wonder at the subject change, looking down at Kinsley's hand in mine. "You really want to talk about this right now?"

She shrugs. "I'm just curious. That's all."

"She wasn't ready to settle down and I was."

"But you guys were together for so long–"

"Yeah, but she–she just wasn't ready."

"How much more settled down could you be? You guys were practically married in high school."

I look out at the orange-gray sky, like a quiet apocalypse approaching, and remember the night Jessica ended things. "It's one thing to be a couple, it's another to be a family."

"Family?"

"Look, I don't want Annie to know this, okay?" I peek over my shoulder and lower my voice. "But, Jess wasn't ready to be a stand-in mom for her. It was just too much responsibility. Annie was devastated when she left. I couldn't tell her the real reason she said no."

"Said no?"

"I–" Jessica's words break free from the grave, coming to life again in my head and my heart. *Marrying you wouldn't just make me your wife,*

I'd basically become a mom to Annie. I'm not ready to sign my life away to that.

"I proposed. That's when we broke up. And Annie knew about the proposal. She was so excited."

"I'm sorry, Caleb," Kinsley whispers, squeezing my hand.

I close my eyes, forcing back the memories that flood the surface. It was the first time I could relate to my dad, the first time I could understand the need to lose yourself in the only thing that numbs the pain. I spent my entire paycheck trying to drown the heartache, and when Gram found me, she lit into me like a cat on a June bug. *You know what this does to the people who care about you. You're better than this.* Then she reminded me, in her not-so-subtle manner, that she wouldn't be around forever and Annie needed stability—not a useless drunk of a father figure. She already had one of those. When I sobered up, I promised Gram, and myself, that I'd do better. The last of the liquor remains buried in the freezer. I haven't touched it since then.

* * *

Light rain patters outside the windows as Kinsley snuggles up to me, laying her head on my chest. "Caleb, can I ask you something?"

"Mm-hmm." I kiss her head, breathing in the scent of her shampoo.

"Did you ever think of me in high school?"

"Think of you?" I trail my fingers along her arm, bringing goosebumps to the surface. "I've known you since I met Ben in sixth grade... I—"

"I guess I'm asking *what* you thought about me. How did you see me back then?"

"Ben's little sister, Landon's girlfriend...quiet, maybe a little sad sometimes, but you seemed to have everything."

"Did you ever think of asking me out? I know you were with Jessica, but..."

"I never let myself think about it..." I sense by her silence that's not what she wanted to hear, but it's the truth—and not because I was dating Jessica. "It's just... Landon wasn't someone any of us guys wanted to piss off, and he made it known you belonged to him from the very beginning. Regardless of how it might have looked."

"What do you mean, regardless of how it might have looked?" She lifts her head and turns to face me.

"You know, the times when you guys were fighting or he was hooking up with someone else…"

Kinsley lets her head rest just under my chin and traces the letters on my shirt with her fingers. The quiet settles like heavy fog. "I wish I had though," I say, holding her closer as my shirt dampens under a quiet tear.

FORTY-ONE

Kinsley: July 30, 2000

Eight years earlier.

I hear footsteps running down the hall and wonder if Ben has come home to surprise me, but when my bedroom door flings open, I know it isn't Ben.

"Kins, have you heard?" Nikki asks, hurrying to my side and plopping down on the bed.

"Heard what?" I grab my head and sit up against the headboard. Nikki must know a miracle cure for the morning after. "You're so loud."

"Gabe never came home from the party last night."

"Are you kidding?" I rub my eyes, blinking the world into focus.

"No. Did you and Landon see him after you left?"

I shake my head, bringing on a hint of vertigo as Nikki continues. "His parents have been calling around, asking anyone who saw him last night to talk to the police. I guess they're hoping to piece something together so they can figure out where he went."

"Have you talked to them yet?"

"No, I came to see if you wanted to go together."

* * *

At the police station, we tell the officer everything we can remember from the night before. Well, maybe not everything. But what does Smirnoff have to do with anything anyway? When we get back to my house, Landon is waiting for me in the living room.

"Where were you? I tried calling." He stands up from the couch, gripping his Nokia in one hand.

"We were at the police station."

"What for?"

"Didn't you hear about Gabe?"

"Yeah, but what does that have to do with you?"

"They're just trying to piece the night together so they can find him," I say, kicking off my shoes and taking a seat cross-legged on the couch. "You should go down there. Tell them what you remember."

"I don't remember anything." He sits down next to me, letting his head drop against the oversized cushions.

"You don't remember fighting with him," Nikki asks.

"We didn't fight, Nikki." He whips his head to face her before turning to me. "What did you even tell them, Kinsley?"

"Just that you two had been fighting and he seemed upset when he left."

"Kinsley, why would you say that?" He rubs his face in frustration, but I don't understand what I did wrong.

"What? I just told the truth."

Nikki's phone rings and she answers it, walking out of the living room. Landon stands up, pacing the floor. "If something happened to him, they're going to look at us because of what you said."

I catch his hand as he walks by. "I was just trying to help. We didn't do anything, so what does it matter if they look at us or whatever?"

He jerks his hand away. "God, Kinsley, you're so naive."

"Guys," Nikki cuts in.

"What are you talking about?" I stand up, following him.

"You should have talked to me first–"

"It's not a big deal–"

"Guys," Nikki tries again, louder this time.

"Yes, Kinsley, it is a big deal."

"Guys," she shouts. "They found him."

I turn to look at Nikki, but her face doesn't match the good news. Fear catches in my throat. "What is it?"

"He was hit," Nikki says. "I guess he was walking home from the party and someone hit him and left…" She stammers, "I don't–"

Broken flashes from the night before crowd my mind. The swerve, the thud, the screeching tires. "Oh, my god, Landon–" I collapse into him.

"Shhh." He holds me so close I can barely breathe, let alone speak. "Hey, Nik, I think Kins needs some time to process this. I'll have her call you later, okay?"

When the front door shuts, he releases me. My head is wobbly and heavy with fractured images. There isn't enough air to fill my lungs as my body becomes lighter and lighter. "I think… I think I'm–" I struggle to push words from a dry mouth. Landon helps me to the couch.

"You're having a panic attack, just breathe." He tilts my head forward between my knees and rubs my back. When gravity returns, I sit up and look at him, his eyes unreadable.

"I hit him," I say. It's barely a whisper.

"No, Kinsley." His voice is firm. "You didn't hit him."

"But Landon." I shake my head, tears rolling down my cheeks. "He was walking home from–"

"I know, Kinsley. I heard her, too. I'm not deaf."

"But–"

"I told you last night. It was a deer."

"What if it was…" Fear chokes me. "How do you know it was a deer?"

"Because I saw it." He grabs my hands, smoothing his thumb over my knuckles. His blue eyes soften, melting my fears. "I saw it." He wipes a tear from my cheek and pulls me close, kissing my head. "You need to get a hold of yourself. Now what did you tell the police?"

Through shaky breaths, I recount my statement as Landon sits silent, nodding in contemplation. "But, what if he dies?" I ask, tears breaking through again.

"That would be sad, but it would not be your fault." His voice is calm and steady as he smooths my hair, looking me in the eyes. "You hit a deer."

FORTY-TWO

Caleb: July 31, 2008

Why did I agree to this? This is what happens when you sell your soul to the devil. You end up in hell. I open the truck door and step out into the blazing heat.

Inside, the receptionist behind a green marble counter directs me. "Through the lobby, take the elevator to the fifth floor and follow the curved hall to your right."

When I reach my destination, I knock on a large wooden door, and it opens seconds later, revealing that son of a bitch Landon. "Hey, Caleb. Good to see you, man. Come on in."

That good old boy shit may work on everyone else, but it ain't fooling me. We're not friends.

"Caleb, please have a seat." Richard gestures to the black velvet chair in front of the desk as he sits down. Landon closes the door and follows, positioning himself in another chair, flanking the desk. "I'm sure you have an idea of why I called you in today," Richard starts.

"No." I offer nothing more as stoicism takes over in the face of my opponents, but of course I know. I only agreed to the meeting because I thought I might somehow be able to help Kinsley. How? I don't know, but I can't stand the thought of her giving up her life to work for her asshole father.

"Of course you do." Landon smirks. "Kinsley." The sound of his voice wearing her name stokes a fire inside me that threatens to burn down all traces of stoicism.

Richard clears his throat. "Look, Caleb, I know what happened with the accident and how Kinsley owes you money. I hate that she didn't come to me for help. I would have done anything she asked."

What a load of shit. Might as well be back on the farm mucking pens.

"Would have saved us all a lot of trouble," Richard continues. "What, with you two getting married just for the trust fund money–completely avoidable." He waves his hand. "And now, well, I know your life is in shambles and it's all Kinsley's doing. So I want to make it right. I'm ready to write you a check for every penny she owes you. We'll get this cleared up today, what do you say?"

"What do you want from me?" I ask, cutting through the bullshit.

"I'm sorry. Did I offend you? I'm just trying to do the right thing. Clean up another one of Kinsley's messes."

"That's it, huh? Just cleaning up her mess. Not asking me for anything in return."

Richard shrugs. "That's it."

"What happens to Kinsley?"

"No need to concern yourself with that. Family matters, we'll sort things out," Richard says. "But of course, we'll need you to sign this petition for annulment we've drawn up." He slides a stack of papers across the desk toward me. "No need to wait for the trust fund money if you walk out of here with a check, right?"

"You're paying me to leave your daughter?"

"Caleb," Landon says. "We all know that was the plan from the start. You two aren't *really* married. You're not in a relationship. You're just playing house until the marriage certificate comes. Kinsley told me everything." His face is so smug, so condescending. It's practically begging for my fist.

"Everything?" *If she'd told you everything you'd be trying to kick my ass right now.*

Landon nods. "Yeah we had a good long talk Tuesday. A real heart-to-heart, you know? She's sorry for dragging you into her little experiment with independence. We have such a long history. We always knew we'd get back together." He leans forward and winks. "We rekindled the fire if you know what I mean."

His smug face is about to know what my fist means. I grip the armrest of the chair and clench my mouth to hold back the words I want to say. Kinsley *has* been distant the last couple of days, but I'm not ready to believe Landon. Not yet anyway.

Richard clears his throat. "We all knew it would end at some point. This is just a way of expediting it." He holds out a pen. "I just want my family back, Caleb. Surely you can understand."

"Oh," Landon says. "And as a little thank you for taking such good care of my fiancé, I'd like to pay the difference you need to buy the farm."

"I don't want your money, Landon."

"It's the least I could do, Caleb. After all, you've allowed her to live in your home. I know how difficult she can be."

"Nah, it's fine. You don't owe me anything," I say, standing up. Doubt, anger, and disappointment form a tornado of heat inside my chest, and I have to get out of here before I lose control.

Even if the marriage started out as a business arrangement and divorce was always part of the plan, why should Richard be concerned with an annulment? Unless that's what Kinsley wants. Did she see Richard and Landon on Tuesday? Maybe those were the errands she mentioned. She must need *all* of the trust fund money.

As much as I fought it in the beginning, all I want now is to keep Kinsley in my life and Annie's. If she needs all of the trust fund to cut ties with her dad and Landon once and for all, I'll do anything to make it happen. It's not just about my dream anymore.

✳ ✳ ✳

I don't stop at the house for a lunch break but grab a quick bite at the drive through before heading back to the farm. When I knock on Mr. Cunningham's door, I take a deep breath, running through the words I planned on the drive over.

Mr. Cunningham opens the front door of his ranch-style home, the comforting scents of cedar and cinnamon with a touch of vanilla welcome me. "Caleb, come on in, son. What can I do you for?"

"I need to talk to you about our agreement," I say, taking a seat on the well-loved couch to my right. Mr. Cunningham takes a seat in the gingham armchair across from me. "I hate to do this, but I'm not going to be able to go through with it. I'm really sorry."

"Caleb, I… I know moving up my retirement wasn't ideal for you, but is there any way… I just hate to see you give up after coming so far."

"I know." I exhale, wringing my hands together. "But something's come up with the funding I thought I had secured and…well it…" The words resist, but I push through, cutting ties with all I've worked for. "I'm really sorry. It's not going to happen. You should go ahead with the next buyer in line. I'll be happy to stay on as long as I'm needed." I stand to leave, and Mr. Cunningham does the same but with less agility.

"Are you absolutely certain, Caleb? There's no other way?"

I nod and extend my hand. "I can never repay you for all the kindness and support you've shown me. Aside from Gramps, you're the closest I've had to a father figure. I hope you know how much I appreciate you, Mr. Cunningham."

He takes my hand, shaking it with a firm grip, just like he and Gramps taught me. "I love you, son," he says, pulling me in for a hug. The frailty under aging skin, the plaid-collared shirt that smells of leather and mint, it reminds me so much of Gramps that I almost cry.

FORTY-THREE

Kinsley: July 31, 2008

I pick up to-go orders from Buddy's with what's left of my earnings, and when I arrive back at the house, Eric's green Ninja is parked in front of the garage. *What the actual fuck?* I'm ready to give this kid a piece of my mind, but when I open the front door, I find Annie and a shirtless Eric tangled up in each other's arms, making out on the couch.

"What the hell is going on?" My voice takes on an authoritarian tone I never could have imagined.

"Oh, my god, Kinsley," Annie says, face burning red as she scrambles away from Eric. "We made up—"

"You made up?" I'm shouting now, and though I only meant to send my anger toward Eric, I can see it has landed on Annie as well.

"Why are you mad?" she asks, standing up from the couch as Eric pulls his shirt over his head.

"Annie, you told me he cheated on you."

"It was all a misunderstanding." Eric stands up, arms out as a gesture of peace.

Not falling for it punk, I know your type.

"Kinsley, please. You don't understand. He explained everything to me."

I watch as Annie defends him, the boy who tore out her heart just days ago. I've been there—naive, confused, hopeful. The rumors, the incriminating photos. I begged Landon to tell me the truth, but he would say over and over again that I was just being insecure or it was a misunderstanding. There was always a convincing explanation. And eventually, I would drop it—in part because I wasn't entirely convinced he had done anything wrong, but if I'm being honest, I was terrified of losing him. Like Ben, like my mom.

"What's going on here?" Caleb asks as he walks through the door. His voice is rough and his eyes zero in on Eric.

"We're just hanging out," Annie tells him.

"No. You were not *just hanging out*." I shake my head, knowing exactly where this *hanging out* was going if I hadn't come in the door when I did. Caleb turns to me, eyebrows pulled tight. "They were full-on making out when I walked in–"

"Kinsley!" Annie's face takes on a deeper shade of red. "Oh, my god. I can't believe you would–"

"What? Tell your brother what I saw? Annie, this isn't okay. Don't you remember anything from yesterday? You were so hurt–"

"Shut up," she yells, tears rolling down her cheeks. "Come on, Eric, let's go." She takes his hand and starts for the door, but Caleb blocks them.

"You're not going anywhere with him."

"Whoa, hey–" Eric says.

"You got something to say, boy?" Caleb takes a step closer to block their exit, and I wedge myself between them.

"Don't," I whisper, glancing over my shoulder at Caleb before turning back to Eric. "Look, we have some things to discuss as a family, so you need to go."

Still holding Annie's hand, Eric turns to kiss her right in front of Caleb. This kid is playing with fire. Does he actually have a death wish? I press my back against Caleb's chest, a warning not to try anything, and I can feel the anger emanating from him. When the screen door slams, I let my head fall back and relax for a half second.

"Annie," Caleb and I start at the same time.

"You go ahead." I say, closing the front door.

"Annie, why are you doing this? You were crying over him yesterday. You said he cheated on you and–"

"You don't understand!"

"I understand he's a little asswipe coming in here–"

"No he's not, Caleb! He's my boyfriend and I… I love him. So deal with it." Annie stands her ground, arms crossed like a toddler as she wells up with tears.

"How did this even happen?" I ask, leading Annie to the couch.

"He came over to apologize, he even brought me flowers," she says through tears. "It was just a misunderstanding."

"But how, Annie? You saw them together with your own eyes. You told me so."

"It wasn't what it looked like." Annie sniffles.

"What else could it have possibly been?"

"You don't know anything, Kinsley. You weren't there!"

Ouch. I didn't expect Annie to lash out at me like that. At Caleb? Sure, but not *me.* "It just seems like he's playing you, Annie. You deserve better than that."

"He's not playing me, okay?" Her voice elevates as tears run down her face. "He loves me, and I love him, and it's none of your business."

I look at Caleb, who's hunched forward in the armchair, rubbing his temples. "Annie, maybe you should let us have a minute. I need to talk to Caleb, okay?"

"Whatever," she says, stomping off to her room and slamming the door behind her.

A dozen pink roses sit on the coffee table. Apology gifts, explanations, charm—it's right off a page from Landon's playbook. *But what if it isn't?* I didn't see what Annie did at the rec center. There's at least a slight margin for error.

"I don't like him," Caleb says as he leans back against the chair, dropping his arms.

"I don't either, but what can we do?"

"Tell her she can't see him anymore."

"Do you think that will stop her? My god, she was convinced he was cheating on her yesterday and she's already forgiven him, Caleb. Telling her she can't see him isn't going to work. Trust me."

"Then what?" He looks at me and he's exhausted, broken, helpless in navigating this new terrain with Annie. I want to help, but I don't know what to tell him. Annie deserves better than someone who's going to make her doubt herself and their feelings for her, but how can *I* make her see that? I've only this summer come to see that better *is* out there and that I deserve it too.

FORTY-FOUR

Landon: July 30, 2000

Eight years earlier.

"Remember what I told you, son," my dad says as he pushes the elevator button, illuminating the circle with a number five in the center. "Let me do the talking. If I need your input I'll ask for it."

When the metal doors slide open, I follow him down the long hallway to Richard's office. We haven't even had a chance to knock when Richard ushers us into the room. "Devon," Richard says, extending his hand.

"Richard, I'd say it's nice to see you, but under the circumstances…"

"Yes." His tone is grim, but he attempts the social standards anyway. "Would you like a whisky?"

"No thank you, we have more pressing concerns."

"Right." Richard gestures to the chairs in front of his desk, and we each take a seat.

"Look Richard, I'm sure you know there was an incident last night," my dad says.

"Terrible news."

"Yes, has Kinsley mentioned anything to you?"

"Nothing specific, no."

"Well, Landon told me everything." He looks at me but relays the information himself. "Kinsley was upset, drinking too much, making a scene. Landon tried to calm her down but she was irate, uncontrollable–you know how she can be."

Richard nods with shame, and my dad continues. "She stole Landon's truck keys and was nearly gone when he caught up with her. She refused to pull over, screaming and crying hysterically. Landon did everything he could, even jerking the wheel to avoid the collision but, well…"

"I see…" Richard says, horror washing out the natural color of his face.

"She was out of control to begin with, and Landon was quick in his thinking, I'll give him that." He gives me a firm pat on the back. "Considering the challenge he had on his hands with your daughter, he managed the situation quite well. He convinced her to let him drive after that." My dad clears his throat. "After she hit the *deer.*"

"Deer?" Richard stammers. "But I thought you–"

"Let me finish, Richard."

I watch my dad, always calm, contained. Nothing like Richard who blubbers under pressure, weak and scared. "Now I've spoken with my brother-in-law, Chief Birmingham, and he's doing everything he can, but there are risks, of course. We have to be smart about this. My companies and yours have a lot to lose. Do you follow?"

Richard's eyes dart between us. "I–I think so."

"Last I heard, Gabe was in surgery and has multiple more to go. He's in for a long fight if he's going to make it. There's no way of knowing if he'll remember anything, that is, if he even lives." A heaviness settles in the silence, all that is unsaid but understood.

"We think it would be best to do something for the family," my dad says. "After all, Gabe is a friend of Landon's and Ben's. And his father works here, doesn't he?"

"Yes, lower management." Richard says.

"The medical expenses will be substantial if he pulls through. They could be looking at long-term care, and if he doesn't, then there's the funeral cost. It would be good to set up a fund for the family. Something other businesses and individuals can contribute to if they like. Hawk-Reynolds will be putting in 200k. Can CHI match that?"

Richard's eyes widen and he flusters a response. "Oh, yes. Of course. That's–that's only fair."

"Good to hear. Now as for the truck, yes it's Landon's, but let's not forget who was driving it… Kinsley. Drunk. And without a license. Nonetheless, we're dealing with the vehicle. Landon was planning to get a new car before school starts anyway, and we've made arrangements for the truck. But like I said... *Kinsley.*"

"Yes, yes." Richard leans forward on his elbows, eyes full of submission. "What... What do you need from me?"

My dad takes a deep breath. "As I mentioned, my brother-in-law is doing what he can, but he could use a little...incentive to make it worth his while."

"I see," Richard says, his voice lowered. "And how much would that be?"

"Well, I don't know exactly, Richard. What's your daughter's future worth to you?"

FORTY-FIVE

Kinsley: August 1, 2008

I open my eyes and the room is dark. I'm not sure why I'm awake—Caleb is sleeping next to me, it's not raining, and the house is quiet. I flip on my side, curling up next to him, and close my eyes. My phone dings, signaling a new voicemail, and I'm hit with a wave of anxiety. No one calls at this hour to chat or sell you an extended warranty. No, this hour is reserved for emergencies—for matters that can't wait until morning.

I grab my phone from the nightstand. The missed call is a local number—not Ben. *Thank god.* My dad? Nikki? Landon's mom? Holding the phone to my ear, I listen to the recording. "Kinsley, it's me. It's um… Annie. Look I'm really sorry about all this but…" The background noise bleeds through, making it hard to hear everything she says. Music, crashing, laughter. A party. And my heartbeat doubles with the realization that Annie isn't here.

Annie. Isn't. Here.

"I just… I need a ride, okay? I'm sorry. I know you're gonna be mad and Caleb's gonna be… Just can you…I need a ride and I don't…" Annie's words are slow and heavy. Likely from drinking.

Panic grips my chest, and the recording ends. *Where the hell are you?* I look at the number and type it into the browser on my phone. It's a landline listed under Helen and Frank Marcoby.

"You okay?" Caleb asks, pushing himself up on his elbows.

Shit. "No. Umm… Well, I am, but Annie's not."

"Is she sick?" He sits up completely, rubbing his eyes.

"I don't know, but she needs to be picked up from–"

"Picked up? She's not in her room?" He shoots out of bed, storming through the house. Doors open and shut as he calls out her name. I throw on a pair of shorts and sandals while calling the number back, but no one answers. Caleb returns to the room, red faced and wide awake.

"What the hell? Did you know about this?"

"No, Caleb, of course I didn't." I would be offended, but I understand his concern. I feel it too. "She called from this number, it belongs to the Marcoby family. I'm trying to find the address." I struggle to type without error, my hands as jittery as if I chugged a triple shot espresso. "Okay, here–it's out by the lake."

Caleb dresses and I toss him the keys, then hold out my phone to show him the address. "I'll keep trying the number while you drive."

* * *

The ride is a long string of unanswered calls with worry building the more distance we cover. I want to tell Caleb I'm sorry—that it's all my fault, but I can't bring myself to speak what I already know he's thinking.

"This is it." I point to a craftsman-style house, the curved driveway packed with cars. Caleb pulls the truck over by the curb and parks, hopping out before I can unbuckle.

"Annie," he hollers as I run to catch up with him. The house is ridiculously full of people. Music blaring and kids drinking, laughing, making out—it's like I stepped back in time.

I call Annie's name, but it's no use, I'd need a bullhorn to be heard. Caleb charges on through the front room, so I head upstairs. Standing at the top of the landing, I scan the party below but can't see her. Behind me, a bathroom door is open and a group of girls are primping in front of the mirror. "Do you know Annie Lewis?" I ask them, but they don't.

I turn back to the hall. Three lanky guys in Von Dutch hats walk toward me, laughing and smelling of weed. "Have you seen Annie Lewis? Or Eric Birmingham?" I ask. They offer no help, but they do offer me a joint.

Shit. I proceed down the hall, peeking inside room after room—no sign of Annie. Someone taps on my shoulder, and I turn around to find one of the girls from the bathroom mirror. "I don't know Annie, but I heard you ask those guys about Eric. I saw him earlier. You might check the game room. It's up one more floor." I thank her and run upstairs.

The landing is small with two doors and a tall window. I try the first door, but it's a closet. I reach for the knob on the second door and place my ear against the wooden panel. I hear a muffled conversation—no screaming or crying. Nothing to alert suspicion. But when I try to open the door, the knob won't turn. I knock and jiggle the handle again.

"Room's occupied," a male's voice calls out, followed by laughter.

"I'm just looking for someone. Is Eric in there?" I ask.

"Who wants to know?"

"Just a friend... I've got some weed." I don't plan on handing over the joint, but it works. Seconds later, the door opens and I'm face to face with Eric. He's barefoot, wearing only his jeans, his hair in disarray, and eyes glassy. It takes him a minute to recognize me, which I use to my advantage and shove past him.

"Where's Annie?" The room is a mess of bottles, cans, and a few pieces of clothing crumpled on the floor. "Where is she, Eric? I know she came here with you."

"Annie?" Caleb calls from the hallway. His voice grows louder with his approach. I turn and he has tackled Eric to the floor. The other two boys scamper out of the room, leaving Eric to fend for himself.

"Caleb, stop!" I try to pull him off the kid. "You'll go to jail."

"Fine by me."

"No, not fine. We need to find Annie and he can't help us if he's unconscious." Eric's face is pure trepidation. Caleb lets out a sharp huff and stands up as Eric cowers against the wall.

"Stay right there, Eric." I point to him. "Don't move or I'll let him go another round." The kid wipes his face and nods.

Caleb looks like hell. Behind him is a door, probably just a closet, but I move past him and try it anyway. It's not a closet but a bathroom, and Annie is balled up on the floor.

"Oh, god. Annie." I bend down beside her, grabbing a towel from the rack and covering her body. "Annie, can you hear me?" Her eyes flutter, she's breathing at least, though nearly unconscious it seems.

"What the hell did you do to her?" Caleb roars at Eric on the other side of the doorway. I look back at him to make sure he's not killing the kid, though I'm not sure I'd stop him at this point. I leave Annie to search for her clothes in the game room as Caleb shouts obscenities and potentially criminal threats at Eric. I have to get him out of here.

I find a sundress Annie borrowed from me. It's crumpled up in the corner, and I take it to her, helping her into it. "Can you walk?" I ask, but she's groggy and weak. I peek my head out of the bathroom and call for Caleb to help.

He scoops Annie up into his arms and I look around for any more of her belongings but see none. My eyes settle on Eric. Caleb's tongue lashing has had an effect, but as pathetic as he looks, all I can think about is slugging his pretty-boy face. "This isn't over, Eric," I tell him and slam the door behind me.

I catch up with Caleb and Annie at the bottom of the stairs and follow them out the front door. We make our way through the maze of parked cars under the black sky, dotted with stars. When we get to the truck, I jump in and hold my arms out to collect Annie as Caleb places her in the cab.

* * *

Back at the house, we transfer Annie to her bed, and I sit with her. In case she wakes up or gets sick. When she starts to stir, I reach for her hand. "Hey, shhh. It's okay, Annie. You're home now."

"What?" She squints, taking in the dim room, and when her eyes find mine, they're wide with a mix of shame and heartache. "How did I... What?" Annie asks, propping herself up against the pillows.

"I got your voicemail. We came to pick you up—"

"You what? You... How did you..."

"Annie, you were in trouble. You called saying you needed a ride. We came to—"

"How could you?" she shouts. "You mean Caleb too?" She spirals into a hyperventilating bundle of tears and hysterics.

"We came because you needed us. You were..." I don't want to speak the words aloud.

She doubles over, hands cradling her tears. "It's not what you think," she whispers. "It was just a game, Kinsley. It's not a big deal—"

"I found you nearly passed out and naked in the bathroom at a party. That is the definition of a big deal."

"I was fine. It's just part of the game."

"What the hell kind of game is this, Annie?"

She doesn't speak but sniffles into her hands. "Annie," I say, rubbing her back. "Come on, talk to me."

"It's called flip, sip, or strip," she says and I wait for more because I haven't heard of this game. But the name says it all.

"Someone flips a coin and you call it. If you're wrong you take a drink or take off a piece of clothing." *Shit.* She sits up, wipes her face, and takes a deep, shaky breath, avoiding my eyes. "The guys asked me and Brittany to play, but after two rounds, Brittany and Dustin went off to hook up. So it was just me, Eric, and two of his friends." She pauses, still refusing to look at me, and fumbles with her hands. "After two more rounds I didn't have anything left to strip…"

She stops for a moment, wrapping her arms around her waist. *Fuck, this isn't good.*

"So they made up a new rule," she says quietly. I'm nauseous. I want her to stop talking. I want to wake up—this has to be a nightmare.

But it isn't.

"I mean, it was okay at first, because it was mostly Eric, and I wanted him to… You know." She wipes her cheeks and pulls her knees to her chest. "But then things got foggy, and I don't really know *exactly* what happened. I just remember…" Annie shuts down, dropping her head on her knees, jerking with sobs.

"Annie," I whisper, placing a hand on her back. "What *do* you remember?"

She recalls choppy bits and pieces of the night, and it's enough for me to see the whole picture even if she doesn't see it yet. And when she describes the horror of being pinned down, unable to fight back, unable to stop the violating pain that ripped through her, I know *exactly* what she's talking about.

I know Annie's pain and humiliation. I know her shame and disgust. I know her mourning and her heartbreak. I know them because they are also my own. I have known abuse, though I mislabeled it love. But long before that, before I ever dated Landon, a monster snuck into my room and stole a piece of my soul.

It was never a dream.
It was more than a nightmare.
It was real.

* * *

"I'm so sorry, Caleb," I whisper and sit down on the side of the bed
"It's not your fault, Kins."
"Yes, it is. If it wasn't for me, none of this would have happened–"
"You didn't know Eric would–" His jaw is clenched and he exhales through his nose. "You didn't know."
"But I encouraged you to let her date Eric. If you hadn't let me stay here–"
"Don't." He joins me on the bed, shifting his weight so he faces me. "Don't say that. You've done so much for Annie, for me. You're like the missing piece I didn't know we needed." I lean into him and he wraps his arms around me. Even now in the middle of this mess, he feels like home.
"Anyway," he says, rubbing my back. "I called the police station. They said they could send an officer out or she could come in and file a report."
I sit up and take his hand. "I'll talk to her again in the morning, but I think she's still processing. She blames herself for playing a stupid party game."
"But she was drunk."
"She blames herself for that too." I shake my head, knowing he's not going to like what I tell him next. "She said that her plan was to hook up with Eric all along. Then things got out of hand… She doesn't remember saying no."
"That doesn't mean anything." He pulls his hand away and his voice grows louder. "She was drunk. Hell, she couldn't even walk, how could she make a consenting decision like that?"
"I agree with you, Caleb. I do." He's so tense I can see the anger pulsing under his skin. I place my hand on his cheek, running my thumb

over the stubble. "She needs to rest, sleep off the alcohol. We can talk to her in the morning."

* * *

The room is dark and quiet and tense. I'm curled up in Caleb's arms, crying. He thinks I'm crying for Annie, and I am. But I'm also crying for the twelve-year old girl who had to stay home because her friend got sick. I'm crying for the girl who fell asleep reading *Through the Looking Glass* while a thunderstorm raged outside. I'm crying for the girl who woke up to a monster stealing her innocence.

I'm crying for the girl who had no one to tell.

The girl who felt disgusting and alone.

The girl who told herself it wasn't real.

The girl that has carried this nightmare for years.

The girl who, tonight, opened her eyes to the truth.

The girl who still doesn't know who raped her.

I'm crying for that girl.

I'm crying for me.

FORTY-SIX

Kinsley: August 2, 2008

It's morning and Annie won't leave her room. She doesn't want to talk. She doesn't want to go to the clinic. I'll try again in a couple of hours, but I recognize the emptiness in her eyes. Shame, depression, self-loathing. They take up every inch and leave no space for hope or healing.

"You alright?" Caleb asks, walking toward me in the hall.

I shake my head, swallowing back tears. "Just have a lot on my mind." He holds his hand out to me, and I take it, allowing him to pull me into his arms, and I stand here, listening to his heartbeat. Listening for what's true—listening for anything that might put an end to my fear that it was Caleb who raped me the night of Ben's birthday party.

* * *

As usual, Nikki has gone all out decorating for the day. *Happy Unbirthday Kinsley* a banner reads, hanging from one end of the camper to a nearby tree. Nikki opens the door, blowing a noisemaker and wearing a party hat. I climb the steps and hug her. "You're too much, Nik." I roll my eyes, kicking balloons out of my way that float near the floor.

"Yeah, sorry this heat is killing the balloons."

"It's fine. You always overdo it."

"You only have one unbirthday, Kins."

"No, actually I have 364, but we just celebrate this one." I plop down on the mini sofa. I hate my birthday. I'd like to erase it from the calendar. Why celebrate the day that took my mother's life? Clouded with mourning, it can never be a day of celebration.

My dad has never handled it well. It's just too hard for him. So Nikki started a tradition of celebrating my *unbirthday* instead, thanks, in part, to my insistence on watching *Alice in Wonderland* at countless sleepovers.

"How's Annie doing?" Nikki asks, handing me a huge cookie sandwich filled with buttercream icing.

"Not good, she doesn't want to eat or even leave her bed. I get it though, I was the same way."

"What do you mean?"

I set the cookie aside and focus my eyes on my lap. "God, this is hard."

"Kins… What is it?"

"Something happened to me a long time ago, and… I wasn't even sure if it was real. I thought maybe it was a dream, but I've been thinking about it lately. And last night with Annie, it was like I was right there living it all over again."

"Hold on, Kins. Are you telling me you were…" *Why is it such a hard word to say?*

"Remember Ben's sixteenth birthday when I was supposed to sleep over at your house but you were sick?"

Nikki tilts her head. "I think so… Kins, what's going on? Did something happen at the party?"

My stomach is twisting and my heart is breaking. Speaking the words out loud makes it real. "I woke up in the middle of the night and someone was on top of me and they… They raped me."

"Oh, my god, Kinsley. Why didn't you tell me?" Nikki reaches for my hand.

"I was scared, Nik. I didn't– I was so embarrassed and ashamed. And I got sick after he left, so I thought maybe I had a bug like you and it was just a bad dream." I squeeze my eyes to shut out the memory. "I didn't want it to be real."

"Who was it?"

"I still don't know, Nik." I fill my lungs with an unsteady breath. "I woke up with him on my back, pressing me into the mattress. I tried to see, but it was too dark and he was so heavy… I couldn't push him away."

"Do you–was it… I mean, was it a *man* or a boy?"

"Oh, god, it wasn't my dad if that's what you're asking. It couldn't have been. He smelled awful, like fish and dirt and sweat. It was disgusting." I fold forward onto my knees like I've been sucker punched, remembering the night.

"Do you remember who was there that night?"

I nod and sit back up. "Well Ben, of course, and Caleb, Gabe, and Landon."

"Are you sure? Was there anyone else?"

"I don't think so... I found this picture from the party and they were in it." I reach into my purse and pull out the photo I've been carrying around and show it to Nikki. Four boys in typical nineties apparel, plaid shirts and cargo pants. And one of them is a monster in disguise.

"Do you remember what he was wearing?" she asks, squinting to examine the photo.

"I hardly saw him, except when he was leaving and it was dark."

"Think, Kins. Did you feel any clothing? Or maybe hear anything–"

"I don't know, Nik!" I snap at her in frustration and I hate it. I know she's only trying to help, but I can't give her answers. I just don't have them. I drop my head into my hands, leaning over my knees. How can I make any sense of the darkness I'm staring into? Nikki rubs my back, comforting me and bringing me back into orbit. I draw in a calming breath and allow my mind to travel into the recessed corners, the darkest places. The places I've tried to avoid.

Party favor.

The jingling of a belt buckle.

A zipper.

That's all I remember hearing. "Maybe he wore a belt." I take the photo from Nikki, unsure if I'm ready to learn the truth it holds.

"Ben and Gabe," I whisper, pressing my fingers to my lips and blinking out fresh tears. "But there's no way it was Ben. He couldn't–he wouldn't... He just..." Another wave, this one with a sweeping undertow.

"Shhh." Nikki puts her arm around me. "Okay, look, that doesn't necessarily mean it was one of them. We can't see if Landon or Caleb are wearing belts. Their shirts hang over too far."

"Nik," I whisper. "What if it..." My heart breaks as I force the words from my mouth. "What if it was Caleb?"

"Is there something that makes you think–"

"The skating party, remember? He asked me to skate. Maybe he had been waiting for a chance to…"

"I don't know, Kins. The skating– That's not really the same kind of thing. It just doesn't sound like Caleb."

"It doesn't sound like any of them, Nik."

Nikki looks down at the photo in my hands. "Actually, Kins, it does sound like–"

"Don't say it." Of course, she'll try to pin it on Landon. I never should have opened my mouth about our fights, hinting that things sometimes got out of hand. Landon might have been rough and controlling in our relationship, but that was only when he became angry. We weren't together back then. He didn't even pay attention to me at that age. Caleb *did*.

"Sorry for ruining the unbirthday celebration," I say.

"Don't be. This is more important, Kins. You should talk to someone–"

"And tell them what? Nik, I don't even know who it was." It's bad enough that I've been haunted by the memory of it, believing it was only a dream. Now I have to accept that it *did* happen without knowing who to blame.

"Okay, you're not ready," she whispers. "But just think about it, please."

FORTY-SEVEN

Caleb: August 2, 2008

In the time since Kinsley left for Nikki's, I've checked on Annie twice, started a load of laundry, and thought of countless ways I'd love to teach Eric and his friends a lesson. I hear the squeaky brakes of the postal truck as it comes to a stop, so I step out into the heat and retrieve the mail. Bills, junk mail, and one very official looking envelope with the county courthouse listed as the return address.

I open the envelope and unfold the document, running my thumb across the shiny gold seal—the marriage certificate. I hadn't forgotten about it, but I chose not to dwell on its impending arrival. What will it mean now? It was never my plan to fall for Kinsley. How do you divorce the woman you're falling in love with? What's the protocol for that—divorced but dating?

But staying married to her, that's another thing entirely. Am I really considering it now? *I am.* But is Kinsley? Since game night, we haven't talked about the plan to divorce, the trust fund, the marriage certificate. I don't know where she's at.

I'll do whatever she wants, even if it means divorcing like we planned. It's only a piece of paper. It doesn't define our relationship, and even if the marriage isn't real, our relationship is. I tuck the certificate back into the envelope, now heavier in my hands. The timing couldn't be better, with Kinsley's birthday tomorrow. I'm going to tell her that the farm deal is off and she can keep all of her trust fund. Handing her the marriage certificate will be the cherry on top.

I've been working on another gift for her as well, and it's almost finished. I enter the garage and tug on the pull chain overhead, illuminating the space. With sandpaper in hand, I smooth out the rough edges before dusting off the debris and opening the wood finish. As I apply the protective coating I think about Kinsley—her smile, her eyes, her laugh. The way she really cares for Annie. How she doesn't give up, even when she's in way over her head. Her tenacity and heart. That's what I love about her. *Love? Maybe.* I want to protect her and cheer for her. To see her happy and following her dreams. I'd do anything to make those things possible. Isn't that love?

Stepping back from my work, I give it a final inspection. The wood-stain fumes are giving me a headache. Dizzy and near nauseous, I clean up the work area, leaving the gift to dry, and step out into thick August air.

FORTY-EIGHT

Landon: August 2, 2008

"Hello?" I answer my cell, holding it between my shoulder and ear as I unbutton the collar of my dress shirt.

"Landon, it's Uncle Malcolm. Just calling to let you know I got my guys lined up for the third week of September. That work for you?"

Shit. I was hoping to have access to the land by now. I flip the pages of the day planner on my desk. "Landon? You there?"

"Yeah, sorry. Bad signal. Mmm, yeah should be okay… You know what, can I get back to you on that?" I walk across the den to the Palladian window framing the perfectly manicured backyard.

"Hell, Landon, what happened? I thought we were all set. I had to move a lot around to fit you in. We're booming down here and I can't miss–"

"I know. I know. It's just…" I turn my back to the view and walk over to my desk. "Never mind. I'll work it out. It'll be fine. Third week of September?"

"Yep, third week."

"Alright."

Damn it. I end the call, and notice a new text message from Sierra. *Almost there. xx.*

Shoving the phone in my pocket, I stare at the mess of schematics and maps strewn about my desk. If I can't gain access to the land through Kinsley, I'll have to convince Richard to lease. It won't be hard to persuade the old man, but my control and earnings will take a hit if I go that route.

The survey results show massive shale deposits under CHI. Tapping into the shale could save Richard's ass five times over, easy. He's sitting on a pot of gold and has no idea. The land might belong to the company, but the mineral rights belong to the family, and it's mine for the taking. After all, everyone expects Kinsley to marry me, and it's a smart move for both of us.

Fuck. She can be so irrational. And after all I've done for her, she repays me by fucking up my perfect plan. My head feels like it's in a vise, squeezing tighter and tighter by the second. Massaging my temples, I walk over to the wet bar and make myself an Old Fashioned. After two swigs and a deep breath, I consider the available plays to secure the mineral rights. Time is running out, and Kinsley is becoming more difficult every day.

The doorbell rings, and I walk to the front entry to greet Sierra. "There's my girl," I say as I open the door and try to cover my surprise.

"Landon, please. I'm not your girl. I just need to talk to you. It's really important." Kinsley brushes past me, making her way into the house. I close the door and follow her into the living room.

"What do you remember about the night of Ben's sixteenth birthday?" she asks.

I approach the subject with caution. "Alright… Random. That's when he got the Roadrunner, right?"

She nods and I take a seat beside her on the couch. "I think we stayed over at your house that night. I remember him driving us around and just hanging out. Can't remember much else. Why do you ask?"

"Do you remember who else was there? I mean besides you and Ben, obviously."

Where are we going with this? I run my hands over my face and exhale. "Gabe, Caleb, and Chase I think? Why?"

"Chase? Are you sure? He's not in this picture." She takes a photograph out of her purse and shows it to me.

"I don't know, Kins. It was forever ago. What's going on?"

Kinsley shifts her eyes downward, staring into the photo. "I think– no, I *know* something happened to me that night," she says, finally peeking up at me. Her eyes are full of questions.

"I don't follow."

"Someone," she starts with a shaky breath, "came into my room that night…and umm." Tears fill her eyes. "Someone did something to me, Landon. Someone raped me," she ends in a whisper.

"What?" I contort my face in disgust. "Who? Who did that to you, Kinsley?"

"I don't know." She sobs, and I pull her into my arms, smoothing her hair away from her face as she sprinkles my shirt with tears. "I never got a good look at him," she says with a sniffle before pulling away to compose herself. "And for the longest time, I thought it might have been a bad dream. I didn't even know if it was real."

I reach for her hands. "Okay, so how do you know it really happened, Kins?"

"Seriously?" She jerks her hands back. "Look, I just need to know if you remember anything from that night–"

"Kins, that was years ago. What could I possibly remember?"

"A lot, Landon. Come on, just try. It's important to me. Who else can I talk to?"

True. It would be better to have a say in the memory. Who knows what shit Caleb will come up with.

"Umm, okay. Like I said, we had been out in his car and came back to the house. Probably to eat or something. I vaguely remember hanging out in the game room, shooting pool, playing video games." I shrug.

"I need to know who did it, Landon–"

"Kins, it's not like anyone came out and said, *Yo, Ben I just fucked your sister while she was sleeping.*"

"How did you know I was sleeping?" Her eyes shoot to me in fear, and anger spikes in my chest.

"You *just* told me you were."

"No–"

"Yes, Kinsley. Remember, you said you thought you were dreaming... Obviously I took that to mean you were asleep. God, do you seriously think I had anything to do with it?"

"I don't know... I mean, no...but–"

"Kins, that's just sick. We've been together for years. I asked you to marry me, remember? Do you really think I'm capable of hurting you like that?" I look deep into her eyes, trying my best to connect with that part of her soul I once held.

She softens, lip trembling with regret. "But *who?*"

I sit silent for a moment, searching my mind and staring at the repeating gold triangles woven into the navy rug beneath my feet. "What do you remember?"

Her face pales and she squeezes her eyes shut. "I remember it was storming that night... Waking up to someone on top of me–it was hard to breathe, and they smelled awful. Like fish and sweat."

"Okay... Is that all?"

"Umm, he put his hand over my mouth to keep me quiet. I tried to bite him, but it didn't help. He just wouldn't stop, and..." Kinsley drops her face into her hands, sucking in a labored breath. I rub her back, and she seems to relax at my touch. A moment later, she sits up and continues. "I think he might have said something to me about a party favor, but I don't know–I'm not sure. And when it was over, he just left."

"Did you see him? Anything you can remember about how he looked or..."

She shakes her head. "It was dark. I was on my stomach, and he was behind me. How am I supposed to figure this out, Landon?"

"I don't know, Kins. I mean, we know it wasn't me. What about Ben–"

"It was *not* Ben. Don't you dare." She breaks into sobs, and I scoot closer to her, taking her hand in mine.

"So it had to have been Gabe, Chase, or Caleb. What does your gut say?"

"I don't know... Sure, I'm a little suspicious of Caleb since he let me move in and..." She stops, wipes her cheeks, and looks up to the ceiling. "But something about that night when Gabe died... The way he was acting and talking to me. Do you think it could have been him?"

I study her face. Her eyes reveal brokenness and vulnerability. She wants answers, and I'll be the one to give them to her.

"Alright, look, Gabe *was* talking shit the night of the accident. You remember he and I had a fight?" She nods and I continue. "He was pissed about some girl dumping him or whatever–I don't know. Somehow my name got thrown into it, and he came up to me talking about how he had you first."

"What–are you serious? Landon, why didn't you ever tell me–"

"Kins, I–I had no idea." I place my hand on her knee, attempting to settle her down. "I thought he was drunk and talking out of his ass. I didn't know he was telling me the truth."

"So, he told you he…" She crumbles into tears again.

"Hell, Kinsley. He didn't say that he raped you. If he had, I would have killed him. He only implied that you guys hooked up before we got together. I figured he was just trying to piss me off. I never believed him."

Kinsley raises her tear-stained eyes to meet mine. "So it was him? It was Gabe."

I offer the slightest of nods and whisper, "I guess so."

"And he's dead…because of *me.*"

*"*Kins, it was an accident. You didn't do it on purpose. But look, if you do something stupid like turn yourself in and the police learn that Gabe raped you, it won't look like an accident anymore. You have to be smart about all of this." Her brows furrow in response, but she nods in compliance.

We sit in silence for what feels like forever. She's as white as a ghost. After a deep breath, she wipes her eyes and stands up. "God, I'm a mess. Be right back," she says as she walks to the guest bathroom by the den. Once she's out of sight, I hurry to send Sierra a message. *Something came up. I'll let you know when I'm home.* No more than ten seconds later, she's calling me. I hop up, taking the call to the front porch.

"Now's not a good time, babe. Just grab some coffee or something. I'll call you back, but *do not* come over yet." I end the call and go back into the house.

"How could you?" Kinsley shouts, waving papers at me.

Fuck. The shale deposits. "Kins, calm down. I can explain–"

"You bought the farm so Caleb couldn't. Just because I won't marry you? You're such an asshole!"

"Whoa, babe." I hold my hands up and step back. "You don't understand."

"Why do you have this?" She shoves the papers on my chest.

"Because your dad and I talked to Caleb last week and worked out an arrangement–"

"What kind of arrangement?"

"Your dad offered him a check to cover the medical expenses, tractor repairs, all that–"

"How do you even know about–"

"Really, Kinsley? Do you think you can keep anything from your dad?" I shake my head, playing up her foolishness. "Anyway, Caleb wouldn't go for it. He refused to sign the petition for the annulment."

She narrows her eyes at me and starts again. "That doesn't explain why you–"

"He wanted *more*, Kinsley. He wouldn't do it without the farm."

"No, that doesn't make any sense." Her face scrunches up in confusion.

"I had to buy it for him," I say. "Just picked these up yesterday, I'm supposed to sign them over tomorrow."

"Why would he–no, we already had a plan, he didn't need you to…"

"Kins," I say softly, reaching for her hands. "Babe, it's never been real for him. It was always about the money and the farm. I told you he was just using you." She crosses her arms, hugging herself, and staring down at the polished wood floor. "You gotta understand, he's not like us. He grew up with nothing. You can't expect someone like him to say no to an offer like that." I tuck a piece of hair behind her ear. "It's not your fault you fell for it. He's always been a leech."

"I just–I don't understand."

I pull her to me, wrapping my arms around her. "It's alright, you don't need to understand. You just need to agree to the annulment and we'll move forward with the merger. Everything's going to work out like it was supposed to all along."

✳ ✳ ✳

July 29, 2000: Eight years earlier.

"You just couldn't stop yourself, could you?" Gabe says, shoving my shoulder, and I almost spill the bottle of whisky.

"Watch it, Gabe." I down a shot of Jack. "What's your problem?"

"You and Stephanie. You hooked up with her last year at the grad night party."

"Dude, I don't know what you're talking about." I turn back to the counter to pour another round, but Gabe hurries up beside me, eyes bugging out like a deranged owl.

"Bullshit! She told me."

I grin at the memory—that chick was wild. "Probably trying to make you jealous. What can I say, man? I'm a bit of a legend." Gabe's fist flies at my face, but I dodge it, knocking over a nearly full bottle of Goldschläger. "Fuck off, man. You're drunk." I say, reaching for a roll of paper towels to sop up the gold-speckled liqueur.

"You knew I was into her and you hooked up with her anyway," Gabe says, voice growing in volume. We've drawn quite an audience. "Your little jailbait piece of ass isn't enough for you? Hell, you screwed half the school. She must be desperate to stay with you—or maybe just fucked up from what you did to her all those years ago."

Alcohol and rage burn together, fuming in my chest. "You're talking out of your ass, bro."

Gabe hitches his upper lip. "You know exactly what I'm talking about."

I start to walk away when Gabe says, "Does she even know it was you? Or did you make up some shit and blame it on Ben? Huh, is that why he left?"

"You should stop talking now, Gabe." I grab him by the collar of his gray Abercrombie shirt, ready to beat the living shit out of him.

"Of course, she doesn't know it was you," Gabe says, jerking away from my hold. "What kind of sick slut would date the guy who raped her?"

I reel back, doubling my fist and aiming for Gabe's face. Instead of landing a blow to the pimple-scarred cheek, I stumble forward, knocking a kitchen chair into the table. Recovering my balance, I twist and wrap my arms around Gabe's waist, wrestling for control. "Shut your fucking mouth," I tell him through gritted teeth.

"You should have left Steph alone. I told you we were together."

The fight leads us out of the kitchen and into the connected den. "Well, she didn't seem to think so grad night," I say, gaining a foothold and pushing Gabe off me and into a bookshelf. Howls of laughter and jeering erupt from the crowd that has formed around us. Gabe's face reddens and his eyes darken as he pushes off the bookshelf, sending trinkets and books crashing down on the white oak panels.

"Piece of shit!" Gabe shouts, pummeling me to the floor.

"Fuck you!" I grunt, using all my strength to push Gabe off me. Black dots spot my eyes and a sting ripples across the left side of my face when Gabe's fist slams into it.

"Come on, man. He's not worth it," someone says, pulling me back from the fray.

Two underclassmen I remember from high school hold Gabe by the arms, walking him backward down the hall as he shouts, "You're not gonna get away with it, Landon."

Head pounding and sweat beading on my forehead, I collapse into an oversized club chair and soon, a familiar blonde is perched on the armrest, holding a bag of ice to my cheekbone.

FORTY-NINE

Kinsley: August 2, 2008

I park in front of the little white house that just yesterday felt like home. Now, looking at its weather-worn siding and dark streaks running down the roof like mascara tears, I can't believe I ever imagined being happy here. Taking a deep breath, I step out of the car and march inside.

"Why did you do it?" I ask, startling Caleb who's standing in the kitchen.

"I'm sorry?"

"You lied to me. I know about the farm."

He shakes his head. "Kinsley, what are you talking about?"

"I know about your deal with my dad and Landon. I know he bought the farm for you."

"Hold on." He approaches, but I back away.

"I never agreed to anything. When I–"

"Stop lying. I saw the papers at Landon's house."

"What papers– Wait, why were you at Landon's house?"

"Cut the act, Caleb. We're not really married, we're not really together. This was never real and you know it." I fight back tears. I'm so stupid for thinking I had it figured out. For thinking Caleb actually cared about me. He was only using me.

"Kins," he says carefully as he approaches again. "This is real for me. It might not have been at first, but it is now." He tilts his head, trying to meet my eyes, but I refuse. *Don't fall for it.*

"Whatever Landon told you, he's lying."

"You're the one lying, Caleb. Did you meet with Landon and my dad?"

"I–yes, I did, but–"

"Why? There was no reason to. We had a deal, and you went behind my back to make a better one. I found the purchase contract, Caleb. I saw it with my own eyes. He told me about the pay off and the petition for annulment."

"Kinsley, I'm telling you I never agreed to–"

"Right, you wanted more than just the money my dad offered you. You wanted the farm too. Well, congratulations, you got it." I storm past him and into the bedroom to pack a bag.

Caleb follows, continuing his defense. "No, I never signed–"

"Stop it, okay!" I turn around to face him. "I'm tired of everyone lying to me and using me. Just leave me alone." His hazel eyes mirror the heartbreak I feel in my chest, but I can't deny what I saw at Landon's.

I pack quickly, shoving anything I can into my duffle. Before I slip out of the house, I leave a scribbled note on the little wooden table.

Annie, I'm sorry. I know you're hurting, and it's my fault. If you can forgive me, I'm always here for you. You have my number. Call any time. —Love Kinsley

* * *

I race down the dusty path leading to Nikki's camper and slam the Jag into park next to the Range Rover.

"What is it?" Nikki asks, coming out of the camper as I run to her in tears. I assume my position on the little pink sofa and tell Nikki about Caleb accepting the payoff and demanding the farm. "I don't believe it, Kins. Why would he do that when we already worked out the deal with the trust fund?"

"I don't know, Nik. I guess because he saw an opportunity to get more out of us and he took it. He's no different than anyone else."

"This doesn't feel right. I don't–"

"Nikki, I saw the deed, okay? Stop defending him. He's not who you think he is."

"I'm just saying, maybe Landon was trying to–"

"Would you leave him alone? God, you're always attacking him. Why can't you just let me make my own decisions? Look at the mess I'm in because of you!"

"*Me?* What are you talking about?

"The marriage. Caleb. I wouldn't have done any of that if you hadn't planned it all out and talked me into it."

"Kinsley, you wanted to find a way out and I helped you. I never–"

"It wasn't about helping *me*, Nik. Your little plan helped Caleb–and Chase, and his dad. I wouldn't be surprised if there was something in it for you too."

Heartache, resentment, and confusion fill every inch of the little camper. *Who can I trust?* I search my brain, my heart, my memories, hoping to find at least one single thing I know to be true, something I can cling to—an anchor, but I come up short. They all lied, or at the very least allowed me to believe something contrary to the truth. Nothing is ever as it seems. That's the only constant.

"I need to be alone," I say, rushing out of the camper as Nikki follows close behind, begging me to stay. But there's no way out. I've been fooling myself, thinking there was an escape route. Believing Caleb cared for me. It was a lie. Now the light is cracking over the horizon and the truth can't be ignored any longer. There's only one path—the one I tried to avoid —the one I thought I had freed myself from. Dirt clouds fill the rearview as I drive away, the glaring path of surrender stretching out before me.

FIFTY

Caleb: August 2, 2008

The Jag races down the road. It's an echo of the night my mom left, tail lights fading slowly like a comet in the dark. When we were kids, James and I would torment each other like all brothers do, and one of his favorite maneuvers was to come up behind me when I wasn't expecting it and kick in the backs of my knees, making my legs buckle beneath me without warning.

This feels like that.

Annie's bedroom door opens and I brace for impact. "Caleb, what's wrong? Where's Kinsley?"

We've been here before—when Annie found out Jessica left. I never wanted to repeat that night, and I hate myself for letting Kinsley in. The heartbreak is never mine alone.

"Is she coming back?" Annie asks through tears, joining me at the screen door.

"I don't know, Annie." It takes all of my strength to say the words without crumbling.

"Can't you go after her, Caleb? Please, I need her." She tugs on my sleeve like she did when she was little.

"I know, Annie." I pull her into a hug. *I need her too.*

It's a double punch that Kinsley believes Landon over me and that she can just walk away from Annie. Like Jessica, like my mom. And the final blow is learning Landon bought the farm. Everything I worked for is gone, and for the second time in my life, I'm ready to give up. To follow my dad's path—lose myself in alcohol. The life I worked for has been taken from me without warning, and the woman I love has walked out the door. What's left?

Annie.
Annie needs me.
I won't give up like my dad.
I'll do better.
For Annie.

* * *

Once Annie is asleep, I open the freezer, not to drink the last of my reserve but to pour it out, knowing the temptation I'm facing isn't worth the price we'll pay. I shuffle items around but can't find it. *Annie?* I can't rule it out after last night, but the discussion can wait until another time. I walk into the living room, peeking out the window one last time for any sign of her return. June bugs and moths dance in the street light. Nothing more. I turn to look at the corner where Kinsley stacked her boxes when she moved in. I approach the faded bed sheet that covers the mass and gently pull it away, revealing the art desk I restored and set up for her. "Happy birthday," I whisper.

FIFTY-ONE

Kinsley: August 3, 2008

Dust particles float in the sunbeam that casts through my window. I roll over and try to surrender myself to sleep again, but my mind refuses to cooperate. The house is quiet, and my dad is at the office. It's the anniversary of my mother's death and my birth. I was nine when I fully realized the connection, and ever since, there has been a small voice hidden somewhere deep inside that asks if it was my fault. Once, I asked Ben, but he told me it wasn't. I never had the courage to ask my dad.

I shuffle downstairs and into the pantry to collect a K-pod and notice a pile of mail in the wire basket Carlita set up for me. A colorful birthday mailer from one of my favorite boutiques downtown catches my eye. *Make a wish*, it says. I toss it in the trash can, grab a coffee pod, and go back into the kitchen. *Make a wish?* I wish I'd never been born. That's it. Then all of my problems would be solved. My mom would still be alive and maybe my dad wouldn't have bankrupted the company. Ben wouldn't have left. Annie wouldn't be hurting. Every mistake I've made, every failure, every hope that I've crushed, every dream I've watched die—they would all be made right. The pain would be erased.

I place the little white pod in the coffee maker to brew. Looking at the clock on the stove, I calculate the time in Afghanistan. Ben will probably give me a call soon to wish me a happy birthday. Taking the coffee and sitting at the granite bar, I add sugar and cream. The weight of hopelessness settles on me as the caramel-colored liquid swirls around the spoon. *How can the absence of something create weight?* The absence of gravity makes you float, the absence of pain creates peace, but the absence of hope—it doesn't follow the same rules as the rest of the universe.

I take my coffee to my bedroom, shutting the door behind me. When my dad kicked me out, I couldn't take everything with me, so there are some art supplies in my closet. I place a blank canvas on the easel and pour my confusion and hurt onto it with broad, heavy strokes of black and gray, smudging speckles of white like fallen teardrops. An hour later, I put the paintbrush down—the torment of love, shame, hope, and fear held captive in the canvas fibers. My cell phone rings. It's Ben, and I answer with a tearful smile.

FIFTY-TWO

Twelve years earlier.

The game room is a mess of crumpled pop cans, greasy pizza boxes, and empty chip bags. Ben has passed out on the sectional, a partial bag of Doritos tucked under his arm and drool forming a Rorschach shape on the tan microfiber. "Dude, look what I found," Gabe says as he walks into the room carrying a bottle of vodka.

"Yo, Ben. Wake up," Landon says, poking Ben's foot with the pool cue. The birthday boy rolls over, facing the back of the couch and crushing the bag of chips.

"Oh, well." Gabe shrugs. "More party favors for us."

"So what's it gonna be?" Landon asks as he takes a shot at the eight ball and misses.

"Truth, Dare, or Drink," Gabe says. "You boys in?" he asks Caleb and Chase, who are sitting on the floor, battling it out on Modern Warfare.

"Whatever, man. We're in the middle of a match," Caleb says, fingers moving frantically over the controller.

Gabe rolls his eyes and joins them on the floor. "Come on, guys. One round with us, then you can go back to COD."

Rapid fire blasts before the screen goes black and white with the game stats. Chase drops the controller and nudges Caleb. "Dude, let's get it over with."

Landon joins the others on the floor and grabs the bottle from Gabe. "You're up first, what'll it be?"

"Dare," Gabe answers.

"I dare you to dial a random number and make a booty call." Landon laughs, reaching for the cordless phone on the end table and handing it to him. Gabe starts to punch in numbers but stops after Landon reminds him to block the caller ID first. After a raucous call and laughter that Ben manages to sleep through, Chase is in the hot seat.

"Truth," he tells Gabe when asked.

"What a pussy," Landon says and slumps back against the wall, taking a swig of vodka.

"Alright," Gabe says. "How far have you gone with a girl? And who?"

His cheeks turn red as he tells them. "Second at summer camp with a girl you don't know."

"Lying," Landon says with a smirk and holds out the bottle. "Drink up."

"I'm not lying, man–"

"Come on, a girl we don't know–sounds like a cop-out."

"I'm telling the truth, Landon."

"Whatever man, just take the drink," Gabe tells him with a nudge. "He's not gonna let it go." Chase glances at Caleb and shakes his head in defeat before taking a swig.

"God, that's nasty." He coughs, wiping his mouth as he shoves the bottle back to Gabe.

"And since you lost your round, you forfeit the ask, so I'll go again," Gabe says. "Caleb, what'll it be?"

"Don't puss out and say truth like Chase," Landon says.

"Fine." Caleb straightens his back and takes a deep breath. "Dare."

Gabe leans over to Landon and whispers something behind his hand. They both crack up laughing. "There's no way he'll do it," Landon says, shaking his head.

"Okay, Caleb," Gabe says through laughter. "I dare you to kiss Ben's sister."

Caleb scoffs. "No way, man. You're crazy."

"Told ya." Landon cackles. "He's probably too scared. He'd rather play video games all night like a little kid."

"I'm not scared. It's a stupid dare," Caleb says. "What, I'm just supposed to go knock on her door and say, *Hi, Kinsley. I'm going to kiss you now*?"

"Dude, don't be dumb. She's asleep. Just go on and get it over with. She'll never know."

"How do you know she's asleep?"

"Duh, it's one o'clock in the morning," Landon says.

"Yeah, go on, man. Do it," Gabe says, patting Caleb on the back. "She might even wake up and jump your bones."

"No way, dude," Chase says.

"It happened to my brother," Gabe continues. "One night after a party at his frat house, he saw this chick sleeping on the couch. So he started kissing her, and she horned up and jumped him right there in the living room."

"Your brother's full of shit," Chase says, grabbing the Xbox controller. "Rematch?" he asks Caleb.

"Forget it." Landon stretches his arms out and folds them behind his neck. "He's too chicken shit to do it."

"No, I'm not. I just... I don't want Ben to kick my ass for messing with his sister."

"Whatever, dude. You're either gay or a pussy," Landon says. "Or maybe you just prefer the livestock at the farm." He howls in laughter and Gabe joins him. "Go on, drink up." Landon pushes the bottle into Caleb's chest.

Caleb looks at the bottle as if it were a dead rat. Taking a sharp breath and clearing the disgust from his face, he removes the lid and holds the bottle to his mouth. With his eyes squeezed shut, he takes a quick drink.

"I'm done with this game," Caleb says, shoving the open bottle into Gabe's hand, spilling some. He grabs the Xbox controller and starts a new match with Chase.

"So lame," Landon says.

"Come on, let's see if Ben's dad has any Goldschläger." Gabe stands up, swinging the half-empty vodka bottle as he walks away.

FIFTY-THREE

Kinsley: August 4, 2008

With my birthday behind me, I take the first steps into a new year—and with more optimism than I expected. Talking to Ben last night helped me to finally see a flicker of hope in the darkness. There's still work to do, persuading my dad to make cuts and liquidate, but if I can pull it off, if I can make things right, maybe I can convince Ben to come home. Of course, he didn't jump at the idea when I mentioned it, but he's warming up to it. And it didn't hurt to remind him how close he is to thirty. Maybe I have learned a thing or two about persuasion and reading people. Thanks, Dad.

Dressed in a black Chanel shift dress, one of the few pieces I left behind when I moved out, I step into the elevator. I'm taking on more responsibility than I ever wanted, but it's the right thing to do, and the only thing I can do to reduce the collateral damage. After all the messes I've made, now it's my turn to clean up one for my dad. When I told him I would take the CFO job, relief washed over his face. I could almost see the burden of ruin lift from his shoulders. And while he may think my compliance is the bandaid on his wound, my intentions are surgical.

I spend the day acquainting myself with stacks of paperwork and the depths of my dad's mistakes. By midmorning, it feels like I've fallen into a rabbit hole so deep I can't say for sure which way is up. Looking around the office suite I've inherited, I wonder if I can give it a minimalist makeover and sell off the excess. It wouldn't make a dent in the big picture really, but I have to start somewhere. That and reducing my salary are the first items on my list.

I work through lunch, ordering in a salad. *Lunch account spending should be addressed.* I make a note, planning to cut mine entirely. It's a tightrope walk—I have the power as CFO to dictate changes company-wide but still have to contend with my dad. And laying down a new set of rules on day one isn't a good look, especially since I know how he'll respond to someone else calling the shots.

Though my dad might argue the contrary if he knew my plans, I don't aim to tear the company down. I'm trying to save it. To save jobs. To save my dad's undeserving ass. And maybe a piece of my soul that can only be salvaged through sacrifice and penance.

And with penance on my mind, I know where I have to go after work. I left a trail of destruction and heartbreak all over town. Recovery and cleanup efforts will take time, as with any storm that blows through, but I'm ready to work.

❋ ❋ ❋

I stand before the door, my heart aching with regret. I knock, and as soon as the door opens, my apology pours out. "Look, Nik, I'm sorry for last night. I shouldn't have lashed out at you." Face to face with Nikki, I see the hurt in her eyes. Maybe I've gone too far this time—pushed away one of the only people to have ever really cared about me. I can't make it without her.

"I'm–"

"Come here," Nikki says, pulling me into a hug. "You're going through a lot. I get it."

"But it's not okay. I was an ass."

"Well, it's not the first or last time you're going to be an ass," she says, and I chuckle despite the ache in my heart. "You're more than my best friend Kins, you're the Lucy to my Ethel."

"I don't deserve you." My shoulders drop and Nikki ushers me into the camper.

"True. But you have me anyway, and you're gonna have to fuck up a lot bigger than that to get rid of me." Nikki winks. "So what's this?" She points to my outfit. "Someone die?"

Oh, maybe just a little part of me.

"It's one of the only outfits I left at my dads. I had to find something professional to wear to the office." I kick off my shoes and sit on the little sofa.

"Hold the phone. The office? You mean…"

I nod. "I'm only doing it to see if I can help fix things. I'm not okay with what he's doing, but I can't really make a difference from the outside."

Nikki joins me, cross-legged on the couch. "You could report it, Kins."

"But what would happen to the employees? Think of how many families would be affected, Nik. I can't stand the thought of being responsible for that. Like how things turned out for Caleb and Annie when their dad was laid off. I just can't."

"Caleb and Annie?"

"Yeah, their dad worked for CHI and–"

"I know about that," Nikki says. "I'm just surprised you're–never mind. Continue."

I raise an eyebrow at her *surprise*, but choose not to follow that trail, wanting to keep the space between us free of tension. "Anyway, I have to make changes from the inside. It's the only way I can control the potential damage. So last night, I told my dad I'd take the job. I just finished my first day–hence the funeral clothes. Which, now that I'm thinking about it, you wouldn't want to save me the humiliation and swing by Caleb's to pick up some of my stuff would you?"

"You're still set on believing Landon then, huh?"

"Nik, I saw the papers."

"Right, but that doesn't mean–"

"Look, Nik. I don't want to fight with you." I pull my hair up into a ponytail and continue. "Landon's been really helpful with figuring out what happened at Ben's birthday."

"Landon knew about it?" Nikki nearly shouts.

"No, not exactly…"

I walk her through what we discussed, the fight at Lainey's and what Gabe said to him. "I mean, yeah it sucks that he's not here to pay for what he did, but he's not hurting anyone else now… You know? And I kind of feel, well this sounds bad… I'm not *glad* he's dead, but at least he's…"

Nikki nods in silence, which concerns me. "What? I know you have an opinion. I can see it all over your face."

Nikki shrugs. "I don't know. It just sounds like the perfect solution to the problem, that's all."

The perfect solution? What does that even mean?

I sigh. "Sure, I guess… If there even is such a thing." I let my eyes drop to the black kitten heels I kicked off. "I'm just glad it's behind me now, you know?" Nikki nods, but I know she's holding back. "So, you think you could pick up a few things for me? From Caleb's? Just whenever you're free…"

"Yeah, I'll swing by tomorrow."

I thank her and stand to leave. "I better go. It's supposed to storm tonight, and I brought home some work to do."

* * *

Not long after I arrive back home from Nikki's, a deluge breaks through the heavens. Electric veins light up the black sky and the pounding of thunder shakes the house. I sort through the file box of papers, receipts, and contracts until I can't see straight. With tired eyes, I turn off the light and settle into bed. As I drift off to sleep, I suddenly feel a cold metal against my collarbone. Gasping, my eyes snap open as I reach for it, but nothing is there—only the cotton tank top lying against my skin. I exhale a shaky breath and close my eyes, letting my mind wander through the dark maze of memories. Outside, the rain continues all night as if to wash away the sins laid bare.

FIFTY-FOUR

May 19, 1996, 1:13 a.m.

Twelve years earlier.

Chase and Landon shuffle glass bottles of liquor quietly as they search for gold in the downstairs wet bar. "I knew he wouldn't do it, man," Landon says, holding up a bottle for inspection in the dim-lit room. "He's such a puss."

"Whatever, man. I don't blame him. If Ben found out, he would kick his ass."

"Please." Landon scoffs. "Ben would never find out. Besides, it's just a kiss. Not like he would have gotten any. He's not man enough for that." He sets the bottle of brandy back on the shelf and looks around. "He doesn't have any."

"Dude that's harsh," Gabe says with a laugh.

"No–I mean there's no Goldschläger, but, yeah–Caleb doesn't have any balls either." Landon laughs and nudges Gabe. "Let's go."

When the boys return upstairs and step onto the second-floor landing, Gabe turns left toward the game room and Landon turns right. "Where are you going?" Gabe asks. A quiet rumble of thunder and light pattering rain hardly cover his whisper.

"Come on, you'll see."

Gabe hurries to catch up with Landon, who stops at the knotty pine door, his hand resting on the knob. "Dude, are you serious?" Gabe asks.

"Why not," Landon says with a shrug as he turns the knob. "It's nothing."

"What if she wakes up? She'll freak out."

"Nah, she'll be happy to see me. Trust me. I can tell when a girl's into me." He pushes the door open, peering inside.

"Whatever man, you're trippin'. You think every girl is into you."

"Because they are, Gabe." Landon offers a smug grin and pats Gabe on the shoulder. "I don't expect you to understand."

"What's that supposed to mean?" Gabe almost shouts.

"Are you trying to wake her up?"

"Yeah, maybe I am." He straightens up but still isn't eye-to-eye with Landon's taller frame. "Then we can find out if she's really into you or if you're full of shit."

Landon narrows his eyes on Gabe, releasing a sharp puff of air from his nostrils. "You don't think she wants me? She couldn't keep her eyes off me when we came back from the creek. Look," he says, pulling Gabe into the doorway. "She's probably dreaming about me right now."

"God, you're a conceited prick."

"Nah, bro, I'm a man, and you're just a little pussy." He steps into the bedroom.

"Dude, she's gonna wake up," Gabe whispers across the room.

Power and pride feed off one another, building with adrenaline and the alcohol racing through his veins. "Yeah, and she's gonna love it."

"Nah, man. You can get your ass kicked alone, I'm out." Gabe panics and scrambles away.

FIFTY-FIVE

Kinsley: August 5, 2008

All that remains of last night's storm are puddles and a heavy blanket of humidity. I dress in a sleeveless gray mid dress, the coolest professional attire I can find from the picked-over options I have to work with, and pull my hair back into a bun to keep it off my neck.

The work day is a near duplicate of the one before—nodding, smiling, agreeing politely in the public eye, but once behind closed doors, I skim budgets and purchase requests for any little thing I can cut without making too big of a wave. What I don't expect to find is the record of a check made out to Chief Birmingham for *consultation* back in 2000. At first, I brush it off—it's filed under "security" after all. But really, sixty-thousand? It seems a bit excessive. Was it an up-front payment for years' worth of consulting services? I try to imagine the kind of security training and advice he might have offered Mr. Jeffries—even back then he wouldn't have been a young gun. *After hours patrol, maybe?* But when I call the police station to inquire, they don't have a record of it. Of course, Chief Birmingham is retired, they remind me, and it's possible he offered the services privately.

As I sift through files, I get a text notification on my phone. *Come by my place asap. I have something to show you. Nik*

I hope she wants to show me the little camper filled to the brim with everything I left at Caleb's house, but I'll settle for a few outfits and my favorite peep-toe Chanels.

It's nearing five-o-clock, and I slip my shoes back on, straighten my dress, and leave the office. "Goodnight, Ms. Holland," Mr. Jeffries says as I approach the main doors and his little security station.

"Night." I smile and continue toward the exit, then stop and turn around, approaching him with hurried steps. "Mr. Jeffries, do you remember Chief Birmingham's security consultation some years back?"

"Security consultation?" His bushy gray eyebrows crowd together. "No, dear. I don't believe I do."

"Well, maybe it wasn't a consultation. Night patrol, perhaps?"

Mr. Jeffries protrudes his thinning lips into a frown and shakes his head. "Not that I can recall. Sec-Guard has been handling that for years."

"I must be confusing it with something else then." I thank him with a smile and head outside where the humidity cloaks me immediately, and by the time I make it to my front-row parking spot, trickles of sweat roll down my back.

❋ ❋ ❋

"Tell me you got the Chanels," I say, stepping inside the camper and noticing the absence of boxes, tubs, and bags. "Wait– Did you not go to Caleb's at all?"

"Of course, I did. Your stuff is in my car. Figured I'd just unload it at your dad's house." Nikki hands me a Diet Coke.

"Thanks. What did you need to show me?"

"So, when I was doing research for the article–Mitchel Sawgrass, remember him? AV guy?" Nikki plops down on the little rug in front of me. "Well, he gave me this old tape from the night of the party. You know, when Gabe and Landon were fighting. When I first watched it, I was only trying to see what time Gabe left the party, but it didn't show him leaving." She waves it off and refills her lungs before surging on. "But, it *did* show the fight, and I rewatched it last night. Maybe just to confirm what Landon said–"

"Oh, my god, Nikki. Really?" I take a seat on the sofa. *Here we go again.*

"Listen, if everything had checked out, I would have been happy to go along–"

I shoot her a look, calling out her bullshit. "Okay, I would have *tried* to go along with it, but it didn't happen like he told you, Kins." She swivels on her butt and grabs the remote, turning on the TV mounted to the camper's wall. "Alright, it's not the best audio quality, but listen to what Gabe says–"

"Nik, I *know* what he said–"

"Humor me." Nikki side-eyes me and pushes a button on the remote. Lainey Evan's living room comes into focus as laughter, indistinct conversation, and music crackle through the speakers. The camera zooms in on a couple making out on the couch, then back out, panning toward a small group of guys huddled near the kitchen.

"What's going on over here?" the cameraman asks.

"Shit's about to hit the fan," one of the guys says.

"You hooked up with her anyway," a voice from inside the kitchen cuts through the noise, and the cameraman pushes through the group, jarring the videos' focus. When the vertigo blur fades out, I recognize Landon, hands full of wet paper towels. He tosses them across the room and the camera follows, documenting a missed shot. Another group crowds by the kitchen's opening to the den.

The camera pans back to Landon, who now stands face to face with Gabe. The onlookers' jeers overlap with the argument, but I pick up a few phrases: "jailbait piece of ass...screwed half the school." I can't identify the voice, but the context tells me it's Gabe. *I'm* the "jailbait piece of ass," and Landon "screwed half the school." Nikki turns up the volume. *Oh, good. Make sure I don't miss a single syllable of humiliation, Nik.*

Then Gabe says, "Desperate to stay with you–or maybe just fucked up from what you did to her all those years ago." The camera wobbles in unsteady hands as a head brushes past, blocking the view momentarily.

"Hey, watch it," the cameraman says and refocuses the shot on Gabe mid-sentence.

"–know it was you? Or did you make up some shit and blame it on Ben? Huh, is that why he left?" Landon takes hold of Gabe by the collar and leans in close as if to say something—or threaten him, more likely. Then Gabe jerks away from him. "What kind of sick slut would date the guy who raped her?" he says, and my heart drops, sinking into my core like a heavy stone. *No.* I must have misheard it.

"Rewind that, Nik."

But there's no mistake. I heard him correctly, and the look on Landon's face confirms his guilt. I've seen that look too many times before.

As the tape plays, Landon and Gabe wrestle and curse. Their war continues in the background as another rages inside me. And when Gabe says, "You're not gonna get away with it, Landon," the last piece of the puzzle clicks into place. Landon didn't want me talking to Gabe that night, I remember that, and now I understand why. He wanted Gabe to stay quiet. That's why he grabbed the wheel.

There was never a deer.

It wasn't an accident.

And it wasn't my fault.

I pull out the photo of Ben's birthday party, scanning each boy's wrist. One by one, I rule them out, until I come to Landon's wrist and his James Bond watch. The heavy metal band stares back at me, sending a phantom chill across my collarbone.

* * *

The air is thick with humidity, and a new round of storm clouds hang low in the sky, suffocating in their approach. I knock on the front door, but no one answers. So I follow the path hugging the magazine-perfect flower beds and punch in the security code on the garage pad. The garage is empty. Landon isn't home from work yet. I take out my phone and text him. *We need to talk. It's urgent.*

Once inside the house, I help myself to a glass of his wine to settle my nerves and appease my anger, though I don't really want the anger to go away. Not yet—not before I can push it back on the one who caused it all. The pieces have fallen into place this time. I knew Landon could be cold and manipulating, but I never wanted to accept that he was the monster I saw when things got out of control. Now, I can see it all. He took what he wanted from me long before I ever knew how to give it. That alone is bad enough, but then, when Ben left and I was broken and lonely, he swept me up into his arms, made himself a savior and imprisoned my heart, letting me think it was given freely.

I check my phone for a response, but Landon hasn't replied. I try to walk off the nervous energy bubbling in my chest. The living room is clean and unencumbered by magazines or books or newspapers, unlike Caleb's house where there's no shortage of things to read. I open the double doors to Landon's den, thinking I might find a *Time* magazine or *Forbes*—something. As I peek under stacks of papers and files on his desk, I notice the address of CHI on a geological survey. I don't understand all the technical aspects of Landon's work, but I know enough to make sense of the schematic map and cross-section inset labeled *shale*. That and the nearby papers detailing plans to implement the horizontal drilling he has been harping about clue me in.

Hurrying back to the coffee table where I left my phone, I call my dad. Did they figure out a way to get the money together without a merger? But when I ask him about the shale, he's clueless. *What the hell is going on?* I go back into the office and grab the paperwork. It looks like Landon has signed a contract with his uncle's drilling company.

When the alarm chirps and the front door opens, a jolt of adrenaline hits me. I tighten my grip on the papers and return to the living room, shoving them into my purse.

"Back again baby? You might as well just move in," Landon says, walking into the room, loosening his tie. I don't speak at first, taking a moment to look the monster right in the eye, blinders off.

"What's going on?" he asks as he lays his suit jacket aside. "Still upset about the whole Gabe thing?"

"I know everything, Landon."

"What are you talking about?" He takes a seat on the couch, offering me a condescending smile.

"You lied to me." The memory of Landon comforting me when I told him what happened at Ben's birthday guts me like a hot knife. "Gabe didn't do it…"

"Jesus, Kinsley, what are you rambling on about?" He stands up and walks into the kitchen to pour himself a drink. Outside, crackling thunder rolls across the sky.

"I'm telling you that I know Gabe didn't rape me, Landon."

"One day it's a dream, the next day it was Gabe. Now it's not. Do you hear yourself? You need to get some help. You–"

"You were the only one wearing a watch."

"You take those pills of yours?" he asks and takes a swig of his drink.

"It was you." His silence challenges me to bring the accusation. "I woke up and *you* were on top of me, Landon. I told you no." The haunting memory I long believed a dream chokes me. I'm exposed and vulnerable once again with the same monster.

Landon takes two steps, closing the distance between us and stares down into my eyes. "You're sick. Like, mentally unwell, Kinsley. You need help."

Allowing the anger and hurt to fuel my courage, I refuse to break eye contact. "You said it was my party favor. I tried to bite your hand and you squeezed my neck." The words pour out over shaky breaths. "I remember your fucking watchband digging into my collarbone."

He holds my stare, his eyes empty, unmoved, like stones. "I was just a kid, Landon," I whisper.

"You're delusional," he says without emotion.

"I'm not." I shake my head. "In the picture from Ben's party, you're the only one wearing a watch."

"Okay, I'm guilty of wearing a watch. That doesn't mean it happened, Kinsley."

"I know it happened, Landon, and I have proof—"

"Last time we talked, you said you didn't even know if it was real," he says with a smug grin. "How could you have proof all of a sudden?"

I swallow, ready to show my hand. "I have a video to prove it."

"A video, huh?" He takes a sip of his whisky and shifts his eyes to the storm beyond the window.

"Someone caught the fight on video—you and Gabe at Lainey's party. He knew about it, Landon! I heard him say that you raped me before Ben left."

He returns his eyes to me, seething with hate. "You're crazy if you think anyone will believe you."

"You feel good taking that chance?" An exhilarating energy boils over in my chest and pumps through my veins.

"What are you saying?" He sneers.

"I'll go to the police—"

"Right, Kinsley. Tell them how you all of a sudden remembered something that happened when we were kids. You think it'll hold up?"

"Yeah, with the video and the photo. It would be enough to draw negative attention at least. For you–your dad. Maybe, if I'm lucky, a trial, but either way, it won't look good for you."

"What is this, then? You here to blackmail me?"

"What do I have to lose, Landon?"

"Manipulative bitch." He runs his hands over his face, now growing red in defeat. "What is it you want?"

I want my innocence back, but he can't give me that. So, I'll settle for retribution. "A few things," I say. "But first, what's all this?" I retrieve the papers from my purse and hold them out.

"That's something I've been working on with your dad, Kins–"

"Stop lying, Landon!" I smack the papers down on the granite countertop. "My dad doesn't know anything about this. How do you even– you know what, never mind. I'm taking these." I shove the papers back into my bag. "Tell Malcolm the deal's off."

"That all?" Landon's lips pinch tight as he glares at me.

"Of course not. We're just getting started. For CHI, you're going to sign a silent investor agreement with a five-percent return, all of which you'll donate directly to the local women's shelter. As CFO, I can have those papers ready for you by morning. Or if you'd rather, I can just stop by the police station on my way home." I take a deep breath, proud of myself for delivering the ultimatum with conviction and courage.

"I'll sign your fucking papers, but this isn't over, Kinsley." He glares at me.

"You're right. There's more. You're going to sign the farm over to Caleb."

"God, you're such a doormat." He laughs, and downs the whisky in his glass. "It's really pathetic."

"You know what, I *was* a doormat, Landon. Yours, for far too long, but I'm not anymore. Now, I'm taking back a fraction of what you owe me."

"Oh, I owe you? What about everything I've done for you? All the money I've spent–what about the damn ring I bought you?"

I'm sick with anger at this man for lying to me, using me, cheating on me, abusing me, and worst of all, making me think I was the problem. I turn away and dig through my purse, pulling out the so-called symbol of his love for me. "Here, you can have it. I'm not the same person I was when you gave it to me." I place the little black velvet box on the countertop and let myself out.

FIFTY-SIX

May 19, 1996, 1:28 a.m.

Twelve years earlier.

"What the hell was that?" Gabe whispers from the dark hallway, startling Landon as he closes the door to Kinsley's room.

"Where the fuck did you come from?"

"I never left, Landon. I saw–"

"Damn, Gabe, you whacking off to me? Jesus, we gotta get you laid." He smacks Gabe on the back.

"That's not what I was–Landon, she...sh–"

"What? She loved it, just I told you she would." Landon starts toward the game room.

"Dude, that's not how it looked to me."

"What would you know about it?" Landon stops and turns so that Gabe nearly runs into his chest.

"But she... I thought I heard her say *no*?"

Landon ushers Gabe down the hall. "Let me explain something to you, Gabe. When a chick is with a guy as big as me, she's gonna say *oh*. A lot." He shakes his head. "Jesus, have you never watched porn?"

"Of course I have, but you were like... Were you choking her?"

"It's called BDSM. Really, Gabe. You don't have a clue, do you?"

"Landon... She didn't," Gabe sputters. "She didn't even look at you. I don't think she–"

"What? Please, enlighten me with your virgin knowledge."

In the dark of the hall, they stare at one another, both knowing what transpired, refusing to give truth a voice.

FIFTY-SEVEN

Kinsley: August 5, 2008

The summer storm is raging in full force by the time I make it to my dad's house. Rain beads bounce off the pavement like marbles poured from the sky. I let myself in, removing my rain-soaked shoes in the entryway and find my dad in his office.

"I need to talk to you," I say when I enter the room. He motions for me to have a seat, but I stand. "I just spoke with Landon, and we've come to an agreement."

My dad's eyes light up, and he pushes his chair back from the desk, giving me his full attention. *Here we go.*

"Landon is going to sign on as a silent investor to cover the deficit."

He's elated. I've never seen him so happy. He stands up from his chair and starts toward me. "This is wonderful news. Thank you–"

"I'm not doing this for you," I say, my hand out to stop his approach. He tugs his brows together and sits back down.

"What you did was wrong, Dad. Not just wrong—*illegal.* And who knows how many people you've hurt with your choices." *People like Caleb and Annie.*

"Kins–"

"No, Dad. There's no coming back from this. Not for you. Landon's investment will shore up the accounts, but I can't let you run the company into the ground. It's not fair to the employees."

"But, I–"

"You're going to step down as CEO."

He tries to object, but I don't give him the opportunity.
"Immediately. And I'm going to take your place–just until Ben comes back.

He's agreed not to re-up when his contract ends." The confusion and hurt in his eyes beckon my empathy, but it has to be this way.

"You'll have your retirement package," I say, an attempt to soften the blow before I hit him where it hurts—again. "But I've made *significant* modifications to it."

"Kinsley, honey, please be reasonable." He stands.

"Reasonable? It would be *reasonable* for me to turn you in. My arrangement with Landon has nothing to do with keeping your ass out of prison. The company will stand even if you fall."

"But–but, this is my life. This is all I have." He gestures to the plaques and framed photos championing his success.

"All you have?" I shake my head. He's pathetic and an asshole—I know this—but it doesn't stop the words from piercing my heart. "No, you have a son and a daughter."

"You know what I mean," he scoffs.

"I know that your greed and your poor choices are the reason Ben left. The reason you wanted me to marry Landon."

"No, he loves you, Kinsley, and you love him that was just–"

"That wasn't love, Dad. I'm done making excuses for Landon, and I'm done letting you make decisions for me. This is our endgame. You get to choose if it's messy or clean."

* * *

August 6, 2008

I park in front of the little white house, pausing for a moment to gather my courage. When I step out, I smooth my dress, and tuck the file folder under my arm before wobbling across the gravel in my favorite Chanels. Caleb's truck is in the drive, but Annie's bike isn't in its typical spot. Of all the hard things I've done in the past few days, confronting Caleb and Annie will be the most difficult. I climb the little porch steps and knock on the front door. With every second the door remains closed, I'm more convinced that Caleb knows it's me at the door and chooses not to answer. The idea takes root in my heart and I turn to leave.

"What are you doing here?" Caleb says as he walks around the side of the house, and my heart breaks with hope. He's in his stained work jeans and a stupid cotton tee shirt speckled with dirt.

"I umm… I have some paperwork for you, and…" I desperately need to look him in the eye, but I'm terrified of the heartache it will bring. I hand him the file folder.

"What is it?"

"It's the farm. It's yours–"

He tries to hand it back. "I didn't ask for this."

"I know you didn't, Caleb," I say, stepping back, arms crossed, refusing to take the file. "Landon lied to me, and I should have known better." With each second that he doesn't speak, sorrow tightens in my chest. "Mr. Cunningham told me what you did, and how Landon swooped in… But it's yours now."

"You don't owe me anything, Kinsley."

"I owe you an apology. And the money for the repairs and…" I peek at him, but he avoids my eyes. "Caleb, please, I fucked up, okay? I got it all wrong. I'm sorry."

"I never lied to you."

"I know," I say and swallow back tears. "Please, just take the farm–"

"I'm not making a deal with the devil." He shakes his head and tries to hand me the file again.

"I'm not asking you to… I already did."

He stares at the ground between us, pushing a stray piece of gravel away with his boot. "What's that mean? You marrying him?"

I shake my head and try to discern the meaning in his question, meeting his eyes and hoping to find it there.

"Working for your dad then?"

"Not exactly… It's complicated."

"Complicated, huh?" A hint of a smile curls on his lips. My stomach tangles with both desire and trepidation, and I want more than anything to throw myself into his arms and kiss him.

"Wanna get out of the heat and tell me about it?" he asks. I nod and turn quickly to wipe a fallen tear.

Inside, I take a seat on the couch while he sits in the armchair across from me. Starting with Ouranos Group and Ben's leaving, I trace my dad's infractions, leading to the forced abdication of his throne. I explain how Landon knew everything all along, how he wanted in on the shale deposits, and finally, how I learned that Landon raped me the night of Ben's birthday.

"I threatened to report the rape and blow the whistle on my dad if they didn't do what I asked."

"But why would you let them get away with it, Kinsley?"

"They're not getting away with it. This is their punishment–losing control. They can't hurt me anymore now that I have their secrets."

Caleb looks at me from the other side of the room. The distance between us hurts. "Anyway," I say, fumbling with the hem of my sundress. "Umm, there's another set of papers in there if you want to sign them." I never thought signing the divorce papers would be so hard, but it's nothing compared to this moment, awaiting the verdict.

"Oh," he says, shuffling the papers. "The gig is up, huh?"

"I'm just trying to clean up my messes." I try to hold it together as every memory made in this room slams into my heart. "I don't have a pen…" I say, looking around and noticing a bed sheet over my pile of boxes in the corner. *He doesn't even want to be reminded of me.*

"Is that what you want?" he asks, joining me on the couch with a pen in his hand. I can't answer him or look at him. I can't watch him sign the papers.

He leans forward, trying to look me in the eye, and my heart races in response. "Can I tell you something?" he asks, and I nod. "The day you ran me off the road, yeah, that was a mess… When you asked to move in, and Annie heard about the marriage. Another mess." I shift my weight, trying to hide my face and the tears that track down my cheeks.

"Burning dinner, flooding the laundry room," Caleb continues. "Messes." I bury my face in my hands as if to collect the heartache I can't hold back anymore, but he isn't finished reading me the record of my wrongs.

"Annie dating," he says with a sigh. "Big mess." He snips my heartstrings, one by one with each memory. I close my eyes tight, but the tears won't stop.

"You want to know the biggest mess of all?" Caleb pulls my hands away from my face, tilting my chin up to look at him. "The biggest mess was when you said none of this was real. When you left and told me to leave you alone."

I open my eyes to find Caleb looking at me the same way he did on game night before I kissed him. It's the way he looked at me when we went fishing at the creek. It's how he looks when he holds my body to his. It's the way he looks at me when he loves me.

"That's the only mess I'm interested in cleaning up," he says and pulls me into his perfect kiss, welcoming my heart back home.

* * *

"I love you," Caleb whispers in my ear before rolling over to lie beside me, tucking me into his hug.

I love you. I've lost track of how many times we've said it this afternoon. The first was on the couch after he kissed me. Then there was the *I love you* he whispered into my neck. And the one I breathed on his shoulder. Another when he slipped the strap of my sundress off and kissed my collarbone. I'm fairly certain there were a handful as we undressed each other, stumbling into the bedroom. And there was most definitely an *I love you* when he entered me and our bodies became one. But there's no way of counting after that because they exploded like confetti. *I love you. I love you. I love you.*

"I love you, too," I tell him, closing my eyes and breathing in this moment. I'm home. Not in this little house. Not in this little bed. I'm home in Caleb's arms, surrounded by his *I love you.*

Caleb lifts his head, looks at the alarm clock on the nightstand, and lets out half a groan. "Annie will probably be back soon, and when she sees your car on the drive, she'll bust down the door to find you, I'm sure."

I laugh and kiss his chest. "You're probably right."

We dress and Caleb leads me back to the living room. "I have something for you," he says. "A late birthday gift."

I'm not sure what to expect, but he walks toward the pile of boxes covered with a bed sheet and pulls it back. Except it isn't my pile of boxes. It's a large wooden art table with an adjustable tabletop and drawers and cubbies for storing supplies.

"It's not brand new," he says. "But I tried to make it look new and everything works–the drawers, the adjustable top–"

"Caleb, it's perfect," I say. I've never seen him so worried about my opinion of something. I wrap my arms around his waist and lean my head back to kiss his stubble, then his lips. "I love it."

We sit on the couch, waiting for Annie to come home. He tells me how he found the table and shows me the "before" pictures—battered wood, rusting hinges, and derailed drawers. It was a wreck, a complete mess. I can see why the owners tossed it out as useless. I look over to the corner where it sits. It's hard to imagine this is the same table. I don't know how, but Caleb saw the potential in the broken pieces. And it means more to me than if he had saved up to buy a brand new one.

When Annie busts through the door, she barrels into my arms. "You're back! You're not leaving again, are you?" I literally cannot answer because she's hugging me so tight, or maybe it's the other way around. "Please stay, Kinsley," she says, her voice muffled by our hug. Her tears dampen my shoulder.

"I'm not leaving." I'm choked by emotion—remorse, relief, love, and pure happiness. "I'm so sorry... For everything, Annie. I love you."

"I love you, too," she says, pulling away and wiping her freckled cheeks. "I'm so happy you're back."

"Me too," I tell her and reach for Caleb's hand. He pulls me into him, tucking me under his arm instead. Annie sits cross-legged beside us on the couch, taking a deep breath and wiping her cheeks again.

"So, does this mean you're getting married?"

I look over my shoulder to Caleb, who wears the same confusion I feel. "What? Annie, you know we're–"

"I know you *got married*," she says with air quotes. "But, like–for real this time?"

"Wait," Caleb says. "How did you–when did you..."

"Please, Caleb. I'm fourteen, but I'm not an idiot. I knew something was up from the beginning."

"But you acted like... You didn't say anything?"

"Why would I? You two needed all the help you could get, and I wasn't about to let you drop the act. Haven't you ever watched a rom-com?"

I laugh and think back to the night she questioned why I was sleeping in the living room, and the game of truth or dare when she asked about our first date. Nikki has competition—or a co-conspirator.

FIFTY-EIGHT

Kinsley: October 31, 2008

Twelve weeks later.

Stepping inside the elevator, I take out my phone and dial Caleb's cell. "Hey, you finish the proposal?" he asks after one ring.

"I did. Just sent it off, so fingers crossed they'll like it and we can move forward."

"I'm sure they will. This town needs a community arts center–"

"They might not see it that way, Caleb."

"If they don't at first, they will by the time you're done with them. I know first-hand how convincing and tenacious you can be."

"Isn't that just a fancy way of calling your wife stubborn?" I ask, holding the phone with my shoulder so I can fish the keys out of my purse.

"I would never," he says with a chuckle. "Are you heading home?"

"Almost. Have everything we need for the bonfire?"

"Yeah, Chase is here now. We're about to set it up. What time are Annie's friends coming over?"

When the metal doors slide open, I step out into the lobby. "I think she said seven–I'll double check when I pick her up. Hey, do we have enough candy for the trick-or-treaters."

"Oh, yeah." Caleb laughs. "Nikki just got here. She went overboard."

"Sounds about right–just a sec." I walk up to the security podium by CHI's main entrance. "Mr. Jeffries, Ben said you didn't need to wait on him. But you can walk me to my car if you'd like." Mr. Jeffries nods, and slips on his jacket, shaky hands reaching for his car keys in the podium.

"Hey babe," I say into the phone. "Mr. Jeffries is walking me out. I just have to make one stop after I pick up Annie. Love you."

The little downtown street looks like a painting come to life with hay bales and pumpkins outside every shop door and fallen leaves sprinkled around like confetti. I take a deep breath and pull the file and VHS tape from my purse. "Ready?" I ask Annie.

The cool October wind whistles through what's left of the trees and I pull the glass door open to walk inside.

"Can I help you?" the woman behind the plexiglass asks.

"Yes, I spoke with Chief Sanders earlier. He's expecting me. My name is Kinsley Holland."

"I'll let him know you're here. Please take a seat, and help yourself to some candy if you'd like." The woman motions to a big plastic cauldron near the entrance. We sit down in the vinyl-cushioned lobby chairs and poke through the bowl. Annie offers me a Hershey Kiss. I unwrap the foil and pop the candy into my mouth.

"Ms. Holland?"

I turn, mouth full of melting chocolate, to find Chief Sanders holding the door open for me. Smiling and swallowing down the candy, I stand up, motioning for Annie to follow. We take our seats in his office, and I thank him for seeing me.

"My pleasure. In fact, I'd like to thank you for coming forward with this information. It takes courage, Ms. Holland, and it says much of your character and integrity."

I fight the echo of fear that I can't help but associate with the subject. With a deep breath and a glance toward Annie, I place the file and tape on Chief Sanders' desk. "I'm just trying to do the right thing. It's what Gabe deserves, and so does his family."

* * *

It's nearing dusk as we pull away from the police station. "So, Annie, what do you think?"

"I guess it wasn't too bad... It's not exactly the same, Kins."

"I know, babe, but I'll be with you the whole time, I swear." I reach across to take Annie's cool hand in mine as I slow to a stop at a red light.

She chews on her lip, eyes set on the floorboard. "It's just... I still think they'll say it was my fault, and what if I get in trouble for drinking?"

"Annie, look at me. It was *not* your fault, and you've already been punished for the drinking. That's not what this is about. This is about Eric and his friends learning that they can't get away with shit like that. *Even if* someone is drunk." She squeezes her eyes shut, and I continue. "If we don't speak up, they may never stop. It could happen to someone else at the next party."

"I'm scared," Annie whispers.

"I know babe. I was too, but we can do it together."

"Tomorrow?"

I nod and squeeze her hand. "If you're ready."

"I am," Annie says.

The light turns green, and I drive back to our little white house, knowing I did the right thing. It wasn't easy handing over the evidence to implicate Landon and even myself in Gabe's death, and furthermore, showing my dad's part in the cover-up. But it was the last mess I had to clean up, and maybe the most important one. Chief Sanders assured me that my cooperation and honesty, plus the fact that I wasn't aware of the cover-up or even that I *had* hit Gabe, earned my immunity. He wants the real criminals to pay—the ones who knew what happened and kept their mouths shut for nearly a decade.

I didn't tell Caleb about my plan to meet with Chief Sanders. I'll tell him tonight, but I wanted to handle it on my own—to prove to myself that I'm capable of taking responsibility. But I wanted Annie to see me do this hard thing so that she would know she can do hard things too. Growing up in a world of men, I didn't have a mother-figure looking out for me, a woman to show me how to navigate the lies and manipulation that awaited me. I see that now—I didn't know I *could* do hard things. I might not be able to go back in time and tell my twelve-year-old self that what happened isn't her fault. That Landon deserves to pay for what he did. That she doesn't have to carry the guilt and shame he saddled her with. But I can help Annie understand those things. I can be the woman to lead Annie, the woman I needed but didn't have growing up. I can lend Annie my strength because I know just how hard it's going to be.

According to RAINN, one out of every six women in America has been the victim of attempted or completed sexual violence. Typically, but not always, the victim knows the perpetrator, and over half of the time, the assault occurs near or at the victim's home. Furthermore, more than two out of every three sexual assaults go unreported.

More information, statistics, and resources can be found at RAINN.org.

Give truth a voice.

ABOUT THE AUTHOR

T. R. Hill

T. R. Hill is an Oklahoma native and lives in a small town with her husband and three children. A book-lover since childhood, she now spends her days writing stories of her own.

You can follow her on social media and subscribe to her email list for updates on Always, August, a second-chance romance, coming soon.

www.ingramcontent.com/pod-product-compliance
Lightning Source LLC
Chambersburg PA
CBHW021503110726
47899CB00001BA/270